Single mother Alison Aronov-Lockewood has just found herself face-to-face with a ghost. A living, breathing, ghost—of her lost wife Sasha, and mother to her daughter Lidi. After she manages to get her anxiety under control, she realizes that this apparent apparition is a wonderful woman, a woman of wit and charm, a woman who cares about being an advocate of the children, just as she has become a representative in the legal system of children in honor of Sasha's death in the line of duty as a social worker. And more importantly, like herself, she is a lesbian. After feeling nothing but pain inside for the last six and a half years, Aly's heart beats once, twice, three times in quick succession. Could this be love again? Could this be that special person that she's waited all these years for?

A HOLLYANNE WEAVER NOVEL

Elaina J. Wright, you are and ever will be a part of every book I write.

My creativity, my passion, and my empathy were given to me by mother, Emily. Without her, even today, I am nothing.

My spirit guide is René, my younger sister, who is herself half wolf. When I need direction, it is her whom I seek.

To Sara Cunningham, you have no idea how much you give of yourself and to how many others. You are truly a gift to the world. We are all truly blessed to have you among us. You are a shining light where there is darkness; you are the instrument!

HOLLYANNE WEAVER

AFTER SASHA

Published by:
Shadoe Publishing
Copyright © June 2016 by HollyAnne Weaver

ISBN-13: 978-0692729137
ISBN-10: 0692729135

HollyAnne Weaver is available for comments at hollyanneweaver618@gmail.com and https://hollyanneweaver.wordpress.com as well as on Facebook, or on Twitter @HAWeaver618. Check out her new website at www.hollyanneweaver.com if you would like to follow to find out about stories and books releases or check with www. ShadoePublishing.com or http://ShadoePublishing.wordpress.com/.

www.shadoepublishing.com

ShadoePublishing@gmail.com

Shadoe Publishing is a United States of America company

Cover by: Cover design for this book was the brainchild of Marie Sterling. Thank you so very much!

Edited by: Deb Amia

AFTER SASHA

CHAPTER ONE

I don't go to benefits as a rule, but I'd just finished my first full year as a child advocate attorney with Kings County, New York. It seemed as though I was constantly running into new faces of people who work *with* the system, but who weren't part *of* the system. After about forty-five minutes at the gathering, I'd decided it was probably not such a good idea and considered leaving, especially since it was Tuesday evening and I had to work in the morning. Why not have these things on the weekend, I wondered? I walked over to the drink table and was picking up a glass of wine when I heard a voice to my right. I turned, and immediately my heart skipped a beat. No, that wasn't it. I think it momentarily stopped. I just stood there and stared straight ahead, looking foolish no doubt.

"Are you all right? Is there something in my hair? I'm always getting things stuck in my hair with all my curls."

"No, it's not that. It's just that...Um...Well...I uh...."

"Seriously, are you all right? Do you need some help? You look like you've just seen a ghost," said the woman.

"For a moment, I thought I had. You have no idea."

I couldn't stop staring at the woman. Very tall with dark brown, curly hair, bright blue eyes, wearing blue serge slacks and a sports jacket over a turtleneck shirt. It was her. But how?

"I'm Kárin (pronounced KÁH-rēn) Zajac. My first name means rabbit in Polish, by the way," said the woman as she extended her hand.

"I'm sorry. I didn't mean to stare at you like an idiot. I'm Aly Aronov-Lockewood. Very pleased to meet you."

"Don't worry about it. Pardon me for saying so, but you don't look very Slavic."

"I shared my wife's name when we got married. She was Ukrainian."

"Was?"

"Yes. She passed away when we'd been married a little over a year and a half."

"Oh, I'm so sorry. I feel terrible now. Please forgive me and my big mouth," Kárin said.

"Don't worry about it. It was over five years ago now and Lidiya and I have gotten along pretty well. I've had a lot of support, especially from Sasha's family…and some from mine."

"Lidiya's your daughter?"

"My heart's delight. She's the spitting image of her mom. Sasha was the one who got pregnant first. After she died, I never got the chance, so it's just Lidi and me." By now I was smiling. I always did when I got a chance to talk about my beloved Sasha and my little Lidi.

"Am I correct in assuming that I'm the ghost?"

My smile diminished significantly.

"You could be Sasha's sister. In fact, you look more like her than her two sisters do. Tall, slender, your eyes, your hair."

"Ugh! My hair. Now there's a story unto its own. I hated my hair all my life; from kindergarten through high school. It wasn't until I got to the university that I noticed other girls like me. Not just university, but moving here to New York. There just weren't any Jewish girls where I was raised."

While she was talking, Kárin was combing out her curls with the tips of her fingers.

"Where were you raised?" I asked.

"Denton, Texas. What a total cesspool—a tiny, smelly, ignorant, redneck cesspool. You wouldn't think it would be quite that bad, being so close to Dallas, but it was. Dad was an accountant for an oil company based there. I couldn't wait to get out."

"Well, Kárin, if you don't mind me saying so, I think you have absolutely beautiful hair. Not just because it reminds me of Sasha. I really think so."

"Well, thank you for that. I'm sort of proud of it now. My leefa hair...," Kárin said with a laugh.

"Sasha was Jewish as well. We practiced her traditions as well as mine. We were married in a dual ceremony with both a rabbi and a minister. It was totally cool."

"That's better."

"What is?" I asked.

"Your smile came back. You're very pretty when you smile, but when you get sad, it makes me feel sad too. So for the rest of the night stay happy, okay?"

I laughed.

"So the Star of David? You wear it for Sasha?"

"My first present to her at Christmas and she bought me the cross. Neither of us knew that we were going to buy a necklace for the other."

"That was sweet."

"I don't know *anybody* here and that was the whole point of coming. I wanted to meet some of the people that I run into once in a while through work. I know they exist, but they seem to be very cliquish. I guess that's always the case when you've got money. My father-in-law is a bit that way, but he's changed tremendously since he and Sasha made amends, and he's helped me and Lidi tons since then. If it weren't for him, I don't know how we'd have gotten through everything. I have friends, close friends, but he's opened up not only his heart, but also his pocketbook for us. He even gave me a job at his firm while he put me through law school. I couldn't go back to what I was doing at that point, I just couldn't. I guess that makes me weak, and if we would have had to, I guess we would have just done it, but things have worked out pretty well. Sasha was a social worker working for Child Protective Services mostly and me becoming an advocate is my living tribute to her."

I was running at the mouth, I realized suddenly, and went silent and took a sip of wine.

"Don't stop on my account. I think you're delightful. If it weren't for you, my night here would be a total ruin."

"So what's your connection to this soirée?" I asked.

"I work for a group of non-profits: Partnership for Children's Rights, Children of Promise, Children in the Arts, and K.I.D.S., among others. And PFLAG, separately from my involvement with children."

"PFLAG?" I asked.

"Parents, Family & Friends of Lesbians and Gays."

"Do you have gay family members?"

"Nope. I'm the one in my family that's gay. I assume that won't offend you, with what you've told me so far," Kárin grinned.

I genuinely smiled.

"Of course not. I just hope you didn't wait until you were almost 25 years old to come out like I did."

Kárin laughed, loud enough for several people near us to turn their heads our way.

"I started dating girls when I was fifteen. Unfortunately, there was only one other girl in school that I knew was gay, and we had to be very careful. But after we got driver's licenses we used to drive to Dallas and spend the weekend in a hotel room. It was pretty popular for girls to do that for shopping trips...totally straight girls. They'd pack enough clothes for a week and go to expensive hotels just for the weekend so they could go 'shopping.' When they weren't spending daddy's money, they were getting drunk in their rooms and picking up guys. Laura and I just went to cheaper places and spent the weekend going to restaurants, movies, and gay bars," she laughed again.

"I wish I'd had the courage to do that. I was bottled up for over ten years."

"But you're squared away now, right? I mean, you don't *have* to be gay or anything. I just mean you're getting to make your own choices and decisions now."

"Oh, trust me. I've *definitely* been gay for a long time. I think everybody just thought I was asexual. I'd been asked out by a few guys, but always said I wasn't ready for a relationship."

"Have you seen anybody since Sasha..." Kárin asked.

"No. Well, no...strictly speaking, that's not true. There's one other person I've been interested in since I met Sasha, and I met her through Sasha. She is a beautiful and delightful woman from Argentina. I had a double major in college: Information Technology, which was my last job, and Spanish Literature. Immediately we chatted in Spanish like old friends and pissed everybody else off because they couldn't understand. When we did, Sasha started talking Russian until we stopped," I laughed.

I stopped talking again, and my mind went off into a corner somewhere until I realized there was this awkward silence.

"Estefanía and I found out after a couple of casual dates that we loved each other deeply, but like sisters. Thank God we didn't have sex and ruin that. I talk to her at least once every week or two. We're incredibly tight," I said as I finished my thought.

"She sounds wonderful. I wasn't trying to pry, by the way. You're just naturally interesting."

"Oh, give me a break! Hardly."

"To me you are."

"So what's your story, other than making a jailbreak from Denton?"

"I came to New York to attend The New School to get my degree in Social Research. Even though my parents were paying for school, I got a job at my first non-profit while I was going to classes and got the bug. Been there ever since."

"My sister-in-law, Veronika, graduated from there. She's working for a U.S. congressman here in New York. Even though I think her degree is in finance or business or something like that, she's the information director."

"A Democrat, I hope!"

We both laughed.

"Of course, of course."

"Because I'd hate to have to end this conversation and walk away right now when we were getting along so well."

We both laughed again. We were getting along famously, in fact.

"Kárin, I know that we've only known each other for a little under half an hour, but can I ask you something personal?"

"Absolutely. I'm an open book."

"Are you involved with anybody?"

Suddenly, Kárin's smile disappeared.

"I'm sorry. I had no business asking you that. Please forgive me."

"There's nothing to forgive. At all. And no, I'm not involved with anybody. Can I ask you a question in return?" asked Kárin.

"Of course. Anything."

"Do you see me as getting Sasha back?"

"Oh, no. Nothing like that. It's true that you look like her twin, and your personality is very similar to hers, which is what attracted me to her in the first place. I wondered if maybe sometime you would like to have a cup of coffee or something, but I didn't want to bother you if you are involved."

Kárin's smile returned.

"Just so we're clear. I've been a consolation prize before, and it's not a very good feeling when you finally find out."

"I would never do that to another person. No matter what."

"I would love to have lunch with you on the weekend. We could make a day of it. You and I and Lidi."

"I can get a babysitter if you'd like."

"Don't be silly. I love children. That's what killed my last relationship...I wanted children. She said she did, but lied about it. After a while, I gave up on it."

"That's too bad. Okay. Saturday? One o'clock? It just so happens that one of my brothers-in-law owns a restaurant up toward The Village. I'll text you with the address and time. Give me your number," I said as I handed her my phone.

Kárin entered her information into my phone, then handed me her phone. I entered both my cell and work number. I don't know why I gave her my work number. It was a totally unconscious thought. I made a mental note to call Valery tomorrow and see about coming around to his restaurant, Тарелка, The Plate, this weekend.

"Cool. I'll wait for your text then and make sure nothing else pops up on Saturday," Kárin said.

"It's no big deal. If you have something come up and have to bail, just send me a note, and I'll understand."

"Aly? Please don't think I'm predatory. I didn't come here to pick up a girlfriend. And I'm not trying to pick you up now. I just like you."

"Uh, I'm sorry, but wasn't I the one that asked you out?"

We laughed again.

"Well, hopefully everything will work out and we'll meet this weekend. I so look forward to meeting Lidi," Kárin said as she held out her hand again.

I shook her hand once again. I couldn't be sure, it seemed almost imperceptible, as if there was a slight hesitation prior to our hands disconnecting. I had butterflies in my stomach. Was she a ghost? Was this a new passion? Until I figured that out, I had to be careful. It was the last thing in the world I'd want to do...I'd never forgive myself if I hurt somebody, especially my little Lidi! No more would I want someone to hurt me, but there was something special about Kárin. For the first time in seven years, I went a whole hour without thinking about Sasha even though I was talking about her. After the first few minutes, I was relating my history with Sasha, but not feeling Sasha's presence.

After I left the conference room at the hotel, I began to feel incredibly guilty. I knew that was silly, that I had nothing about which to feel guilty. I'd been in mourning for over five years. And it wasn't as if I was trying to jump into bed with Kárin, this new goddess I'd just seen for the first time that night. How strange. To find somebody that looks like Sasha...that acts like Sasha...that is Jewish.... It was too much for me to take in. I called for the car service and waited in the lobby to be picked up. I wasn't having a good time inside anyway. Gideon, my father-in-law, never let me go anywhere anymore without either being in my car or having me driven. There was a parking garage a block from our place—Sasha's and mine—where I could park, and money wasn't quite as big a deal anymore. Just the same, Gideon also paid for the parking ramp. I didn't make a lot of money, but we certainly did okay. But Gideon built a trust fund for Lidi and bought me a car, not to mention constantly feeding me a check here and there. He claimed it was all for Lidi, but we grew to love each other very much, even before Sasha passed.

I couldn't wait to get home now. I practically ran from the parking ramp to the apartment. The sitter, Melanie, was sitting up on one end of the couch, and Lidi was laying with her head in the girl's lap. Melanie was gently stroking her hair as Lidi slept. I moved over to the couch and leaned over Lidi, kissing her on the forehead.

"Hi there, my little angel. Mommy missed you so much tonight."

I picked her up and took her into her bedroom, laying her down on the bed and covering her with her duvet. I kissed her again and gave her a hug. She moved a little bit, but stayed asleep. I walked back into the living room.

"Did she give you any trouble at all tonight?"

"None at all. She was a perfect doll."

"Good. Let me get you some money," I said as I fished into my billfold for a pair of twenties.

"Oh, Aly, this is way too much!"

"Nonsense. Tonight you helped me out with no notice, and on a school night to boot. You deserve it. Go buy yourself something nice."

"By the way, my mom heard me call you Aly on the phone. She gave me an ass-eating for that. I'm not sure what I need to call you. I don't want to offend either of you. I guess I just have to be careful where I am and use the right name."

"Bologna. If your mom has a problem with it send her downstairs, and we'll straighten her out."

"I do like babysitting for you. It's in the same building. I never have to go anywhere. That's pretty cool."

"I'm just glad I found you. You've helped me out so many times. I can't thank you enough."

"Lidi is the best kid I've ever gotten to babysit too. She's never been fussy, not even once."

"I'm glad. Well, have a good night. See you later. Say hi to your parents for me."

"Okay, bye, Mrs. A."

"There you go. Mrs. A. Your mother will think it's short for Aronov-Lockewood, and you and I will both know it's for Aly."

Melanie giggled.

"Night-night."

I went to the bedroom and kicked off my shoes. I still hadn't had anything to eat, so I went into the kitchen and made a sandwich. I made a big effort to make a wide variety of food for Lidi, and tried to keep it healthy as well, but for myself it was either a salad or a sandwich. Time and circumstances had taken their toll on me. I sat on the couch and ate and watched television. When I had finished with my sandwich, I went into the bedroom and got into my pajamas.

I picked my phone up from the table and held it for a few minutes before putting it back down. God, I had to stop this. And I meant right then. About thirty minutes later I still hadn't fallen asleep. I picked up my phone and entered a text message.

'Don't take this for any more than it is. I just wanted to say, tonight I enjoyed myself more than I have in quite some time. Thank you.'

I began to get a little nervous when I didn't get an answer in reply. But around forty-five minutes later I finally got the tone for an incoming message.

'Sorry. First I was in the shower, and then forgot to turn my ringer back on. It was on silent when we were at the fundraiser. You must think I'm a bitch!'

'No, far from it. You have a very calming effect on me.'

'I'm glad. In fact, I'm glad I met you tonight. I almost didn't go, but I sort of have to attend these things.'

'Didn't mean to bother you in any case. I'll see you on Saturday.'

'Believe me when I say you're not a bother by any means. And I'm *really* looking forward to it. Sweet dreams.'

Sweet dreams. Okay, I've been through this once. Feeling things too fast...imagining things that might not have been.... The first time things worked out better than I ever could have imagined. And as short a time as Sasha and I had together on this earth, I wouldn't trade that time for anything. Ever. I held the phone in tightly to my chest and smiled to myself, drifting off to sleep finally.

CHAPTER TWO

Between interviewing two clients on Wednesday morning about ten o'clock, I called Valery.

"Tariylkuh. This is Michaela. May I help you?"

"Hi. This is Aly. Is Valery in this morning?"

"Hi, Aly. Sure, he's in. Let me see if he can take a call right now. One sec..." she said, putting me on hold.

"Aly, how is one of my two favorite sisters-in-law today?"

The younger brother, Grigory, had gotten married about two and a half years ago to a woman from Barbados he met in New York. Her name was Gabrielle. He was a machinist at a ship yard and doing quite well for himself. His wife was Val's other 'favorite' adopted little sister.

"I'm good, Val. How about you? Been staying busy at work? Business is good?"

"Beyond my best dreams. When we started this place, we had a five-year plan that we passed in the first three years. We keep updating our plan each year and every year we exceed our expectations. I know that there will eventually be a ceiling, but we're putting a lot of money in the bank for when that day comes. And we already have some ideas for a new restaurant when we close this one and change the sign," Val laughed.

"Say, I've got something pretty serious to talk to you about if you have a few minutes."

"Sure. Are you having troubles?"

"Yes, but not the kind you'd expect. You see the thing is, I may, and again this is too soon to tell for sure, but I may have met somebody. I'm at least wanting to pursue it. And I want to make sure that you're okay with that."

"Aly, we all love you. We want nothing better than for you and Lidi to be as happy as you can. Why would any of us have a problem with that?"

"Well, here's the thing...the new woman, Kárin, she looks like she could be Sasha's twin. And before you ask, that's not what attracted me to her. She's completely her own person. I just didn't want you to freak out. I feel stupid even bringing it up because you're so sweet to me. You always have been. Everybody in the family has. I just didn't want you to see her without a warning and go into an instantaneous meltdown the way I did. When I first saw Kárin, I couldn't breathe. My heart just stopped working for a minute, or so it seemed. All I could do was stare. Anyway, she's pleasant and funny, and extremely nice. And I want you to know that if I fell in love with her eventually, she would never take Sasha's place in my heart. I will never love anybody that much, ever again. I can't. Sasha was...is...the absolute love of my life."

"When were you thinking of coming?"

"Saturday, about one o'clock if that's okay."

"I'll make it okay. You just show up, and we'll take care of everything."

"I'm not looking for a free lunch, Val. I just wanted to talk to you first. I owe you that much. I love you."

"Don't make me start crying now, damn it!" he laughed.

"Okay. See you on Saturday then, ya big lug. Bye."

"Bye."

I immediately texted Kárin with the address and confirmed one o'clock. I wasn't expecting an answer immediately, but it was less than thirty seconds when it came through.

'I'll be there with bells on. And don't forget, you bring Lidi along. If you leave her with family or a babysitter, I'll be pissed. We got a play date?'

'Is that what we have? A date?'

'I've never been on a first date with a woman with kids before. That should be interesting. What if she doesn't like me?'

'First off, I assure you she'll like you. She and I like and dislike the same things. And I like you. And secondly, does that mean this is a date?'

'It is what it is. See you at one on Saturday. TTFN.'

'Tiggers are the most wonderful things....'

'Yup.'

I couldn't stop smiling, which made it so, so hard to talk to my next client, a little girl whose parents had moved in the middle of the night leaving her to wake up on her own. She was fourteen, and we were in the process of determining whether we could emancipate her or if she'd have to be put into the system. Her grandmother already told her she could move in with her, but if we could get her declared emancipated, there wouldn't be any legal paperwork to deal with, she could go and do what she wished.

It was so hard to be happy while dealing with tragedy, but it was part of the job. You have to maintain your objectivity and keep your life compartmentalized or the walls could come tumbling down both in your private life and at work, thus reducing any efficiency you had for performance.

On Friday, at ten past twelve, my phone vibrated in my pocket. I was just eating my lunch so I pulled it out and looked at the text.

'So, still on for tomorrow?'

'Why wouldn't we be?'

'Just giving you a last chance to back out.'

'What in the world would make me want to do that?'

'Truthfully, the question was insignificant. I just wanted to hear from you.'

Instead of texting her back, I pulled up her contact and hit the call button. I hoped she was where she could talk.

"Hi. You didn't have to call me, you know. A text would have been fine," Kárin said.

"Naw, it wouldn't have. I've been fighting the urge to call you all week long. I must appear either desperate or creepy. Or both. Now you gave me an excuse to do it."

"You're silly."

"Probably. See you tomorrow then. Don't be late. Just joking. I don't care if you are, just as long as you are there."

"I'll be on time, believe me."

"Okay. Bye for now."

"Bye."

I hadn't felt like this for years. Literally. I'd been deeply in mourning until this week. Today was the first time I wasn't. Even when Estefanía and I went out a few times, I was still deeply mired in grief and we both knew it. I'm glad that Estefanía found somebody two years ago, María-Elena, and they are now living together. They're doing famously well, and she's getting far more from her partner than I could ever have given her. It worked out for the best.

CHAPTER THREE

"Come on, Lids, why are you so pokey this morning? I told you that we're going to have lunch with somebody at Uncle Valery's restaurant."

"Who is it, Mommy?"

"It's a woman that I met this week named Kárin. She's very special and she's very nice, but there's something that you and I need to talk about first."

I continued to get Lidiya into her dress and sweater while we talked.

"When you see her, I don't want you to be surprised. Because, well, it's the way she looks."

"But, Mommy, you told me that people can't help the way they look and we shouldn't judge them."

I had to laugh at that. It's moments like this when you are so proud of your children.

"It's not that exactly. It's that she looks very, very much like somebody else."

"Who does she look like?"

I stopped moving for a minute or two while Lidi just looked me in the face wondering what I was going to say.

"She looks very much like Mommy Sasha. Is that all right with you? Are you going to be able to do this for Mommy?"

"Why is that a bad thing? I think Mommy Sasha is pretty. Don't you? You always told me that she was the most beautiful person in the world along with me. That's what you said."

"I did say that. I still think that. Nobody will ever be prettier to me than you and your Mommy Sasha. I just didn't want you to be too surprised when you met her."

"I don't care. As long as she's nice to me, that's all I care about."

"That's good, baby. Let's go now. We don't want to be late."

We walked to the car ramp and got our car. The trip up to the village was horrible—busier that I'd seen a Saturday in years—but we finally made it and parked. When we walked inside, Michaela went up to Lidi and gave her a big hug.

"How are you today, sweetie pie?"

"I'm good, Michaela. How are you?"

"Couldn't be better. Come with me and I'll get you a table."

Michaela walked us to the back of the restaurant and took the small sign off the table that stated 'Reserved.' It was really busy today. I was glad Val saved it for us so we didn't have to wait. It would probably have been about forty minutes to an hour. We'd been sitting for about five minutes and were drinking some iced tea when Kárin arrived at our table. Immediately Lidi looked up with her eyes open wide in surprise and her mouth gaping, her hands on her chest.

"Mommy Sasha! Mommy Sasha!"

"No, baby, this is Kárin. But I told you that she looks a lot like Mommy Sasha, didn't I? Sorry, Kárin. I talked to her, but like I told you last Tuesday night, you are the spitting image of Sasha. Please, sit down."

"Hi, Lidiya. I'm Kárin. I'm very pleased to meet you. Don't you look pretty today?" Kárin said as she put her hand out for Lidi to shake.

Slowly Lidi put her hand out and shook hands with Kárin, her eyes as big as saucers.

"I'm very pleased to meet you, Kárin."

"As I am to meet you. I've heard a lot about you from your mommy. And I want to tell you something, so you won't have to worry. I'm not here to try and take your Mommy Sasha's place. I would never try to do that. Okay?"

"Are you going to be Mommy's new girlfriend?"

"Lidi!" I shouted.

"Well, that's a legitimate question, isn't it, Aly? And to tell you the truth Lidi, I don't know. That would be up to your mommy and you."

"I don't care. If it makes you happy, it's okay with me."

"Apparently it depends on what Lidi and I think? Don't you have any input in this equation?" I asked Kárin.

"Let me tell you a little something. Like I said, I came out to myself when I was fifteen and to the world when I was eighteen. I've dated a few girls along the way—one in particular for less than two weeks— but in my entire life I've never dated two people at the same time. That's just not me. I'm not asking for a lasting commitment, but I haven't been able to get you out of my mind all week. Coming here is all I've been able to think about. And I think Lidi is just adorable. If I went shopping for a little girl, this is the one I'd pick, I think. She is smart and observant like her mother, and I like that. So, yeah, if the two of you want me to be your girlfriend, I wouldn't mind that. But both of you have to want to have me."

"What do you think, Lidi? Would you mind if Kárin *were* my girlfriend? Maybe came over for dinner once in a while? Maybe we could go out and do things on the weekend?" I asked.

"Yay! That would be fun. Then you wouldn't always be so sad, Mommy," exclaimed Lidi.

"Baby, I've always been happy with just you and me. You are everything I need. I've told you that."

"But it's not like on television. You need a big person too, not just me," said Lidi.

"Oh, how precious is that?" asked Kárin.

I reached across the table and took Kárin's hand in mine for a moment. While I was holding her hand I reached out and held Lidi's hand. Then Kárin reached across the table and held Lidi's hand at the same time.

"See, I told you, Mommy. This is better," Lidi said.

Just then Valery came up to our table from his office.

Да, Боже мой! Невероятное! (Yes, my God! It's unbelievable!)

I laughed out loud. Kárin had a strange expression on her face and Lidi giggled.

"Look, Uncle Val, she looks just like Mommy Sasha!"

"You told me on the phone to warn me, but I would never have believed how much so! I'm Valery Aronov. Welcome to my little restaurant. I hope that your dining experience here today is most enjoyable."

"Valery, your whole family has been delightful. I feel privileged just to have met you all for a day, much less how much time we may get to spend in the future. And as far as being a 'little' restaurant, I'd like to know what you'd call a big one!"

"Believe me when I say the pleasure is all ours, but let me also warn you. Aly may only be my sister-in-law, but I have connections in the Ukrainian mafia. If you break her heart, you will disappear in the middle of the night and never be seen again."

"Val, leave her alone. You're going to scare the poor girl!" I laughed.

"Uncle Val, you're funny," giggled Lidi.

"You'll notice that I'm the only one not laughing here," said Kárin with a strange look on her face.

Valery laughed at her response, then bent down and gave her a bear hug.

"Welcome. Don't be afraid of anything. I would use my connections to keep you safe too."

"Just don't do anything to go to jail on my part. That would keep me up nights."

That made all the adults laugh.

"Mommy? What does that mean?"

"It just means that Uncle Val is glad that Kárin is here with us today."

"Oh. So am I," she smiled.

"Val, она еврейского." ("Val, she's also Jewish.")

"Действительно?" ("Really?")

"I believe you mentioned Spanish?" asked Kárin.

"And German. But I've picked up a couple of phrases here and there," I countered.

"I assume that was Russian?"

"Yes," said Valery.

"And what did she say that's so secretive that I shouldn't understand it?"

"She said you were Jewish!"

"That I am. Is that a good thing?"

"Oh, that is a very, very good thing. Not the most important thing, of course, but a special added bonus!" gushed Valery.

"I'm glad you approve."

"Aly, this is a keeper. I've talked to her for only ten minutes and I can tell. You see, Kárin, I am the world's best judge of character. I've only made one mistake in my entire life. Ever."

"Am I allowed to ask what that mistake was? Or is that taboo?" asked Kárin.

For the briefest of moments, Valery became very somber.

"For denying my loving, adoring, kind, and beautiful sister. Because I didn't understand...because I was stupid...."

I took both of Val's hands into mine.

"Val, that's in the past. Keep it there. Stop punishing yourself. Let it go. Sasha did. So should you," I said.

Val wiped his eyes quickly as if nobody would notice.

"Is there anything that you don't eat, Kárin?"

"Nope. Pretty much anything. I'm pretty easygoing. I keep the traditions, but I'm not kosher."

"Aly, what was Sasha's idea of a perfect day of sinning?" asked Val with a broad smile.

"Of course, going for breakfast food at lunchtime and ordering lots of bacon and sausage!"

Everybody laughed, including Lidi, even though she had no idea what we were laughing at. She was just an incredibly happy child having an incredibly happy day. As was I...for the first time in ages.

After we'd had an awesome lunch of bread, salad, soup, pasta, and wine for the adults, Valery came to our table again, along with Jorges René.

"Permit me to present my partner and your personal chef for today, my oldest and dearest friend, Jorges René."

"So this is the nest of lovely ladies whom I've had the pleasurable experience to serve!"

"Jorges René, you can cook for me anytime!" effused Kárin.

"Believe me, it has been my pleasure, but alas, my fans adore me and I cannot keep them waiting!" Jorges said with a faked swoon, disappearing into the kitchen from whence he came.

"You ladies have a great day. I'm glad you came by."

"Val, where's our bill? I told you I wasn't looking for a handout; I only called to warn you."

"Pish-posh. It's done. And seriously, I'm not trying to be pushy, Kárin, but Aly is the real deal. She's my flesh and blood as far as I'm concerned. In fact, even better than some of my flesh and blood," waving a quiet disapproval of Katya, his sister, and Antoniya, his mother, neither of whom had yet changed one iota.

Katya and her mother were true homophobes who had not only shunned Sasha, but had convinced the rest of her family to do it for five years before they had all made up.

"I'll certainly keep that in mind. Thank you for a glorious lunch. I hope to see you again. You're a wonderful host," said Kárin.

As we were walking to the car, Lidiya was walking between Kárin and I, holding both of our hands. I felt a pang in my heart at that moment, feeling as though it should have been Sasha and I that were walking down the street like that. I told Kárin.

"I know I'll get feelings like this from time to time. I know I will for the rest of my life. I don't want to upset you. It will be very transient in nature, I assure you, and doesn't reflect on you at all. I want you to know that it *absolutely* doesn't mean that I've settled for you. I've chosen you…at least for now, as long as we continue to develop. I know it's pretty early in a relationship to talk like this. I just want to avoid giving you any false impressions. Okay?"

"I get it. Look, if you didn't have any feelings like that at all, especially involving your daughter and her mother, I would say that you didn't love one or both of them very much. I'm actually impressed."

"Impressed?"

"Remember, I told you that I wanted children."

"Are you shopping for a ready-made family?" I laughed.

"Not shopping, but not opposed to it either," she smiled.

Kárin stopped walking for a moment.

"Lidi, would you take your hands and cover your eyes for a minute? Just for a minute?"

"Okay," she answered letting go of our hands and covering her eyes as directed.

Kárin took a step toward me, put her fingers under my chin turning my face up, and kissed me gently on the lips.

"I heard that, you two kissed!" yelled Lidi.

People around us turned their heads to see what the commotion was all about.

Kárin and I both smiled, and Lidi giggled out loud.

"Kárin, if you're a woman, does that mean you're a lesbian like Mommy?"

"Lidi! That was rude! Apologize right now!"

"I'm sorry, Kárin. I didn't mean to make anybody mad at me," said Lidi with a look of total dejection on her face.

Kárin bent down to Lidi's height and pulled her close.

"It's okay. You can ask me anything, anytime, anywhere. I'm your special friend. And I hope that no matter what happens, we'll always be friends. No matter what," and gave Lidi a big hug and kissed her cheek.

Kárin stood back up and being so tall, towered over Lidi…and me for that matter. Lidi looked up at Kárin, her smile having returned. This time I held Kárin's hand and she held Lidi's.

"Thank you. I must be the luckiest woman in the entire world," I said.

"How so?" asked Kárin.

"I've only had two girlfriends in my life and both have been so wonderful. Well, at least it's looking very favorable at this point in time for number two. I don't even know what to tell you. You probably think I'm an absolute nutter, feeling so much for you in less than a week."

"It's just fate. When things click, they just click."

"I'll have to take your word for that. Even with a family, I've had very little experience with people. I've never dated a boy. I've only really dated one girl, and I married her. If you're serious about being my girlfriend now, you'll be the second. I'm not very experienced so I must come across like a freshman. Even with Sasha, I'd decided that I was going to give her six months to ask me to marry her, and if she didn't, I was going to ask her. I didn't wait six months. I bought her a ring and got down on one knee and proposed in front of some of our friends. You still want to be my girlfriend?"

"Yup. You still want to be mine?"

"Yup."

We got to the car and stood in silence for minutes. Finally, Lidi spoke first.

"Why are we just standing here? What are we going to do next?"

"I was just thinking the same thing. Do you have plans for the rest of the day?" I asked.

"None. I told you I was going to keep my calendar clear."

"How did you get here?"

"I took a cab. I don't usually, but I figured this was a special occasion."

"Would you maybe want to come with us? And I'll take you home later?"

"That would be nice."

"Lidi, do you want to watch a movie with Kárin? We could cook some popcorn and hang out at the apartment," I said first to Lidi, then looked at Kárin, hopefully.

"That would delightful."

The three of us got into the car and headed for the apartment. It was too late. I had lost my horizontal control and vertical stabilizer, the plane was going spinning down. Oh, God! Not now! It was too soon!

We parked the car and headed for the apartment. I'd had Estefanía and Detective Martha Devonshire, a very close friend of mine and Sasha's, over. Also several women friends and a couple of guy friends who were straight and had wives or girlfriends, but nobody whom I was romantically involved with had been in my apartment. This was the first time I'd had a girl 'over' to my place since Sasha's passing. I was nervous as hell. And also at that very moment I wished I'd spent a little more time cleaning.

"Kárin, please believe me that I'd like to say it doesn't usually look like this, but the truth is it usually does look this messy. I'm trying to get Lidi in the habit of doing a better job of cleaning up after herself. I think even my stuff was a lot straighter when I lived alone!"

"Oh, puh-*lease!* If only my flat looked like this. I'll trade you. By the way, this is a beautiful apartment."

"It was Sasha's for a few years before she met me. I moved in with her. Then we got engaged. Then we got married. Then we had Lidi. It isn't much, but it's our little castle."

"Don't be silly. It's wonderful. So, so nice," Kárin said, walking through the apartment.

"Checking us out completely?"

"Of course not. And not snooping either. Just interested. After all, it is my girlfriend's apartment, isn't it? I need to know the layout in case I'm here late some night and the power goes out, so I can navigate."

"That's the lamest excuse ever."

Lidi took Kárin's hand and practically dragged Kárin into her room.

"Come and see my room, Kárin. It's pink."

"Of course it is. Aren't all little princesses' rooms pink?"

"Kárin, you're funny," said Lidi.

"I'll put the popcorn in the microwave. The two of you pick out a movie and I'll be in when it's done. Kárin, drink? Wine? Beer? Tea? Coffee? Dr Pepper? Water? Juice box?"

I added the last one for effect and Kárin laughed.

"Dr Pepper would be great since we're eating popcorn."

"In a bottle or in a glass with ice?"

"A glass, if it's not too much trouble."

"You got it."

I put some of the popcorn in a small bowl for Lidi and put the rest in a big bowl. I took our drinks and the bowls into the living room. 'Airplanes' was already running on the DVD player. Lidi got in the chair on the side of the couch so that she could sit her juice by Kárin's glass, and slowly ate her popcorn and watched the movie as if she'd never seen it. I bet she'd seen it fifty times if she'd seen it once. I sat on the couch next to Kárin and put the bowl in her lap.

"Isn't this cozy?" asked Kárin.

"I'm sorry. I didn't mean to be presumptuous."

I sat back from her and gave her some space and put the bowl on the couch between us. She picked the bowl up and put it back in her lap, pulling my arm to get me to scoot next to her. I smiled at her.

"I'm sorry if I'm moving too fast. I'm not trying to. I guess I just don't know how else to act. I have no experience dating. I don't know what's 'proper' or the correct 'etiquette' or whatever. Just let me know whenever I do something that makes you uncomfortable. I'll always respect your wishes..."

Kárin put her fingertip over my lips and quietly shushed me, smiling.

"If I promise to let you know, will you promise to shut up and relax? Just let it flow. That's what my years of experience have taught me, in any case."

"How old are you?"

"Thirty. Why?"

"I'm thirty-two. That's how old Sasha was when we first met. I was just wondering how far apart we were."

"Do you have a thing for older women? Is that it?" she asked laughingly.

"No, I just have a thing for delightful, pretty, charming, witty, and smart women," I laughed.

"Good to know."

"And they have to be Democrats or Independents at the very least."

I got a return laugh.

"What about Libertarians?"

"Good in concept, but they don't believe in social responsibility. I do. That's why I do what I do."

"Nice," said Kárin.

I looked over at Lidi. She was enraptured with her movie. She paid us little to no attention whatsoever. I casually put my arm on the back of the couch, laying it against Kárin ever so lightly. She turned her head toward me and smiled, then turned back to the movie. We both ate out of the bowl until it was empty. Finally, the movie was over, and Lidi bounded out of the chair.

"I'm going to pick another one, Mommy. Please?"

"Okay. How about Aladdin?"

"If that's what you want."

"That's what I want, baby."

"Do you have a thing for Aladdin?" asked Kárin.

"If you ask me, it's a great little musical and overall a quiet movie, unlike the last one."

We watched Aladdin, and I sang along with most of the songs. I have a pretty decent voice. I was in choir in junior high and high school. It amused Kárin, so I kept doing it. Then I started talking along with the dialog since I'd memorized every single word of the entire movie.

"Mommy! You said you wouldn't do that anymore! Stop it!" Lidi shouted.

"I take it she doesn't like you competing with the movie."

"I do it partly to annoy her, to tell you the truth. Not in a big way, just to make a little fun. But partly, I do love the movie. As I said, it's a great musical."

"I'm having a great day."

"Watching children's movies and eating popcorn at somebody's house with her daughter."

"What could be better?"

"I think both of us think about the same thing as you," I replied in return.

Kárin and I had our stocking feet up on the coffee table all this time. She picked up one foot and put it over mine, looking down at our feet together. I moved my foot up and down for a minute caressing hers with mine. Kárin looked up at me for the millionth time today and smiled. Then she leaned into my ear and whispered very quietly, "Somebody's got a giiirrrlfriiieend."

It tickled a bit, so I reacted by pushing my head into her face, and she kissed my ear several times surreptitiously. Or so I thought.

"You're kissing again! I saw you!" said Lidi, pointing at us with her finger.

"Does that bother you, Lidi? Would you like me to stop?" asked Kárin.

"I don't care. It doesn't bother me. You can do whatever you want to."

"I'm glad. Come here for a minute," Kárin said.

Lidi ran over to Kárin and crawled up on her lap, pulling Kárin's arm around her.

"What are we going to do now? Is it time for dinner?"

"By the time it's ready, it will be ready. Don't be so impatient, wee little one. How about I go in the kitchen and start it?" I said.

"Here. I'll come help you."

"Nonsense. You and Lidi find something on television and let me handle it," I said.

"Mommy is a wonderful cook. Just wait. You'll think so too."

I moved into the kitchen, trying to decide what to cook. I decided on East Indian butter chicken. I used chicken breasts, garlic, both garam and tandoori masalas, heavy cream, a whole cup of butter, tomatoes, onions, cayenne, and a couple of other things. I chose to use Basmati rice to give it a nuttier flavor than short grain. It took about forty-five minutes to finish. Kárin and Lidi seemed to be getting along well. I peeked in a couple of times and Lidi was still on Kárin's lap. I went in to tell them to come and get it and found Lidi asleep, with Kárin stroking her hair slowly and softly, just like Melanie had last Tuesday.

God, that felt like years ago and it had only been four days. How quickly life can change. I found Sasha in an instant...I lost Sasha in an instant. Now, just maybe, I'd found Kárin in an instant. I motioned to Kárin to come into the kitchen. I'm not sure why I didn't wake up Lidi myself. I later wondered if I wasn't somehow testing Kárin, or the chemistry the two of them might have. In any case, Kárin tickled Lidi's tummy lightly and softly talked to her, "Hey, sweetpea, time to eat dinner. Come on, let's go eat. Time to open your little peepers."

Slowly, Lidi opened her eyes, then turned around and looked at Kárin. When she saw her, Lidi smiled and held onto Kárin's arm.

"Good. I'm hungry. Let's go eat."

Lidi jumped up like a shot and headed for the bathroom.

"Where are you going, baby? We're going to eat now."

"Mommy, I have to potty!"

"Well, she sure as hell told you, didn't she?" Kárin laughed.

We had a minute to ourselves while the door to the bathroom remained shut. Kárin approached me and put her arms around my neck, leaning in and giving me a long, slow kiss. When she stopped, I heard her make a noise.

"Mmm..."

"Is that a good mmm?"

"Mm-hmm."

I poked Kárin in the stomach, grabbed her hand, and hauled her to the kitchen.

"Sit. I'll bring it to the table."

Lidi came to the table right about then. I served up the plates.

"Smells delish," said Kárin.

"Mommy's food is always delicious. You'll see."

"I don't doubt it at all."

Kárin started digging into the food.

"Oh, my God! This…food...is...amazing! *Totally* amazing! Did you go to school for this or what?"

"No, I just watched a cooking channel, surfed the web a lot, and bought books. Anybody can do this."

"Uh, no. Anybody *can't* do this."

"I told you Mommy's cooking is good."

"I'll never, ever doubt you, Lidi. I promise."

We took our time eating and then I cleaned, putting the extra food in containers in the fridge, cleaning off the dishes, and loading the dishwasher. Lidi had gone to her room to play with her dolls.

"Are you ready to go home? If we leave now, I'll get Lidi back in time for her regular bedtime."

"Yeah, I'm ready. Truthfully, I don't want to go, but it's time. You're not just trying to get rid of me, are you?"

"Sure, that's it. I'm just trying to get rid of you. Seriously, I don't want you to go, truth be told. One of these days I'll tell you something Sasha taught me several years ago, but I can't yet. You'll just have to wait."

"You're evil. Bait and switch at its finest."

"No, no switch. Just bait. If you want to hear the rest of the story, you'll just have to stick with me for a little while."

"Don't trust me?"

"Explicitly. But the story explains itself. There's a format to the story. Everything in its time."

"You intrigue me. So, are we a thing? Are we, at least for now, actually exclusive? Because as I've said, that's the only way I can live."

"Oh, I'm the same way. And as far as I'm concerned, we're definitely a thing. You're delightful. Thank you for breathing life back into me after all this time."

I walked up to Kárin and gave her the biggest, longest hug I could. For the second time today, she put her fingers under my chin, pulled my face up, and kissed me, but this time it lasted much, much longer. The butterflies were definitely working overtime that evening.

"Baby, get out your Plimsoles and put them on! We're going to take Kárin home now!" I shouted through the apartment so Lidi would hear me.

"Plimsoles?"

"Crêpe rubber soles and a Velcro strap. You can also buy them with laces. I got these for her when we went to London early in the summer."

"Oh, so Lidi's a world traveler already. What a clever girl."

"She had so much fun, I can't tell you.... I don't think she ever had more fun. Roni—Veronika—is my sister-in-law. She went with us so that when I was in my conferences the two of them could go around the city and see things. And then every day in the afternoon when I got out, the three of us palled around. We were there from Saturday to the next Sunday. I was so jet lagged when I got back. It took me almost a week to adjust."

"I've never gone anywhere but Mexico and Canada. Do you have any conferences you can go to in Poland?"

"It wouldn't work. I don't speak Polish.'

"I do. I'll translate."

"You actually speak it?"

"Sure. Both sets of my grandparents came here in the thirties since they were Jewish. They left just before the war when there was already the smell of conflict in the air, which was so fortunate since the Germans overran Poland first. Both of my parents were raised speaking Polish at home. And even now when I go to my grandparents' houses, English is rarely spoken."

"How will I understand them then? Will they grudgingly speak it when we visit?"

"You want to visit my family, huh?"

"Isn't that what I would do with my girlfriend? Where do they live?" I questioned.

"They have a small farm in Maryland. You know, for somebody without any experience, you sure know a lot more than you let on. I think you may have this process down pretty well."

I hugged her again.

"Lidi? Do you have your shoes on?"

Just then Lidi came out of her room, walked over to the wall, and got her sweater off the hook.

"I was waiting for you and Kárin to stop kissing."

"Who said we were kissing?"

"I told you I don't care if you do."

"Were you watching us?"

"No, but that's what they do on television. Don't you want to kiss Kárin?"

"You're sure that doesn't bother you?" asked Kárin.

"Nope."

Kárin looked at Lidi.

"Lidi, does anybody, maybe at school or something, ever make fun of you or tease you because your mommy's a lesbian?"

"Sometimes, but I just tell them that they're jealous because they only have one mommy, and I have two. Even though Mommy Sasha died, Mommy Aly always tells me that now she's an angel and watches down on me, so it's like she's with me all the time."

"Amazing. Simply amazing. You've done a perfect job bringing her up," Kárin said.

"Sometimes I question it, but most of the time I couldn't be prouder of her."

We drove Kárin to her apartment and pulled up to the curb. When we stopped, Kárin unbuckled her seat belt, turned around, and halfway climbed over the seat. She gave Lidi a hug and kissed her on the cheek again, mussing up her hair.

"Bye for now, little one. Hopefully, we'll see each other again very soon."

"Do you promise?"

"I do. I do."

Kárin turned back around in the front seat. Then she leaned into me and gave me a tender, lingering kiss while holding one hand against my cheek.

"That's the way, Mommy."

"Lidi, hush. You're being rude again."

Kárin winked at Lidi, waving bye at her. Lidi waved back. And with that, my first date in five years was over. Only four dates left to go. Then I'd be able to tell Kárin the lesson I learned. No, not tell...share.

CHAPTER FOUR

Sunday, just after noon, Lidi and I were sitting at the dinner table at Gideon's house. Roni and her husband, Michael had come as well as Valery and his wife, Diya. It was common for there to be lunch at Gideon's house on Sundays. Since his divorce, he had started going to temple on Saturdays, so lunch was usually on Sunday. It was relatively special this week since Valery had taken some time off from the restaurant. The restaurant was closed on Tuesdays since that was the slowest day of the week, and was open all other days. Whenever Val took off an extra day, it was usually a Wednesday to give him two days off in a row.

Diya brought two of her nieces, Greta and Karolina. They were ten and eight. Since Karolina was only a year older than Lidi, they loved to play together and we tried to get them together whenever we could. Sometimes we'd pick Karolina up and bring her to our apartment and sometimes we would drive over to their house and spend the afternoon. I think that they believed they were twins, although they didn't look anything alike at all. This was the moment I wanted Sasha by my side.

To share in this wonderful, fulfilling, glorious, loving moment. And yet, I had other feelings at the same time.

Lidi was sitting over by Karolina, and next to me sat Kárin, whom I had called after I found out we were going to have a family lunch today. Luckily she wasn't doing anything and we picked her up on the way. I know she could feel all the eyes on her throughout the meal. Everybody was so amazed at this...apparition, this amazingly different person who happened to look so much like the woman in the framed photograph with me and our little baby in the entry to the condominium.

I wasn't the only one who had someone new in my life. Sitting by Gideon was a widow that he'd met when he started going to temple again, Esther Horwitz. They had been seeing each other for almost six months. She was incredibly nice. She wasn't old enough for retirement, but had been a housewife and was now financially secure and in very good health. She received her late husband's retirement benefits and he'd had a sizeable insurance policy. Her car and her home also had an Accidental Death &Dismemberment rider, so they were both immediately bought and paid in full. She only needed enough money for bills, food, and day to day activities.

Gideon's condo was fairly large. He had his master bedroom, two guest bedrooms, and Lidi had a permanent room as well for whenever she visited her da'dushka. He did so much for his granddaughter that it truly filled me with awe at times. I was so utterly grateful.

Without warning, Lidi and Karolina ran screaming into the living room and both jumped on Kárin at the same time.

"Lidi! Stop that!"

"Oh, hush. She's not hurting anything," said Kárin as she put an arm around each of them and pulled them up into her lap.

It had been playing on my mind all afternoon. Kárin and Lidi were so good together. I couldn't help but be happy as this was only our second date. I needed to put a little pressure on the brakes, but not too much. I had to think of more than just Kárin and me. I had to think about what would happen if things didn't work out for Kárin and me, but Lidi got too attached. It could break her little heart, and that I couldn't bear. I would never be able to forgive myself.

All of us women gathered in the kitchen for cleaning duties, and the men brought everything in from the table to us. We had a regular assembly line going and managed to whip the chore out in no time at all. In handing dishes off, Kárin and I managed to brush hands fairly often. Roni was the first to speak up.

"If you two want to use one of the guest rooms, nobody would know. And you could tell the little girls that you had a 'headache' and had to take a nap," she mouthed off with a huge grin while making air quotes to the word headache.

I punched her lightly on the arm.

"I didn't say there was anything wrong, did I? I was just saying..."

"Yes, I know what you were just saying. We're just starting to see each other. You should back off," I said.

Roni leaned into my ear once we had moved out of range of everybody else, "Have you two done it yet?"

"*Roni!* First off, stop it! And secondly, no, we most certainly have not! I'm not a total tramp."

"No, but you're a beautiful, adult woman about whom I care very much and who has been alone far too long. I'm only looking out for you, you know."

"I understand, but good intentions aside, I'm not saying I'm not going to, but I want to take it a little slow. Okay?"

"No problem, sis," she said, although she winked at me at the same time.

"Lidi? Come on, baby. It's time for us to go home. Get your sweater and say goodbye to the girls."

"Oh, do we have to go already?"

"Yes, we do. Tomorrow's a school day. You have to be in bed on time."

"Bye, Grets. Bye, Kars. See you later."

"Bye," the sisters said in chorus. Everybody gave out hugs all around. I guess I got the seal of approval from Gideon. When he hugged Kárin, he held on tightly and for a long time. She patted his back while he did so, and he kissed her on the cheek.

"By the way, Kárin, if you break her heart, I'll send the..." Gideon started to say.

Kárin gave a huge belly laugh.

"I know. You'll send the Ukrainian mob after me! I've already been warned once by your number one son."

Val put his hand over his mouth to muffle a little laugh. Diya elbowed him in the stomach.

"You, oaf. Did you really?" asked Diya.

"Well, I sort of may have..."

"Muchachos. Que pueden ser tales asnos," Diya said in my direction, indicating the men could be such asses,

Kárin smiled at me.

"Yes they can," she replied.

Fortunately, her apartment was closer to mine than Sasha and I had been originally. As well, our offices were only about twenty blocks apart. We would be able to grab a bus quickly and lunch together during the week...hopefully. Thinking about that, I reached into my purse and pulled out my phone. I punched in a text to Kárin.

'Free for lunch on Wednesday?'

Kárin's phone beeped. She picked it up and saw the text was from me and put it back into her shirt pocket. Once we got in the car and were on our way, she texted me back. I got the tone indicating I'd gotten it.

"Don't text and drive. It's the law. And it's the morally correct thing to do. Or to not do, I guess," she said.

I just grinned.

I didn't hear anything out of Lidi.

"Baby, are you all right back there?"

Not a peep. Kárin turned around to look at her.

"She's out. They played hard all afternoon. She's tuckered out."

We found ourselves in front of Kárin's apartment for the second time in two days. I could stand this being a habit. I picked up my phone and started to read my message.

"No, read it after you're home. Inside. Okay?"

That gave me a bad feeling. My stomach started to turn into knots. I didn't take this as a good omen, but then I was totally turned around when Kárin leaned into me and pushed me back into my seat and started hungrily kissing me. Forcefully. She licked my lips with her tongue and pushed it inside my mouth, but only a little bit...just enough to draw my tongue into her mouth and share. That's what I felt at that moment. Sharing. Totally equal efforts, molding each half into one whole that was bigger than the parts. My heart was pounding in my chest so hard, I felt it was making an audible noise. I was sent soaring although it gave me very mixed emotions. Don't read the text until I'm out of Kárin's sight, but kiss me and pitch woo to me in open view in public. I was confused. And apparently I would have to remain so until I eventually got home, if I was to be true to my word and wait. Finally, we came up for air and Kárin put her forehead against mine, breathing heavily. She talked to me in barely a whisper, "Bye for now, love."

My heart started beating double time now. 'Love,' she'd said. Skipping beats. Doubling beats. Fluttering. Christ, I was messed up and I knew it. I was suddenly seventeen again, without the wisdom I'd gained over the years, and totally running on emotions alone. Suddenly Kárin was out of the car and into her building. My stomach was now an empty pit, yearning for her to come back, to throw herself into my arms. I was acting immature and childish, but I didn't care. I took in a deep breath and put the car in drive, looking back into traffic for oncoming cars.

I woke Lidi in the parking ramp so that we could walk inside. She was getting so big I could barely pick her up anymore. I knew she would be tall like her mother. Sometimes I thought if I sat and stared hard enough, I could see Lidi grow right in front of my eyes. Finally, we were inside. I helped Lidi get her sweater off and she did a great job of remembering to put it on her hook on the coat rack. She walked straight into her bedroom, got on top of her bed, and fell immediately back to sleep. For a change, I didn't bother her about changing into her pajamas or brushing her teeth. I took off my shoes and carried them into my bedroom. Finally, I took out my phone. With a huge, cleansing breath, I looked at Kárin's text message.

'Promise me that I'm not your second choice. Don't make me regret falling madly in love with you.'

I started crying, holding my phone to my chest, sobbing and shaking. After about fifteen minutes, I finally pulled myself together. I typed out a response.

'Are there rules on how long you're supposed to wait before you tell someone that you love them?'

A few minutes later my phone beeped.

'Yes, but I won't tell you what they are until you tell me what wisdom you've gained.'

'Soon. Very soon. I promise. No, you're not my second choice. You're my only choice.'

I didn't get an answer back for over a half an hour. I got a little nervous.

'Sorry. I couldn't see the screen. I couldn't much for a while.'
'Why not?'

'Because I was crying.'
'Please don't cry. Now you've made me sad.'
'Don't be. They were happy tears. I love you.'
'I love you too. You've brought me back to life.'
'Wednesday?'
'Yes. I think I can wait that long.'
'Call me before you go to sleep. No matter how late.'
'I will. Hey.'
'What?'
'I love you.'
'Remember, I said it first.'
'But I thought it first.'
'Wanna bet?'
I laughed openly.

CHAPTER FIVE

It was so hard to wait until Wednesday. I remembered how hard it had been waiting only hours at a time to be with Sasha. It was a strange feeling. I loved Kárin just the same amount as I missed Sasha. I hoped that I would always miss Sasha the same amount. I wanted her memory never to wane, not one iota. I kept glancing at my watch during my eleven o'clock meeting.

"Ms. Aronov?"

"Yes?"

"Do you need to be somewhere else? I'm not keeping you from another appointment, am I?"

"No, Jacob. You're fine. I'm so sorry for not doing a very good job of concentrating today. Would you rather do this later this afternoon, after I've had lunch? Or even tomorrow? I promise that I'll focus myself and give you my undivided attention. I am so truly apologetic."

"That would be fine. How about we push this out until Friday. I'll talk to Fran and see what's open on your calendar. Don't sweat it. Take care of whatever needs you have and we'll reconnect. It's not urgent. We've still got about three weeks."

"Thanks a lot. I'm acting very unprofessionally. I've never done this before."

"Hey, I understand. It happens to everybody once in a while. I go through the same thing two or three times a year it seems like."

"You're fabulous. I'll talk to you later."

We both got up from the table in the conference room and said our goodbyes. I scurried to my desk and quickly brought up Kárin's contact entry.

'You totally trashed my last appointment.'

'Why?'

'Because I couldn't stop looking at my watch and kept having to ask "What?" Not good!'

'LOL. Deal with it.'

'See you in fifteen.'

'Cool. I love you.'

'I do too.'

I leaned over onto my desk and closed my eyes. Our third date. It would be our third date. Only two more to go. Then I could share.

Since I wasn't doing anything, I left early and walked down the street to the restaurant. It was warmer than it had been. I didn't need a jacket today at all. The day developed into an Indian summer afternoon. I went ahead and got a table. Just as the waitress was coming to ask me for my drink order, Kárin walked up behind me and put her hand on my shoulder. I must have jumped an inch out of my chair.

"My, my, aren't we wound up today."

I stood up so quickly I almost knocked my chair over. I wrapped my arms around her and squeezed as hard as I could. Kárin put her hand behind my head and pulled me in close.

"Hi there. I missed you so much. Talking twice a day on the phone and a million texts is just no substitute for being able to hold you," she said.

"I know. I love you."

"Me too. Me too."

We sat down. It was then I realized that the waitress was still standing there, waiting for us.

"Oh, I'm terribly sorry," I said.

"Don't be. I think it's sweet. What can I bring you girls to drink today?"

"I'll have an iced tea and water, please," I said.

"The same for me, if you would."

"Sure. I'll be right back," she said, handing us our menus.

I took Kárin's hands in mine across the table. For the longest time, we just stared into each other's eyes.

"So. We met eight days ago, and we're on our third date. Pretty amazing, isn't it?" I asked.

"I've never fallen for anybody as fast as I've fallen for you," Kárin said in return.

"Please don't take this the wrong way. I know I shouldn't make references to Sasha. So let me just apologize once for every time I do it from now until forever and the end of time plus a day. And feel free at any time to kick me in the shin to make me stop. But that's what Sasha said to me, that she'd never been with anybody that she'd fallen for so fast. If it hadn't been for her passing, we would have stayed together forever. And I'm only bringing it up for this reason: I think it's almost an omen. I just know that we'll get there. However long it takes, and whatever roads we have to travel, we'll get there. You're not angry with me, are you?"

"No. In fact, I think that based on your life and Lidi, and your family that I've met so far, that's the sweetest thing I could imagine hearing."

"I'm glad."

"Out of curiosity...what happened to Sasha?"

"I told you she was a social worker, right?"

"Yes."

"She went on a home visit to remove some children from a home up in the projects. It wasn't even her case, but there were several children and they were short-handed at the other office, so they asked her to go up and help out. Of course, she said yes and jumped right into the fray. Right after they got there, there were shots fired and somebody called 9-1-1. They responded with S.W.A.T. and a negotiator. They had no response for thirty minutes, which is the limit, so they stormed the apartment. The father, who didn't live with the family, shot the mother, his children, two police officers, and three social workers. Shot them all in cold blood, then turned the gun on himself and pulled the trigger."

"My God. That's terrible. I'm almost sorry I asked, but I would have had to eventually. You understand, right?"

"Of course. You'd think I would get used to telling the story. I've told the same story to so many people, but it still pulls at me. Every time I have to talk about it, I have to stay detached or I get sucked down."

"You, poor baby," Kárin said, squeezing my hands.

"I'll be all right."

"I know anything can happen to anybody, anywhere, anytime, but you have me now…for as long as you want me. Just know that."

"You told me there are rules on how long you should wait before you tell someone you love them. You didn't tell me what the rule was yet, but you told me you loved me anyway. Are there rules on how long you should wait before you tell them that you want them around forever?"

"Yes. There most certainly are."

"Want to give me a hint?"

"Not until you divulge your secret first."

"Then to hell with the rules. Kárin, I think…no, I know…I want you around forever."

"As happy as that makes me feel, make sure that's really what you want before you say that. Sometimes people think they want something, and they have displaced emotions or are somewhat confused even to themselves…"

"Kárin, shut up. I want you around forever."

"Have I told you lately how much I love you?"

"One hundred times a day."

"I'll keep doing it. Wild horses couldn't drag me away from you."

I smiled.

I hated having to walk back to my office after lunch. I'd already stayed a half hour over, but I didn't have anything set in my schedule until three o'clock, and if Fran really needed me she would have called me. Part of me was walking ten feet off the sidewalk, but part of me was ready to turn around one hundred and eighty degrees and run as fast I could to catch up with her and hold on for dear life.

I thought I could sneak past Fran and get to my desk unseen. I knew better, but I tried anyway.

"Aly, that asshole Brook, called from the D.A.'s office. He wants to know what's holding up the paperwork on the Butler kid. What do you want me to tell him?

"Don't tell him anything. I'll take it home tonight. It's almost complete. I won't give him the satisfaction of pushing the point."

"Your mobile plan does have unlimited text, doesn't it?"

"Yes. Why do you ask?" I said, shaking my head slightly with a puzzled look on my face.

"I've seen you typing non-stop for the last three days. From zero to sixty in under ten seconds. It must be love. Are you going to bring her by so I can meet her?"

"I don't know what in the hell you're talking about."

"You couldn't be more obvious if somebody took a felt-tipped pen and wrote in on your forehead. I'm fifty-three years old and I've seen it all: you text non-stop, you can't concentrate, you have a far-away look in your eyes, and since you're gay, it must be a woman. Correct me if any part of that is wrong."

"I guess I'm busted, huh?"

"Yup. Red-handed. You got caught with your hand in the cookie jar, missy," Fran laughed.

I sat in the chair opposite Fran's desk.

"Oh, Franny. I never thought I'd ever feel this way again. Sasha and I weren't just together, we weren't just married. Until the day that I lost her, we were deeply, madly in love. Every single day. Life was perfect. After she was gone, I did my best not to show that to Lidi so that she'd be as happy as she could. I've always made sure she knew everything about her mother except how she died, and it turns out she found out about that at school from some other kid whose dad's a cop and knew about it. I feel like I've been wheeled out of the ambulance into the ER and got hit with the defibrillator. I'm alive again for the first time in years, literally! I've got a girlfriend and it feels wonderful."

"Girlfriend? Aren't you supposed to start out with a couple dates or something first? You'd better be careful, dearie."

"On our first date, within the first twenty minutes and with Lidi there, we had that mystery sorted out. She's my girlfriend. She looks like Sasha's twin and she has a bright, bubbly personality, but that's purely coincidental. I made very sure of that. We just clicked. Instantaneously. In all honesty, it took even less time to be attracted to her than it did to be attracted to Sasha. With Sasha, it wasn't until after we'd been out once. With Kárin, it was within the first fifteen minutes of meeting her. And I have to reiterate…it isn't because they look like each other."

"Just remember, we still expect you to do at least a little work," Fran said with a grin.

"You know I work plenty hard!"

"You know, you're too easy to tip over. You do so need to figure that out. You're not a baby anymore, but you still have a lot of learning to do."

"You got me. Happy now?"

"Pretty much. Now go away and let me get some of *my* work done if you don't mind. Otherwise, my boss will bitch at me."

"I'm your boss and I've haven't bitched at you in over a year. Since I got here, if memory serves."

"Well, there could always be a first time."

CHAPTER SIX

'There are two tears on my cheeks. The one on the left is a happy tear to have gotten an hour and a half with you. The one on the right is a sad tear because I had to leave you,' I punched into my phone.

'I do so love you, but aren't you getting just a little over-emotional?' Kárin responded immediately.

'Are you saying I'm too much drama for you?'

'Not at all. But we've got all the time in the world. Relax, honey.'

'Sorry. I've been storing up love for five years with nobody to accept it. I don't mean to dump it all out at once and get it all over you. I'll rein it in, if it will make you happy. I promise.'

'Now you're upset, aren't you?'

'Not really. Sometimes I have a problem pulling back from my current vista and seeing the whole picture. I can do that at work, but my personal life is different.'

'Let's start over. You calm down a little bit, and I'll understand a little bit more, and we'll be there to support each other as we start this journey through life. Don't forget, if you really want me around you forever, we've got years and years. We won't accomplish everything by Thanksgiving.'

'You're right, of course. So far it's been about my family. Is there anything you want to do with your family? I just realized that you haven't even talked about them much.'

'They still live in Denton. We can go out sometime around Christmas if you want. My sister, Kalista, lives in Seattle with her boyfriend, working as an artist. '

'In that case, do you want to go to my parents' house down in Queens on Sunday? I take Lidi down about once a month and we go to church and then out to a buffet for lunch. You and I wouldn't have to go to church if you didn't want.'

'I don't mind going with you. What time do we leave?'

'Do you have plans on Saturday?'

'Not right now.'

'We usually go down for dinner on Saturday and spend the night. If we did that you'd have to sleep in a single bed with me.'

'I could control myself. Maybe.'

'You'd have to.'

'If that's what you want.'

'Not want, but need for now.'

'I can respect that. What time are you picking me up?'

'Five o'clock.'

'Talk to you before bed tonight.'

'Okay. I love you.'

'I love you too, honey.'

"Ahem..."

My head whipped around. Fran was leaning against the door frame to my office. Oops.

"Um.... How long have you been standing there, Fran?"

"About ten minutes. I was going to go get a hotdog and a soda and just make a show out of it. Care to go back over our last conversation?"

"Oh, my God! I had no idea how long I'd been texting with Kárin," I said looking at my watch.

"I didn't think you did. I was coming in to remind you that you're meeting with Jacob at three o'clock. I was going to say in twenty minutes, but by now it's just ten minutes."

"No, that's three o'clock Friday, not today. We moved it later in the day *and* moved it to Friday. Jacob was the one who rescheduled, wasn't he? If somebody gave you the wrong day, it would have been him. I'm not trying to finger point or get out of the crosshairs, I'm just saying..." I said.

"May I make a suggestion, if I may be so bold?" asked Fran.

"Sure."

"Go home now. You have no appointments this afternoon. Take home two or three cases you can work on through the evening at your own pace and still get the work done. But start by pouring yourself a lovely glass of wine and drawing a nice, hot bubble bath. Maybe a candle or two. Clear your mind. And come in tomorrow with that burning desire to be the lead runner that you always are. I hate seeing you this way, although I see how happy you are."

"Why are you so all-fired sure that I'm over the moon happy? I mean, I have a girlfriend, but it's not like it's the end of the world as we know it, as the song goes."

"Because I got a call from somebody who asked me about you."

"What are you talking about, Fran? I've only had two dates and both times have been with family and with Lidi there."

"Because Kárin called here about an hour ago and talked to me."

"Why didn't you say something? What did she want? Why did she call you?"

"Because she wanted to know if you were going to be in the office."

"What for?"

"I believe your answer is on my desk right about now."

I jumped up and ran around the side of my desk to Fran's. There on the top of her desk was a long, sort of narrow, white box with a wide, bright red ribbon on the top. I picked the box up and gently opened it. It contained two dozen Black-eyed Susans. I smiled widely.

"Now, please take your flowers and get the heck out of here. I'll see you bright and early tomorrow. Right?"

Without even acknowledging Fran, I went back to my desk. I got my purse out of the bottom left hand drawer, put six or seven folders in my messenger bag along with my laptop, and locked my desk. Fran stood in the doorway smirking. I walked up to her on my way out.

"Thanks, Franny. You're the greatest. I always feel safe with you covering me. I hope you know how much I appreciate all you do for me."

"If you *really* meant that, you'd get me a nice, fat, pay raise."

"I tell you what, the very next time I get called into the County Commission office, I'll ask them why they're dragging their feet on that," I laughed.

When I hit the streets, my spirits were high. I headed for the grocery store. I'd been so out of it, depressed, distracted, whatever you want to call it, that the kitchen wasn't very well stocked lately. Not too far from our apartment is a wonderful grocery store. You can call in an order and have it delivered, or shop in the store and have it delivered. It doesn't cost very much for the service, and since I was going to get a ton of stuff without having anybody help me, I decided to shop in-store and have it delivered.

I picked up wine, beer, milk, cereal, and various cheeses. In addition, I got beef, chicken, juice boxes, bread, paper towels, TP, frozen vegetables...it would actually be shorter to tell you what I didn't pick up since I had basically let everything at home run out. As a last minute thought, I went to the Health & Beauty Aids department. I selected two different designs and sizes of soft bristle tooth brushes. I was not only hoping, but confident, that one would soon be used at my house and I would leave one in Queens. I also got a travel size tube of toothpaste in case she didn't like mine and a travel size organic deodorant.

'Tell me to stop bothering you and I will.'

I hoped that Kárin wasn't in a meeting or something. Usually it wasn't urgent, but I needed her to pick up now.

'Now you're starting to scare me. You can't even go an hour without talking to me?'

'I'm so sorry. It can wait.'

'I was only joking! What is it, my love?'

Whew! Back to 'my love'. She had me for a second.

'I know we had lunch today and I said I didn't want us to spend every waking hour with each other, and you said we had plenty of time, but something came up.'

'What do you need?'

'What would you think about coming over to our place tonight for dinner? I was going to cook poo cha stuffed crab for Lidi tonight. You can't make it for less than four people really. And it doesn't keep at all. If you came over, it would be a lot better. I might even get Roni to come over with Michael, if they don't already have plans. With or without them, would you want to come over, maybe?'

'Beg for me.'

'Oh, pretty please, would you please, please come over? Would you?'

'ROFL. Consider it done. What time?'

'Six thirty would be good. Come earlier if you want and hang out. I promise we won't keep you up too late on a school night, so to speak.'

'Be there with bells on. Love you.'

'I loved you first.'

'But I said it first.'

'Are we always going to argue this one, even when we're old and grey?'

'Probably.'

'See you when you get here.'

Then I pulled up the contact for Roni.

'Hey. You where you can talk?'

'Sure. Are you okay?'

'I just wanted to know if you and Michael were free to come over tonight for some stuffed poo cha crab with Kárin, Lidi, and me.'

'Sorry, we have to go to a mixer for the Party Headquarters tonight. Black tie. I'd probably rather be there.'

'Liar. You live for that type of political gathering. You're a natural. You're in your element.'

'I am, aren't I? I'm embarrassed, but it's true. Rain check?'

'Always. Love you, baby sister.'

'Right back at you, Auntie.'

'Call me old again and I'll spank you.'

'Promise? Won't that make Kárin jealous?'

'Go have fun. TTFN.'

I smirked to myself. After Roni had graduated she went to work for a fairly large company in a business department, but within a year was running that department. She was already involved with the party and politics from her college days. While she was at one of these party conference meetings, she happened to bump into somebody that worked directly for the party. They started talking, which led to a direct introduction to the Congresswoman and her Chief of Staff. Within three months, she was the Director of Information in that office.

I headed back to the fresh fish section of the meat department and bought two pounds of King crab legs and a half pound of uncooked medium shrimp. Lidi loved making crab cakes and serving them in giant clam shells on our plates. I also picked up a pound of freshly ground sausage that they ground right in the store. It was high in sage content, which I liked. Lastly, I bought a couple of lemons and limes and a sack of tangerines. Finally, after about three full circuits of the store, I was finished. I hadn't been very efficient tonight in my rounds of the store. I spent over an hour and a half. I checked out. Two hundred seventy-four dollars and change. Ouch!

I hurried home and changed clothes. About thirty-five minutes later the delivery truck came by with my groceries. The two deliverymen brought them up in one load with their large cart. I spent my first twenty-five minutes just putting the groceries up, leaving out everything I would use cooking tonight. I got out three pans to start working. I'd prepare all the ingredients and then bring the dish together right before to keep it fresh and warm.

Poo cha is from, among other places, Malaysia. There they use a higher pork to seafood mix, but I prefer it in basically the opposite proportion. I cooked all of the sub-sets of the meal and added short grained rice just to give us something to go with the crab. Another thing I did to change the basic standard recipe for the poo cha was, instead of two tablespoons of fish sauce I used one teaspoon. It does add something unique to the dish, but I'm not a huge fan of fish sauce as a rule. And of course, as always, a couple of baguettes that I'd sliced, then painted with melted butter, and heated up with freshly minced garlic. I wrapped the bread in foil so I could just pop it in the oven while the crab was cooking. After I got dinner to that point, I cleaned up everything I'd used so far and put it away to minimize the work later. I got out plates and set the table, got a serving tray for the bread, and pulled the clam shells down to wash the dust out of them. I hadn't used them in forever so I was sure they needed a quick rinse. I stacked them on the counter in readiness.

It was still only four forty-five and Lidi wouldn't be home for another half an hour. I opted for a quick shower. The hot water felt wonderful. One of the things I love about our building is that the heating and hot water all come from a boiler—that meant an endless supply. Back when it went out on Sasha and me, it meant we not only didn't have heating in the apartment during the winter for an entire weekend, but we also didn't have hot water for showers. For those few days, cleaning was done with a cold, wet cloth, but it was still preferable to being pelted with cold water. It's strange how you think of things like that, how the memories come from nowhere. Most of the time, they were pleasant memories.

After my shower, I dried my hair and put on light makeup so I didn't look totally hideous. I got dressed in a Mets jersey and some jeans with holes in the knees. It would be a change-up from how Kárin had always seen me. A test to see if she'd still want me after she'd seen the real me. I laughed inwardly. When I finished, I opened the second drawer of my dresser and took several items of clothing and put them in the top and third drawers. I also moved some things over to the left. The dresser was a double wide, so it was roomy. Now the right-hand drawer was empty. I placed the two toothbrushes, the toothpaste, and the deodorant in the drawer. I'd surprise Kárin when the time was right. It was important to me that I waited.

I heard Lidi come running through the apartment.

"Mommy, Mommy, Mommy! You're already home!"

"I sure am. I left early today."

Lidi came up to me and wrapped her arms around my legs, almost tackling me.

"Hi, Esther. You don't know how much difference it has made in our lives for you to be able to pick up Lidi from the after school program and bring her home. You're such a lifesaver."

"Don't be ridiculous. She's an absolute gem. So, have you given any more thought to planning her bat mitzvah? It's never too early to start training."

"Esther, you're incorrigible. She won't take it until she's fourteen, and she still has until she's about twelve to start taking her classes. And like I've told her before, I am going to wait until she's ten or eleven and let her make up her own mind. Once a month we go to temple, and once a month we go to a Protestant church. She's going to be raised observing both traditions no matter how she leans, unless of course she goes off to college and decides to turn Buddhist!" I laughed.

"Wouldn't that be something?"

The door buzzer rang. I walked over to the panel and pushed the button.

"Yes?"

"If I tell you how much I love you, will you let me come upstairs?"

I pushed the entry button for Kárin. She came up quickly, carrying her briefcase and a box. She set them on the floor by the door and come over to me and gave me a huge hug and a long, slow kiss. She smiled at me and said it again.

"I love you so much."

"I love you, too. You have no idea."

"Actually, I think I do!"

"Esther, is Gideon working late tonight?"

"Yes, he's got some quarterly tax thing that's giving them fits. The company that makes the software found an error. They had to reship the software to everybody that uses it, and now they've got to re-enter all the data and re-run it. Apparently they can't even pull the existing data out of the old software and just insert that into the new software. Something about overwriting and thinking that it hasn't."

"Circular crosslinking files. Most people don't know that there are two directories on a computer system. It writes one, then writes the data, and if the data is verified, it writes the second table. It compares the first directory to the second, and if they match then it completes the process. If the first and second don't match, it fails. If the second one doesn't get written it's because the initial process failed," I said matter-of-factly.

Esther and Kárin looked at each other as if I had just spoken Japanese, then together looked back at me in unison.

"Wah wah wah-wawa wah wah."

"What?" I asked.

"In Peanuts cartoons, when the adults talk, it sounds like a trumpet with a mute."

I laughed.

"Sorry. I keep forgetting that most people don't know, and quite frankly, don't care about computers. They just use them as a tool. And when they don't work, they call somebody like me and expect it to be fixed yesterday and in perfect order."

"Pretty much. I mean I set up hotspots and wee, small networks and install software for all kinds of groups that I work with, but that doesn't mean I understand anything that goes on under the hood. It more or less makes me able to change tires and repaint the outside."

"Esther, I haven't heard yet. Do you eat pork?"

"Not very often, but I don't run away from it. It's more out of respect that I limit how often I do eat it."

"Want to stay for dinner? I'm making some stuffed crab with shrimp and pork sausage. It's a Malaysian version of crab cakes, so to speak."

"Ooo, that sounds yummy. Let me call Gideon and let him know where I am," she said, picking up her phone and going into my bedroom for some privacy.

"A little early, but since Lidi goes to bed early during the week, you want me start putting everything together now?"

"Sounds dreamy. A bitch that can cook for me. It *will* be good, won't it? I'm not going to get ptomaine or anything?"

"You'll just have to wait until about one or two in the morning and see how your stomach feels," I said.

I held one arm around the small of her back, rubbing my other hand in small circles on her stomach. I had taken up running to try and take my mind off Sasha's death, and am in a lot better shape than I was. I've gone from a size twelve down to a size ten, and even then they fit pretty loosely, but Kárin had some hard abs. I mean rock hard.

"Well, well, well, it looks like somebody works out regularly."

"Yes, I do. There's a gym in our building and I go almost every day. Mostly I run the treadmill, but I do the machines as well. No free weights though. No intentions of bulking up," Kárin said while I pulled her by the hand into the kitchen.

I already had the filling ready to go and pulled out a flat sheet, covering it with a layer of foil. I placed all the clam shells on the sheet then I used a brush to cover the inside of the shells with a layer of ghee. Next I spooned them to heaping with the meat mix, covering them with fresh lemon juice and pepper. After sliding them into the oven, I dropped the rice into the already boiling water and put the bread into the oven with the clamshells.

Esther came in and sat down at the table to visit while waiting for dinner to come together, which only took about ten minutes. I poured three glasses of white wine for the adults and got a juice box out for Lidi.

"Mommy, I don't want juice. I want iced tea with oranges in it," she said as she got up to go to the bathroom.

"Okay, baby," I said, getting up to make the exchange.

"So, Esther, I hope you're not obligated to ask permission from Gideon every time you do something," queried Kárin, and I knew she was asking a serious question.

"Pish-posh. I've never been that way my whole life even though I was, for the better part of it, a housewife. My house was a damned matriarchal society, and I let it be known daily," she laughed.

"Good for you!"

"Gideon is such a kind and caring man, and he worries about me. He's asked me to move in with him, but I want to make sure it's for the right reasons. I don't want him to feel sorry for me. I want him to do it because he wants me at his right hand all the time."

Kárin and I passed a knowing glance at each other. It seemed we'd just had a couple of talks about this very same thing. Lidi came back in, got up in her booster seat, and we all started eating.

"Hey, Kárin, have you seen Mommy's necklaces?" asked Lidi.

"I know, they're so pretty," answered Kárin.

"Mommy Aly gave Mommy Sasha the Star of David at their first Christmas, and Mommy Sasha gave Mommy Aly her cross at the same time. The cross is the same one as in a movie."

"What movie was that?" asked Kárin.

I was just about to step in and quash this discussion, but for whatever reason I didn't. Was I testing Lidi? Was I testing Kárin? Or was it even possible that I was testing myself?

"Loving Annabelle. It's a movie about lesbians," said Lidi off-handedly.

"Lidi! How do you know all of what that movie is about? You haven't watched it, have you?" I shouted.

"No, one of the girls at school watched it with her sister."

"Well, I think it's probably a movie that you wouldn't understand yet, Lidi, but I've seen the movie, and it's one of my favorite movies. The woman in the movie that had the same exact necklace was named Simone, but it's probably a movie that you want to wait to watch until you're older. And you want to watch with your mommy so she can answer any questions you have while you're watching it," interjected Kárin.

Nice save. Brilliant. And I agree, Lidi wouldn't have any way of understanding the storyline or the emotions or the significance of the interaction between the characters.

"Holy cow! This is some wickedly awesome food, girl!" exclaimed Kárin.

"I agree. Roni, Michael, Valery, Diya, Grigoriy, and Gabrielle. Even Gideon. They all say she's a great cook. And coming from Val, who owns a restaurant, that's a supreme compliment," offered Esther.

"I guess I do all right."

"Well, I texted our driving service a few minutes ago, so he should be downstairs already, or if not, in just a couple of minutes. So, like a prom dress...I'm off!" she retorted.

Both Kárin and I laughed heartily at that.

"Have a great night, Esther. See you tomorrow."

"Good night, everybody," she said pulling on her sweater and picking up her purse.

"So what I said earlier goes, huh?" asked Kárin with a wink.

"I guess so," I winked back.

After we got the dishes cleaned up, Lidi went into her room to color with crayons for a while before bedtime. Esther thanked me for a wonderful dinner and made her leave. Kárin stood toe to toe with me and tilted her face into mine. It took us over five minutes to come up for air.

"I love you," Kárin said, for the hundredth time today.

"I love you too, sweetie," I said as if in a call and response.

"What time do you go to bed during the week?"

"Anywhere from ten to midnight. I don't like to go to bed any later than that, and I try for eleven in bed and read or listen to music or watch television. Why?"

Without responding, Kárin turned on the television and flipped through the streaming movies until she found one she liked. A rom-com. Then she grabbed my hand and pulled me over to the couch. She lay down first, putting one of the throw pillows under her head, then patted the cushion in front of her. I lay down in front of her and snuggled back into her. Since I'm so short and she's so tall, it wasn't a problem for either of us to see the screen okay. I pulled her bottom arm under my neck and her top arm over my upper body and held both her hands in mine, pulling all four of our hands together into my chest. I forgot about the movie for a few minutes. I closed my eyes and sighed. I just took in the love I was getting and sending at the same time.

"Hey, honey, are you awake?"

"Yes, my love. I'm just lost in you for the moment. Is that okay?"

In answer, Kárin snaked her lips down through my hair and kissed me on the neck. It absolutely sent shivers down my spine. Three full sets of shivers.

"I love you so much."

"I know. I can feel it. I can tell."

I parted my legs and used my foot to pull her top leg forward, capturing her thigh between mine, holding tightly. Not even in a sexual way. That had to wait. We finished the movie and got up, stretching. Kárin, without being asked, went to the door and put her shoes on and picked up her purse.

"Thank you for such a totally wonderful meal. I can't wait for the day when I can get that every day," she smiled.

"I don't cook like that every day, so have no illusions," I laughed.

She came and put her face in mine once again.

"Honey, take as much time as you need. I'll wait forever for you. I hope you don't want to make me wait forever, but just so you know, I now belong to you. I'm willing to wait if I have to."

"Thanks. Don't worry. There's just a couple of things. It's nothing major. Have faith in me. That's all I ask."

"I'll call you when I get home just to talk to you for a few minutes before you go to sleep."

"Okay. And don't forget, Saturday night we go to Queens. I'm not sure what you normally sleep in, but make sure you have pajamas—or long shorts and a tee, not a tank or crop top—something relatively demure."

"I know. Lidi."

"Oh, hell no. When it's been really hot in the summer on muggy days, and the air conditioner isn't able to keep up, we've been known to take a cool shower together. Then we'll dry each other off with the hair dryer and climb in bed together with just a sheet over us. The sheet's only to keep your own body from sticking to itself. She's perfectly comfortable with human bodies. It's my parents. They've come a long way, but they're still basically ultra-conservative. How I ended up ultra-liberal in that house is a question I still have no answer to. My initial 'coming out' party wasn't very spectacular; didn't go well at all. Their house is a pretty small two-bedroom, so Sash and I had to bunk together when we stayed over. I guess one of us could have stayed on the couch, but I just pretty much, in my own way, said this is the way it's going to be or we're not going to stay."

"Hardcore. So does that mean we'll be bunking together when we go there this coming weekend?"

"Have a problem with that?"

"Not at all. I already told you that earlier when you asked me over for the weekend."

"Do you think you can do it and keep your hands off me?"

"If that's what you want. It'll be hard, but I can do it. I'm an adult."

"Thank you."

CHAPTER SEVEN

Kárin and I talked on the phone every lunch and every night, and texted in between for the next two and a half days. I could barely stand the wait until Saturday evening. It seemed like somebody had put the batteries in the clock upside down and the hands were turning counter clockwise. I had to force myself to clean. Lidi did a pretty good job for a change, but she couldn't remember from one moment to the next what her task was, and I had to keep prodding her. Of course I could only give her one task at a time. Then there was the problem that every ten minutes I couldn't find her, and I had to look through the apartment, and she was playing with Lilly and Puppet, our cats. Lilly was getting so old she could barely move now. I didn't expect her to live very much longer, to tell you the truth, but Puppet was around seven years old and she was full of life. It was only about four o'clock when Kárin showed up.

"Sorry I'm so early. I would say something quaint like I wasn't sure what traffic was going to be like, or something to that effect, but the plain truth is that I couldn't stand waiting another minute. So I came early. I hope that's all right."

I walked up to her and put my index finger to my lips to quiet her. Then I put my hands behind her head, pulled it down to me, and embedded my lips into hers. I broke our kiss for a moment.

"You talk too much," I said, returning to her mouth, my arms wrapping around her back, feeling her, drinking her in, sucking her chi and her karma, tasting her soul.

Lidi came in while we were intertwined. I went over and sat on one end of the couch.

"Baby, come here to Mommy for a minute. We need to talk, okay?"

"Okay," she said as she crawled up onto my lap.

"When we're over at Grandma and Grandpa Lockewood's this weekend, they'll be sleeping in their bedroom, and you always sleep on the couch with blankets. Well, there aren't any more places to sleep, so Kárin is going to be sleeping in my bed. Is that okay with you?"

"Kárin's your girlfriend, why would she want to sleep somewhere else?"

"You'll find out as you get older, baby, that just because you have a boyfriend or a girlfriend doesn't mean that you sleep in the same bed as them. At your school, isn't Drew sort of your boyfriend?"

"I guess, but we're just kids."

"I know, you're just in the second grade now, but even with adults, sometimes men and women who are in love don't sleep together. I know it's complicated and you don't understand it yet. Your problem is that for you everything has an easy answer and is simple. If only the rest of the world thought like you did, it would be a better place to be."

"Aly, tell me now. Is this going to be awkward? Would it be better if I skipped this one?"

"Unequivocally no, for several reasons. The most important of which is that my parents had to learn to accept me and my decisions once, and they'll have to do it again...or rather, still. In addition to that, I just plain want you with me this weekend."

"Me too! I want you with me and Mommy," said Lidi, practically shouting it.

"Lidi, use your inside voice, please. And there are another couple of reasons."

"Like what?" asked Kárin quizzically.

"You'll see. It will all come clear very soon. Anyway, there's still a little bit of time before we go, so I have to make a couple of phone calls."

"My love, your hand," said Kárin, pointing to my left hand.

I held it up and wiggled my fingers. They were bare where I'd taken off my rings.

"I promised till death do us part and, unfortunately, that happened. Now I'm a widow and I'm dating a wonderful woman. I don't want to insult her by wearing my wedding rings from the previous marriage."

"For me, would you at least wear them on your right hand? I insist. I'm not kidding. I want you to."

"Okay."

I got up and walked into my bedroom. I opened my jewelry box containing my diamond necklace and earrings, my pearls, my costume jewelry, and Sasha's and my wedding rings. I withdrew my wedding rings. Hopefully they would fit my other hand. Fortunately, they were a perfect match, so that was that.

"Better?" I said holding up my right hand, palm inward.

"Much. Thank you. Both for offering to remove them, and for wearing them again."

I walked up to Kárin and scratched her cheek, then gave her a peck on the lips. I grabbed my phone and sat down on the couch. I pulled up Brianna, my best friend of the younger crowd, first. Not only was Bri my best friend, but her husband, Danny, was the sperm donor for Lidi.

"Well, hello, stranger. We were just talking about you. You seemed to have dropped off the face of the earth for a week. Nobody's heard from you at all, which is pretty weird. You usually talk to me or Lexa or somebody. What's going on?"

"Is Danny there?"

"Sure."

"Put me on speaker."

"Okay, we're here."

"Are you ready for this? You might want to sit down."

"Is everything all right?"

"More than all right. Lidi and I are going to Mom and Dad's this weekend, and we're taking something with us."

"Okay. Are we supposed to try and guess?"

"Well, it's not so much a some*thing* as it is a some*one*."

There was only silence on the other end of the line.

"Well, what do you think?"

There was still no sound on Bri's end.

"You guys still there?"

"We're here. Danny and I both could have sworn you said you were taking 'someone' home with you for the weekend."

"Her name is Kárin Zajac. She's a non-profit coordinator for several different charitable organizations. Well, what do you think?"

"Aly, I think I'm blown away. If somebody had walked up to me and said that Alison Aronov was dating again, I'd have called them a liar and punched them in the face."

"We're not exactly dating. That's the thing. It's been sort of a weird week."

"If you're not dating, why are you taking her to meet your parents?"

"Because she's not my date, she's my girlfriend."

"Oh...My...God! OhmyGod. OhmyGod. Are you serious?" Brianna screamed out.

"Yes, I am. I never thought it could happen again, but it has. Anyway, we're going to shove off now, and I still need to call Lexa and Bobby really quick. I'll talk to you on Sunday night, all right?"

"Aly? Be careful. Don't go too fast and get caught up and get shot down."

"I appreciate your concern, but it's a little too late for that. For both of us. Anyway, talk to you Sunday night. Love you."

"Love you too. Bye."

Before I even gave Bri and Danny a chance to close their gaping mouths, I connected to Lexa.

"Where have you been, girl? We've been trying to find you. It's like you were kidnapped by a band of brigands and exiled in transportation."

"Your language has gotten so colorful since you got your doctorate and you're teaching literature. You know that?"

"Damn it, Aly. We're not here to talk about me, we're here to talk about you. What's your excuse? I'm waiting."

"Like I just told Bri, Lidi and I are going to Mom and Dad's this weekend, and we're making it a special trip."

I looked over at Kárin. She was grinning from ear to ear. I think it was getting very real for her now, and she realized that I was as serious as I said I was.

"What the hell are you talking about? Screw the riddles and start speaking English."

"Lexa, I'm taking my new girlfriend to meet the folks."

"You're *what?*"

"Lidi and I are taking Kárin Zajac to meet my parents. Kárin just happens to be my new girlfriend. Not my new date, my girlfriend."

"She's *what?*"

"Okay, this is getting repetitive. Either pay attention or put Bobby on and let me talk to him."

"Wait just a minute."

"Hey, Aly. What's up? Everybody has been wondering why we hadn't heard from you in maybe ten or twelve days."

"I was trying to tell Lexa, but she wouldn't listen."

"She's standing here with her hands on her hips and a stupid look on her face. So what's the deal?"

"I tried to tell her that I'm taking my new girlfriend to meet my parents in a few minutes."

"Let me get this straight. She's not somebody you're starting to date. This is your girlfriend. And you're taking her to meet your parents already. And this is in a period of less than two weeks?"

"Actually, this will be our fifth date in eight days."

"Hey, it's me again."

"So Bobby didn't want to talk, huh?"

"No, he's right here. He just made me take the phone back. I'm not sure whether to be happy for you or pissed at you."

"What?"

"We've all thought it was way overdue for you to get back on the horse, but for you to do all this without a single call.... That's not very considerate of you, if you ask me."

"Oh, Lexa, hunny bunny, I've been trying to start a relationship with this wonderful woman and still be Lidi's mom, and still try to work...I've just been overrun. That's why I made time, even though it will put us a little late getting to Queens, to call you and Bri. Okay? Don't be cross with me. Pretty please?"

"You know I'd never truly be mad at you. It's just a hell of a shock, you have to admit."

"It was meant to be, Lexa. I was meant to be alone for all those years, which let me finish law school, let me get a good start on raising Lidi, and gave me the chance to meet Kárin. Right?"

"That's a beautiful way to think of it, actually. Well, don't be late on my part. Get moving. Just call me when you get home. Sometime after Lidi goes to bed on Sunday. Okay?"

"I promise."

"Okay. I forgive you."

"I'm not worthy."

"Don't be catty."

"Give Bobby a kiss for me."

"I will. Give Kárin a kiss for me," she giggled, and disconnected.

I walked over to Kárin and kissed her twice.

"That's from Lexa and Bobby."

"This is a good thing, I'm hoping. Both Brianna and Lexa seemed to be a bit concerned about your welfare. You probably should have called them, if you already call them that often. It would be different if you talked to them once a month or every six weeks, but you probably scared them all. Is there anybody else you should call?"

"Ah, yes. Give me one more second..."

"Detective Captain Martha Devonshire. May I help you?"

"Hi, Martha, Aly."

"Hey, where have you been hiding? Communications blackout there?"

I laughed. Such a cop. She was the greatest.

"How's your girlfriend? What's her name, Burly, Berry, what is it? And what kind of name is that for a firefighter? She should have a real manly name."

"Beryl. And stop it. She works for the fire department, but she's in IT, just like you were before you sold out, you brat. And for your information, there's not one manly thing about that chick. She's as soft and sweet as they come. She is one groovy chick! Anyway, one of these days she's going to hear you and she'll leave me because of my bad taste in friends. Either that or come to me and expect me to take my gun and put three rounds through your foot. How's Lidi?"

"Great. Growing like a weed every damn day."

"So is this a business call or a social call?"

"Social. Well, sort of business, but not work, business. More along the lines of personal business; about the running of things. How things are. Maybe workflow of personal life..."

"Damn it, woman, either speak with some clarity or I'm hanging up!" she barked into her phone in her gruff way.

"When's the next Last Order of the Dames of the Round Table going to happen?"

"I don't know. We're due this week which means it will be either this coming week or the following week."

"Give me a two-day notice if you can. Okay?"

"You just have the need to get with the girls, or is something particular going on? Your voice is giving you away. Remember I'm a Detective Captain. I can read people even when I can't see them. I can tell in your voice. What's the angle? You can tell Auntie Martha now. Why are you so keen on a meet? You've got something up your sleeve, don't you? Or someone. That's it. Ha! You've found somebody! I told you I could figure it out! Goddamn I'm good. Too bad the pay brackets don't come anywhere near my true worth to this sorry ass department."

"You know, Martha, you suck. You just truly suck!"

"Okay, how about this. I won't tell anyone. Not even Estefanía. You know, she's been living with María-Elena for over two years now. And even though you two went out a couple of times and found out that you were destined to be life-long friends and not lovers, this is going to break her heart. You know that. Be gentle with her. We all love her so much. Make sure you pay a lot of attention to her. Deal?"

"How could you even think that I would do any less? Remember, I love her at least as much as anybody in our group. And probably more than most of the girls. Anyway, give me a call. I'll be looking forward to it."

"10-4."

"Okay, everybody, enough diversions let's get on the road to Grandma and Grandpa's house," I said as I picked up my purse and my overnight bag.

I had clothes and everything else we needed in my bag for both me and Lidi. I had also picked up the toothbrushes in the dresser and stuck them in the bag so that Kárin could pick one out once we were there. Lidi and I already had toothbrushes we left there, and a few changes of clothes. We even had pajamas we left there. Kárin picked up her small duffel and made for the door. We had already fed the cats so they would be okay until tomorrow with no problem. We walked over to the parking ramp, put our gear in the back, got in, buckled up, and fired up the engine. I inched out of the parking space and we were on our way. Traffic was unusually light for a Saturday. We made it to Queens in almost record time.

I'd fought all week long with whether or not I should call and tell Mom and Dad I was bringing Kárin. The decisive factor is that we always had leftovers they sent home with me, so there would be enough food, and I think I was just ornery so I 'neglected' to call them. Strangely enough, it was exactly at the moment in time I was pondering this that Kárin spoke up.

"Your folks do know I'm coming, don't they?"

I hung my head and looked up with sad, puppy dog eyes and stuck my bottom lip out in a pout while still trying to keep my eyes mostly on the road.

"You're kidding me! You're submarining your parents, and you're making me an unwitting accomplice! I can't believe you. This is inexcusable."

"Don't judge me until you've walked in my shoes. Believe me, with my mother, the way to teach her to swim is the old-fashioned method where you just pick up the kid and throw them in the water. I came here a few years back and came out to them. Then I brought Sasha home. Then on another trip *after* that, the big blowup came. It's best to get it over with. Yank the bandage off the wound, that's the way to go."

"I'll play it your way…for now, but make no mistake, I won't put up with any drama just for the sake of drama!"

"Thank you. Believe me. It's the right way."

We pulled up to the curb and parked in the street since Mom and Dad's driveway was just a single car. We got out, picked up our things from the back, and headed up onto the porch.

"Do they at least know that you and Lidi are going to be here?" asked Kárin.

"Oh, yeah, they know that somebody's coming. They just don't know that Sidney Poitier is coming along as well."

Kárin giggled at the reference and barely managed to regain her composure just as the door opened.

"Grandpa! Grandpa!" shouted Lidi as she went running and jumped up into his arms.

"Oof. You're getting too big to jump on Grandpa."

"Lidi, what did I tell you about that? Hmm? Do you want to be responsible for hurting Grandpa by doing that?"

"No, Mommy. I forget. I'm so happy to see him, I just forget."

"Well, let's not stand out here on the porch, everybody come inside."

As we shuffled into the house, Dad held out his hand to Kárin.

"Welcome. My name is Franklin. I'm glad you could be here tonight. Funny, Aly didn't mention any guests."

"Kárin Zajac. And I think I was a last minute addition to the expedition. Forgive me if I've put any undue burden on this weekend's activities."

"Nonsense. Always room for one or two more. Always."

Mom walked in from the kitchen just as we were taking off our sweaters and jackets.

"Hello, I'm Eliza. Welcome to our humble abode. And you would be?"

Kárin extended her hand to Mom.

"Kárin Zajac. Like I was telling Franklin, I hope I'm not imposing. I understand that Aly possibly neglected to add me to the guest list in the excitement of this last week."

"Pretty much. I just wasn't thinking. Things have been hectic at work and everything. But we're here and if you don't mind, we'd like to eat dinner and stay the night," I said.

"Oh, don't be ridiculous. You can bring a guest anytime you wish dear. It's no trouble at all. Why your father and I just last month were talking about how it's about time that you brought a little friend home with you."

"A 'little friend'? I can't believe you just said that! You mean a 'gay' friend? A 'lesbian' friend?"

"No dear, I didn't mean anything at all by it, just that you should bring a friend or two home with you. You've been alone for so long now."

"Okay, here's the deal. As it happens, Kárin *is* a lesbian. And she's also my *girlfriend*. And yes, it happened faster than I ever thought was humanly possible. And no, I'm not rushing into things. But that being said, I'm totally in love with this brilliant woman," I said as I took her hand and pulled her next to me and wrapped my arm around her.

To tell you the truth, I think Dad was happy. And mom pulled the same 'If I ignore it, it won't exist' crap as last time. I'm sure that she thinks that someday I'll meet a nice young boy who will unbend me.

"I'm terribly sorry if I've caused any tension. Aly, maybe you could leave Lidi here, drive me back to Brooklyn, and then come back."

"Don't be daft. You're here, you're going to be fed, and you're going to get a place to sleep. In the morning, some of us will go to church, although you're not required to. But you will be required to join us at the buffet for lunch afterward. It's not the best food, but it is decent food at a decent price. No problem at all," said Dad.

"You're very kind, Franklin."

Mom took that exact minute to turn around and open her stupid mouth.

"You know you are the spitting image of Aly's dead wife. Aly, are you sure you're not dating this girl because she looks like Sasha?"

"Tactful, mom. Go ahead, ask her if she's a Jew too, like Sasha. The answer is yes. Maybe that's why I like her. I'm into Jews with blue eyes and curly hair. Could that be it? Jews with blue eyes turn me on."

"I think that's enough from both of you," interjected Dad.

"Look, I'm really not feeling this tonight. I'm going to call a cab and just go home. You all need to work this out and then get back to me. I'm not in the mood for all this."

Dad quickly pulled Kárin aside.

"Kárin. Please, I beg you. Stay. Ignore Eliza. She's having a terribly bad day today. They're getting closer together than they have been in the past, and the medication isn't working as well as it used to. Things will calm down as soon as we eat dinner, and when I can diffuse Aly. Okay? Please? If for no other reason, for me?"

Kárin sighed deeply.

"Okay, but if it starts again, I'm bailing. Just so you know."

"If it starts again, I'll drive you back myself."

It's a darned good thing that Lidi was playing in the other room with the toys that stayed at my parents' house, while all this was going on. Kárin came over to me, leaned in, and whispered in my ear, "I need to see you upstairs. Now!"

We climbed the stairs. I dreaded getting to the top. I had been acting liked a seventeen-year-old instead of my age. I got sucked in. When you let yourself get sucked in at all, you lose, no matter what else happens. Kárin entered the guest bedroom and flipped on the light.

After I had walked into the room, she shut the door behind us. She immediately shoved me in the chest with both hands, palm outward.

"What the fuck are you doing?"

"You tell me," she said, pushing me again, this time almost successfully knocking me off balance.

"Stop it. What are you doing?"

"Exactly what you are doing, and stop it! *You* are letting her get to you. If you give her no reaction, it's no fun anymore to pitch a fit. She'll take her ball and go home. So, what's it going to be? One simple question: do you want to spend the night in this bed right here cuddled up next to me? Yes or no?"

Kárin was genuinely pissed, but she had a much more adult reason to be pissed than I did. I moved in close to her and wrapped my arms around her.

"Baby. I'm so, so sorry. Yes, I want to share my bed with you tonight. More than you know. And just so you know, tonight's the night when I reveal the knowledge and lore of my experience, and it has nothing to do with being at my parents' house. You'll understand later tonight when we're alone. Okay?"

"Now calm down, you hear me? One more of those and I swear, as God is my witness, I'm outta here for the night! Not forever. Something this simple isn't going to scare me out of your life. Not now. I'm too deeply vested already. You're mine for life. Don't forget." Then she kissed me. And I kissed her back. I think it may have been about twenty minutes before we stopped.

"We better get downstairs. They're going to think we've had makeup sex," said Kárin.

I laughed. True. True.

Kárin and I made our way back downstairs. We went into the kitchen and I got a pair of sodas out of the refrigerator, handing one to Kárin. I put mine down on the table, then walked up behind Mom where she was preparing dinner along the countertop. I leaned my head against Mom's back and reached around on the side of her with my hand around to her stomach.

"It seems like we've been down this same road once before, doesn't it?"

Mom didn't say anything. I pulled back from her, took her hand, turned her around, and pulled her over to the table and sat her in a chair.

"Truth time. Don't tell me what you think I want to hear. Don't tell me something that isn't true because you don't want to admit it. This is just straight up time for some serious answers. Okay?"

She said nothing, but looked me in the eyes; not aggressively at all, but somewhat passively.

"After Sasha died, did you hope that I would meet a man and fall in love 'normally' and get married? I want the plain, honest truth."

For the longest time she said nothing, then leaned forward and started to talk, then just as abruptly she stopped. Finally, she started in earnest. "Alison, would it have made me a bad mother to hope for that? I understood you and Sasha, but I thought that maybe it was just her particular personality that attracted you. I thought maybe if you found a man with a particular personality, you would be just as interested in him."

"Don't you get it yet? I'm gay. I'm a lesbian. I like women. I have men that are my friends, but I never have been and never will be interested in a man romantically. Lidi will never have a father. She will have two mother figures, but rest assured she won't miss out on anything. She has uncles and three grandparents, two of whom are men. She'll be loved and cared for by two different people who will give her all the care and attention and love she'll ever need to become a wonderful woman in her own right. And me? I'm fine with what I am. I don't want to change. I love what I am. I love who I am. I have to tell you, as much as I shouldn't have let you get to me earlier tonight, you said 'little friends.' You implied my gay and lesbian friends. It's no different than if you would have said 'why don't you invite over your colored friends?' Don't you get that? I seriously have a free support group that you need to start going to. It's called PFLAG. It stands for Parents, Family & Friends of Lesbians and Gays. I think you need to look at being gay from my perspective for a little while. Maybe that will help you understand. Kárin happens to work with them in some way and she could get you more information. You wouldn't have to participate. You can just sit in the back and observe if you want, but I want you to try and go. I want you to do it for Lidi."

"I'll try. That's all I can tell you for now. I'll try. Kárin, before you leave tomorrow, give me the contact information and maybe let me know where I can get some literature. Aly, I do accept what you've gone through. I just still don't understand it. It makes no sense. It's not that I think a bolt of lightning will come down from the clouds and strike you dead, it just doesn't make any sense to me. But enough for this weekend. Can we try and just have a civil weekend? As you say, for Lidi's sake."

We had baked chicken and whole baked potatoes with some asparagus for dinner. After everything was cleaned up, we all went into the living room for a little while. Then Mom and Dad went to bed early, at about eight o'clock. I made up Lidiya's bed on the couch with her blankets and her pillow and got her into her PJs and tucked in for the night. I gave her a hug and a kiss and told her good night.

"Kárin? You forgot to give me my good night hug and kiss," said Lidi.

"No, I didn't, sweetpea, your mommy was just in the way and I didn't have the room to get in yet. I'm coming over there. Don't worry."

After I picked up everything in front of her, I had Kárin pick up one end of the coffee table and we moved it farther away from the couch so that if Lidi should happen to roll off the couch in the night, she wouldn't hurt herself on the table.

"Now what's this about not getting your hug and kiss from me, little one? MWAH," she kissed Lidi and then squeezed her tightly for the longest time, the two of them holding on for dear life.

Well, the test was coming in just minutes. Kárin and I went up to the guest bedroom, my old bedroom, to get ready for bed. As we walked in, I reached behind me and flipped the lock shut on the door.

"So, are we supposed to go into the bathroom and change into our jammies?" asked Kárin, standing there holding a pair of shorts and a tee shirt. I had gotten out the pajamas that I permanently kept in the guest bedroom dresser.

"I've got something for you," I said to her as I reached into my bag and pulled out the toothbrushes I'd bought.

"What's this?"

"Pick one to leave here permanently. The other I'll leave at my place. When we leave, leave your shorts and top here. If that's all right with you."

"So this means?"

I moved over to the dresser and lit both of the table candles, moving one over to the nightstand on the other side of the bed, then turned off the lights in the room. I reached up quietly and started unbuttoning Kárin's shirt. I took my time. After all, we had the rest of our lives, didn't we? After I had gotten the cuffs unbuttoned as well, I slipped it off her shoulders and let it fall to the floor. Kárin wore a dark blue bra adorned with lace. I unbuckled her belt and loosened it so that I could open it up. I unbuttoned her jeans then slowly slid the zipper down. After I had her jeans loose, I put my thumbs in the waistband and started forcing them down her sides until I had them in a puddle around her ankles. I leaned down and picked up one calf at a time to take the pants leg off while she put her hands on my shoulders for balance. I pulled her socks off at the same time.

Kárin was now wearing only her underwear. The dark material looked so amazing against her pale skin. I stood up in front of her and came to a complete standstill, my arms held slightly up and away from my body, allowing Kárin access to me in return. She reached out and unbuttoned my jersey, tossing it into a great pile with all the other discarded clothes. Then she undid my jeans and took them off just like I had done for her. I had already taken my socks off when I removed my shoes coming into the house. Now I stood wearing only my underwear, the difference being mine was lavender in color.

"You put on more perfume. I like it. What is it?"

"Burberry Red," I answered.

"Mmm.... It's magical."

"I also redid my lip gloss. I don't know if you can see it in this light."

"I noticed, believe me. It's a darker color. It really stands out in this light."

I moved up close to Kárin and reached my arms behind her. I undid the hooks on her bra, then pulled the straps off her shoulders ever so slowly, finally pulling it off her and letting it fall. I lifted my arms over my head so that Kárin could do the same to me, and my bra went into the pile as well. I moved up to Kárin and pressed my body into hers fully, rubbing my face into her neck, her chest, between the swell of her breasts. I finally ended up with my ear up against her listening to the beating of her heart.

"What are you doing?"

"I'm listening to something I just got."

"What's that?"

"The heart beating inside here…it belongs to me. At least that's what you said."

"I meant it."

"You better have."

I reached down and started pushing Kárin's panties down her hips and over her thighs. She stepped out of them, then did the same to me. I walked backward to the bed and pulled Kárin on top of me. I reached up with my hands and cupped her face in them, kissing her deeply over and over and over.

"Do you want to hear my knowledge?"

"I've been dying to hear it."

"Don't have sex until at least the fifth date. The relationship has to be built out of love and admiration, not sex and heat of the moment responses. By waiting, even though for us it's only been eight days, it's made it much different. I firmly believe it."

"I'm beginning to be intimidated by Sasha. Maybe she's the ghost, not me. She sounds like such a smart, wonderful woman."

"She was. And I'll practice everything she taught me. But I'll practice it only with you, and with no one else in the world. Forever and ever."

"Are you sure about this permanent a commitment though? Are you ready?"

"Aren't you?"

"Of course, but you were married and you have Lidi, whereas I have no one. That's more of an investment than I've ever had in any relationship."

"Sweetie, I knew it was going to be special after fifteen minutes talking to you at the benefit. After talking to you less than thirty minutes, I was doubly convinced. I was totally out of my element when I asked you out. I had to force myself because I'm really shy, believe it or not. But I knew that if I didn't act immediately, I might lose any chance at all that I had."

"I love you."

"Me too."

I reached down and pulled one of Kárin's legs up, pushing my leg up between hers and squeezing mine together, creating friction. Kárin reciprocated the movements.

"I'm torn between wanting to do one of two things."

"What are they?" asked Kárin.

"The obvious is making love to you. For our first time."

"And the second?" she asked further.

"Fuck me!" I replied.

I think maybe we found some middle ground, and we found it until the very small hours of the morning. We were, of course, careful to try and keep our noise to a minimum, but periodically there was a whimper or an inexplicable guttural, throaty sound emanating from one or the other of us. As we lay there completely exhausted, I was stroking Kárin's cheek delicately with my thumb.

"Do we have enough for you?" I asked.

"I'm not sure how much of 'what' you're referring to, but whatever it could possibly be, I'd say yes, so far as I'm concerned," she beamed back.

"Chemistry?"

"Definitely. Honey, I'm speechless. Can't say one thing that would explain how I feel right now except to say I know more than ever I want us to be together forever. However that ends up manifesting itself."

"Stand up."

"What for?" asked Kárin.

"Just do it. Come on, stand up."

She gradually pulled the sheet back and stood. She looked so lovely standing naked in the subdued light, the difference between now and when we first undressed being her totally wild and unruly hair at this point. Her leefa hair that first drew us together. I got up right behind her. I reached behind my neck, unclasping my Star of David. I moved up close to Kárin, behind her back.

"Remember, this is not a hand-me-down. This necklace is an unbreakable bond between you, love of my life of the Jewish faith, to me, love of your life of the Christian faith. You don't have to do this if you would prefer not to. I'll understand. But consider it, if you would. Please. Pull your hair up off your neck," I nearly pleaded.

Kárin did so, showing me her lovely neck in all its glory, a few stray tendrils of her curly hair cascading around. I reached around her from one side and held the necklace in front of her, then took one end in each hand bringing them back around her neck where I fastened the clasp in the back. I made sure the clasp was in the very middle of the back of her neck. I wrapped my left arm around her bare waist holding her tightly and with my right hand I reached around and centered the Star in the middle of her chest. I hoped beyond hope that she'd accept this gift like I offered it and didn't think she was living in Sasha's shadow.

I twirled her around so that she was facing me.

"Sasha never took it off from the day I gave it to her. Ever. And after she died, I've never taken it off until now...not even for an instant. I think of this more as my connection with my beloved. My truly beloved. It's sort of like, if we were American Indians and I had six arrows, I'd give three of them to you. I guess I'm rambling, and I'm not making any sense, am I? It seemed like a good idea, but I guess however well intended, I'm making a muck of things. I'm so sorry, Kárin..." I managed to get out before I started crying.

Kárin pulled my face up with one of her hands, kissed me on the lips, raised the Star to her own lips and kissed it, then placed the Star on my lips, then kissed it once again, before centering it on her chest and smiling at me. Then she turned her head slightly and brought her lips to mine. We kissed deeply for an eternity. When she finally let me go, she picked up our bed clothes from the top of the dresser and handed mine to me while donning her own. She was in bed first and held out her hand to pull me in beside her. We lay there on our sides, facing each other. Kárin reached down and picked up what was now her Star of David and kissed it again, then held it in her fingers.

"I finally have come to terms with Sasha's ghost. Just this moment. Everything you two had, whether it was before or after her passing, has formed who you are. After all, that's over a quarter of your life. How could you not be affected? And now the torch has been handed to me. I'm now your guardian. Your lover. Your everything. And not only for you, but for Lidiya. And it makes me so happy. Sasha, like you, I'll never take it off," she said to her memory as tears of joy started to run down her face.

I reached up to wipe them dry. It was hard because no sooner than I swept one away, a new one would take its place. Kárin pulled my hands together in hers and wrapped them up in a ball under her chin and closed her eyes, smiling ever so slightly. Finally, she emitted a huge sigh, beginning to relax.

"I love you, my darling," I said.

I pulled one of my hands from the mix and started stroking Kárin's lovely hair. Pushing it behind her ears where it strayed, fluffing it up, smoothing it back out, scratching her scalp, just playing in general. Within less than five minutes, Kárin was completely asleep. She'd had it partly right. Yes, she was my new guardian, but I was her guardian in return; equal shares in all things. I put Kárin's hands down quietly and she stirred slightly, but didn't awaken. I tiptoed over to the bedroom door, trying to keep the floorboards from squeaking. I unlocked the door, then tiptoed back into bed. I took Kárin's hands into mine once again and balled them up under her chin where she had originally put them. She nodded up and down a couple or three times caressing our hands with her chin, and was immediately back out like a light. Within two minutes, so was I.

I was startled awake by a light knocking on the door.

"Mommy? Grandma says you need to get up and come down to eat breakfast. She says we need to get up early and have some oatmeal before we get ready for church."

"Come on in, baby. We're waking up."

That might have proven to be a mistake. Lidi had the door open and was running the short distance across the floor to the bed and did a flying jump onto Kárin and me. Thank goodness it was across our legs.

"C'mon you sleepy heads. Get up and come down for breakfast. We have to get ready for church. Don't make us late. Oh, and there's coffee too," Lidi managed to get out before she froze in her tracks focusing on Mommy Sasha's necklace.

She crawled up onto Kárin, looking only at the necklace, not actually at Kárin. She was enrapt with the necklace being on Kárin. She reached out tentatively and took the pendent lightly in her small fingers, considering it for some minutes. She finally looked slowly up at Kárin's face with a giant grin.

"Are you really going to be my new mommy, Kárin?"

"We're working on that for now. Would that be okay with you? You know I won't ever try and take your Mommy Sasha's place. It would be a different place, with different memories. How would that sound to you?" Kárin responded.

Lidi jumped up and wrapped her arms around Kárin's neck, knocking her head back against the headboard.

"Baby, be careful. Don't break Kárin before we can even get her all the way into our family."

Lidi didn't saying anything. She just hugged Kárin's neck, hanging on for dear life. From downstairs I heard Mom holler at us to hurry up and get down to the kitchen. Lidi pulled her head back and kissed Kárin. Then she crawled over me and kissed me. Then she jumped off the bed as quickly as she had jumped up, paused in the middle of the floor, turned around, and waved us to follow her.

"Come on. I told you we're going to be late!"

"Well, does that mean I passed that deal breaker?" Kárin directed toward me.

For a response, I leaned over and kissed her before turning my legs out of bed and forcing myself upright.

"You know, this used to be easier when I was only twenty-four."

"What was?" asked Kárin.

"Having sex all night, getting only about two hours of sleep, then popping up and going through the next day. I need a nap, lover."

"You and me both. I feel your pain," Kárin said as we laughed together.

When we got downstairs, everybody else was already at the table and our bowls were sitting in saucers, already in place along with two steaming cups of coffee.

"Kárin, are you allergic to nuts of any sort?"

"Nope. I don't have any food allergies at all, and there isn't anything that I don't like to eat...except the stuff you see on Andrew Zimmern's food shows. I swear! The stuff he eats from other countries? My stomach swirls just watching it. There are even people from those countries that don't eat some of the things he does! I'm glad television doesn't have smell."

"The coffee is hazelnut. If you'd rather have regular coffee I can make you some instant really quickly."

"No, this is perfectly fine, Eliza. Thank you very much for breakfast. Just don't make fun of me eating like a pig while I try and get this down so we can get going to church."

"Oh, so you're going with us?" asked Dad.

"I figure I'll start going to services on one weekend a month and to the temple another weekend, along with Aly and Lidi."

Then Mom's gaze fixed on my cross. It didn't have Sasha's Star of David with it. She turned to Kárin and saw it hanging from her neck, then she looked me straight in the face with a panicked expression.

"I haven't found a replacement. It's a bonding of my past, present, and future. Do you understand now I was serious when I said that Kárin is it for me? Forever?"

"I think so..." she trailed off, but she was nodding her head with her brow furrowed.

Wow, I may have just made an inroad.

"Well, I think it's wonderful. Just wonderful," proclaimed Dad.

I wonder if he would have still thought so if he knew, not just guessed, that Kárin was banging his little girl under his roof. I laughed out loud.

"What's so funny?" asked Kárin.

"Little ears," I said as a way of explanation and it was immediately dropped.

We hurried through breakfast, just rinsing the dishes and leaving them in the sink to be cleaned after we got back after lunch. Getting ready upstairs, Kárin and I shared the bathroom. She took her new toothbrush and held it up to me.

"You know this was pretty romantic. A small gesture, but very thoughtful. I brought my own, but this is better. Are you bathroom shy around your partners?"

"What do you mean, 'partners'? I've only ever had one. And not particularly. Go ahead."

"I didn't mean anything by it. I'm just so used to using the plural with people. You have to remember, you're just not natural," she laughed at me as she sat down to pee.

When I finished washing my face and brushing my teeth, we switched places. Then we crowded each other sideways trying to get enough mirror space to get our makeup on. When we were done, we went back into the guest bedroom, with me locking the door behind us. I grabbed Kárin's hand and spun her quickly around, then shoved her hard in the chest, knocking her back on the bed and almost knocking the wind out of her as I did. I pulled down on the waistband of her shorts and she lifted her hips off the bed assisting me with my mission.

"Can you get off quickly?" I asked.

"Sometimes."

"This had better be one of those times," I managed to get out.

I used my fingers and my thumbs and my lips and my tongue and quickly had her arching up off the bed, beginning to spasm violently. Finally, she pushed my head back away from her and did her best to sit up on the bed.

"Go get me a washrag really quickly. We're surely going to be late now. And wash your hands while you're at it. Nobody else needs to know what we did," Kárin said as she took my fingers into her mouth and licked them.

I still had my clothes on so I just ran to the closet at the end of the hall and grabbed a cloth. Somebody was in the bathroom, so I sprinted down the stairs into the kitchen and got it wet with warm water and sprinted back up to our room.

"Here you go, sunshine," I said, holding it out to her.

I put on a top and a skirt, and Kárin donned slacks, a tailored button down, and a sport jacket, also tailored. Finally ready, I had to make sure Lidi was ready. Usually she did a good job of dressing herself, I just had to fine tune it and brush out her hair, which was finely curled like Sasha's. I finished that task quickly and luckily we were right on schedule. Dad had bought a booster seat for his car to leave it there permanently. He was on the third one since Lidi had grown so much and the seat requirements had changed. By now she already passed the minimum height and weight requirements, but for her safety we continued to use it.

"Kárin, it's too bad you two didn't meet a couple of years ago. You would have met Pastor Robinson. He's been our pastor for more than half of my life, although we weren't regular attendees. He was the one that co-officiated Aly's wedding. Ah, sorry, that was a stupid thing to say. I wasn't thinking," said Dad.

"You and Eliza have to stop apologizing to me for Sasha. I get it. Sasha was a wonderful person who deserves to have her memories kept alive, especially for Lidi's sake. It doesn't bother me in the slightest. Believe me. Don't worry about it."

Everybody was pretty much quiet on the ten-minute ride over to the church, with the exception of Kárin and Lidi. Kárin was keeping up a lively conversation with her, asking her questions about her church and things they did in the children's part of the services. She asked how she liked going (which she did immensely) and things like that. Walking into church, we assumed what had so quickly become our standard formation: Lidi in the middle and Kárin and I each holding one of her hands, just like any two parents would hold their child's hands. Mom and Dad brought up the rear. We got into the foyer and had to wait for people ahead of us to get seated, or in the case of the younger children, move to the teaching wing for the youth ministries.

Dad held up his mobile phone. I wondered when he'd finally gone to a smart phone. To say that Dad is technologically-challenged is an understatement. How was it that I came from him and I'm a techno geek? I have to wonder. He pulled up three photos, although taken from the back, of the three of us walking hand in hand all dressed up. He was far enough to the side that when the wind blew and the three of us turned our heads slightly to one side, it made us turn three-quarter profile into the camera so you could see us.

"I'll email them to you and Kárin."

"Thanks, Dad. It's the small things like this that are very important to all of us."

"It's nothing."

"No, Dad, it's a huge thing. So much more than you could imagine. If you were in our place, you'd be able to understand it fully. Since you're not, the most I could hope for is partial understanding."

After everyone but the absolute last of the stragglers was seated, Pastor Douglass got up and walked to the dais. He'd been here for the last two years after Pastor Robinson's stroke left him unable to speak very well—certainly not well enough to lead the congregation, which forced him into retirement. It uplifted me to know, however, that Pastor Robinson had recovered relatively well enough to function and was nearly always to be seen at the first position in the right front pew, week in and week out. He was also in the greeting line after services.

"Good morning, everybody! Blessings be upon each and every one of us, and all of God's creation. I want to start today's service by talking about something that many people have some questions about, or perhaps misgivings, or maybe even misinformation. Halloween is coming soon. Remember that Satan is a force that tried to lead us astray from the true teachings of Christ. And witches and goblins are the creations of unlearned, scared people from our far distant past trying to explain things that they otherwise couldn't. So let your children dress up however they want and go out and have a good time. You just might, on the other hand, want to ration out how much sugar they get to eat at any one time, so you don't have to scrape them off the ceiling with a spatula."

That last comment got a resounding laugh from the entire congregation. Kárin looked over at me, took my hand in hers, and smiled. I smiled back, my heart warm and joyful. I had grown to love church and temple both. And sharing with somebody just made it that much better. I mean, I went to temple with the Aronovs once a month, and occasionally Roni or Bri or even Lexa would go to church with me. Heck, even Martha took me with her girlfriend to Our Lady of Lourdes Church, a Roman Catholic Church in Manhattan.

Today's quoting of scripture and surrounding sermon was on the subject of forgiveness. About half-way through, I leaned over to

Kárin's ear and whispered quietly to her, "I'm asking in advance for forgiveness from you, my love."

She put her mouth near my ear to find out what I meant, "What do you need to be forgiven for?"

"For the small things that haven't happened yet, but that I know will happen. The first time I actually call you Sasha. The first time I talk about a memory that we shared and it wasn't a memory you and I shared, it was Sasha. I still love Sasha as much as I ever did. She's a living memory, and I hope she always will be, but finally, her memory has told me to move forward in my life. And that life is with you. I love you."

In response, Kárin brought my hand, still clasped in hers, up to her mouth and kissed it. She put our hands back down, never letting go, and looked me straight in the eyes. She smiled as big as I'd ever seen her smile. I leaned my head over onto her shoulder and stayed that way until the sermon was over. Then it was time for my favorite part of the service. The choir had sung one song prior to the sermon and the congregation had sung one, but now we were going to sing four together, with short talks between each one lasting only three to five minutes. Whatever shortcomings I had (all jokes about me being altitudinally-challenged aside), my voice was not one of them. I was in choir for years and I was very good at it. I even had medals from state competitions in solos, duets, trios, quartets, women's choir, and mixed choir; I'd won competitions in every position I'd ever sung in.

After we'd finished the first song and sat back down, Kárin turned to me. "I was pretty impressed by that first hymn, but that was fantastic, girl! You have some serious pipes. You should consider becoming a Jewish cantor. There are starting to be a few women. You'd be great at it."

I made the sign of a heart with my two hands together, holding it over my chest where my heart is located. Kárin rubbed her leg up against mine in return. After the fourth hymn, they passed the offering plates. It was normal for the pianist, or the organist, or even both to play during this time and usually the choir sang softly, creating a calming atmosphere. It wasn't unusual for people to talk quietly during this period. When the plate came by me, I dropped in a twenty, which was my usual monthly donation. I also always gave Lidi a five to give in the youth ministry class. I was handing the plate across Kárin to

Mom when she stopped me. She reached into her purse and pulled out a twenty herself and dropped it on top of mine.

"You don't have to do that. We can alternate."

"Don't be silly. It's not very much at all. Think of all the people that give several thousand dollars a month to the church in a single check that goes straight to the office."

"True, but thank you all the same."

"For what? Being reverent? For caring? For being a human? I don't deserve thanks for that. That's my moral obligation, but one I fulfill gladly, my sweet love."

"Next is the sacrament. You don't have to participate if you don't want to. At least in our specific church membership they pass it around instead of making you line up as you do at the Catholic Church. And everybody can take it or pass it on. No worries either way."

"It's just a rite. Why would it bother me?"

"Because the bottle it came from may have said grape juice, but after it's blessed and crosses your lips, it becomes the actual blood of Christ, and the wafer becomes the actual body of Christ."

"Christ was a Jew, a prophet, *and* a great leader of men. What's wrong with paying homage to him in any way? With worshipping him?" Kárin asked.

"Are you going to show me a new way to love you every time I see you?"

"I certainly hope so. I can't wait to get you to temple. That place rocks. Now if I only knew more than five words in Hebrew. Everything I learned for my bat mitzvah, I've already forgotten. Most of it, anyway," she giggled quietly.

"I know a few in Yiddish, so maybe that will help us out."

Finally, the service had come to an end. We waited on the side of the Sanctuary for Lidi to show up. She came up and took both mine and Kárin's hands without saying anything. I suspect she was a little tired and a little bored by that time, and raring to hit the buffet. We passed through the pastor's greeting line where he and his wife shook hands and exchanged pleasantries with everybody as they left the building.

"Franklin, Eliza, always welcome. You are such pillars in our church. And Eliza, don't let me forget to thank you more often for all the volunteering you do here. You're an enormous help to us. Aly,

Lidi, this must be your weekend out of the city. Welcome home. It's always a pleasure."

"Pastor, this is Kárin Zajac, my partner. We've just gotten together, and just so you know, she and Lidi get along famously."

Pastor looked at Kárin and noticed her necklace.

"Is this Aly's necklace, avowing her allegiance to her wife, God rest her soul?"

"Uh, yes, it is."

Pastor fished into his pocket and pulled out some change, taking out a quarter

"Kárin, hold your hand out, if you would. I could do this one of two ways...I could just drop it in your hand (dropping it in her open palm) like this, where its possession merely passes from me to you (he then picked it up from her hand). Or I could put the object in my hand like this, and we could interlock our fingers. I would turn my hand over onto your hand giving us a living bond, even a bond watched over by God, and release into your possession after our hands have inverted. You get possession in either case, but always embrace both the past and the present, and the bonds will be stronger than any person could possibly break. And it will assure you two that you will be together until the end of time."

"Father, we haven't exactly gotten to that point yet, you know? This is still very new to us," I said to him.

He wasn't listening. He was giving Kárin a hug and kissing her on the forehead.

"Welcome to our family. Hopefully we'll keep it interesting enough that you'll want to keep coming, and even more that you can take something away for use in your daily life. I guarantee I won't try and convert you. Maybe you can give me advice when we read from the Old Testament and Mosaic Law!" he laughed.

"I'm just happy to be here. You can count on me coming back...for a long, long time. We'd better move though, we're holding up your line. See you in a few weeks. I had a wonderful time. Bye for now."

"Drive safely going back to the city," he called after us.

As we were walking, we fell in our normal, little formation with Mommy Aly on one side and Mommy Kárin on the other. I'd determined already I didn't mind a sleepover, but I didn't want Kárin moving in until we got married for Lidi's sake. It would be hard enough to explain her mommy living with another woman, but it would make it a little easier, I thought, if the other woman were her stepmother.

We drove to the buffet. It was a popular place to be after many of the local churches let out so there was a long waiting line, but fortunately it moved quickly.

We were sitting at the table and I had a few grapes on my plate, but Kárin didn't. She reached over with her fork and stabbed two of them and ate them in a single bite.

"Hey, that's my food. Get your own."

"Do you have a weird phobia like my cousin, where if somebody eats from his plate, he has to throw the food away and get a new plate?"

"No, just keep away from my food. It's a buffet for goodness sake. Go get some grapes if you want some. Just leave mine alone."

"Bite me!"

Lidi broke out laughing uproariously.

"Kárin, you're so funny. Isn't she, Mommy?"

"Eat your lunch, Lidi."

Kárin reached out and stole a piece of macaroni and cheese off Lidi's plate and ate that.

"Now she took something from my plate, Mommy. She's so funny."

"Lidi, remember to user your inside voice. Yes, Kárin's just too funny to imagine. Your food's getting cold."

Dad was sitting on the other side of Kárin from where I was. Her fork darted out and she picked up the piece of meat he'd just cut off into a bite and swallowed it, barely chewing it. Mom moved her arms around her plate with a strange look on her face and drew it as far back to her edge of the table as she could, keeping her arms around it as a guard.

"I've got to tell you, Kárin, it's been utterly delightful having you here with us. And it's helping Aly so much having you in her life. It's evident in her every movement. Even Lidi seems to have taken quite a shining to you. I hope you decide that despite any momentary insanity you want to stick around for very long time."

Wow. From the mouth of Dad to the ears of God. I was blown away. She knew how to woo Dad, she knew how to push Mom's buttons—short of causing a meltdown, and without letting anything bother her—and Lidi was totally in love with her.

"I hate to be a total killjoy, but we need to get going pretty soon. I have a little work to finish before tomorrow that I didn't get to on Friday night. And Kárin and I have to talk about a few things. But we've had a great time this weekend. We have. All of us."

"We have things to talk about?" asked Kárin.

"Yup," I said and luckily Kárin let it drop for now.

We drove back to my parents' house and grabbed all our clothes after changing back into comfy ones, gathering everything we'd brought with us. Well, except for Kárin's toothbrush and sleepwear. We were quickly on the porch in our jackets and sweaters, heading back up the Interstate for home. Kárin didn't ask questions when we drove past the turn for her apartment. Finally, we were in the parking ramp at home and the three us traversed the short distance quickly.

Once upstairs, Lidi went into her bedroom, turned on television, and leaned back on her pillow. She would be there for quite a while, I knew.

"So, we have things we need to talk about, huh? I've got to tell you Aly, that sounded a bit ominous, and you've had my stomach in butterflies ever since. What sorts of things do we need to discuss?"

I was on the end of the couch closest to the chair and patted the center cushion to get her to sit next to me. She looked like a train wreck just ready for a place to happen.

"You told me you had a girlfriend once for only two weeks. What's the longest you've ever had a partner?"

"About 15 months, maybe. Then I'd go for a long time before I dated again. I've maybe had 10 girlfriends total going back to high school. Not too many, I hope."

"No, not at all. That's comparatively low. You know that I've only ever dated one person.

"Sure."

"You see this plant? Sasha gave me this plant after our first date. And look at it, it's thriving, even though Sasha's not here. Lidi's thriving, even though Sasha is no longer here. In fact, Lidi was only a few months old, so photographs and a few video tapes are the only memories she has to go on of her mother. But the thing is, while Sasha left a lot of good in this world, she did exactly that. She left. Now it's up to me to take all of the good she did, and venture out into the world and spread that goodness. And the thing is, I want to spread that joy with you. You remember when you said that even if it was only a two-week long fling, you were a serial monogamist? Well, I'm a serially 'married-ist', if that's even a word. And that's the only way I can work. So in looking for a partner, I have to first make sure they're compatible with my daughter, which clearly you are. You two are simply made for each other. The other thing that's a deal breaker, for me anyway, is that I'd have to get married. It would be no different than if I were a woman who was dating a man who wouldn't commit fully to a relationship or was unwilling to be married. Do you understand where I'm going with this?"

"I think so," Kárin said, although still looking relatively confused, she looked a lot more relaxed at this point.

"There's no pressure. We don't have to do this next week, next month, or even by the end of this year.   I'm not asking you for a specific date. And I'm not asking you to marry me. Actually, I'm the one that asked Sasha. I took the lead on that one. All I'm asking you is if we'll be married sometime in the future. I have to have that commitment. I understand if it's too much for you take in, and I hate to bring it up so soon, but with Lidi, I don't want her to get any more invested than she already is if this can't happen and then things go terribly awry."

Kárin sat motionless, staring at the floor, saying nothing. Finally, she got up.

"Do you still have Sasha's wedding rings?"

"Yes, they're in the bedroom, why?"

"May I see them?"

"I guess so..."

I led the way into the bedroom. I opened the box and took out Sasha's wedding rings, holding them out to Kárin.

"You gave me Sasha's pendant with no hesitation whatsoever. Right?"

"Right."

Kárin took my left hand and pushed Sasha's rings up onto my finger. Fortunately, the size was only about a half of a size different than mine so they fit pretty well. Then she took my right hand, took my rings off, and put them on her left hand. She took my face in her hands and kissed me gently. Finally, she looked me right in the face, only about six inches away.

"You pick the location, the date, how many people, what type of wedding you want, and all the details. And I'll be right there with you.

I'll let you plan it all, I'll plan it all, we can do it together, or we can hire a planner to do it for us. It just doesn't matter. I promise that we'll be married."

"Okay," I answered.

She held our left hands up together, showing our rings.

"Are you okay with this? Would you rather get different rings? I certainly would understand that, a thousand percent, but this way I can always be a part of you. And you can always be a part of not only me, but carry Sasha with you wherever you go in life as well. Everybody wins."

I wrapped my arms around Kárin, standing up on my tiptoes to be up to her height, and started bawling like a baby.

"Shhh, shhh, shhh. Honey, calm down. I thought this would make you happy. We don't have to do this."

I pulled my face from Kárin momentarily and punched her in the arm.

"Shut up you dumb ass. This tied for the three happiest moments in my life. When Sasha said yes, when Lidi was born, and right now. Don't ruin my moment!" I yelled at her.

I buried my face back into her shoulder, and within thirty seconds I was back to bawling my head off. Lidi came in to see what all the commotion was. She tilted her head to one side like a dog being given a new command, not knowing what to do with it.

"What's the matter with Mommy? Why is she crying?" asked Lidi.

"Lidiya, come sit over here with me for a minute." Kárin disengaged me and went over to the chair and sat down, getting Lidi to sit in her lap.

"So you know that I love your mommy, and your mommy loves me, right."

"Uh-huh."

"And you know, just like the first day we met, I want you to know that I'll never take your Mommy Sasha's place, right? Well, I get to wear the Star now so that I carry around all of the good things from Mommy Sasha with me, to share with other people. Just like that, we are using her wedding rings for your mommy, and I'm wearing your mommy's rings to take all the good things from her. Do you understand that?"

"Sort of like a good luck charm, right? I saw something like that in a movie one time."

"That's a good way to look at it. Anyway, I have something really important to ask you. And before you just blurt out an answer, I want you to think about it very carefully. Would it be all right with you if I married your mommy? I would live here with you and I would adopt you so that would be my real daughter too. The whole thing. How would you feel about that?"

Lidi jumped immediately and grabbed Kárin around the neck yelling "Yay!" over and over, jumping up and down, again and again.

I slowly walked across the living room, pulled Lidi off, which was no easy feat, and then sat crosswise on Kárin's lap. After I got settled, I held out my arms for Lidi, who scrambled up on top of the two of us and leaned down with an arm around each of us holding on for dear life. Oh yes, my checklist was complete.

"Aly, are you good with me adopting Lidi? "

"I wouldn't have it any other way."

"So that only leaves one question."

"When?"

"Nope. Lidi, what would you think about having maybe a little brother or a little sister, or maybe even more than one?"

Lidi literally squealed so loudly both Kárin and I cringed. Clapping her hands together, she was totally manic right now. Even more than the two adults in the picture.

"Kárin, this is what I meant. If it weren't for Sasha, we wouldn't all be sitting here right now together. And I have to tell you that the best ten minutes of my life is this very moment in time. The very, very best moment in time ever. More even than the two I mentioned a few minutes ago. You've made me so happy."

"Don't you think that just maybe, that's the way you've made me feel?

CHAPTER EIGHT

"Lidi, you have to get off Mommy for a minute. You're making my leg go to sleep. Okay, baby?"

After she had gotten up, I got up off Kárin and held out my hand to her. When she took my hand, I pulled her up out of the chair and without letting go, dragged her into the bedroom. I stopped at the dresser and I pointed to the top drawer.

"Open it."

Tentatively, she slid the drawer out. She saw the empty drawer with the toiletries.

"You can put that stuff in the bathroom. I cleared out the entire right hand mirror cabinet for your stuff. You might want to consider getting some extra makeup to leave here."

Kárin ran her hand along the bare bottom of the drawer smiling. I opened the drawer in the night stand and pulled out Sasha's keys.

"Please get a new key ring and put all the keys on it. I want to give that one to Lidi as a memento. She's already got a big tin of things of Sasha's like that. It's all she has. So I try every time I can. Roni even got me some photos of Sasha as a baby, a little girl, and into junior high. Of course, that's when she began her 'fall from grace.' About the same time as you," I chuckled.

"Don't remind me. I thought I knew everything back then, and I didn't know jack shit," she laughed.

"Do you own your apartment?"

"Have you heard one word I've said? Remember, 'non-profit'."

"Are you attached to your place, or would you consider moving in with us after we get married? Or would you rather get a different place that's bigger than our place. Hell, I don't even know how big your place is. It may be huge inside for entertaining clients. I've never been upstairs."

"Come over for dinner on Tuesday and find out for yourself. And no, it's maybe fifty square feet bigger than this because it has two additional small closets."

"Is it rent controlled?"

"Oh, hell no! It's killing me too."

"This one is."

"I love this place. This is perfect!" she cackled gleefully.

"You don't want something bigger?"

"Three bedrooms would be nice, but if this is already rent controlled, I doubt you would be able to find a three bedroom without at least doubling the price."

I moved backward until I was laying down on the bed—a nice, big queen-size mattress. I curled my finger indicating I wanted Kárin to come to me. She slid in beside me and we stared at each other, smiling.

"What are we going to do for names? Aronov-Lockewood-Zajac?" asked Kárin.

"How about Lidi and I stay the same, and you take Zajac-Lockewood?"

"This could get messy!"

We both laughed.

"How about all three of us just change it to Aronov?" suggested Kárin.

"I don't think Lidi would go much for that and I don't want to rob her of anything either. How about I change her name to Lidiya Marie Zajac Aronov-Lockewood, I change mine from Alison Jeanette Aronov-Lockewood to Alison Jeanette Zajac Aronov-Lockewood. What's your full name, by the way?"

"Kárin Cecylia Zajac. My middle name is my grandmother's name."

"How pretty. Well, you can change your name to Kárin Cecylia Zajac-Lockewood. Just food for thought."

"I'm'a thinkin' I like this food you've got. It sounds pretty tasty."

"I'll be right back."

I shot out of the bedroom and fished my phone out of my purse, then returned to the bed and lay back down by Kárin.

I selected the contact and hit dial, handing the phone to Kárin.

"What in the hell do you think you're doing?"

"Just answer it."

"Hey, Aly, how did your weekend go? Aly? Aly? Is everything okay?" Bri questioned.

"Uh, hi. This is Kárin. Kárin Zajac. I sort of got forced into this conversation against my will, but you're Aly's best friend, so it must be okay. And I was sitting next to her when she called you yesterday afternoon."

"You're her! You are, aren't you! You devil woman! You've done in two weeks what nobody has been able to do in five years. You've breathed new life back into my best friend. So you're Aly's girlfriend, huh?"

"Not really. We're no longer girlfriends."

"Oh, I'm so sorry. What happened? She seemed so lit up and happy."

"Actually, she's still lit up and happy, but I'm no longer just her girlfriend...I am now her fiancée."

"*What?* Are you *kidding* me? This is wicked crazy! You two are certifiable! Okay, when are you coming for dinner? I've got to meet you. I have to see you together...and it better be damned soon."

"It can't be Tuesday because we'll be at my apartment for dinner. Hang on.... Aly, do you have any other plans this week, honey? Apparently there might be something on Thursday. I'm not sure what. Any other night though. Or next weekend might even work better."

"I know what Thursday night is all about, but I'll let her explain that one to you. I think that'd be best. It's great to talk to you though. And congratulations! Wow. Engaged. Does Aly want to talk to me or was it just an ambush for you? Okay, have her pick the night and let me know. Bye now."

"That was just plain vicious of you!" said Kárin.

"But you still love me. Get ready to do it again, only this time you'll be ready. Anyway, you're good at public speaking. It's your job. It should come naturally."

"Not when you're telling a person that you're marrying her best friend. That's different. Okay, give me the phone."

"That's more like it. That's my lover."

I brought up Lexa's info and handed the phone over. This time I let Kárin hit dial.

"Hey, you. Did your weekend go well, introducing your new bee-otch to your incredibly uptight parental units?"

"Hello to you, too, Lexa."

"I'm sorry, who is this?"

"Kárin Zajac, Aly's new bee-otch. How's things, Lexa?" she said, trying incredibly hard not to burst out with laughter.

"I'm so, so sorry. I didn't mean anything by it. It was just girlfriend banter between me and Aly. Or who I thought was Aly. And I don't mean girlfriend like you guys, just friend that's a girl, you know."

We'd had the call on speaker. Both of us finally broke out laughing hysterically.

"You both truly are a couple of bitches, you know it? Not bee-otches. Just plain cold-hearted bitches! Thank you very much! Is this what you've been reduced to? Calling best friends and messing with their minds just for fun? And anyway, where is Lidi? Do you think this is stuff you should be doing in front of her?" Lexa demanded.

After we finally regained a semblance of composure some number of minutes later (thank goodness Lexa didn't finally just hang up the phone), I poked Kárin and told her to go ahead.

"So, Lexa, I'm supposed to tell you that I'm no longer Aly's girlfriend. Really, I'm not. That's past history."

"Did you two break up? Was it just too fast and got out of control? From the way things sound over there, you're at least good friends."

"Oh, we're more than just friends."

"You mean...friends with benefits type of thing?" asked Lexa nervously.

"Um, more than friends with benefits."

"Then I don't get it. Just what exactly is going on?"

"As of a little less than an hour ago, I became Aly's fiancée. What do you think?"

Silence. Just like the previous call.

"Do you need to get Bobby back on the phone, chicky? You there, Lexa?" I called out.

"Have...You...Both...Gone...Stark...Raving...*Nuts?*"

"And it's not hormonal. I had waited until our fifth date before we had sex, to make sure it wasn't a relationship based on sex and transient emotions."

"When are you getting married?"

"We don't know. Next week, next year, whenever. No hurry. And Kárin is going to adopt Lidi. What do you think?"

"Well, you're a grown-ass woman, so you can do whatever you want. Don't get me wrong, I'm happy for you, but also remember I'll be here for you if something goes terribly awry. Just so you know."

"Thanks. Well, we have to run, just wanted to keep you up to date."

Kárin disconnected and held out the phone to me. I put it on the night stand.

"Let's just order in a pizza for tonight so we can eat pretty soon and there won't be any cleanup. I can skate out of here early. Everybody can get lots of sleep tonight. Everybody needs it, especially you and me," she laughed with a wicked little smile on her face.

"You're bad."

"I try."

After we finished eating and the plates were cleaned and the extras stored in the fridge, we sat in the living room, relaxing. I sat next to Kárin, and Lidi was stretched out across both of us.

"When are you and Kárin going to get married, Mommy?"

"I don't know yet, baby. There's a lot of things we have to get done before we can do that. There's a lot of planning yet."

"When is Kárin going to move in?"

"When we get married."

"Then do it pretty soon."

Kárin and I looked at each other. What a sweet child.

"You have attorneys, I'm assuming, all over your organizations, right? Get with one of them and have them go over all of your investments, your retirement, your bank statements, your car, your apartment lease, everything. Make sure you're protected so that in case of an emergency you'll be covered."

"You're an attorney, why don't you do it?"

"It would be easily struck down as a conflict of interest. I'm not just talking about us breaking up, I'm talking about living wills for both of us. What my responsibilities will be for you and what your responsibilities will be for me. Everything. Even though most of this will be covered under The Marriage Act of New York, having it specifically delineated keeps families from fighting over things. Especially in the case of mutual demise. Have your will updated so that anything that's joint goes into a trust for Lidi, to be handled by Gideon. Anything that I brought in goes to my parents and Lidi, and anything that you brought in goes to your parents, or however you want it. It will only take about a half a day total work and will be totally worth it in the long run. Okay?"

"If you say so. I mean, it makes sense."

"Now, before I change my mind and make you stay all night, get the heck out of here and go home. I'll lose all willpower. And when you come back, you'll need to bring some things with you to leave here," I said with a smile, which she returned.

"Throwing me out," she said as she changed from a smile to a fake pout.

"Kiss me, my love."

She did. Quite well. I held our rings up together.

"Thank you for this. So very much."

Kárin picked up her pendant.

"Thank you for this. Temple in two weeks?"

"Definitely. Which one?"

"Wherever Gideon and Roni go is fine with me."

We gave each other a lasting hug and multiple kisses goodbye. I called Lidi in to say goodbye for the night as well. Lidi was all over Kárin, smothering her legs with her arms at first, then holding her arms up to indicate she wanted to be held. She gave Kárin the 'Hug of Death' and kissed her a couple of times while Kárin mussed her hair, causing Lidi to laugh raucously. Suddenly Kárin was gone for the evening. And for the first time, even though I missed having her right by my side, I didn't feel awful when she left. I looked at my new ring, Sasha's ring.

"Hey, that's Mommy Sasha's ring, isn't it?" cried Lidi.

"Yes, and Mommy Kárin has my old ring."

"Why don't you buy new ones?"

"First, they're very expensive and I don't make that kind of money anymore. Uncle Val bought my ring or I wouldn't have had such a beautiful ring. And second, by wearing this ring, I carry Mommy Sasha's heart with me all the time, just like when she's watching over you as your angel."

"Oh."

"Now it's time for you to go put on your PJs and get into bed. You can read a book for thirty minutes, but then I'm coming in to turn out the light."

"Okay," she said and turned one hundred and eighty degrees and tore through the apartment.

"Lidi, don't run! You're going to step on Lilly some day and hurt her. She's old."

I just shook my head. The perfect child, probably, but still not quite seven years old.

CHAPTER NINE

Monday morning, my walls came tumbling down. I was at Sasha's old office, meeting with a Social Services caseworker, Tamara, whom I'd been introduced to by Sasha. I faced a situation that Sasha would have to deal with every once in a while. In fact, I was paired with a caseworker specifically regarding this issue. It just tore at my heart strings. How do these things happen? It's so terrible I could barely even talk about it with the caseworker. An eight-year-old girl had taken a loaded gun she found in her house and shot her three-year-old brother in the chest twice, just to see what would happen. She had no other reason than simply to see what would happen.

I dropped my pen, got up, and left the interview room. I understood that the other two children were removed from the home until their safety could be assured, but it was too late for the toddler. And my predicament now was that I was the child advocate for the eight-year-old girl. I was supposed to get her the lightest sentence, try and get her committed to a mental health facility instead of a juvenile facility. As a rule, the child had to be ten years old to enter a juvenile corrections facility, but that wasn't necessarily true for kids younger than that who have committed Class A felonies.

I wiped my eyes clear, hoping I hadn't streaked my mascara, and re-entered the room.

"This is one of the more onerous cases I've ever gotten. No, make that tied for the top two. I had a twelve-year-old once that got jealous of his ten-year-old brother so he picked up a chair and threw it against the window several times until it shattered, then tossed the younger one out the window. I feel for you on this one. This isn't going to be easy by any means," Tamara said as she patted my shoulder.

"We better get started. So, Tamara, as her representative within Child Protective Services, what are you willing to do for her long term to get them reunited, regardless of the penalties she receives? What will I have to do as far as rehabilitating the girl to get to that point? Second item of business, of course, is the parents have had their two other children removed, at least temporarily. I need to follow the children and their care, along with if they're returned to the parents and when. Also look into therapy for both parents. And the last point is solely mine, but I'll keep you appraised. The D.A. decides what the charges will be against the little girl, but I get a huge say so in the charges against the adults. And from where I sit right now, whoever's prints are on the gun gets negligent homicide. If both parents have prints on it, then for the sake of the other two kids, I hope they have family willing to take custody, at least temporarily, because Mom and/or Dad are going away for five to ten. That's what gun locks are for!"

"I was thinking a little while ago about what I wanted to do for lunch. I think I'm just going to have a cup or two of this building's shitty coffee."

"I'm with you, Tamara."

"Aly, I have to say that what you've done as far as a career change is just wonderful. We're so happy you've done this. And I also want you to know, hon, there isn't a day that goes by that we don't think about Sasha. You know she has a plaque on the wall of the main building, don't you?"

"Yeah, I've taken Lidi to see it a couple of times."

"I notice you're wearing Sasha's rings. Just decided to switch for a while?"

"Erm...Well...Funny you should say that. On one hand, it's like a living tribute to Sasha. I'll keep wearing these rings...and my new fiancée will wear my old rings."

"What? Are you kidding me? Oh, give me a hug, give me a hug! That's such good news. None of us thought you'd ever get over all your tragedies. This is a happy day after all. What say when we finish this then we go get that lunch after all?" she squealed and hugged me and pulled me up off my feet with her arms and spun me around.

"Okay. I guess so," I shot back, beaming, momentarily forgetting the savagery of which we were just speaking.

We worked for the next two hours or so researching and looking up and inspecting and detecting...all the things we could do to get as much information as possible to make the best-informed decisions regarding the little girl. I stopped to text Kárin.

'Total shit day. Worst case I've ever caught. Can't talk about it though, sorry. Just don't worry if I'm off my game. It's not you. It's this case. Pure tragedy.'

'I understand. Just know that I love you. BTW, everybody loves my new rings. They also think I'm effing nuts!'

'Isn't that what Lexa told us?'

'Maybe she was right.'

'I *am* nuts about you, sweetie.'

'Me too. I miss you so much. With every hour that passes, more and more I want to move this wedding thing up.'

'I know what you mean. Got to run. Love you.'

'Me too. X O'

I got a call from Brianna just as I was walking back in my building. Tamara had gone for the day, returning to her office.

"Can you come by on Saturday afternoon?"

"Sure. We don't have any plans at all for this coming weekend other than going to temple."

"Man, you've sure gotten into this, haven't you? Both church and temple. Twice a month."

"I want Aly to grow up with a strong foundation, and I want her educated enough to know which she prefers so she can make her own choice about whether she wants a baptism or a bat mitzvah. "

"Are you and Kárin going to bring Lidi with you?"

"Of course. She and Ingrid will want to play with each other," I replied.

"You have time to talk for a minute?"

"Sure I do," I responded.

"Tell me about her. What's she like?"

"She's wonderful."

"What does she look like?"

"You'll just have to find out later this week."

"Nothing, huh? It's going to be that way, is it?"

"That's my story and I'm sticking to it."

"What does...what was her name? I was in too much shock to remember, to tell you the truth. What does she like to eat?"

"Kárin Zajac."

"You mean like Pat Sajak from the television game show?"

"No, she spells her name Z-a-j-a-c and it's sort of pronounced with a mix of a 'ts' and a 'zh' at the beginning. You'll get it. Don't worry about it."

"What does she do for a living?"

"She works for several non-profits. She's a fundraiser, among other things."

"So, you really are going to marry her? After less than two weeks? Do you really think that's healthy, hon? I mean, I know you were dark and depressed for the longest time. Way too long. But are you maybe, just a tiny wee bit, trying to overcompensate now?"

"Wait until you meet her and answer that for yourself."

"I'll take your word for it, for now, but just the same, I do want to see her for myself. I want her fully vetted before I turn her loose on you."

"If you say so."

"I say so. See you on Saturday. Come over about four thirty, so it will give the girls time to play."

"Will do."

"Over and out."

"Bri? How many times have I told you...you can't be both over and out? Over means my transmission is complete, and I expect a reply. Out means my transmission is complete and I'm discontinuing the communication."

"Nerd."

"Wuss."

For the first time today I had a smile on my face. I gathered up a few folders and put them in my courier bag and made for the door. I had started carrying just my courier bag instead of a briefcase, to be different, maybe a little more 'hip.' I used it for my purse since it had a couple of dividers. I had a notebook PC, so it was very slender and fit in the center section quite well. I slowly walked to the garage in the back of my building. In a way, I missed taking the buses and the trains and mixing it up with all the people on the street. It's just not the same from your car.

I once heard that the difference between Los Angeles and New York was that in LA there are millions of people crowded into a small place all going from Point A to Point B, bumper to bumper, but in New York there are millions of people crowded into a small place all going from Point A to Point B, shoulder to shoulder. It was so true. I don't know if I would be able to live in any other place in the world, with the exception of maybe Seattle or London. I thoroughly enjoyed my venture home tonight. My little angel would be home soon. And one of these days, God willing, my big angel would be coming home to the two of us with my original big angel looking down upon all three of us and watching over us. I couldn't help but smile.

After finding a stall in the parking ramp, I pulled out my phone.

'I know I said I was going to wait until later to text you, but I couldn't wait. I sound like a little junior high girl, don't I?'

'No more than I do. All the experience I thought I'd had with women has been thrown out the window. I'm in completely new territory. Damn you!'

'LOL. I've heard that before.'

'Where?'

'I'll tell you later tonight. Are you free Saturday to go to Bri and Danny's?'

'I won't be able to shake loose until about five o'clock. Got a luncheon that I have to go to, followed by some awards thing.'

'You can meet us there. Better yet, let us drop you off. That way you can throw a bag of things to keep at our place in my car and you won't have to get a cab back to our place. You'll just catch a cab to Bri's.'

'Sounds like a plan, if you don't mind dropping me all the way down in midtown Manhattan.'

'More time to talk.'

'Call me tonight.'

'Yes, ma'am!''

'When I say jump, you say, "How high, Sergeant?"''

'I'm going in now. C U l8ter.'

'I L Y'

'♥'

When I got into the apartment, Lilly was crying out to be fed. Puppet was playing by herself, running along the back of the couch from one end to the other and back. I put my bag on the coffee table and went to the kitchen to open a couple pouches of food. Puppet came running, but Lilly just walked around meowing. 'Great,' I thought. I knew this day was coming. She was starting to have trouble with her GI tract. Hungry, but couldn't eat. I'd have to take off during lunch tomorrow and take her to the vet. For now, I just scratched her head and along her back. She seemed to enjoy it, but didn't purr. That certainly was a bad sign.

Lidi came in within about fifteen minutes, running up to me and wrapping her arms around both of my legs, nearly tackling me as she did almost every day.

"Hi, Esther. How are you today? Can I make you some tea?"

"No, thank you. Roni and I are going to a gallery tonight for wine and cheese."

"That should certainly be fun. You deserve to get out like that."

"Yes, I do!" she said chuckling.

I made Lidi hang up her windbreaker and put her shoes up.

"Have fun tonight. Drive safely."

"No designated driver tonight…no need. We're using Gideon's service to drive us. How handy is that?"

"Esther, can I ask you something very, very personal?"

"I don't see why not. We're all family here."

"That's just it. How serious are things between you and Gideon, if you don't mind my asking?"

"Let me put it this way. He's working about fifty hours a week, maybe twenty less than he used to. That should give you some clue. He wants to be home much more than he ever has and he's putting more of the work off on the other partners and younger staff members," she said, with a twinkle in her eye.

"Is there a toothbrush at his place for you?" I asked with a grin.

"A lady shouldn't kiss and tell. You know better than that! But then again, I'm not so sure I'm that much of a lady. Let's just say there is a toothbrush…and a little makeup. And maybe a change or two of clothes…in case I got 'caught out in the rain' sometime."

"I was just wondering. I think you two really deserve each other. I'd so like to see you two stay together for a very long time."

"That's what Roni and Val have said. I think Grig thinks pretty much the same thing, but he's so seldom around. Did you hear about his big trip?"

"I haven't heard anything about any trip. Where's he going?"

"He's going to be crossing the Atlantic en route to Hamburg. He's going to take that new navy cruiser on its extended sea trials as the master machinist representing his company. He's going as the consultant for the CNC machines in the engineering section. His voyage is supposed to be about two weeks in transit going, however long maneuvering, two to four weeks in the docks there, back for another stint in maneuvers, and two weeks back home. Then, however long back in the docks for final repairs for final adjustments after sea trials for ship commissioning. Gabrielle and Diya are going to take a trip to Europe together for about three weeks while he's gone. They're supposed to be able to meet with him a couple of days in port over there. Val and Diya's two little ones are going to have a live-in nanny with them while Diya is on vacation."

"That sounds cool. I know we are a sort of melting pot in our family, but how did Gabi end up growing up in Barbados, born to English parents with English passports, and married to a Ukrainian she met in New York? That's the hardest stretch of the whole group. I don't know, I guess I was a young American girl living in Queens that found a Ukrainian woman living and working in Brooklyn. Now I'm engaged to a Polish woman whose grandparents left before the war broke out and still speaks Polish at home."

"I guess you've never heard about me then?"

"I can only imagine what tales you must bring," I smiled at her.

"I was born in Haifa."

"You're an Israeli? I never knew that! How interesting."

"My father's tattoo read SB102329 and my mother's was BK41798. It meant that my father was in Spitzbergen and my mother was in Berkinau. When they were freed in 1945, they remained in Germany and helped in the rebuilding. They were still persecuted and had to fight harder for everything they got: food, shelter, water, clothing...everything. But they waited, and they waited, and when the British Mandate was reiterated in 1948, they immigrated to Haifa. I came to New York when I was 22 so that I could find somebody better off to marry. Our family was a little old-fashioned I guess. My three sisters and I all came here, and I've been here ever since. I married my Bernie less than two years after we arrived, and was married for years and years. After Bernie died, I don't know what I would have done if Gideon hadn't rescued me. And that's what he did, he rescued me."

"Are your sisters all here in New York?"

"My oldest sister died about 10 years ago in an automobile accident, but everybody else is still here. My parents are in an assisted living facility that's entirely comprised of elderly Jewish people. I see them every week. Gideon likes to take me over there."

"Do you still speak Hebrew?"

"Of course, child. I've used it all my life: with my family, at temple, and sometimes even at home with Bernie. My children learned enough for their mitzvahs and promptly forgot everything," she laughed, throwing her hands out in a gesture.

"Look at me, you're going out for the night and here I am talking your ear off. Get up and get moving or you'll be late."

"It's good to see you again. Take care."

"You too, Esther," I said as I gave her a hug.

"Lidi, come in here and give Auntie a hug and kiss," I shouted through the house.

Lidi came running in and made sure she got to her before she left without saying goodbye. After talking to Esther for about half an hour, I went back to the kitchen. Lillibeth was lying on her side on the rug in front of the counter.

"Lidi, I need you to do something for Mommy. I need you to go, really quickly, into your bedroom and shut the door."

"Why?"

"Just be a good girl and do it for Mommy, okay?"

She did as I asked. I immediately got my phone out.

"Melanie, Aly here. Are you available for an emergency? It could take up to three hours or so. I'd need Lidi to come to your apartment."

"Let me check with my mom....Sure, she said it would be just fine. I'll come down and get her in five minutes if that's all right."

"Super. See you then."

Melanie came and got Lidi. I tried to keep the mood light and get her moved through without letting her go into the kitchen. I got the cat carrier out and put Lilly inside it. I looked for the refrigerator magnet that had the vet's information and put it in my purse. I took the carrier with Lilly to the car and drove in the rain to the vet clinic. They took the carrier and asked me to have a seat. Lilly was about fourteen if I calculated correctly. That shouldn't be too old. Should it?

A technician finally came out to the waiting room, but instead of talking to me, she took a seat next to me and held out her hand and took mine. I immediately started crying.

"What would you like to do with the remains, Mrs. Aronov?

I sat for the longest time, not saying anything.

"Could you please handle it for me? I can't. I just can't."

I got up and ran out the front door and just kept running…past the car and down the street. I didn't have an umbrella or a raincoat, but I scarcely noticed. I finally stopped and just walked. I ended up completely circling the block.

I drove around for almost an hour, trying to calm myself down, but it wasn't working. Finally, I drove to Kárin's apartment and called her from in front of the building.

"Hi, honey. You're calling awfully early tonight."

I was sobbing. I could barely string two words together, much less a sentence.

"Kárin, I…I need…Need to see…See you…" I wailed.

"Tell me where you are and I'll be right there."

"I'm…Downs…Downstairs…At your apartment."

I sat holding onto the steering wheel for dear life, sobbing like a little girl. Within moments, Kárin was around the car on the street side, in her bare feet and sweats, trying to open my door. I forgot the locks automatically engaged when you drove. I unlocked the doors and Kárin hauled me out of the car. She was much stronger than she looked. She held out an umbrella and covered my head. She pushed me ahead of her to the elevator, up to her floor, and inside, locking the door behind us.

"Okay, Lidi's okay or you would be at the hospital. I know you'd never leave her side. Anything else can't be as bad as that, so let's sort this out. What's wrong with my sweet Aly?"

I threw my arms around Kárin's neck, still wearing my rain-drenched clothes, and just cried into her tee. I couldn't tell you what her apartment looked like, what Kárin was wearing, anything. I was just so abjectly sad. She kept patting me and rubbing my back and shushing me.

"Tell me what is making you so sad, my love. I can't help you unless you help me understand what it is."

"Lilly died tonight," I said, without lifting my head up at all. My crying increased by about five times the ferocity."

"Oh, honey, don't worry. You always said you knew that she was living on borrowed time. You gave her the happiest home a cat has ever had in the entire world. You have to think about that and remember the happy times and all the good memories you had with her. That's what you'll have to do. Who's watching Lidi?"

"Melanie, a girl from upstairs," I finally managed to get out.

"When do you have to be back?"

"In an hour or so."

"Give me just a minute," and she disappeared.

Within five minutes, she showed up with a hang-up bag and a small duffle bag.

"Come on, let's go."

"Where?" I asked through my tears.

"Home. We need to go be there for Lidi. I'll drive."

I reached around and hung onto Kárin once more and started crying all over again. This time though, partially because she was taking care of me so well, I just let go for the freefall. I let her lead me down to the car. I still had no idea what the apartment looked like. I couldn't get the tears out of my eyes for even a second. Kárin drove us home, then grabbed her bags from the back of the car. We walked into the building. She opened the apartment, hung up her work clothes, and emptied the duffle bag into the drawer I had cleared out for her.

"Now, what apartment does Melanie live in?"

"Four-K."

"I'll be right back."

I started to wonder about them when they hadn't showed back up in almost half an hour. I was beginning to regain some composure. Finally, they walked in together holding hands. Lidi came over to me where I was lying on the bed, my shoes off, but still wearing my wet clothes and my soggy jacket as well. She crawled up on the bed and laid down practically nose to nose with me.

"I'm sorry that you're so sad, Mommy. Mommy Kárin told me that Lilly wanted to go and live with Mommy Sasha, to keep her company so she wouldn't be so lonely."

I wrapped my arms around my precious, precious Lidi. So big and brave, and so understanding of the ways of the world.

"Lidi, what would I do without my little princess?"

"Let's go get you in your PJs, Lidi, and get you to bed. Tomorrow's a school day and you're going to be so, so tired."

Lidi got up and took Kárin's hand. I could hear the water running, so I knew she must be getting Lidi to brush her teeth. I heard the toilet flush, so she made her go to the bathroom. I heard the cabinet shut and the water from the kitchen running for a few seconds, so somebody got a glass of water.

"Good night, sweetpea," I heard Kárin say to Lidi.

"Good night, Mommy Kárin."

I heard the sounds of a hug and a kiss. Then Kárin came into my bedroom and pulled me up out of bed.

"I really don't want to get up right now."

"Get up! Don't make me fight you. I'll win."

She pulled so hard I thought she was going to pull my shoulder out of its socket, so I relented. After pulling the wet duvet off the bed, Kárin fished underneath my pillow and pulled out a pair of shorts and a tank. She proceeded to strip me completely naked. I didn't give her much of a fight. She had me step into the shorts and pulled them up for me, then pulled the tank down over my head and pulled the hem down. When she was done with me, she opened the drawer where she had put all her clothes and pulled out a pair of boxers and a tee shirt. She stripped down and put on her night clothes. When she was done, she picked all the wet clothes up off the floor, took them in the bathroom to hang them on the shower curtain rod to dry, then got a blanket out of the closet and spread it out over the bed.

She grabbed me by the hand and picked up a small makeup bag. Dragging me into the bathroom, she put her makeup away behind the mirror on her side, pulled out a toothbrush for her and me both, and loaded them with toothpaste. She handed one to me and started brushing with her own. She was moving a lot faster than I was and quickly rinsed hers out and put it up, then sat on the toilet and peed. I finally finished with my teeth and she moved over, sort of pushing me towards the toilet. I went to the bathroom too, then she took me by the hand and led me into the bedroom.

Kárin pulled back the covers and put one of the pillows on each side of the bed. She reached into her purse and pulled out a travel alarm, setting it to get up in the morning.

"Is your alarm set to go off the same time every day?" she asked.

"Yes."

She turned out the light and pulled the covers up over us both, settling in and putting her arm out so I could lay my head on it. She reached over the top of me, grabbing my hand and pulling it in tightly.

"I'm sorry, Kárin."

"For what? What could you possibly have to be sorry for?"

"For falling apart. I don't know what I would have done tonight if it weren't for you. Helping me. Helping Lidi. Explaining it to her so brilliantly."

"It's my job. You're going to be my wife, and she's going to be my daughter. Why wouldn't I take care of you both?"

"If you break Lidi's heart, I'll kill you," I managed to say, barely managing to get half a laugh out, and sending snot out of my nose onto the bed in doing so.

"If I break Lidi's heart, I'll kill myself," she said as she squeezed me tightly.

"Kárin?"

"Yes, love?"

"You don't have to wait. You can come over any night you want to. You don't have to move in yet if you don't want to, but, I mean, you could if you wanted. And we don't have to get married yet. It's all up to you. Just let me know."

"What did you think about my place?"

"I didn't see it."

"What do you mean, you didn't see it?"

"I was crying too hard. "

Kárin laughed at that.

"Don't make fun of me. This is the first meltdown I've had since Lidi and I have been on our own. I've managed all these years, and I don't think it would have been so bad tonight if I didn't have you for my safety net. I feel so good having you."

Kárin pulled her hand back from mine. Then I felt her cool fingers move below the material of my shorts and run across my bottom, stopping when she had her hand flat against me. She didn't try and move it. She didn't try anything sexual in the least. She just wanted direct skin to skin contact. It was so pleasant. I put my hand down the back of my shorts and covered her hand with mine, which is how we fell asleep just a few minutes later.

When I woke up in the morning, neither of us had moved. My hand was still over hers inside my shorts. Her arm was still under my neck, with that hand holding my other hand, curled up together toward my collar bone. When the alarm went off, Kárin pulled her hand up and rubbed her eyes. I turned over so that I could face her.

"I wish I could call in today, but I couldn't if I wanted to. I have a hearing today," I said

"And I have to press the flesh today with a couple of smarmy, but very rich people...see if I can pick their pockets a little. The big trick is just to dress pretty and act sexy. Hell, knowing I'm a lesbian, and especially meeting you when you do some of this stuff in the evenings with me, their typical view of girl-on-girl sex will get them to give even more."

"So, is this the voice of experience speaking?"

"Uh...busted. But I think I can get you inside some of those cliques that have so far been very elusive. That would work, wouldn't it? When do you have to get Lidi up?"

"About now."

"Does she pick out her own clothes or do you pick them out for her."

"Actually, she picks them out herself and gets them on with no help. The hard part is getting her eyes open and getting her standing up."

"Be right back."

I tried to listen as best I could without getting out of bed yet. I just wasn't prepared to face the day.

"Hey, Lidi, wake up, sweetpea. You've got to get up now, pumpkin."

Then I heard the strangest noise, followed by protestations from Lidi. Then I heard them again, and again, and again, followed by laughter and giggling from both Lidi and Kárin.

"Hi, Mommy Kárin. Did you sleep all night here?"

"I sure did. I think Mommy Aly needed me to be with her last night to keep her from being so sad. Is it okay with you that I was here?"

"I can't wait until you live here all the time."

"We'll get to that in time, but for today you need to get up and get your clothes on. Don't forget to brush your teeth and go to the bathroom. What do you usually eat for breakfast?"

"Toast and jam. Uncle Val gets me black current jam. It tastes really good. Have you ever tried it?"

"Not before today, but it sounds like it may be my first time. Do you eat before you get dressed so that you don't get anything on your clothes?"

"Most of the time."

Lidi got up out of bed and got her clothes, putting them on the bed. Then she ran into the kitchen and climbed up into her booster seat. By that time, I had gotten up and wandered in. I thought my hair was a mess. Wow.

"Look at that!" I laughed, pointing at Kárin's hair.

"Sure, laugh at the little JAP."

"JAP?"

"Jewish American Princess."

"No, it's adorable," I said as I walked up to her and ran my fingers through it.

"Leave me alone, I'm fixing breakfast. You want anything?"

"I'd take a cherry chip bagel from the bread box. On the top shelf in the fridge there's some cream cheese."

I took the chair next to Lidi and sat with my arm around Lidi while we were waiting for Kárin to make breakfast.

"Mommy, do you know what Mommy Kárin did to me this morning? She blew on my tummy and made motorboat noises. She's funny."

Kárin turned her head around to me and smiled, and then turned her attention back to her preparations. When she had everything ready, she brought the plates to the table, including a glass of orange juice for everybody.

"I'd take some coffee, actually."

"You can drink some of that ratty carcinogen once you get to work. You start your day with OJ. I do, and I follow it with a coffee chaser when I'm about fifteen feet inside the door at work. Now eat, drink, and do it quickly. Lidi needs to get to school, and you and I need to get to work. Mach schnell!"

"Wirchlich? Sprichst du?"

"Natürlich. Im meinem Familie alles kann."

("Really? You speak it?

"Naturally. In my family, everybody can.")

"This just gets better and better! Why didn't you tell me that you spoke German when I told you I had a minor?"

"It didn't seem relevant at the time. How do you feel today, honey?"

"Like a train wreck. I feel so guilty about last night."

"There's nothing to feel guilty about. Forget it."

"I certainly didn't act like an adult, like the mother of a nearly seven-year-old child."

"But you had me to do that for you, and I suspect that gave you license to let go. You know what they say about having a good cry now and then. Maybe you'd been long overdue and it was just too much to control. Anyway, like I asked you, are you okay today?"

"Thanks to you," I smiled.

I reached my hand across the table and held hers. Lidi was oblivious, eating her toast and drinking her juice. When she was done, she simply slipped down to the floor and went to go wash her hands and face, brush her teeth and hair, and get dressed for school. She so had Sasha's independence.

"So, how does this thing work with the pickup and delivery of our daughter to school? Private or public?"

I had to smile at that. 'Our daughter.'

"Not related to our church, but it's a Presbyterian school for now. They know that Lidi is half Jewish and they don't bust her chops at this school. They also don't mind at all that her mom is gay. There are actually a few other kids there that have gay parents. And the other parents are always open and helpful. When they found out I was a single mom, and especially the circumstances, every one of the parents in Lidi's class made some effort to make sure if we ever needed anything to let them know. Gideon's driving service takes her to school. After school is out, she's in an after school program for a couple of hours, then Esther brings her home. I like the school. It helps Lidi maintain a good social atmosphere."

Kárin started clearing the table, and out of habit, I started to get up and help.

"Nah, nah, nah, nah! You sit right back down. I've got this."

"Kárin, you're so good to me. How is it that we didn't meet sooner?"

"I'm a firm believer that it was necessary for me to go through a few bad relationships and you to go through some time alone in order to prepare both of us to be standing in front of each other. And now, we're in this particular moment, both of us finally ready, able to not only live life, but succeed."

"And among your other talents, can we list philosopher?"

"Go get ready for work. You're going to be late. And don't forget, you two are having dinner at my place tonight. Six thirty sharp."

"Good enough."

I got up from the table and went through my morning routine. Lidi was out the door with the driver's service. I always thought it was over the top, but Gideon was already at work, and the driver got paid for full days. He had an office at the law firm, where he read the paper, surfed the net, read books, or whatever. Then when someone needed him, he drove. While everybody in the family calls it the driving service, it's not an actual driving service in the normal sense. It's a service that caters only to the Aronovs and only has one employee. There was always somebody from an agency to cover vacation and sick days, but Frenchy was a full timer for the firm, who was a retired veteran. Actually, he was twenty-six years Army Special Forces, so he also sort of doubled as security, in a sense.

Kárin and I were working around each other getting on makeup, brushing teeth, going to the bathroom, etc., while each of us was in our underwear. Suddenly she got behind me and got down on her knees. She slowly began pulling my panties down over my hips, lowering them over my thighs, then further down my legs. She leaned in and gently ran her tongue from the small of my back, lower, until she had run a trail all the way to the juncture of my upper thighs.

"What are you doing?"

"Letting you know how sexy I think you are."

"You have exactly ten seconds to stop that. And if you don't, I'll give you another ten, and another ten, and another ten...."

I turned around to face her, held out my hands, and pulled her to her feet.

"Kiss me," I demanded.

Without waiting, I grabbed her face by her cheeks and pulled her into me, passionately kissing her.

"Oh, my God, how I love you," I said into her open mouth.

"Baby, so do I. Remember, forever and a day," she said as she pulled back.

We walked slowly—too slowly based on our lateness leaving the apartment—hand in hand to the parking ramp. I picked up my phone and dialed Fran.

"Hey, Franny, last night there was a little bit of an emergency and we're running about a half hour late coming in this morning. If anybody needs me, make my apologies and tell them I'll call them as soon as I can."

"What's the matter, your dog die?"

"Actually, it's the cat that I've had since I first started college."

"Aly, I didn't know. I'm so sorry. I didn't mean anything by it. Please forgive me."

"Don't worry about it. How could you know? I'll be there in a bit." I smiled as I hung up the phone.

Kárin was smiling at me.

"What?"

"My fiancée is driving me to work. How cool is that?"

"Pretty damn cool. I guess I owe you one, huh?"

"I don't keep score, but if you feel at any time you want to do something for me, you feel free to go right ahead," she snickered.

"Are we still going to come over to your place tonight for dinner?"

"I hope so. Otherwise, there'd be a ton of food that would spoil."

CHAPTER TEN

When I dropped Kárin at the front of her building, I was amazingly happy. Drained, but happy. Last night was devastating, but what a trooper Kárin had been for me. And as for Lidi? Lidi was already calling her Mommy Kárin. I knew that whatever happened along the way, we'd have to make it work. For Lidi, my little Lidi, and now *our* little Lidi. It occurred to me at that very moment, I'd committed the ultimate 'Breach of Lesbian Protocol.' One date and we're a couple, two dates and we've hired a U-Haul to move her in. What did I know about Kárin? I'd been to lunch with her, but I'd never been to her main office much less any of the other offices where she had a desk to work. I didn't get a chance to see her apartment last night, I was so wrecked. Her parents lived in Texas so I wasn't going to get to meet them until at least Christmas, if then.

Strangely, I started making a list in my head of things I should learn more about. Yet, as I was doing it, I had no trepidation whatsoever. I was very...confident. This was just going to be. That was all there was to it. Period.

I parked the car in our office garage and slowly made the walk to my office. For being so broken up last night, I was at my best in what seemed like forever. It wasn't as if I hadn't already thought about how much longer Lilly would live. And she'd already been to the vet twice in the last four or five months. Somehow it was a relief to put closure to that worry.

But Kárin, last night and this morning, taking care of both me and Lidi. Then making breakfast this morning and making sure we were both up and going. The things that a mom was supposed to do. And she did it with a big smile and tons of compassion. How could I have any doubts at all? Then it hit me like a ton of bricks…it was prank time.

"Detective Captain Martha Devonshire. May I help you?"

"Martha? Hey, you. I need you to do something for me. Do you have time to spend about an hour and a half working with that little thing that you figured out the other day?"

"Actually, this would be a perfect day for it. There are about four meetings I'm trying to get out of. If you gave me an excuse to be 'called away on urgent business,' I'd be eternally grateful."

"I don't want to give too much away before Girls' Night, but run a quick background check on Kárin Zajac. K-a-r-i-n Z-a-j-a-c. It's pretty unusual, so I don't think you'll have any problem with finding more than one. If there are any red flags, stop and call me, but I seriously, seriously doubt there will be. I just have the best gut feeling on this one. After you get it, have a detective drive around to her office and ask to interview her, but don't tell her why you're doing it. Grill her about last night…big time. Make a show of it. I know how to drive to her building, but I don't know the exact address. It's on my phone. I'll forward her contact information to you as soon as I get upstairs in my office. If she gets too hysterical, pull off. I suspect she'll be able to take anything you dish out though," I laughed at Martha.

"You are one mean pussycat. I'm going to make sure you're declawed one of these days, aren't I?"

"If what I think is right, she'll pass with flying colors. It would mean a lot toward making sure I'm making a good choice, not for me but for Lidi. I have to think about her too."

"You're right there. Send me the information and I'll run it down. Then I'll call you this afternoon. Deelio?"

"Right on, sister."

"10-4."

I felt positively wicked. Isn't this sort of what I did to Sasha the first time I saw her? No, different circumstances. I already knew Kárin, and it was already beyond casual. I walked by Fran's desk on the way to my office.

"Excuse me, Aly. Could you come here for a moment, please?"

"Sure. Give me a sec...."

I put my bag down, pulled my notebook out, plugged it into my docking station, and turned it on. I walked back out to Fran's desk.

"What is it?"

"What are you up to?"

"What do you mean?"

"You had a rough night last night. You didn't say 'I' will be a little late this morning, you said 'we.' Both are things that are understandable, but the look on your face blowing through here...you're scaring me. What's the catch, and how much backlash is there going to be?"

"Nothing gets by you, does it?"

"I hope not."

"To start with, last night was the most devastating night I've had in several years. Maybe just a stored up...whatever...anywho, Kárin came through for me like a champion and took care of me. And even more importantly, she took care of Lidi. And she did it like she'd been doing it for years! And now...I'm pranking her."

"So this magnificent woman that you've recently met, that has bonded not only with you but with your child, and who picked up the pieces for you last night and took brilliant care of you...you're going to prank her?"

"Something like that."

"Is this really a prank or a test?"

"Yes."

"Funny. So what's the prank? Or aren't you saying?"

"Remember Martha Devonshire, Captain in the NYPD? She's going to have one of her detectives mosey over to Kárin's office this afternoon and question her."

"You are *so* mean. You'll be lucky if she doesn't dump you straight away."

"If she's made of the stuff I think she's made of it won't phase her."

"Remind me never to date you."

I laughed out loud at her. I laughed so long and hard I could barely breathe. I walked back to my desk still gasping for air, pulled myself together, and pulled out my first case.

About two thirty in the afternoon, Fran forwarded a call through to me.

"This is Alison Aronov-Lockewood. How may I help you?"

"You've *got* to be fucking *kidding* me? Sending a cop over to harass and intimidate me? As if. And did you really think I wouldn't figure it out in an instant? It didn't take me two minutes to crack him like a raw egg. How dare you, Mrs. Alison whatever-your-name-is! You should be ashamed!"

I started all over again with the laughing. I couldn't talk at all. I heard a lot of hollering from the other end of the conversation, and I'd break up again. Every time I managed to compose myself to some degree, she started in, which set me off again.

"Oh, sweetie, I'm so sorry. I don't know what got into me. And you took care of me last night in my darkest hour. I don't deserve you. I swear I don't."

"You got that shit right! I'm not sure what I'm going to do with you, or to you, regarding this little stunt."

"You're going to feed me tonight?"

"You expect me to invite you over still?"

"Please? Pretty, pretty please? May I still come over to your house and play?"

"You can come over, but while Lidi and I sit at the big people's table, you're going to be at the children's table where you belong. Damn it! Did you *really* think I was that stupid? I don't think we've ever actually sat down long enough for the conversations to happen that will eventually be those loving conversations that will fill in between all the bricks of our relationship, but you might be interested in a bit of information. I graduated summa cum laude with my Bachelor's in Classic Studies. I also have a Master's in Letters, not in English Literature mind you, in *Letters*, where I graduated, surprisingly, summa cum laude. I'm halfway to my Ph.D. in Political Science, also from The New School, one of the top schools in the country for that major. And the only 'B' I've ever gotten *in my life*, I got back in seventh grade from a teacher who got all pissed off at me for proving him wrong in class in front of the other kids. I speak English, German, Spanish,

Polish, and Hungarian fluently. Put that in your pipe and smoke it, missy!"

I sat there with nothing to say. I was trying to find words to string together and not sound stupid. So I said the only thing I could.

"So I guess that means that I'm a complete idiot. I accept the mantel thrust upon me to be worn in public attesting to my lack of knowledge about the ways of the world and my marvelous, magnificent, beautiful fiancée."

"You remember the age-old adage about judging a book by its cover?"

"But sweetie, I never, ever judged you. When we meet up with Martha and the girls next week, ask her exactly what I asked her to do and ask her exactly what I told her your response would be."

"She was in on it? And what do you mean *the girls*?"

"Yeah, the detective you talked to works for Martha. You'll find out next Thursday. Never mind for now, just don't schedule anything for next Thursday night."

"I remember, you already brought it up and I've reserved the whole night on my calendar."

"Have I told you lately how much I love you?"

"This morning, if memory serves. Although I'm not so sure how much I still love you after this one."

"Don't say that, sweetie. I was just playing."

"Playing is watching a movie or coloring with Lidi. Playing is closing our bedroom door and taking off our clothes. Sending the NYPD by my office unannounced is certainly not playing. I'll give you this though, the detective did it behind my closed door, so it was discreet. And he never once cracked a smile until I told him I knew what it was all about and he knew the gig was up. When he left my office there were several people standing around trying to poke their nose into my business. In front of them all, he reached out to shake hands and said, 'Thank you, Ms. Zajac. I'm sure our case will be quickly resolved. The information you've provided will be of immense value, and I'm sure that apprehension is no more than one or two days away with your assistance.' He was totally cool. He could work a scam as well as anybody I've ever seen. He is one smooth dude. I can see why you want Martha on your team when you pick sides."

"Bri and Lexa helped me so much when I lost Sasha. And Gideon and Roni. Even my parents. But Martha...Martha is the reason I didn't leave Lidi at a firehouse, find a gun, and blow my brains out. In our network of people you'll meet, they never let me have a minute needing anything...and Martha was the one leading the way. All kinds of people gave me moral, physical, and financial support, but Martha coordinated the entire effort. She has such a huge heart and a gentle soul, despite her hard outward appearance."

"I don't know why, but for whatever reason I get the impression that Martha's gay as well, isn't she?"

"Oh, yeah! In the biggest way. I certainly don't mean a bit of disrespect to her, but she's the quintessential bull dyke. Definitely wears a lot of denim and flannel off duty, and she goes for cute, young things. Not too young. She's about fifty, I'd guess. Her current little fling of about six months isn't a day over thirty-five. She never gets overly-attached and never dates anyone for more than six to nine months. Then she'll go for several months with nobody. She's happy as a lark. She's never wanted more."

"Not me. I've been looking for the silver bullet my whole life. Who knew it would take this long?"

"And now you found it?"

"What a stupid question. I didn't just find the silver bullet, I found the whole box of ammo and they're all silver tipped."

"What a sweet thing to say."

"I have to run. I've got a meeting over at the McBride Underwriters Group. I may be able to squeeze about ten grand out of them for the year. They've been pretty steady over the years, and I've already pulled up their financials, since they're publicly traded. They had a boring, but above industry average year, so they might still be in a giving mood."

"I'll see you tonight, sweetie. Love you."

"I love you too, honey. Ta."

I buried my head back in my cases and was able to seriously focus the rest of the day.

"Maybe this was a good thing for you to do today," Fran said as she turned off the light switch on our way out.

"How so, Franny?"

"Because you're back to being a serious lawyer. I'm not saying you shouldn't have fun along the way, but your feet haven't hit the ground for the last two weeks. Really! You should have your mother stripe the backs of your legs with a willow switch."

"I suppose. But it's been fun not having to be an adult with responsibilities for the last little bit."

"I wish I could say the same thing. Arsène would simply cease to exist if I didn't play his mom every day. We have three grown children and both of the boys are just like him; relying on their wives to run everything or it doesn't get done. Oh, all of them have jobs, but they're just so juvenile. It gets tiring sometimes."

"You've never said, but is Arsène's family French or did they just name him that."

"How did you know that Arsène's a French name?"

"Are you kidding? Arsène Wenger is the manager of my team! Arsenal Football Club, English Premiership League."

"Oh, God, tell me you aren't a total sports nut just because you're gay."

I nearly laughed my ass off.

"No, but I also like the Giants and the Mets. Yes, the Mets. I'm a sucker for punishment."

I was biting at the bit to clear the building to get home today. I had Esther pick up Lidi early today so that we could scoot over to Kárin's apartment. They were waiting when I got home.

"Lidi, go put on one of your striped shirts, baby."

"Why?"

"Because I asked you to. Would you do it for Mommy, please?"

"Okay."

"Aly, she is so well-behaved. That's why I love helping you out in the afternoons."

"You're such a huge help to us, in case I haven't mentioned it lately."

"You keep mentioning it every week and I tell you every week that I don't mind. You really have to stop that."

"I'll try. So you and Gideon are going out to eat tonight?"

"Erm...um...He called me and told me he canceled our reservations. We're going to get Chinese takeout delivered and watch a movie. We may even put a sock on the door handle."

"Esther!"

"What? I may be old, but I'm not dead."

"I guess I always wanted to ask, but thought it wasn't any of my business."

"Well, now you know," she grinned at me.

She took off to Gideon's for what I assumed would be the entire night. Lidi and I took off for Kárin's place. I was so amazed. First, that it was so modern. Second, that it was so clean. It had hardwood and tile floors throughout and not a speck of dust. Amazing. But it was also relatively plain and unadorned.

"Hi, honey. Give me a kiss."

"I'm coming," I said as I was putting down my bag.

"I wasn't talking to you, you bonehead. Come here, my little pumpkin and give Mommy Kárin a big hug and a kiss."

As if Lidi wasn't already on a tear running to greet Kárin. Kárin picked her up and twirled her around in her arms several times while Lidi giggled, then put her down.

"Now, come over and give me a kiss, bonehead."

I gladly complied.

"I couldn't help but notice that there is decidedly less clutter in your beautiful apartment than there is at our place. Are we going to have to go through and gut the apartment and give everything to the Goodwill people?"

"Don't let the looks deceive you. When I finally found out that Leyla was stringing me along and split up with her, I moved out and got this place. What you see is a year and a half of not unpacking anything that's in the second bedroom. Come look."

She led me back to the second bedroom. It was practically stacked from floor to ceiling with unopened boxes. I let out a long, low whistle.

"Holy Mother of God. Where are we going to put it all?"

"I've thought about that. Everything of real value can probably be narrowed down to about ten or fifteen boxes. I was thinking about getting one of those little spaces at a storage facility, one of the tiny closets. It will hold everything I want and won't cost much at all. Unless you want me to keep this place as our 'little loft' where we can escape periodically."

"Wow, this would be a pretty expensive place. Wouldn't it just be cheaper to go to the Park Plaza twice a month?" I chuckled.

"I think it would. No doubt. Come sit down. Dinner is just about ready."

"What are we having?"

"Moroccan fish with mango sauce, couscous, stuffed harcha, and lamb tagine. Wine for the adults."

"Wow! So I guess I'm not the only cook in the family, huh?"

"Apparently not. Before you come to any snap judgments, maybe you'd better taste it."

"I haven't been dissatisfied with anything else so far. And I do mean *anything*," I told her giving her a wink and a poke in her side.

Lidi had grabbed the television remote, turned the screen on, and found her favorite channel. No instructions needed even though it was a different brand and system.

"Our daughter is a precocious child, isn't she?" remarked Kárin.

"You have no idea. Just you wait and see," I intimated.

"By the way. I've already talked to an attorney at one of my associated companies. He totally agreed with you. I already have him getting me a list of things I'll need to submit to him, and he's going to start right away to get everything in order. I told him that when we pull the trigger, I didn't want anything standing in the way."

"I'm glad."

Kárin pulled the lid off a saucepan and stirred the contents, did the same with another, and opened the oven and checked that. When she was done, she went and sat on the couch next to Lidi. She bent down with her face in front of her, which irritated Lidi. She tried to move around her to see the television. Kárin moved in the way again and Lidi got ever more frustrated, leaning way down to see. Kárin then slumped down over Lidi, completely blocking her view. Lidi pushed Kárin off with her arms, turned her body, and kept pushing until she had Kárin sitting upright. Then Kárin climbed in Lidi's lap and looked nose tip to nose tip.

"You're in my way."

"No, I'm not. You're in my way."

Lidi squealed.

"Mommy Kárin, you're silly!" and grabbed her by the neck, wrapping both her arms and legs around Kárin.

This was a moment that would forever be emblazoned in my memory. One of so many to come.

We finally sat down to eat dinner. The food was delicious. It was nice to have such an extravagant home-cooked meal without being the one to have to cook it. Don't get me wrong, I've eaten many wonderful meals at friends' and family's houses, but not exotic. This was definitely exotic.

"Mommy? Are you and Mommy Kárin married?" asked Lidi with a quizzical look on her face.

"Not yet."

"Are you going to get married?"

"Someday."

"When?"

I laughed and wondered where this was all coming from.

"Why do you ask, baby?"

"Scarlet at my school said that I can't have a Mommy Kárin if you aren't married."

"Well, baby, we just don't do things exactly like everybody else."

"William has two mommies, but he only calls one Mommy. He calls the other one only by her name. They're not like us though. They all live together with William's little sister and brother."

"Baby, sometimes when women get married, they still don't call both people Mommy. Most don't, but we do. It's just to show each other how much we love each other."

I thought she'd let it go. She got very pensive, just eating and furrowing her brow, but it wasn't to last.

"Why can't Mommy Kárin come and live with us? Doesn't she want to? Kárin, don't you want to live with us?"

"Shhh...baby, just be patient. When the time is right everything will happen just like it's supposed to. Be patient. Don't worry so much. And when kids at school ask you questions that they shouldn't...."

"I know. I'm supposed to just ignore them or get a teacher."

"That's right. You know, Kárin, I've already had the big white wedding: two wedding dresses, at the temple, with several hundred people there. We even had the thing video recorded; I've got the ceremony on DVD. A group of graduate students from the NYU Film School paid a lot of the costs for letting them film it. In any case, I don't care what kind of wedding we have. Big, small, temple, courthouse, whatever. I've had my dream, now you deserve your dream. Any thoughts, or do you want to think it over?"

"I want to wear a white evening dress, and I would like you to as well. Small would be fine with me, but I'd like to have the ceremony at a temple, if you wouldn't mind. I know you're a Christian and everything, but you didn't seem to mind last time, so I didn't think you'd have a big hang-up this time...unless you felt cheated the first time."

"I was the one that planned the last one! I just want to make you happy, sweetie."

"You know, I take back most of what I said about you today," Kárin retorted.

"You have to admit it was a brilliantly hatched scheme. Did the detective freak you out at all? Even for a minute?"

"Not really. I was pretty confused at first, but that's the sum total. It also helps when you know that you didn't do anything. If I'd have known that Martha is who she is, I would have laughed right in his face within the first thirty seconds, if not sooner. I finally asked him if the City of New York was in the habit of using public funds to prank its citizens. He assured me it was no prank and that he'd thank me to take his business more seriously. I told him I would take it more seriously if you and your obvious connections would try playing with the big kids. I told him to take his ball and go home. He got a chuckle out of that, but I'll tell you that up until that second he played it deadpan. Totally deadpan."

"One of these afternoons when we're just sitting around doing nothing, I'll tell you how I met Sasha. It's a funny story, one for the books. And it's the day I officially came out, because of my encounter with her. My encounter with a silly plaid skirt in a store. My life-changing metamorphosis."

"Come with me, my pretty, and you too, little Toto!" Kárin cackled as she took both my hand and Lidi's and led us back to the big bedroom.

She turned on the television and found Nickelodeon. Then she got up on the bed and laid down, pulling Lidi up beside her and patting the blanket on the other side indicating I should lie down too. Lidi pretty much paid attention to the show. She was lying up on top of Kárin's arm. Kárin's other hand was paying more attention to my hand, my cheek, my neck, my hair, my ear, and eventually she surreptitiously dropped her hand lightly down, covering one of my boobs. I placed my hand over hers. I rolled my head over to the side noticing that Lidi was enraptured with her show. I squeezed Kárin's hand underneath mine and held it like that for about five minutes before releasing it. Kárin moved her hand back down and took Lidi's hand in hers next, playing with Lidi's hands. Lidi's hands were enormous for her age, like a puppy. She was definitely going to be tall when she got older, no doubt. Both Sasha and Danny were extremely tall, so no wonder there. Lidi enjoyed playing with Kárin, but never broke her concentration.

When the show was over, Kárin got up and turned on the lamp on the nightstand.

"Everybody up and go home. Tomorrow is a school night. Right?"

"Oh, do we have to go now?"

"Lidiya Marie, what is the rule about whining?" I chastised.

"I know, Mommy, don't whine. Nobody likes it."

"That's right, my sweet baby," I said, pinching her cute little cheeks.

"Stop. You know I don't like that."

"I know. That's probably why I do it."

"Well, don't."

"Go get your sweater on, baby. Time to go."

"You know I don't want you to go," emphasized Kárin, to me.

"I don't want to go. If you came to our place tonight, I'd give you some 'happy time.' "

"As delicious as that sounds, I know that I'd be up until the wee hours of the morning, and I have to be at the Manhattan Towers building at seven o'clock in the morning. I'm taking a helicopter ride down to the Hamptons to hold a meeting at some big dog's house; his 'other house.' One of them, anyway. The one that's not in Aspen and the one that's not in Zurich and the one that's not in Tucson when it gets too cold and nasty."

"Oh, *my gosh!* I never realized. You've got such a *tough job.*"

"You want it?"

"Me? Oh, *hell* no. How do you go out and throw a sales pitch with no product to sell? I would so totally suck at your job. No, thank you."

I was facing Kárin with my arms around her, hugging her, kissing her, when my hands started sliding lower until they were over her butt.

"You're going to have to stop that. Either that or come with me into the bathroom and let Lidi watch another show."

"No, we should go. We'll get there in time. Someday we'll share a bed, and all it will take is somebody reaching over to the other one, and the sparks can fly anytime we want."

"See you later, my love."

Barring anything major happening, I wouldn't see Kárin until Saturday. That would be the longest we'd gone without seeing each other since we'd met. Well, tied for it. The wait for our first date was the same length of time. From Tuesday to Saturday. I sighed out loud. I wasn't going to be a happy camper this week.

CHAPTER ELEVEN

"Hi, Diya. How are you guys doing?"

"I'm *exhausted!* I can't get over it. I thought I wanted kids. I have to tell you, having one was a chore, but having the second one has just wiped me out."

"Are you going to come to temple this weekend?"

"I hadn't decided one way or another. I still need to talk to Roni to see what she and Michael are doing."

"Can you come even if Roni doesn't? Lidi and I will take care of the little ones for you, if you like."

"What gives?"

"I need you to bring a dressmaker's kit with you."

"You need a dress?"

"No, I need two of them. Just formal evening dresses. Nothing too awfully fancy either. And this late in the year it's going to be hard to find white dresses unless you go to a bridal shop."

"Who are they for?"

"Me. And a friend of sorts."

"You. And a friend of sorts. Wouldn't happen to be a certain someone that had dinner with us over at Papa's house, would it?"

Everybody in the extended family had taken to calling Gideon 'Papa' out of respect. And unlike his storied past, he showed the utmost respect and care for everybody around him. Val said that's the way he acted when the kids were growing up, especially the older ones, even though he'd always worked too many hours.

"I don't know. It just might be."

"Aly, didn't you *just* introduce her as your girlfriend?"

"That's changed. What would you say if I told you I'm wearing Sasha's rings and Kárin is wearing my rings? It was even Kárin's idea. I told her it wouldn't be fair to her to 'recycle' the rings. She said that if I wore Sasha's rings, it would be as though Sasha were my guardian angel, and with me wherever I went. And that she in turn, wearing my rings, would have an eternal bond with me. When you think about it, it's actually sort of romantic…and saves about ten grand to boot!"

"I'm stunned. Aly, you'd better be careful. Remember, if you get burned, so does Lidi."

"Oh, you should see her with Lidi. They're wonderful together. Sometimes I don't know who she loves more."

"Are you sure that she wasn't just looking to have kids and you were the perfect solution?"

"If you'd been in bed with us, you'd know how ridiculous that sounds."

"Okay, TMI. My ears are bleeding now. *La la la la la la la,*" she said laughingly.

"Laugh if you want, but it's the real thing. I just thought you might want to do a little work for us. I'll pay you for them, of course."

"You will not."

"At least for the materials. It's the least I can do."

"I won't hear another word of it. But, uh, just out of curiosity. The thing about being in bed with her? It was good, yeah?"

"Oh, yeah, *baby*. It was so good. Want me to draw you a picture?"

"Not necessary. I can probably figure it out."

"It's not really what you'd picture. I mean it is, and it isn't. Have you ever seen a lesbian scene in a porn movie?"

"Without ratting myself out, yes."

"Well, everything you see in the movie is everything that isn't real. I mean, some of it is mechanically, but it's just not that. It's completely different. If you ever wanted, I could get you a demonstration. Not from me, of course. That would be almost like incest. But I've got a couple of friends."

"Okay, that's enough. Sorry I asked. Jesus! I'm sorry I asked."

"Jesus? I thought you were Jewish?"

"Don't forget Judaism is an enate tradition and religion; it comes from the mother's side. Recuerdes, mi papá es Católico." (Remember, my papa is Catholic.)

"I keep forgetting about that. Then shouldn't you be saying 'Jésu Cristo'? Isn't that the Latin mass for it anyway?"

"You're a pain, but I love you just the same. I'll bring the kit with me and I'll be there."

"Diya?"

"Yeah?"

"Not because you're doing this for me. Not because you guys bought my rings. Not because you've fed me both at home and at the restaurant. But because of how much you've meant to me and Lidi...how much support you've given us, mentally, morally...everything. I love you to death. You know that, don't you?"

"Sure I do. And I'm pretty fond of my little sister-in-law."

"Hey, you're only five years older than me!"

"Yeah, but I'm six inches taller!" she laughed and hung up on me, not letting me get in the last word.

I'd bring it up after temple and probably after we'd gone to see Rabbi Abrahamson, but I planned on suggesting we might want to find a room and take a couple of measurements. I didn't know how long Kárin wanted to wait, but last time I got married, I pretty much picked up the ball and ran with it. And I even slowed myself down. I was prepared to back off at a moment's notice, but I didn't plan on it if I didn't have to. I was thinking about a December wedding. That would give us about eight weeks to plan. Plenty of time for seasoned veterans like me and Bri-Bri.

That night when I made my bedtime call to Kárin, I pressed her about her friends.

"You haven't ever talked about any friends. And I never took the time to pay attention properly to them. Do you have any good friends?"

"None, for the most part. Most of my friends I met through my exes. When the girlfriend goes, the alliance with her friends goes with it. Sort of left me without anybody in particular. I have a couple of acquaintances at work, but they're barely more than that. Friendly, but I never go to their houses and they never come to mine. An occasional dinner out, but that's almost always in relation to a collaboration or a fundraiser. It's certainly never drinks after work."

"We're going to fix that."

"Oh?"

"Next Thursday night we're going to meet a couple of people for drinks…and chips if you want. Eat first, you'll need it. Plan on coming home with me for the night. It will be logistically easier that way."

"No problem. What else went on with you today?"

"Oh, nothing to speak of," I lied.

I just picked your dress designer, my filly. Bwahaha. And I've set our wedding date and I'm not telling yet. You'll just have to tag along and see. Wasn't it Bette Davis who had the line, 'Fasten your seatbelts, it's going to be a bumpy ride!'? I felt like Bugs Bunny talking to Elmer Fudd, making fun of the way Fudd talks, 'Ain't I a wascawwy wabbit?'

My night was filled with fitful dreams. Every time I woke up, I knew that I had been startled awake, but I couldn't remember what the dream itself was about. About four in the morning, I started to get up to go to the bathroom and found a lump in my bed. I hadn't even noticed when Lidi had decided to crawl in with me. Note to self: after move-in, always get dressed after sex. I chuckled to myself as I bumped into furniture and walls making my way to the bathroom. I'd already turned on the light when I thought it would be a mistake and I would blind myself. Too late. Damn! That was bright. I made my way back to bed when I was done. I crawled back under the covers and snuggled up to my little baby girl. My mini-Sasha. She was such an angel. Mommy's perfect little girl. I finally fell back asleep.

It made for a hard time getting up in the morning. Lidi and I were both dragging like we had lead in our back pockets. We managed somehow to squeak out the door just on time in spite of this. As I walked into work, I was practically running to play 'Beat The Clock.' Fanny barely looked up at me and was polite enough to give me about ten minutes to get settled in and signed onto the network before bringing in messages and our working calendar.

"I hate to do this to you, Ms. Aronov, but you're not going to like it."

AFTER SASHA

"Can I assume that the formality is your way of letting me know this is really bad?"

"It actually came yesterday in the four thirty mail run. I didn't have a chance to look at it until today. Judge Baker has denied your petition to remove the Hudson children from the family environment. She determined that you didn't show sufficient cause and that, in her estimable opinion, 'The children's continuity in their present circumstances outweighs the consideration of them being placed into foster care.'"

"What does that stupid bitch need? Two broken legs instead of one? Wasn't that enough convincing for her? I wonder how Her Honor would like it if I showed up in her chambers with a couple of thugs that held her down and snapped one of her legs? Would that help? Really? Best for the children?"

"Aly, calm down, I'm on your side. I was just trying to ease into it. Here are the records," she said, handing them to me.

I briefly reread the document that I'd had in front of me twice before this last incident.

"I always thought the third time was the charm. What the hell is this? I don't care. I'm filing a complaint with the Judicial Review Board requesting she be removed from this case, and I'll re-present. Whatever it takes."

"If you do that, you could just make it harder for the next child's case you have that goes in front of her. And you can't always get another judge. You're going to be stuck with her. She's only two years older than me if memory serves. She's going to be on that bench for a long, long time."

"Franny, do me a favor and turn the lights off on your way out. I want to meditate for about thirty minutes and consider my options. I don't have any appointments until eleven if I remember correctly," I said with a deep sigh.

"Aly, keep in mind, our job is to do the best for these kids that we can, not cure everything that's wrong in their lives. Sometimes it just can't be helped. There are circumstances beyond our control. Remember, 'God grant me the serenity...', right?"

Fran turned to leave and had just flipped off the overhead light switch when I turned on the desk lamp.

"Fran?"

She turned back to me, waiting in the doorway.

"Thank you. If ever you think I don't appreciate all of what you do for me, just come hit me square in the head and ask me what I think of what you've done lately. Just so you know."

Fran smiled and pulled the door shut on her way back to her desk. I dialed her extension.

"Unless it's Lord Buddha calling, take a message for the next half hour, would you?"

"Okay," she said before she clicked off.

I got a bottle of water out of my mini-fridge and took some prescription migraine medication, then put my head down on the desk, resting on my arms folded in a circle. My phone started flashing Kárin's picture and playing her unique ringtone.

"Hey. I thought you were going to be choppered off to the Hamptons this morning. Change of plans?"

"Nope. Delay in plans. They're going to bring somebody from the Bryant Foundation along for the ride. He's being taxied over right now. We should be taking off within a half hour, maybe less. I just wanted to call and tell you how much I'd rather be eating lunch with you today."

"Mmm...that sounds delish. I thought yesterday's case was a crap deal. I've got one today that the judge pushed back on and is allowing the parents to maintain custody."

"Bad parents?"

"We don't know which one of the two broke her leg. Therefore, ergo, to wit: we can't charge either of them. At least we can still seek to charge both with conspiracy, which is easier to get a conviction anyway, even if it doesn't carry as big a sentence. Keeps it a misdemeanor; just let me get the kids out. But even without that, a pattern of violence with a parent intentionally breaking a bone should have been enough, and this is the third incident in the same household in two years. It's so frustrating at times."

"I would think that a good anecdote to consider is the number of children that you've been able to help over the last year and a half or so that you've held that job. Don't you think?"

"Maybe. I just don't know this morning. I haven't figured out what to do. I was going to get all up in that bitch's crib and show Her Honor what I'm made of. Word! But Fran told me that maybe it wouldn't go so good when I was back in her courtroom and needed a favor. It's sort of like being back at college and pissing off the dean only to find out that your grant request needs to be amended to include more than the original figures. You know what I mean?"

"Still don't want to change jobs with me?"

"The things that keep me going in times like these is the memory of all the selfless years Sasha put in with the system working for the kids...damn. Kárin, I'm so sorry. I didn't mean that like it sounded. I don't mean to always bring her name up."

"Honey, don't sweat it. I understand. Truly, I do. I get it. And some of my fundraising is for charities that do just exactly what you're working for. Just relax. I can't wait for Saturday, to see you and Lidi again."

"Kárin? I don't deserve you. You're so spectacularly wonderful. I love you so much."

"I know."

"That's all you have to say? I know? Being catty are we?"

"You know it, girlfriend. Meow."

Finally, I laughed. She'd managed to draw it out of me. How could she tell I needed it at this very point in time?

"There's the last passenger. It's a tough job, but somebody's got to do it. There's a Sikorsky S-76 with my name on it warming up on the helipad. I'll call you when we get back. And, yes, I do miss you, my love."

"Do you love me or do you love Lidi and want a kid and I'm just the process to get her?"

"Yes."

"Well, meow, meow again. What a morning!"

Kárin giggled in my ear. She brought me so much happiness, it was indescribable. After she had hung up, I kept the phone in my hand and clutched it to my chest, returning my head to my arms on the desk. A few minutes later, Fran rapped quietly on the door, then pushed it open a few inches.

"I hate to bother you, Ms. Aronov, but there is a Rob Briscoe from the County Court System here to see you. Shall I show him to a conference room?"

I raised up and pulled myself together, taking a big swig from my water bottle.

"Put him in 2A and I'll please tell him I'll be right there."

I picked up a writing tablet and walked into the conference room. Rob rose and shook my hand. I'd never met him prior to today and wondered what he wanted.

"It seems as though Her Honor, Judge Baker, has been stricken with a pretty serious case of food poisoning and won't be able to return to her duties for several days. She'd already decided the disposition of some cases, but hadn't yet found the time to sign them. One of them is the motion you filed on behalf of the Hudson children. Thus, it's still in request status, and we're now over the time limit prescribed for the resolution. I'm here for two reasons. One is that I'm new to the Family Courts, and I wanted to meet you in person since we'll be working together periodically, and I thought it would be nice to do a meet and greet. Secondly, I took it upon myself this morning, at about seven thirty, to hand carry five cases over to Judge Horace's office. I've already gotten dispositions on them: both the Hudson case and the motion for the Brandywine children are included in those. For the Brandywines, he's going to block their mother from contact, giving the father temporary sole custody until they've been able to allow their divorce to play out in court. Judge Horatio has also reversed the decision on the Hudson children and has given you the green light on the other three cases: King County vs. Rainwater, King Country vs. Trenton and Trenton, and King Country vs. Green. I thought this might help you out," Rob said, smiling.

Yes, I could say my day immediately got brighter and my mood was elevated, but the headache had already been triggered, so that I'd have to deal with the rest of the day.

"Thanks, Rob. And, by the way, please call me Aly. After all, we'll be working together periodically, as you said."

"Okay, Aly. By the way, nice rings. I'd guess your husband must have a job much better than the state jobs that we have," he said laughing.

"Actually...these are my wife's rings. She passed away about five years ago."

"I...I...I don't know what to say. Please accept my apologies for speaking out of turn. I'm so sorry for your loss."

"Don't worry about it. Actually, I'm getting married again in a couple of months, but nobody knows it yet. That's weird. I don't know why I just told you that. I haven't told anybody outside our family and my admin that I'm remarrying, and I've only told one of them when it's planned. I haven't even told my fiancée that I've set a date. Maybe you'll want to reconsider being friends with me once you find out all of the strange things about me," I said laughing.

"What's her name? Your fiancée? I assume that you're still going to marry a woman?"

"Her name is Kárin Zajac."

"My partner's name is name is Nathan Carlsen. His office isn't too far from here. He's a fundraiser for non-profit organizations. Maybe we can grab a lunch together sometime? I mean, if you'd like…or not."

"Wow! Kárin does the same exact thing as Nathan. I kid you not! Isn't that the most bizarre coincidence?"

"Totally. Way cool. Anyway, if you have any questions going forward, call our office, but ask for me. I'm the new case coordinator. Nate and I just moved down here from Buffalo so we haven't met a lot of people yet. It would be our pleasure to get together with you two," he said, handing me his card.

"Definitely. We'll just make it happen, simple as that," I smiled, extending my hand.

We shook warmly as he walked down the hall to the front door. I was watching after him, smiling. I turned into the vestibule and was walking past Fran's desk.

"My, my, I thought you preferred girls. You certainly seemed taken with that young man. I can see why, he's pretty handsome."

"Don't be ridiculous. He brought us some very good news, and besides he's gay. He and his partner are going to take me and Kárin to lunch sometime. They're newly arrived from upstate and don't know that many people yet. I think we may have just gotten an inside pull, of some magnitude, within the courts. And one of his first acts was to handle the Hudson case. Judge Baker is sick, and she's out! I'd say that was fortuitous. Wouldn't you?"

"If you came looking for a fight, you came to the wrong place. Has his office already taken care of the notification to Child Protective Services for removal?"

"Done, done, and done!"

"There's service. That should take care of your headache."

"Nah, not in the least. Once it's triggered, it's hell getting it back down. And it started by having a really bad night last night. I barely got any sleep. Coming in was just the icing on the cake."

I sat down in my chair in the now fully-illuminated room and pulled out my phone. I sent a text message to Kárin even though I knew her phone would be off for the flight and on silent afterward, but I sent it so that she would be able to see it later.

'FYI – crisis averted, kids ok, switched judges w/o repercussion. BTW, do you know Nathan Carlsen?'

I needed to get some research finished before my eleven o'clock showed up. It took me a little under a half hour. I put the tablet into a folder, neatly put it in the stack on my desk, tidied up the desk overall, and sat back in my chair. I pulled out my phone and looked through the contacts.

"Hello, Mrs. Schiffman. I need to find out if we can schedule a conference after second services this coming Saturday if the rabbi has any time available. We'd be willing to wait for a couple of hours if we need to."

"What type of conference are you looking for, so I could check and see how large a block of time I need to look for?"

"It's for pre-marriage counseling."

There was a short silence on the other end of the telephone.

"And who would be involved in the conference, might I ask?"

"Me, and Lidiya, of course, and a woman named Kárin Zajac."

"Kárin? From Children's Beneficial Finances, among other groups?"

"Well, she certainly seems to have a reputation that precedes her!" I laughed.

"Oh, we know her. We've worked with her, raising money, and she's been able to get outside money for our children's programs. Very beneficial for both, really. How is she doing these days? I haven't talked to her in probably a year and a half or so now, I think. It's been quite a while, in any case."

"She's doing fine. I've no doubt that we'll see you during second service this coming weekend. She's coming with Lidi and me, Roni and Diya, and Gideon, and even though Gabi is a Roman Catholic, she might be here this weekend since her husband is going overseas."

"Tell her she is always welcome. All children are God's children, no matter what you would think by watching the evening news," she tittered.

"No doubt. I hear you there."

"Well, services should end about one thirty, and I have a block of time open between two thirty and three thirty if that would do?"

"Very well indeed. We have a couple of things to do in the Activity Center and we can just do those things prior to meeting the rabbi."

"You know that Rabbi Abrahamson always enjoys any time that he can see Lidiya."

"I'm so blessed. Everybody feels the same way. I'm so lucky that she takes after her mother so very much."

"Oh, come now, Aly. She takes after *both* of her mothers. She who bore her passing along nature, and she who raised her passing along nurture. You've been exemplary. Trust me. I deal with children all day long almost every day. I would take one Lidi over hundreds of other children."

"That's very kind of you to say, Mrs. Schiffman. So we'll see you this weekend. Have a wonderful day."

"Shalom."

I'd have to tip my hand about the dress, and I'd have to tip my hand by having our pre-marriage conference with the rabbi, but that couldn't be helped. During our nightly bedtime call, I reminded Kárin that we were going to temple and asked her if she was sure she wanted to go with us.

"Of course. Why wouldn't I? Don't you want me to go?"

"I do, babe, but I don't want you to feel pressured. I mean, we've hit this thing pretty hot and heavy. I don't ever want you to think I'm forcing you to do anything."

"Aly, if I don't want to go, I'll tell you I don't want to go. I'm a li'l ole Texas gal after all. You forget that sometimes, don't you? And I won't make up an excuse, I'll just tell you I don't feel much like going and would rather sit that one out and stay home and chill. I won't ever lie to you and tell you that I'm home chilling out and then go do something else. Okay?"

"I guess."

"I said *okay?*"

"Yes, Mother."

"That's better. Are you just going to come pick me up? And maybe I could bring some more clothes with me? Maybe?"

"Sounds dreamy. Why do two days from now seem so far away?"

"Only a day and a half. We'll get through tomorrow, somehow, and then I'll see you when you pick me up on Saturday. Oh, yeah, Nathan

Carlsen? I've met him a couple of times. I've been up to Albany for some meetings with lobbyists and he's been involved with them as well. He's great. How do you know him?"

"He recently moved to the city. His partner, Rob Briscoe, works as a new supervisor over at the county courts. I met Rob today. He said he would love to invite us out to lunch or dinner or something. I could tell right away I'd love it. I have a great feeling about Rob. I think he's going to help us out with our cases."

"Well, if he's anything like Nate, I guarantee he will."

"All right. Nighty-night."

"Good night, honey," Kárin said, then rang off.

On Friday, Fran picked up the intercom on the phone and dialed my office. The door, as usual, was open, but Fran was old school. She was from a time where legal secretaries used a typewriter and telephones were old-fashioned, with rotary dials.

"Yes, Fran."

"Aly, I've had a quick addition to your schedule for noon. Unfortunately, that was their only available time, but they're apparently bringing a couple dozen deli sandwiches for everybody here. Do you have any preference as to meat?"

"I didn't need this today...I guess chicken," I said, after thinking a moment.

"You never know. This may be just the thing you need."

"What do you mean by that? And who is the appointment with?"

"An advocacy group that works with both children and adults of a specific topic. This one is more of a rights group than anything. I'll gather the menu from everybody else in the office and phone it over to the group. I need to get that quickly, so I'll check in when I get done."

"Fran..." but it was too late.

Franny had already jumped out of her chair at a dead run to scurry off around the other warrens of desks. How odd, I thought, and had a nagging feeling that something didn't seem right.

I managed to stay busy until noon, and Franny managed to avoid me fairly neatly until that time as well. She kept telling me 'just a second,' or 'as soon as I do this,' or something or other.

Finally, there was a large commotion going on in the large conference room. I suspected this was the meeting and got up with my pad, pen, and cell phone and walked toward the doorway.

"Ah, there you are, Ms. Aronov," she said as I entered the doorway of the conference room.

At the far head of the table stood Kárin.

"Good morning, Ms. Aronov. I'd like to introduce directing members of several local chapters of PFLAG: Bill Feynman to my right, William T. Wexler to his right, Theresa Sparks to my left, and Shawna Beem to her left. People, I'd like to introduce to you Alison Jeanette Aronov-Lockewood, my fiancée."

You could hear a sharp intake of breath from everybody in the room. Nearly everybody spoke at once, saying things like "I had no idea" and "When did this happen?" or something similar.

"Please believe me, everybody, when I say that nobody could be more surprised than both Kárin and myself. It was a whirlwind romance. And please, call me Aly."

"I have to say, there isn't anybody in the world that would make a better representative for our collective groups. To be one of us, so to speak. Kárin did tell us that you were openly out, but not that you two were an item. This is exciting news! And please, call me Terri."

"So, Aly, after putting our heads together, we thought about different types of support that can be offered. Fiscal, mental health, etc. And one thing that was glaringly overlooked was the support and education available to children who were undergoing problems of both bullying and acceptance by other kids or by family members or others. We thought helping the kids fit in better, getting them in touch with more of the support that's already there for them but could be communicated more widely, and things like that, would be highly beneficial, sort of a list of allies, so to speak, where they know they have friends in their corner, as opposed to just going to any office of a counselor, doctor, psychologist, lawyer, whatever... Whoa, that was a lot to say in one sentence, wasn't it? Forgive me, but I get passionate when I talk about my kids."

"And my involvement here would be what?" I asked.

"Solely this—that you are aware of our resources so that you can incorporate them into the rehabilitation, protection, development, etc., of the children for whom you are their legal advocate. The more information you have, the better a total program you can outline for them, thus being more effective."

"Well, on the surface of it, it sounds like a wonderful idea. In fact, it's something I'd been meaning to talk to you about since meeting that night at the fundraiser. That was the first time I'd ever heard about PFLAG, and it intrigued me. Life's been a little hectic and I've not had a chance to get any of the literature from you, but this is much better. How about you give me a thirty-minute pitch, let me ask some questions based on that, and then we'll go round table for everybody's input. Sound good?" I said as I sat back in my chair and readied myself to be wooed. I wasn't sure if the wooing was the product or the pitcher thereof!

"I don't know if we need that much time, to tell you the truth."

"You may not, but I've gotten a free sandwich out of the deal, and I intend to eat while scribbling notes!"

Everybody in the room liked the food icebreaker and reached for the paper bags laid out by Fran on the sideboard.

It ended up taking almost two hours for lunch, but we'd scratched out an outline to be broadened for not only my office, but others in the five boroughs area as well. Some seriously good work had happened here today. Finally, everybody got up to return to their various offices. Last out of the room was Kárin. I took her hands in mine and looked in her eyes. I had to look up, just as I had with Sasha.

"If you think you're going to get any favoritism out of my office...," I started.

"Yeah?"

"You can count on it," I said, leaning in, going up on my tiptoes, and kissing her lightly on the lips.

"I believe the phrase, Ms. Aronov, is 'get a room,' " snorted Fran.

"Don't you have some work to do, Fran?" I queried.

"After making so many arrangements over the last three days to make this happen for you, you'd better talk a little nicer to me."

I looked at Kárin. Kárin nodded her head at me while looking sideways to Franny.

"I suggested a meeting sometime and she did the rest. It's all on her. Right down to the sandwiches. You've got a pretty hot item working for you there."

"I know. And I tell her that every chance I have. I want her to stay happy and never leave me here on my own. Or worse, trying to break in a newbie."

"Stay happy? You imply that I'm currently happy, Aly."

"I can't give you money, the county determines that, but let me know what else you need and I'll try."

"Let me think. I don't want to waste my one wish on something foolish."

"I'll be back in a minute. I'm going to walk Kárin down to the parking garage."

"Okay. No problem."

Kárin and I slowly walked arm in arm to the garage and then to her agency car.

"Nissan Murano! And you're a charity organization? How do you afford that?" I asked incredulously.

"We have five of them. But they're on a one-year loan, use of vehicle only, not ownership. We still have to insure them, although maintenance is totally picked up by the dealership. We've got bylaws that they have to be rotated between brands and dealerships and that no one can compete for the five years following a sponsorship year. Thus, every brand, but not every dealer of course, gets to be a sponsor on a six-year rotating basis. Cool, huh? Costs us nothing and takes the favoritism out of it. First idea I had when I started working for the consortium. Ain't I a smarty pants?"

I wrapped my arms around her body and squeezed her tightly to me.

"Yeah, I've seen what's in your pants! I liked it pretty much, if memory serves... And, by the way, thank you so very, very much."

"For what?"

"For leading off with the fact that you were my fiancée. Freely and openly. It makes me feel just that much more likely it will come to pass, that it's all real."

"Look at me, honey," she said, putting her fingers under my chin and lifting my face and eyes upwards.

Her eyes captivated my soul at that very moment. Time stood still, and my heart went from beating hard in my chest to skipping beats altogether, I think.

"This is real. This is happening. Give it time. Everything will work itself out all on its own. Believe in me. If anything, it should be me thanking you."

"What do you have to thank me for?

"You. Lidi. Gideon. Diya. Roni. Grigory. Valery. Puppet. My own drawer and medicine cabinet. Where do you want me to stop?"

After holding each other in silence for over ten minutes, I finally broke loose and told Kárin I had to get back to work to prepare for a court hearing this afternoon.

"I'll talk to you tonight, honey. Bye now."
"Bye, sweetie."

CHAPTER TWELVE

Lidiya always wore the same thing for temple. She had several blue dresses, all of different patterns, but all cotton and frilly, adorned with eyelet. And she always wore the white scarf with blue trim that we'd worn that first Chanukah, her mother's scarf. Sasha's scarf. Every time we went to temple, she wanted to wear Mommy Sasha's scarf that she first saw a photo of when she was less than three years old. It was practically growing threadbare. I told her we should get her a matching scarf, but a new one. Lidi would hear nothing of it.

As I pulled up to Kárin's building, I pulled out my cell and called up to see if Kárin was ready. Before it had rung enough times to be answered, a most striking woman came walking out the doors of the building, wearing a lovely hunter green dress with matching low quarter pumps and bag, finished off with a matching ribbon through her hair, holding her exploding locks behind her and keeping her hair out of her face. The woman quickly crossed the distance from the doors of the building and got into my car.

"Are we ready to go? Oh, Lidi, what a pretty scarf. Where did you get that? It's magnificent," Kárin exclaimed.

"Oh, God in heaven! You're so...so...exquisitely beautiful!" I managed to choke out after a few awkward moments of silence.

"What, this old thing? So you thought I was a stone cold dyke, huh?" Kárin asked laughingly.

"It's not that. I've just never seen you..."

"You've never really seen my totally femme side? Is that a better description?"

"I have no words. You look stunning. I'm inspired."

"Now, now, let's not go all potty for penguins, shall we? So, Lidi, where'd you get your scarf? My grandmother wears a scarf almost like that. She's gone through several, actually."

"It belonged to Mommy Sasha. I get to wear it now. I wear it every month when we go to temple."

"How cute. You know, at some point as it begins to wear a little bit, you should carefully fold it and put in a special place with other things from Mommy Sasha. That way you won't tear it and you'll always be able to look at it on special occasions. And you could get a new scarf. I bet you could get one exactly like it if you wanted to. Or maybe even a little different that would make you always remember Mommy Sasha, but would show Mommy Sasha that you are keeping her memory fresh."

I reached across the seat and clasped my hand around Kárin's tightly, driving down the street as we continued to hold hands.

"I've been looking forward to this all week. I went to temple not too long ago with a work associate, but it wasn't a reform temple. The ladies and the men had to sit separately. You don't get to sit with your own families. I much prefer the reform temple. Who is the rabbi?"

"Rabbi Abrahamson!" shouted out Lidi.

"Aram Abrahamson?" queried Kárin.

"The one and only. Do you know him?" I asked, knowing full well that she did.

"Sure I do. We've been to many functions together. He's a delightful person."

"I'm glad you approve. We're going to have a conference with him about an hour after second service this morning. I hope you don't mind waiting around. I sort of wanted it to be a surprise."

"I can only imagine what sort of surprise it will be, coming from you," Kárin said as she leaned over and kissed me.

We pulled up to the parking lot at the temple. I started to get Lidi out of the car, but Kárin shot out and told me that she'd like to get Lidi out if that was all right. I had no problem with that, so I just picked up my purse and watched Kárin. She looked so perfect. And, of course, wearing my old rings and Sasha's Star of David. No, I corrected myself. *Her* Star of David. And *her* rings. I wanted to pinch myself to make sure it wasn't an illusion.

As we entered the temple, several heads turned. Many people here thought they'd just seen Sasha as well. We caused quite the murmur around us. And people kept turning in their seats to look. I shrugged it off. The whole family was here today, even Val, who managed to take a half day away from the restaurant. Esther had come with Gideon. Grig, of course, had already left for sea trials, Phase I, on his ship. In less than six years with his company, he'd gone from Master Machinist to Mechanical Specialist and Boiler and Motor Engineer. Gabi was even here today just to be out and share in the family togetherness. We were all extremely jubilant.

One person's head we didn't turn was the rabbi's. After all, he'd known Kárin for about four years. But the people at temple? Some of them were outright shocked. Everybody here was getting to see "The Ghost" for the first time. The rabbi made a point of introducing Kárin to everyone.

"We on the staff here have worked with benefits and children's programs for many years, but some of you may have noticed that Aly and Lidi Aronov-Lockewood have a guest today. Her name is Kárin Zajac, and she has worked with us hand in hand on those charities. I want to welcome her here as she may become a fixture in the future, if the gracious Adonai answers our prayers the way we wish them to be answered. I noticed on the faces of some of you that our new guest seemed very familiar to you. Let me be the first to admit the similarities and tell you that no, Sasha Aronov did not in fact have a long lost twin sister that has been miraculously found. However, Elohim has provided us a miracle in her presence alone, and she just happens to look like our beloved lost Sasha. They are two so completely different personalities, but Sasha and Kárin were both blessed with a heart of gold and an inner drive to help others less fortunate. So please, everybody, meet Kárin and welcome her after shul today. Shalom."

The entire shul responded.

"Shalom!" the people of the temple replied loudly to the rabbi.

Then the cantor began reciting religious verses. Since this was very much a reform temple, many of the people in the audience sang along with the cantor. Being so adept at languages, it was not hard for me to learn many of them, and I found them uplifting. So periodically, when either the cantor or the rabbi sang a verse, I sang along, although an octave higher. Nobody seemed to mind so I'd continued to do it. Eventually, I'd gotten more and more interested and had gotten the prayer book. I'd attended a couple of classes and learned basic Hebrew, enough to learn the alif-bet and some pretty standard words and phrases, along with proper pronunciation. Then I'd started studying the music in earnest. I had become equally happy at both my church and the temple.

I looked down periodically and patted Lidi on the back, and often found that my hand was over Kárin's. Then I'd smile at Kárin, who was already smiling at me. I'd no doubts left. This was real and was going to happen, and it was going to be as perfect as life with a family could ever be.

After services were done for the day, everybody broke up into smaller groups and said their hellos and greetings. Then even smaller groups mingled longer still. Next to the entrance to the main congregation of people toward the center of the back was the greeting line of the rabbi and his wife, the secretary and her two daughters and one of her grandchildren, the cantor and his wife, the head of Outward Services, as well as a few additional family members.

As we headed to the exit, there must have been over one hundred fifty people stop and greet us. Most of the people were welcoming Kárin into the temple, many assuming this was my new partner and congratulating me, although nothing had been mentioned about that.

"Good morning and welcome, Kárin. Aly. Lidi. Gideon. Everybody. And how are all the Aronovs today? Well, I hope?" asked Rabbi Abrahamson.

"Yes, Rabbi, very well, thank you. Everybody's going home now except a couple of us girls. Mrs. Schiffman said there would most likely be an empty room in the Women's Hall that we could use until our appointment."

"I'm sure there will be one available. If not there, somewhere. We have lots of space. Always obliged to help out."

Diya, Kárin, and I had gone to the end of the hall on the second floor before we found an empty room. It turned out that a lot of the rooms were merely being used as musical practice rooms, also bar mitzvah and bat mitzvah training, etc. Diya dropped her oversized bag on the desktop, got out her notebook, pen, and her measuring tape. Kárin started to sit down, but was rebuffed by Diya.

"No, no, no, no, no. Just stand there for a minute. Do you want a dress, a skirt and top, a suit, or a tux?"

"For what?"

"For the ceremony, you ninny. Now come on, we only have an hour before the meeting."

"What meeting, exactly?" asked Kárin with her eyebrows arched.

"Please answer my question. I don't know you well enough to predict what you'll want to wear. So, what will it be?"

Let it not be said that Kárin isn't absolutely brilliant.

"I would think a simple dress, formal type, no gathered waist, shin length, sleeveless, spaghetti strapped, maybe a simple pearled floral pattern above the breast on the left side? And I absolutely hate empire waists, if you even had a thought about that. Does that sound okay?"

"You're sure you want a dress?" I asked for verification.

"I'm wearing one today, aren't I? And after that night at your parents' house, you know that I'm not a stone cold dyke."

"La-ti-dah!" Diya said under her breath with a grin.

"I meant wearing a dress to church, for goodness sakes!" snapped Kárin, also with a smile.

"No, sweetie, I was just making sure of what you wanted. Really."

"Out of curiosity, if it didn't matter to me at all, what would you have chosen for me?"

"Truthfully, that's pretty much what I was thinking for both of us. I've done the frilly thing already, and I enjoyed it, but I've moved on. Unless that's what you want me to wear. I mean, crap. Is this going to be a big deal of neither of us wanting to upset the other?" I laughed.

"If you wouldn't mind, I'd rather you had a little layering. Maybe a dress mostly like mine, but with a layer of silk organza. And either wide shoulder straps or spaghetti, but I hate strapless dresses. Don't know why. Just not my cup of tea. Mostly I think because they make your boobs take on a life of their own, not moving freely with the rest of your body. And everybody goes around tugging them up all the time. Makes the woman look stupid. Like wearing a pair of pants that's too big without a belt so that you're always tugging them up. Not that I'm picky, mind you, but if I could, that's what I'd choose for you. For me, I'd choose a veil that comes just to the bottom of my hairline, and for you one that comes just to the middle of your shoulder blades. No train, nothing long. Like so."

"So? We're agreed?" asked Diya.

I looked at Kárin. She looked at me. I looked at Diya, who looked at Kárin, who looked back at her. We simultaneously shrugged our shoulders in agreement.

"From this point, it's too late to turn back. Agreed?" asked Diya.

"Agreed," Kárin and I said in tandem.

Diya placed the tablet in front of herself and started taking measurements, working first with Kárin. She took several measurements, then stopped and wrote them down. Then every few measurements she would ask a question about a particular preference and scribble in a note to go with it. When she finished with Kárin, she asked about color.

"Champagne, beige, crème, whipped cream, white, pearlescent? What is your color choice? And do you two want the colors to match or do you care?"

"What is pearlescent? And yes, I want the colors to match," said Kárin.

"It's the color of a brand new Lincoln, Cadillac, Camry, Sentra.... Something like that. Instead of the old style of grinding up pearls in the paint they use a powdered form of plastic. Sometimes polyacetate, sometimes polyacrylon, sometimes polyvinylchloride. It could be other things as well, but it would be something like that which gives it even more of a magical sheen than pearls do, and still makes it a bright, almost shimmery white. Maybe it would be better if you thought of comparing a regular household lightbulb to one of the new compact fluorescent bulbs. Less yellow, more of a pure, clean white...."

"Honey? What do you think? That one sort of speaks to me all on its own. Does it you?"

"That would be plenty good for me. It would make them really pop, really bright, right?" I answered, picturing it in my head.

When Diya finished with Kárin, she went to work on me. I wanted actual shoulder straps on my dress. I also wanted it to come down just above ankle length. But I was good with the rosette on the breast and the shoulder blade length veil.

"Kárin, do you want me in full shoulder straps because you're ashamed of my body and you want to cover it up more fully? Is that it? Are you ashamed of me?"

"Diya, look at the door."

Not knowing what Kárin was driving at, Diya did so. While she was looking away, Kárin slapped me lightly on my right cheek then quickly withdrew her hand. Diya turned around trying to hide a knowing smile. I took Kárin's quickly withdrawn hand into my two, brought it to my lips, and kissed it gently, moving it then to my cheek and nuzzling it.

"Looks like we finished up just in time. We need to get back to the offices for your meeting," Diya pointed out, glancing at her watch.

"I take it our work with you is done here, for today at least?" Kárin asked Diya.

"Pretty much. If you two have time, next weekend we can go through a fitting."

"Next weekend? Are you nuts? Aren't you doing anything for the rest of the week?" asked Kárin with incredulity.

"Oh, these? I'll get the material tomorrow and have them both made by Monday, but only with the seams pinned. That way, when you come over for an hour or so, we can get them both completed."

"Both of them? An hour?"

"Probably won't take that long, but just to make sure, I plan on it."

"I told you. She made her husband a three-piece suit from scratch, without a pattern, in under three and a half hours. Wool, leather patches, silk lining. I've never seen better."

"One of these days I want to find a talent that I've got."

"You can sing, you know foreign languages, and you can squeeze ten thousand dollars out of a clam on the beach if you are in the mood to."

"Okay, I'll give on those points, but none of those make *me* lots of money."

"You know the dresses Lidi wears to church and temple? Diya makes all of those. Usually takes about an hour start to finish. She's a lifesaver."

"I don't know how to thank you, Klavdiya. Like the rest of your family and all the wonderful things you do for each other and are doing for me."

"It's hard to imagine we used to be so messed up and dysfunctional, isn't it?

Diya packed all her things in her oversized bag and headed downstairs with us. Up by the offices, waiting quietly on a cushioned bench, we found Roni and Lidi.

"Roni, what are you doing here with Lidi?"

"Esther felt obliged to stay, but I told her to take Dad away from here and go have a good afternoon doing something fun. They may actually be having a picnic in Prospect Park, believe it or not. Esther has a couple of friends up there. The rabbi wanted Lidi to stay and talk with the two of you today, if that's okay. So we stayed together and have just been talking. Michael's going to a basketball game today at UCONN with some of his friends, so he won't be in until late tonight. I'll take Diya home while you guys talk, and then we'll talk more tomorrow or something. Okay?" Roni ventured.

I hadn't noticed, but while Roni and I had been standing talking, Kárin had taken a seat on the bench next to Lidi, and Lidi had crawled over onto her lap. Lidi gave Kárin a kiss on her cheek and had her arms wrapped around her neck. It made my heart glow warmly.

Moments later, the rabbi walked out into the hallway with several members of another family, which looked for all intents as though they were undergoing grief counseling. He held the door open wide and motioned for us to enter. Then I took one of the middle two chairs in front of the rabbi's desk while Kárin and Lidi already occupied the other one.

"I'm told the purpose of this meeting today, is a life counseling session for a couple nearing the point at which they are considering getting wed in holy matrimony. Is that correct?"

"My mommy wants to marry Mommy Kárin," answered Lidi.

"Is that so, little lady? Well, may I ask you, what exactly do you feel about that? If it didn't matter one way or another to either your mommy or to Kárin, what would you want them to do?"

"It would make them both happy if they got married."

"Yes, I understand that, Lidi, but if they were happy either way, would you want them to get married or just be girlfriends, maybe."

"Oh, no, because Kárin can't live with us until we're married. Sometimes she can sleep over, but she can't move in until then. That's what Mommy said. And I want Kárin to move in with us now."

"Why do you want that?" asked the rabbi.

"Because she takes care of me in the morning and when something is wrong with Mommy. She makes my mommy happier. And she cooks as good as my mommy, and only Uncle Val and Jorges René can do that. And she gives me kisses and hugs, and she tucks me into bed, and she holds my hand. I love Kárin, and she loves me."

"Well, that certainly is something. I'm also told that if your mommy and Kárin get married, they plan on Kárin adopting you, making her one of your two permanent mommies. Just like Mommy Sasha is your mommy forever, even though she isn't here anymore but is always in your heart, Mommy Kárin will have the same responsibilities. And you would have to obey her as well. If she tells you to do something that you don't want to do, you'd have to do it anyway since she would be your real mommy. You can't go to both mommies to see which one has the answer you want. You have to just listen to whoever is next to you and follow her wishes. Do you fully understand this?"

"Yes, Rabbi, and it's what I want. My mommy wants to get married again so she won't be so lonely anymore, and nobody at all in the whole world is better than Mommy Kárin."

"Well, there's that barrier. I think we can safely put that one to rest. Now on to the rest of the inquest. Kárin, although I've known you for a little over four, maybe four and a half years now, it's been strictly from a business standpoint. I believe you are of exemplary character, but this is personal. And I want to know that what I've seen in you so far is aligned with how you are after work, day in and day out. For instance, how many relationships have you been in over the last five years?"

"Three. One that started way before that five years. One that lasted only about nine months. And my last one that lasted for about fifteen months. Between relationships, I was always alone for anywhere from six to nine months before I even dated again. Even dating casually, I'm a serial monogamist, I always have been. I've never gotten this serious about a woman in such a remarkably short time either, before now. In the past, it's taken months of slow and steady progress. And before you ask, I've been openly gay since early high school. No late surprises like my bride-to-be," Kárin smiled at me.

"Aly, you've been alone, maladjusted, emotionally dead, wanting, yet seemingly happy with your life with Lidi, until now. What's changed it? And I want you to consider my next question seriously. Is it the way that Kárin looks?" asked the rabbi.

"Rabbi, I went to a fundraiser and was completely out of my element. I thought it might be a place to meet others that work in my system of being a child's mens rea representative and advocate. Then I saw her. Her visage threw me, and it drew us together, that's true. But we started talking quickly, and it was the most normal thing in the world. I asked her out within thirty minutes, to make sure that if she wasn't already seeing somebody, she might consider going out with me. She was telling me about the PFLAG organization, and I asked her who was the member in her family. She said it was her. My heart fluttered immediately. I had to wait until the following Saturday to go out. It almost killed me. And every time we were together after that I felt like I was dying when she wasn't beside me. On our fifth date, we were at my parents' house in Queens for introductions and church. That night we were...intimate...and from that point I knew it. I missed her when we were apart for hours or days, but I didn't feel like I was going to die. I felt like I was truly alive. And that's why I want to get married, with your permission, of course, Rabbi."

"Well, it seems like the three of you have pretty much thought this through much more thoroughly than it would appear on the surface."

"And I've already instructed Kárin to approach an attorney from one of her organizations to reorganize her estate completely, for her protection. Everything both of us bring in would go to Lidi, in trust, her estate to be handled by Gideon's firm—not him personally. And in the case of our mutual demise, all prior assets would go to our personal beneficiaries, mine being Lidi's trust, and Kárin's being her trust, set up probably to her family."

"And that shows good planning and forethought," said the rabbi.

Rabbi Abrahamson sat for some minutes, quietly, with his fingers folded together into a horse barn's steeple. His brow was wrinkled.

"So when would you want to do this? How many people, etc.?"

"I think probably no more than fifty people maximum, and I was thinking sometime in December?" I replied, looking at Kárin as if pleading for approval. I got no reaction whatever.

"The only problem is that with all the bar mitzvahs and bat mitzvahs and anniversaries already planned, I don't think we'll have any space available until well into March maybe. Will that be a problem?" the rabbi queried.

I almost caught, or thought I did, a hint of a smile from Kárin.

"No, as soon as we can is fine. And nobody coming will need lead time. We already have dresses, as well as a caterer and florists picked. I'd like to ask your wife for that again, if it would be okay with her."

"Oh, I'm sure she'd love it. She did so love doing your last one."

"Okay, so we'll just go into a holding pattern for the moment, and shoot for about March. We'll probably talk again by the beginning of December to firm up the dates?"

"That would be perfect. And let me know if you'll also be bringing your Presbyterian pastor with you for a double ceremony. I know that Pastor Robinson is not in the best of health. Of course, he's welcome to attend; that would be utterly fantastic. Well, ladies, and I mean you too, Lidiya, I give you all three my blessing. L'chaim."

"Thank you, Rabbi," I said.

"Thank you," said Lidi.

"Shalom, rebe. Nie mogę się doczekać, aby to święto. Pamiętaj, że jesteśmy na na drugą sobotę grudnia, prawda?" asked Karin.

"Oczywiście. To będzie nasza tajemnica. I Diya jest. Shalom," said the rabbi to Kárin.

We three girls walked out together. We went to the car and got Lidi loaded into her chair. We originally had considered changing into something more comfortable, but Lidi wanted to go like we were dressed, so we relented. Before we took off for Bri and Danny's, I gave Lidi her iPod so that we could talk in front of her.

"Okay, that was rather conspiratorial. I could only catch a couple of those words. Nasza I think means ours. Szalom, of course, is Shalom. And from what you asked the rabbi, prawda is asking permission. At least I'm assuming so, since pravda is Slavic for truth. Remember, I'm a linguist."

"Lover, remember when you first met me, and I was getting butterflies in my stomach and they were getting worse because I thought that you didn't want to have a sexual relationship with me? And you told me that you had a valuable life lesson, and it would come in its proper time and make sense? This is your turn to totally trust me, relax, and just let me love you. Like the trust game where you stand behind somebody and they intentionally fall, and you catch them, saving them from harm. I will, above all things, save you from harm, for you are mine forever and ever."

And with that, Kárin raised her Star to her lips and kissed it, then resting it down on her chest, re-centered it and grinned the most evil grin I've ever seen. Well, maybe not evil…conspiratorial is more like it.

"You women are nothing but a bunch of bitches!" I laughed.

"Ain't we though? And who do you love?"

"I love you, my precious darling. I love you and only you."

"How long do I have to wait until I can adopt Lidi? Is there a certain amount of time after we're wed? I mean, I'm not trying to set a world speed record, I'm just trying to get a general idea."

"If everything is already in order, we only have to wait about two weeks until the courthouse has caught up with its backlog and gotten our license registered and recorded. Then we can push the paperwork immediately. That should take about two weeks to request. It might take two extra weeks if it goes before a judge, maybe even two more weeks if the judge wants to background it and hold a hearing. From there an additional week to render judgment, then two more weeks to record. Two months, give or take."

~ ~ ~ ~ ~

We made our way over to Brianna and Danny's house for dinner. We were only a little bit late getting there, but still way ahead of dinner, so everything worked out well. It just meant Lidi and Ingrid wouldn't have as much playtime, but it would be okay to stay up late tonight since it was a weekend. We were standing at their door and I was ready to push the button, when I looked at Kárin.

"Nervous?"

"Should I be?"

"This is different. Unlike our family, this is my best friend and confidant. And remember Danny's relationship to..." I said pointing to Lidi with my head.

"Yeah, I remembered that. I'm cool. The question is, are *you* nervous?"

"Yes, I am, and I don't know why."

Kárin laughed.

"Push the button already."

I did. Ingrid immediately answered it.

"Hello? Is that you, Lidi?"

"Hi. We're here. Open the door!"

The door buzzed and Lidi struggled, but managed to pull it open. We walked up to their flat and Ingrid was already halfway in the hallway with the door open behind her.

"Lidi! Hi! Come in, come in."

The two little ones went running and screaming back to Ingrid's room. I led the way into the apartment with Kárin a step behind me.

"Hiya, guys. Let me tell you, girlie, I was scared at first that I hadn't heard from you. After I had calmed down, I got just as pissed at you. Don't you ever do that ag-"

Kárin had just stepped out from behind me and held her hand out.

"Hello. I'm Kárin Zajac. We spoke on the phone briefly."

Bri held out her hand weakly, trying her best, but standing with her mouth half open, unable to move much.

"I know you told me, but damn! It's uncanny. I'm so sorry, Kárin. You must get this all the time when you first meet Aly's friends."

"Pretty much. I'm almost used to it, I guess. I don't get too wrapped up in it. More than anything, it just shows how much Aly's friends care."

Just then Danny walked in. He looked at Kárin, then at me, then back to Kárin.

"So, which one of you do I get to inject first?"

"Daniel Thomas Frost! You total pig of a man!" shouted Brianna as she slugged him hard in the midsection.

Kárin walked up to the two of them standing next to each other and put an arm around both of them.

"Don't worry, I've already been warned. And I've also been told that he has the biggest heart of any man on the planet. Don't sweat it, this time anyway," Kárin laughed.

"Well, I'm sweating it. You'd better shut up, asshole!" said Bri.

It set the mood for an entirely wonderful and delightful evening of sharing with my best friends in the world.

After the cleanup from dinner, sitting in the living room chatting with the little ones in the other room, Brianna turned to me.

"So, are you two planning on more children, if you don't mind me asking?"

"Brianna Cherise Frost, you absolute pig of a woman!"

"Touché. Daniel, I'm very sorry that I yelled at you, even though I still think your timing was entirely inappropriate and though I somewhat regret the force that I used to strike you. While not apologizing for said bellicose action..."

"Bri, the only difference between you and me is that I don't waste time, I just cut straight to the punch line," said Danny.

"Actually, that and I also have very nice breasts."

"Oh, so that makes it all right? You have great boobs?"

As if on cue, all three of us girls sang out in chorus, "Yes!"

"Well, I know when I'm not wanted or appreciated. I'm going to go check on the *little* girls, the ones who still like me!" he said, getting up and walking to the back of the apartment.

"Your man is funny, Bri. He's definitely a keeper," said Kárin.

"He can say stupid things at times, but once you get to know him better, you find out that it's almost always for a reaction. He does actually stop and think most of the time."

Just then Danny came waltzing back in with four beers, two in each hand.

"I didn't open them since I wasn't sure who wanted one and who didn't. But I checked, and the girls haven't stopped chattering since they went back there to play with their dolls," he said holding out his hands.

Everybody grabbed a beer and opened it up immediately. We stayed for probably another two and a half hours and another beer each. Finally, we gathered for goodbyes and hugs all around. As usual, the kids wanted more time, or for one of them to spend the night somewhere, but none of the adults was really into logistics for the rest of the night and we told them maybe another time. Driving back to our place, which wasn't that far from Bri and Danny's, Lidi pulled her favorite trick—falling asleep in her car seat. After we had parked in the ramp, I popped the back open so that Kárin could get the clothes she had brought to leave at our place and was holding them out to her.

"You take my clothes, and I'll carry Lidi."

"Okay, sweetie," I smiled and kissed Kárin before taking her purse as well as mine along with the clothes.

CHAPTER THIRTEEN

I had an entirely boring week at work for a change, which in a way made it go by doggedly slow, but also meant that there weren't any kids in trouble or in danger or anything like that. And that, after all, is the goal of the system, so I was actually pleased. On Tuesday, just before lunch, I called Kárin.

"Hey, stinky. I was just thinking about you. Whatcha doin'?" she answered.

"Wondering if you wanted to take me to lunch."

"Sorry, can't today. I already have a lunch date," Kárin replied.

"Who with, or is that a secret?"

"Another woman. An older woman."

"So you're passing up lunch with me to take out an older woman?"

"No, she's taking me out."

"How much older?"

"Seventy-eight, I think. Do you remember the National Public Radio announcements between shows that give the sponsors' names? Sheila is the daughter of Frederich and Natalia Wørsc, and their foundation's chairwoman of the board."

"Well, I don't know whether to feel stood up by my girlfriend or humbled by her importance to be in the presence of greatness!" I laughed.

"Girlfriend? What's this girlfriend shit? I thought we were affianced?" Kárin snorted.

"Sweetheart, you'll always be my beautiful girlfriend, long after we've been married for years and have gotten old and grey."

"I love you, but I have to go. I'll call you when I get back to the office. Okay?"

"Don't forget. Don't make any plans for Thursday."

"I haven't forgotten. See you."

"Bye, love."

I sat back in my chair and closed my eyes for a moment, holding my cell phone in my right hand up against my stomach, subconsciously.

"That must have been Kárin."

"Fran, who told you that you could come in?"

"It's my job. For this reason, I stopped asking the day after you got here. You're lucky I even gave you that one day as a grace period."

"Look, Miss Nosey Parker.... What can I do for you, Fran?"

Fran wasn't just my administrative assistant, she was also the head admin for our office. She was also the head admin for all of our offices spread across the five boroughs. One of her jobs was to play internal Human Resources.

"I've just done the audit for all of the offices. I have two problem children, it seems. And it's always the same two."

"Sorry, but what in the heck are you talking about?"

"You know as well as I do that if we worked for the state there would be a really high limit for personal time off. And although our funding is through the state, we are only county workers. Thus, we have a ceiling of two hundred sixty hours of time off to be accumulated, or we lose it. You have two hundred forty-six hours. Take Kárin on a three-day weekend. Shoo! Amscray! I have no ability to make exceptions on your behalf. It's the regulation."

"Okay, okay. I know it's been getting close. I'll talk to Kárin about it and get back to you. Just don't be surprised if I take you up on it and bail with no notice."

"That'd be fine by me. Not a worry in the world."

"Franny? Thanks for always looking out for me. You're the best."

"I keep telling everybody that, but still no raise.... What's up with that?"

I laughed as she turned and went back to her desk. Yes, I'd definitely like to talk to Kárin about that. I wondered what she was doing on Friday...

I lay in bed late on Wednesday night, wishing I could have Kárin by my side at that very instant. Lidi had gone out like a light, earlier than normal. I read for a while. I didn't feel like watching television or a movie; I just felt lonely. It wasn't too late to call Kárin for the evening, but I knew that she was at some sort of black tie soiree, glad-handing, and I'd only get her messaging. In spite of that, I sent a three letter text. 'I L Y'. I turned off the lights and lay there in the dark, too glum to even get up and get my jammies on. I must have lain there about an hour, although it seemed like it had been several, when I heard a light knock on the apartment door. Then I heard keys in the lock. I sprang up out of bed and ran into the living room, turning lights on the whole way. A ghostlike hand beat me to the switch there and my hand covered hers, crushing it to the wall.

"Hey, take it easy! That's the hand that I use to take money out of people's back pockets while I'm shaking their hands with my other."

"Kárin, oh Kárin!" I practically shouted as I threw my arms around her and dragged her into the apartment.

"What's all this then? First the message, and now this. What's going on, Chiquita?" Kárin asked me.

"I was just feeling blue and lonely and missed you and had to see you. I can't believe you came. I can't believe you're here."

"You can calm down now. I'm here. But tell me, what's really going on?"

"I don't know. I just missed you so much. I'm in a mood. Maybe hormones, although my period shouldn't be coming on for at least a week."

Kárin took my face in her hands and put her lips over mine to shut me up. She kissed me long and hard for several minutes. Finally, she let go of me, dropped her purse and laptop to the floor, kicked off her heels, and took off her jacket, hanging it on a hook.

"Have you eaten? Can I fix you anything? A snack maybe?" I asked.

"No, please, I'm stuffed. I ate like a damned hog tonight. I foraged all evening. It's amazing that I got to talk to anybody all night long since there was always a bit of food in my mouth."

"Are you sure? It wouldn't be any trouble."

"Honey, calm down. You aren't going to be like this after we're married, are you?"

"Ask me again," I said.

"What, are you going to act like this after we're married?"

"I just wanted to hear you say it again."

"Now you're just plain being silly. Maybe I'll have to remember to throw the word 'married' in casually every day until then just to assuage whatever fears you may have."

"Not fears. More like anticipation. More like, I don't know. I just don't want anything to go wrong."

"Remember when you wouldn't make love to me, but when you finally did, it was like *'wow'*! Out of the ballpark! It was honestly the best sex I'd ever had in my life. I don't mean just sex, either. Love, passion, adoration, the whole ball of wax. When we do finally get there, think about how good it will be."

"I know. What are you doing on Friday?"

"I haven't checked my calendar specifically, but I don't have anything planned, I don't think."

"Check it now, would you?" I begged her.

"Jesus, what is it with you tonight?"

Kárin fished her phone out and went to her calendar.

"Nothing at all. A dead on boring day. Probably trying to line up stuff for the next two or three weeks. Probably try and find somebody to take to lunch."

"Can you take the day off with this little advance notice?"

"Sure, I guess. What did you have in mind?"

"Lidi is going to spend the night with Papa and Esther is going to be there to help. We're already going out, and I want to spend the day with you on Friday. That's all. No big deal. I got told today to take some vacation time or I'll start losing it."

"I'll make sure to let them know early in the day. Speaking of which, what exactly are we doing tomorrow?"

"You'll see."

"What time?"

"Six thirty."

"Where?"

"Meet me here and we'll go together."

"What do you want me to wear?"

"Your pajamas if you want. Wear anything. Dress up nice, dress down, whatever."

"Let me put it this way, what would you prefer I dress in?"

"Just dress the way you would when you go out to lunch with a client. Not one of your black tie thingies, but business dress."

"You're acting really strangely tonight."

"I know. Forgive me?"

"Honey, there's nothing to forgive. But you could do one thing for me..."

"What is that?" I asked her.

"Take me to bed."

"I think we can arrange that, my darling. Come with me."

I took Kárin by the hand and started dragging her back to the bedroom, turning off lights as we went. I lit a candle in the bedroom and turned out the lamps there as well. I reached into her drawer and pulled out a tank and some shorts and placed them on top of the dresser. I got my pajamas out from under my pillow and put them on top of her clothes. Then I pushed her back gently against the bed where the backs of her knees were nearly touching. I unbuttoned her shirt and folded it neatly on the bed. I undid her belt and pants, sliding them down to her ankles. She stepped out of them one leg at a time. Then I neatly folded them and placed them with her shirt. I took off her underwear and neatly placed them on her other clothes, taking the whole stack and putting them in the chair at the foot of the bed.

After she was entirely nude, I took her gently by her shoulders and leaned in to kiss her. Just before her lips met mine, I pushed her really hard, making her scream slightly and fall back on the bed. I laughed at her, then stripped myself. She simply lay there and watched me, taking it all in. When I was also completely naked, she reached up to me with her hands. I grasped her hands, and she tugged me really hard, making me fall on top of her. I buried my face in her neck and nibbled and licked and kissed. We played for the next two hours before finally getting up to go to the bathroom to brush our teeth and pee.

After we had gotten back to the bedroom, we slipped into our bed clothes. I bent over and blew out the candle, then we slipped into bed and into each other's arms. I was no longer lonesome and blue, and we were both asleep within a matter of seconds.

"Mommy Kárin! You're here!" screamed Lidiya as she came running into my, that is, *our* bedroom and jumped up onto both of us.

Ignoring me, whom she obviously saw every day, Lidi went instead for Kárin and wrapped her not so little anymore arms around Kárin's neck.

"Mommy Kárin, I missed you so much! Where have you been?"

"Easy, sweetpea. Don't shout. I'm not awake yet for goodness sake!" Kárin told her.

"Why didn't you tell me you were doing a sleepover?"

"Because I didn't know until after you were already asleep last night. And I didn't want to wake you up. I just thought I'd fix your breakfast this morning though. Is that all right?"

"Why do you have to wait until you and Mommy get married to move in?"

"Well, that's a good question to ask, but it's just because we have to get a lot of things done first. Soon though, soon."

"Where do you sleep now?"

"At my apartment."

"Well, you came here last night, why can't you just come every night?"

"Lidi! Leave Kárin alone, and get going or we'll be late this morning. And don't forget that Esther is taking you to Papa's house tonight after school. You're going to spend the night at his house and come home on Friday night."

"Why doesn't Auntie Esther move in with Papa? They're always together anyway."

"Lidi, it's not anybody's business but their own. Don't ask them."

"I already did. She said she didn't know for sure."

"Lidiya Marie! You don't ask people personal questions like that! You just don't."

"You know, it's that type of inquiring mind that has made it possible for fifty-seven women to fly in space. Don't be too hard on her," giggled Kárin.

"Such a precocious child. And occasionally such a fractious child!"

"What does that mean, Mommy?"

"It means go and get ready, that's what it means."

Kárin lived up to her word and made everybody eggs, bacon, and toast for breakfast. Then Lidi was out the door with Frenchy, the driver, this particular morning, and Kárin and I started getting dressed for the day.

"In a hurry to get the hell away from me after my mercy fuck last night?" I laughed since Kárin was scurrying to get ready.

"Oh, hell no, just having to rearrange my day to accommodate that bitch of a girlfriend of mine. She's so damned pushy. It's a wonder I put up with her at all."

"When you see her, tell her that she's the luckiest girl in the world to have a wonderful partner like you," I said, leaning in and kissing her lightly on the cheek.

Kárin leaned into my kiss, shrugging her shoulder up into me.

"If I see her, I will. I think I'm supposed to see her tonight as a matter of fact."

"I know that will make her happy."

"I'm counting on it."

Kárin got dressed wearing some of the clothes she'd already brought over and left at the apartment. She slipped on a pair of shoes, grabbed her purse and laptop bag, and split. No sir, I thought to myself; I'm not sad anymore. I was floating off the ground right then.

I reached over to the table and picked up my cell.

"Detective Captain Martha Devonshire, may I help you?"

"Aren't you all official sounding?"

"Have to be toots. It's the job."

"I wonder how many people in the entire world know what a soft and giving heart and soul lies beneath that starched and ironed uniform you wear, Ms. Martha?"

"Do you *want* me to get all up there in your shit? Is that what you want?"

"Lover, you held me and my baby on the worst day of our lives, and dragged us crying, kicking, and screaming through it and nursed us back to health. You don't scare me."

"You sound great. It makes me so happy that you're finally happy again."

"I haven't been unhappy. Lidi and I have been great."

"Yeah, but now you're happy in love. And that's going to make for a better relationship with you and Lidi as well. Old Auntie Martha knows a thing or two about the human condition."

"We're still on for tonight, right?"

"I *personally* called everybody either on Monday or Tuesday, depending on when I could get ahold of them and threatened each and every one. Back down and you die. Sort of like that 'Don't Tread on Me' Gadsden flag.

"I'll see you tonight."

"10-4," she said, hanging up.

I decided to wear a regular suit and skirt to work for the day, but had already planned to break out a little early so that I'd already be made up and dressed when Kárin showed up. She'd seen me in a suit jacket and skirt, and she'd seen me dressed for church and temple, but she'd never seen me dressed to kill. And tonight I wanted to kill.

The day dragged on forever and ever. I'd told Franny as soon as I wandered in that I would be out Friday.

"I see you took my advice. Taking the little woman out on a weekender?" she smirked with a grin.

I just smiled and went to my desk, setting up my laptop for the day, settling in for a review of my cases coming up over the next week. I practically cracked my forehead open on the desk a couple ofr times trying to keep from falling asleep it was so dead slow. Some entire weeks were jam packed, and others were beyond tedious. This was one of the latter. I checked out at about three thirty and ran for home.

I know that I'm not beautiful in a model sort of way, but I'm okay looking I guess. And my two best dresses were my LBD (Little Black Dress) and my red dress that I used to 'ensnare' Sasha. I struggled long and hard with the decision, but finally, the day before, I'd dropped the red one off at the cleaners so that it would be fresh. I had stepped out at lunch and picked it up. I jumped in the shower first and cleaned up. I hopped out and blew my hair dry, curled it, and put on my underwear. I removed my nail polish from both my feet and my hands, and redid it to match the dress. I was wearing open-toed shoes, so it had to be a good job, and quite frankly putting on polish just isn't my strongest suit. Still, I managed.

I painstakingly tried to get just the right balance of makeup...not too much, not too little...but more than normal since it was nighttime. I wanted Kárin to love what she saw without going overboard and looking like a tramp. I was finally satisfied, and it was about a quarter to six. I didn't have a heck of a lot of time left. Since I knew I was going to be drinking, I shuffled into the kitchen and made a quick sandwich to help absorb some of the alcohol, instead of just relying on chips and nuts and things at the club. The food at the club was alright, but it was outrageously expensive. As soon as I'd eaten and wiped my face and washed my hands, I went back into the bathroom and put on a fresh swipe of lip gloss. Then it was time to don the dress and shoes. I had barely smoothed the material down and put my feet into the shoes when I heard a knock on the door and heard the keys rattling. I went running for the door. I held back about ten feet and clasped my hands behind my back waiting anxiously like a little schoolgirl, with my feet angled in slightly in a silly stance.

When Kárin walked through the door, my heart pulled one of its old tricks and stopped. Kárin had changed after work before coming over. I couldn't say a word. I was completely tongue-tied.

"Look at you. You're...beautiful. I don't know what to say," Kárin said when she finally spoke after her own silence.

"I don't want you to get mad at me, okay?"

"Why, on God's green earth, would I be mad at you?" Kárin responded.

"I don't have that many dresses, and this is my best one. I debated on whether or not to wear it. I wore it the first time Sasha and I went out together, although we weren't actually seeing each other yet. Please promise me you won't be upset with me? And I debated just not saying anything, but that seemed like a major lie of omission. And I never, ever want to do that with you. I want to be as honest and truthful as I can be, no matter what."

"Honey, don't worry about it."

"There's more..."

"More? How so?"

"You're wearing a blue velvet dress. And you look...you look...I can't even say...you are so, so pretty. Beautiful. Extraordinary. Fantastic."

"Okay, okay, I get it. You like the dress."

"No, I like you in the dress. The first time Sasha and I went out was to the symphony. Not as a date even, just as friends. Well, to her, anyway... I was already falling hard for her. Sasha wore a blue velvet dress. It was a little bit darker than that one, but very close. And like that one it had a halter back. You probably hate me, don't you," I yelped as I started to tear up.

"Oh, honey, come here," Kárin said as she came nearer to me and engulfed me in her arms.

I tried really hard not to cry, if only to keep my makeup from running.

"My poor baby, don't cry. This is supposed to be my surprise date night. Cheer up and let's have a good time. Let me make you happy tonight, and you make me happy. Look in the hall. I've got even more clothes with me. We'll sleep in tomorrow. We'll make love all night. We'll do whatever you want. Just don't cry. How could I be jealous of somebody you loved with all your heart that was taken away from you like she was, so very horribly? And this dress? I got it last week to surprise you. I know you've seen me in a dress before in church and temple, but I wanted to look really good for you. I just happened to see this old thing hanging up in a store at lunch and thought it might look okay if I had it cleaned and brushed."

I kissed Kárin over and over, trying to keep from smudging her makeup or mine. Other than our lip gloss, it didn't get too bad.

"Now, come on. Let's go have some fun. Since you won't tell me what it is, I'm dying to find out. Now come on, shorty, vamanos!"

"Okej. Låt oss gå vidare...." (Okay, let us move on....)

"Svenska?" (Swedish?)

"Japp. You know, your abilities as a linguist are really impressive." (Yup.)

"Nowhere near yours, honey."

"It's not like I'm fluent though. I just know some words here and there. I watch tons of foreign films, and have seen some of them many times. You start picking up phrases, y' know?"

Since we'd be drinking, probably heavily, we took a cab to the club. Half of the gang was already there. I was in the lead and immediately saw Martha stand up to greet us. She froze in her steps. A half second later, everybody in the group stopped talking altogether.

"Everybody, I'd like you to meet Kárin Zajac. Kárin, this is everyone. That's Martha, who we talked to over the phone. That's her girlfriend, Beryl. Mac, short for McKenzie. That's Denise...Dawn...and that especially beautiful lady at the end there is my adopted sister, Estefanía, who is from Argentina. And practically sitting on top of her, her partner, María-Elena, who is serious old money from Uruguay. Just to her right is Brooke. Brooke's girlfriend isn't with her tonight since she had to work late. She might be here later. Then Karen, but pronounced normally, not all messed up like yours...."

"Hey, now, don't make fun of my name!" pouted Kárin.

Everybody around the tables laughed, standing up briefly, holding out hands, smiling and having a wonderful time.

"Por lo tanto, Estefanía, María-Elena, de los otros de Martha, te las dos que he oído todo lo que hay que saber sobre la. Estefanía, Aly dice que son hermanas de sangre, ¿corregir?" delivered Kárin without skipping a beat. ("Mostly, Estefania, Maria-Elena, of all the friends of Martha and Aly's, you two I've heard everything there is to know about. Estefania, Aly says you are blood sisters, right?")

"Oh, for God's sake, there's another one of them. Who started this crap anyway?" asked Dawn, jokingly.

"I have to admit, I help run PFLAG meetings at various locations, I've been to several PRIDE parades, and I've been to tons of LBGT functions, but I can honestly say that this is my very first Dykes' Night Out. This is great. What a wonderful idea," smiled Kárin, warmly.

Everybody laughed again. Everybody.

Martha made a big show of getting up in Kárin's face.

"So, you know who I am, and you know what I do, right?"

"Sure. We've talked."

"If you break her heart, I will use every illegal, illicit, unlawful, underhanded method I can possibly muster to hunt you down, kill you, dispose of your body, and erase your records so it will appear as if you never existed."

"I think I was more intimidated by my first meeting with the Ukrainian mob, to tell you the truth."

Martha emitted a huge belly laugh and hugged Kárin.

"I know you've already heard this over and over so far, but every last one of us was stunned seeing you walk in the door. You have Sasha's blue eyes, her curly hair, and you're tall like her. You even have her dimples. I hope you forgive us."

"I assure you, there's nothing to forgive. I think I'm the one that should ask forgiveness if I ever fail to live up to the living legend of Lidi's mama."

"Well said, it's all about Lidi. Sit, sit, and let's get some booze going here. What'll you have?" bellowed Martha, good naturedly.

"Anything. Anything, that is, so long as it's made with Bombay Sapphire gin."

Everybody froze for a moment once more. Especially me. That had been Sasha's drink. It hadn't occurred to me since the only thing we'd ever had to drink together had been beer or wine.

"What? You asked..." uttered Kárin.

Having no social graces at times, Martha roared from her chair toward the bar.

"Bring us a Bombay Martini and a Tequila Sunrise! Both doubles!"

A waitress quickly came over to our table.

"What exactly is a Bombay Martini?"

"God*dammit*, woman. How hard is this shit? Bombay Sapphire to the top of a martini glass after being shaken with ice and poured off through a strainer, five olives on a skewer, hold the vermouth. You call yourself a bar and you don't know that? How many people do I have to teach that to?" Martha practically screamed at her.

"Erm, you know, it's not that big a deal, really," demurred Kárin.

"No, you don't understand. She's quoting exactly what Sasha said almost eight years ago, the first night she brought me here. Again, before we were a couple, just starting to get along well," I offered.

"Bullshit. The two of you were entangled within the first five minutes of meeting. You just had to sort it out, that's all," said Martha.

"Yeah, but this time, even *I* knew it in the first five minutes. We talked about half an hour at a fundraiser when I asked her out. I didn't want to take the chance that she was single and later that night somebody else might ask her before I got a chance to. It would be too much to take," I said to the group.

"Oh, honey, you're my baby. I love you so much," Kárin said as she kissed me.

Practically the whole group issued a chorus of catcalls.

"Isn't it pretty quick to start with the love talk? Kárin, are you a U-Haul lesbian?" asked Estefanía.

Again the group tittered and snickered. I got up and walked over to Estefanía, asking María-Elena to scoot over for a minute.

"Sweetie, I have to tell everybody something, and I want to make sure you and I are good. Because you know I love you, and I will always love you, so, so much. Right?"

"Yes..." Estefanía reacted with a puzzled look on her face and a slight nodding action.

I held my hand out with Sasha's rings on. Then I motioned to Kárin with my hand to prompt her to show her rings too, held like women do when they're showing off their new engagements.

Estefanía's jaw dropped open, and her eyes got big as saucers.

"You're..."

"Mm-hmm. You're okay with this, right? I'd absolutely die if it caused you any pain at all," I said as I reached over and caressed María-Elena's cheek.

"I mean, of course I'm okay. I love you too. And I always will, just like you. We're bonded for life. We're blood. And besides, I've got my protector here with me," she said as she hugged María-Elena tightly to her.

The two of them molded together, smiled at each other, and kissed.

"So, um...does this mean what I think it does?" asked Mac.

"Yup. It does. Lidi took to Kárin on our first date, when we went out to lunch as a threesome. We're a package deal now. We've even been to the temple to have our pre-marriage counseling with the rabbi. Same place. "

I went back to my seat by Kárin and sat down just as the alcohol showed up. I took the first sip slowly. Then another. Then another. Then I chugged the rest.

"Another!" I shouted through the bar, holding the glass up high.

Immediately after I did, so did Kárin, and the kid working as bar back saw us and nodded in acknowledgment. I'd always promised myself never again, but somehow that particular night, Kárin and I both set out to consume vast quantities of 'sweet nectar of the Gods.' We had two things going in our favor: firstly, we were cabbing it, not driving, and secondly, not being male, there was no chance for poor performance due to libations.

"Any date been set yet?" asked Denise.

"Not yet. We're waiting for a free time at the temple. Uh, everybody, if you'll give me a quick minute here, I need to go to the little girls' room," I advised.

Beryl started to get up to go with me, but Kárin sort of put her hand up as if to say, 'No, stay back.' It looked out of place, but I couldn't figure out what it meant. What I didn't know at the time is that Kárin wanted to talk to the whole group behind my back.

"So, here's the deal. Everybody get your phone out. Put this date on your calendar. Before we went to counseling, I called the rabbi and told him to say there wasn't any available time until March. Aly's sister-in-law, Clavdiya, measured us last Saturday after temple for dresses she's making for our wedding. And other things can be arranged quickly. The truth is, the wedding's going to be the second Saturday of December, just when Aly wanted it to be. She thought she would surprise me with the dresses...she hasn't got a clue that I'm going to surprise her with this. I do believe she may honestly shit a square brick," Kárin said, with a humongous grin on her face.

I did figure something was up when I got back to the table for two reasons. The first was that three of the ladies got up to go to the restroom, including Beryl, who had already started to get up before. The second thing was that everybody was smirking and nobody was talking—like the cat that ate the canary. Rat Bastards. I knew that something was up, but I refused to give anyone the satisfaction.

Since neither Kárin nor I had to work the next day, we lasted the longest. Estefanía and María-Elena walked with us—no, make that staggered with us—out the front door just before closing time. On the street, all four of us very drunk girls hugged and kissed one another a half a dozen times each at least. I don't know how I could have even begun to have a clear thought, and maybe it wasn't a clear thought, but I later had a vague memory of an arm around the necks of both Estefanía and María-Elena, pulling their faces close to mine.

"Hey, it'll be next spring, so it will give you guys plenty of time to plan.... Why don't we have a double wedding? What would be cooler than that?"

Everybody broke out laughing, which confused me at that particular moment. After all, I was three sheets to the wind, falling down, pissed-drunk. Both pairs of us went our separate ways in two cabs to ring out the night. When Kárin and I got back to my apartment, we managed to be really loud going up while trying really hard to be quiet. Oh, well. We made it to the bedroom straight away, stripping down as we went. We still had our underwear on, but that was it. I pushed Kárin back on the bed and put her legs over my shoulders. Kárin started giggling uncontrollably in her drunken state.

"What are you doing?"

"I'm going to pleasure you, Sasha."

Kárin started her fits of laughter all over again.

"Hey, what's my name?"

"It's Sasha."

If anything Kárin laughed harder and harder by the minute.

"No, it's not. My name is Kárin. Remember?"

"Fuck. I'm in shit, huh? Sorry."

"Shut up and pleasure me. You said you were going to."

Over an hour and a half later, I looked up at Kárin and yelled at her, "Hey! What the hell is wrong with you? When are you going to get there?"

Again with the laughing. When Kárin drank a lot, she thought everything in the world was hysterically funny. She casually looked up at the digital clock.

"Actually, I'd have to say I got there well over an hour ago. The first time. And then again, and again, and again.... You're really good at that, you know?"

"Well, you could have said something!" I snapped at her, over-exaggeratedly in my drunken state.

"Why? You might have stopped. That may have just been the best time I've ever had in bed."

Then we both started laughing together, but I didn't stop...not for another twenty minutes. Everything was absolutely hilarious in my state. Finally, I laid down beside Kárin, stroking her cheek, kissing her neck, her collar bone, her shoulder...then somebody turned the lights out on both of us in a millisecond. The next noise either of us made was a pitiful moan with the light streaming in the window Friday morning. My head was pounding and I had to pee. I think I could easily have thrown up with little prompting. I picked up my head and looked at Kárin's face. "You bitch."

She barely cracked her encrusted eyes open a bit, and then quickly closed them to keep the light out.

"Why did you call me a bitch?" she asked.

"Because I feel this bad, and you look so beautiful. It's just not fair! It's just not fair! And to think that you used to hate your leefa hair. It's so pretty, framing your face that way. God, you're so amazing."

"You've lost something, and I'm thinking it may be a gear from your transmission."

"I've got to go to the bathroom. What all I do there leaves to be seen. I feel like barfing."

"Just hurry up and do it, because I need to as well."

"Sure, sweetie."

I got out of the bed and had already turned to leave, when a flash of a memory hit me like a ton of bricks. I turned around and got up on my knees right by Kárin.

"Oh, sweetie, I'm so sorry. Will you ever forgive me? I know I was drunk, but that's no excuse. There's not an excuse in the world."

"For what, honey?" she asked in return.

"For calling you Sasha last night. I'm so, so, so sorry. I love you," I said through eyes that were welling up.

Kárin used her thumbs to wipe both of my eyes, and then pulled my head down to hers and kissed me long and slow.

"If that's the worst thing that ever happens to us, then we'll have the most perfect marriage in history! Stop thinking about it, there's nothing to forgive. And get your pretty, little ass in the bathroom, I need in too!"

CHAPTER FOURTEEN

Kárin and I had both done our morning routines. I did manage to get through without throwing up, and while I was in the bathroom, my lovely girlfriend made coffee…a must-have item this morning. For a change, Kárin didn't insist on OJ. She was standing at the counter pouring up two huge cups, then turned around and handed one to me. She was wearing boxers and a tank top, and had her sunglasses on. Without knowing what she was going to dress in, I'd also gotten a pair of boxers and a tank.

"What's with the glasses?"

"Shhh…don't be so fricking loud!" Kárin whispered.

"And look at us. Aren't we just a couple of dykes?"

Kárin looked at me, then down at herself, then back at me, then started laughing. At that point, she moaned and set the coffee cup down on the counter, and held her head in her hands.

"Do…Not…Make…Me…Laugh!"

I walked up right next to her, pulled her hair back on one side, and very, very lightly kissed her ear. "Okay, I won't," I whispered ever so softly.

We took our coffee into the living room and sat on opposite ends of the couch, turned sideways, with our feet together in the middle. After it was gone, I took both cups into the kitchen and got a refill for each of us.

"What do you want to do today, sweetie?" I asked.

"Whatever would make you happy."

"You want to just get out and enjoy being outside since it's warm this weekend. I can't believe Hallowe'en is tomorrow."

"Sure. And while we're out, maybe a movie?"

"Yeah, that would be good. Have you ever been to the Intrepid Museum? I wouldn't mind going back out there. It's not like it's the exact plane my uncle flew, but they have one like he used to fly in Vietnam. It always makes me feel like I have a connection to him when I'm there. I go probably twice a year. And, of course, all the other planes and choppers, and the tour through part of the ship."

"What does he do now?"

"Who, Uncle Walter? He was shot down, missing in action, presumed dead in 1968."

"Oh, I'm sorry."

"It was before I was even born. It's just that from everything I've heard, he was the greatest character ever."

"Where do you take Lidi trick or treating? Or do you not?"

"Oh, sure. I let her go with the two little cousins you met over at Papa's house the first time we went over there: Greta and Karolina. We'll take them over late tonight, and they'll stay there for the weekend. Then after everybody's on a total sugar high, I'll bring her home and let her wind down all afternoon Sunday."

"What's she going to be?"

"A princess, of course. It's the only thing she has ever done. Every year. The exact costume always changes. Every year it's more complex, but always a princess."

"Naturally. So...that means we have tonight to ourselves after we take her over. And tomorrow. It's going to be like a mini vacation. Wanna drive up to the Poconos and spend the night, just for grins and giggles? It's only a two-hour drive. You can just sit back. I'll even do all the driving."

"No."

"It was just an idea," Kárin said, holding her eyes down.

"I mean, no, you won't do all the driving. I'll let you drive there, and I'll drive home. Or we'll each drive half way in each direction. Let me call Esther or Roni and see if one of them can take Lidi over tonight, so we can get going around lunch time. That way we can spend two nights."

Kárin sighed deeply and started rubbing her feet against my feet and calves.

"Our first romantic road trip. If we could just go to the hardware store on the way home, we could get our official secret decoder rings from the Gay and Lesbian Society!" she smiled.

"It does sound wonderful. This will be my first real, total break from responsibilities in...over six years."

It took little time at all to get a few raggedy clothes and sneaks together and pack an ice chest with food. The turnpike traffic was all going against us, opening up the road nicely. Kárin drove first and for half an hour neither of us spoke. I held her free arm and leaned contentedly into her shoulder.

"Hey, Kárin, you're taking my Pocono virginity."

"You mean you've never made...no, you mean you've never been there?"

"I almost went in college once with some friend trying to 'fix me up' with some guy. I bailed quickly on that one."

"You could have taken the group trip and just told him you were really not interested."

"I don't work that way."

"What would it hurt to sit around a campfire, shoot the breeze, and just enjoy the outdoors?" Kárin asked.

"Maybe not."

"I hope you love the outdoors. I just assumed..."

"I'm happy as a clam."

"So what's different about this trip?" Kárin questioned me.

"Because my friends were all pressuring me. I pretty much push back to anybody pressuring me. I probably still do. Of course, if I'd been out it wouldn't have been near as much of an issue. Don't worry, it wasn't Bri and Lexi or any of my current friends. I pretty much left most of my friends behind at school, except for Benjamin and Rachel."

"I'm going to show you something that will blow your socks off then. You probably needed a long weekend."

"You're right. You're so right. You know, the first fall we had together, when Sasha and I were still living apart, I had her sleep at my place on Wednesday before Chanukah. I told her it was Thanksgiving. Then instead of using chicken for Chanukah, I cooked turkey, but prepared it as if it were Jewish chicken. And I melded the two into a single meal. I got a new menorah, scarves for all of the women there— that's Sasha's scarf that Lidi wears to temple…from that week. That's why she won't wear anything else to temple. After we got everything cleaned up and the guests left, we just had a quiet holiday to ourselves. Somebody in her office had an emergency and she had to work one day on the weekend, but we still had a few days off together."

Kárin squeezed my hand a couple of times without letting go.

"I don't know why I just told you that. I guess it was just a memory that flashed in my brain. Listen, I'm really sorry for calling you Sasha last night."

"You were drunk. I mean, we were both *really* drunk. Remember the old joke about a college girl's mating call? 'Oh, God, I'm soooo drunk!' And I've already told you, I understand. As long as you stand by my side, I'm fine. Okay? Not to mention, you made me into four whole pints of jelly. I'm not kidding. I've never, ever, *ever* been that totally blown away. Not sexually. Not sensually. Not romantically. I think every single neuron in my body hit a synapse last night. What in the world would make me not like that?" she said, squeezing me.

"You say that, but I sometimes wonder how much you'll take before you get tired of me and split..." I said, while the car braked to a violent stop and Kárin pulled off the side of the highway.

"What are you doing?" I asked.

"The only reason I don't slap your Goddamn face is that not only do I do not believe in domestic violence, but it would hurt you, and that would make me cry. I swear, woman, you'd better stop that crap. I mean it."

My eyes quickly averted to the floorboards. I was playing with my thumbs. Kárin leaned over across the console and hovered above my seat, kissing me and holding my face for the longest time. Then she sat back up.

"Now, are we ready for a weekend in the woods?" Kárin asked.

"How woodsy is where we're going?"

"There will be ants crawling up your bunghole if you're not careful. The rest is a secret."

The road went from four-lane divided highway to two lane non-divided highway, to a narrow two lane black top, to a wide single lane blacktop, to a single lane dirt road overgrown with tall grass. We finally came to a big turn, and a large opening in the arbor showed a small log cabin with a porch across the entire front edge. I could see a stone chimney coming up from the back, and there was a woodpile on the side of the house. We got out of the car and I tried to take it all in, nature's regal glory.

"Well, what do you think, hon?" asked Kárin.

I closed my eyes with my arms wide out to my sides and breathed in deeply, turning around slowly in circles.

"It's wonderful. Magical. Magnificent," I answered.

"Are you sure you like it? We can always backtrack a bit and get a B&B for the night."

"Shhh...don't break the spell," I told her as I put my fingers up to my lips.

As I was standing, still breathing in the delightful aromas of the woods, listening to all the sounds, feeling the last of the warm fall days beat down on my face, lost in the reverie, Kárin slowly tiptoed toward me. When at last I opened my eyes, she was immediately in front of me, nose to nose.

"I was hoping you liked it. Wait until you see the inside. We'll get a fire started."

"Isn't it a bit early in the day for a fire?" I asked.

"Not if there's no electricity. And the water comes from a stream about fifty yards behind the cabin. We'll have to boil it before we use it. We do have lanterns though, and there's coal oil inside; enough to last for about two weeks of daily use. And the outhouse is about fifteen feet behind the cabin, out of sight."

"Outhouse? You're kidding me! You mean we're really in the woods. Actually out in the middle of the woods!" I shouted.

"We are indeed. Is that okay with you?"

"Oh, sweetie, it's so okay, you don't know how much. You've now officially taken my 'roughing it' virginity in addition to the Poconos thing! It's just too bad we've only got two nights here."

"You can be so excitable. It's hard to remember at times that you're the older one. You seem so..."

"So juvenile? So infantile? So childish?" I came back.

"No, so pure. So unjaded. So untarnished. So trusting. You're a breath of fresh air."

"Gimme a break! Let's get the car unloaded," I said with a wave of my hand, without mentioning that Sasha said that about me all the time.

We got everything unloaded and then Kárin lit a match to fire up one of the lanterns. We found the two biggest kettles and set out for the stream to haul a batch of water.

"I know you're always supposed to boil it first, but taste the water," said Kárin.

"Oh, Jesus, it's wonderful. Is this what water is supposed to taste like?"

"Mmhmm. Amazing, isn't it. And look..." she said pointing.

About twenty feet away from us were three squirrels working on a nest in the hollowed-out crook of a tree, loading it up with nuts and other food items for the winter.

"That is so cute," I said, taking out my phone from my pocket and zooming in for a photo.

"Give me your phone. Right now."

"No, I want to take photos, and I didn't bring my camera."

"Turn off the ringer then and set it to 'do not disturb' until we leave on Sunday. Or we'll drive right back right now."

"Yes, Mother. No technology, no electricity, not even a proper shitter."

"What do you mean, not a proper shitter? It's perfectly proper," she laughed, joined in by me.

We boiled water, made dinner, and then moved out onto the porch in sweaters. It was a chilly night up here in the mountains.

"Sweetie, thank you. I really needed this," I practically purred to Kárin.

"No problem. I'm happy to do it."

"Do you celebrate Chanukah?"

"Sort of. I usually have some rich donors giving me an invitation every year. About half the time I take them up on it, other years I skip it."

"You want to do it this year? Thanksgiving is on the twenty-fifth, and Chanukah is on the following Sunday. Lidi would like it."

"If Lidi would like it, mark me as RSVP."

"She'll appreciate it. She was so proud of herself the first year that she had memorized all four blessings. Of course, I was prouder than she was, being her mom, don't you know."

"I bet. Can I take our baby girl shopping next weekend? Just her and me?"

"Sure."

"Absolutely sure? Just her and me?"

"Of course. As far as she is concerned, you're Mommy Kárin. And I know that you two bonded the first five minutes together...pretty much as long as it took you and me to come together," I giggled.

My mind went back to that first moment in the restaurant when they laid eyes on each other. Kárin seeing this precious, beautiful, little girl, and Lidi in such reverence of Kárin. It brought a huge smile to my face.

"It's sort of strange. I feel like she is completely one hundred percent yours, and yet she's completely 100 percent mine as well," Kárin said.

"Welcome to being a part of a family and being a parent. Isn't that what you always wanted?"

"It is. Do you think Danny would be willing? I mean, I wouldn't want him to feel obligated, and he doesn't even know me really, and I don't mean tomorrow...."

"The answer is yes. I'm sure he and Bri would be happy as could be. Don't wear him out though. I still want to get pregnant too."

"Sorry. I forgot to use the filter between my brain and my mouth."

"Sweetie, you never have to use a filter with me. Never."

"It's getting cold. Let's go in and get into our jammies,"

"What? You brought jammies? Not a gown or a tank and shorts?"

"Nuts to that. It's going to get cold tonight. The duvets are heavy and we'll be snuggling up tightly."

"Sounds yummy. Too bad we don't have a microwave. I'd love to make some popcorn," I said.

"What do you think they did for popcorn prior to sixty-five?" she said, bending to fetch a saucepan and lid from under a counter, and grabbing a jar of popping corn from the pantry.

She poured a little cooking oil in the pan, filled the bottom evenly with popcorn, and covered it with a lid.

"And you're going to light a fire in the potbelly stove to cook it?" I asked, although I felt pretty stupid very quickly.

She opened the opposite side pantry and produced a Coleman propane cook stove. After pumping it up about thirty or forty times and screwing down the pressurizer, she struck the flint. Voila, fire. As soon as she heard the first pop, she started shaking the pan continuously while holding the lid down. As soon as the popping pretty much slowed to a stop, she pulled it off and set it on a trivet. She took off the lid and showed me the wonderful, white, fluffy goodness inside the pan. Magic.

"Showoff."

"City girl."

We both had no end to our giggling that night. It was really strange that it was only seven o'clock and it was dark outside. The sky gets dark in the city, but it's offset with trillions of watts of lights that come on, illuminating everything. We got into our jammies and crawled into one of the four beds. The cabin itself was very small, with no interior walls, just one large community area for all functions. All modesty checked at the door for this small piece of paradise. A single lantern was on a table between the heads of two of the beds. Well, more than cots, but less than beds, for the most part. We were lying on one, spooning. We'd go for several minutes without speaking, just stroking the other's cheek, arm, stomach, shoulder, whatever. Neither Kárin nor I had said anything for about twenty minutes at one point.

Finally, Kárin spoke, "You told me that you already had what you called 'your wedding,' right?"

"Sure."

"And you said that I could do ours any way I wanted, right?"

"Yeah?"

"What if we had it somewhere other than the temple, but still had Rabin Abrahamson perform the ritual. What would you say to that?"

"Rabin?"

"Sorry, Polish for rabbi. Habit."

"That would be fine. Truthfully, the whole reason for Rabbi Abrahamson to do it is our history. It's not like I'm Jewish."

"So tell me what all you'd want to include if you gave me a list of desires and then left everything else up to me," Kárin prompted.

"Of course, Lidi would be the ring bearer. Gideon would give me away. Do you have anyone to give you away?"

"I do. An older gentleman that I work with about once every quarter, whom I've known for years. I bet he'd be tickled pink to do that."

"And Diya's doing the dresses. I'd probably use the rabbi's wife's nursery for flowers. And I'd get Valery for finger foods. How many people do you think you'd want?"

"Probably about fifty. How many would you have?" Kárin asked.

"About the same. I was thinking half of that, but when all is said and done, I think that is probably about right."

"What else?" Kárin said, adjusting her body to mine, settling in like a child who was listening to a story being read to her.

"The food would have to be kosher, that way nobody would have to worry. Even though I bet there won't be but a handful total who keep kosher, it would be the right thing to do. And I'd want to have movers move everything in during the service so that we'd come home, and it would just be done."

"That's a nice idea. What else?"

"What's gotten into you? Why the fifty questions?"

"Because you got to plan your wedding, and I want to plan ours. I want you to give me all the things you want to include or do a particular way, and then I want to do everything behind your back and surprise you with a fabulous day."

"Sweetie, you're amazing. I wish we could just get a date now. I know, I just have to be patient, nobody's going anywhere."

"Meanwhile, if you think of anything else, just tell me. I'm going to start laying everything out, if that's okay with you, that is."

"Totally. I mean, you're right. I planned mine. No reason you shouldn't have the experience as well."

Suddenly I felt something cold on my butt.

"You could blow into your hands before you put them down my bottoms you know. Your hands are freezing."

"I was actually trying to warm them up on your keester."

"Glad I could be of service to somebody. T'anks for nuttin'!" I said in my best attempt at an Irish accent, which made Kárin laugh.

"Would this help?" Kárin said as her hands slowly started cupping my cheeks and moving lower.

"Oh, now you're trying to feel me up."

"That's the idea."

"Pull your hands out," I said.

Kárin pulled her hands out, and as I flipped over in bed to face her I saw a funny look on her face, which quickly broke into a knowing visage.

"Put your right arm down," I commanded.

She put her right arm down, and I laid on it.

"Now put both hands back where they were," I said as I reached up to palm her cheek with my hand, and began kissing her.

From there we explored and experienced what we would call our 'happy time.' Finally, we both had to go to the bathroom. We put our jammies back on and slipped on some shoes and stepped from the cabin to the outhouse. Finished, we ran quickly back inside, lost the shoes by the front door, and jumped back into bed.

"Promise me something, if you can," said Kárin.

"I'll try, but if I don't think I can keep it, I won't promise."

"Promise me that years from now, when we're much older and grow complacent with each other, we'll still make love all the time. Promise me that you'll let me explore your body for the next fifty years, trying to find new ways to excite you."

"My dear, sweet, precious love. Kárin, I promise you that we'll always have that chemistry in our bedroom that will be like the first time we ever spent the night together."

"Dear Franklin and Liza...thank you for letting me hump your daughter. Love, Kárin."

We closed our eyes and suddenly it was morning, with the birds singing and the sunlight trying to peep through a crack between a pair of curtains on the east side of the cabin.

We went to get water again around lunch time. I picked up one of the kettles and Kárin picked up the other, along with an old wool blanket.

"What's the blanket for?" I asked.

She said nothing, but led the way to the stream. She took the kettles and laid them both on the ground. The next thing I knew, Kárin was kneeling down picking up twigs and pebbles and other small items from the forest floor, tossing them aside. After she was done, she spread the blanket on the ground. Standing up, she pulled my shirt up and reached behind me, undoing my bra. Then she unbuttoned and unzipped my jeans and pushed them and my underwear to my ankles. She held my hands and helped me lie down on the ground, my pants trapping my legs together. Then she took off every single stitch of clothing she had on and knelt on the ground in front of me.

"I think this may be the fastest I've ever been able to get there," I told Kárin.

She put her finger up to my lips to tell me to shush, without moving her position and without stopping what she was doing. I was right. I seriously didn't know I had it in me. I finally had to make Kárin stop. I couldn't keep it up any longer. It was the most outrageous experience I'd ever had. And to think, prior to now, the only place I'd ever had sex was on a bed, on the floor, or against a wall, and always inside at my place or at my parents' house. I can't describe what was different, but being outdoors made it so totally, incredibly intense; it was a completely new experience.

I grabbed Kárin by her hands and pulled her up higher and higher onto me. The entire time she was on me, she didn't once take her eyes off mine. Like me, she achieved ecstasy over and over. Finally, she positioned herself next to me, side by side.

"Well, now. That's a first for me," said Kárin.

"Oh, come on. You with all your experiences?" I responded.

"Don't compare the number of partners with the best experience. I've done it in the bushes, and in a car. Once I even fooled around in the back of a cab with an old girlfriend, just raising our skirts, but this...this...I have no words...."

"I suppose we should get dressed. What if somebody walked by from another cabin or something?" I exclaimed.

"Fuck them."

"Only if they had a vagina. I don't do penis."

Kárin looked me in the eye for a moment, then broke out laughing, her voice seemingly booming through the glen. "You're funny. Let's go get some food."

Kárin helped me stand up since my clothes were still partially on, making it somewhat difficult on my own. We got dressed and heated up a couple cans of soup. The rest of our time passed so quickly I felt robbed. About halfway home, at a convenience store and gas station, we switched from Kárin driving to me.

"This is so strange."

"What?" asked Kárin.

"I'm homesick for the cabin already."

"I don't think that's strange. It's a lovely place."

"It's not just that. It's the fact that I also can't wait to get home. I've never been away from Lidi for three nights. Ever. It's killing me."

"Poor, Mommy. We'll get there in a couple of hours and everything should be well."

"Can I turn my phone back on yet?"

"No! If there's an emergency, you can't get back any faster. If there's not, then you don't need to talk until we get back."

"You're right. Sorry."

We drove for about another hour chatting about this and that.

"Hey, Kárin?"

"Yeah?"

"Have you taken other girlfriends up to the cabin?"

"Would it bother you if I had?"

"I'd like to say it wouldn't, but I don't know if that's true or not. Either tell me the truth or refuse to answer. Just don't lie to me."

"I don't lie. I don't play any head games. And yes, I've been to the cabin with a couple of other girls, but believe me, nothing compared to this weekend with you. Nothing even came close."

"I suppose that's good. Thank you."

Kárin held out her hand to me and I took it. We stayed like that all the way into the city.

"You know that I really loved Sasha. I mean, I was totally devoted, head over heels, puppy dog in love with her. Maybe I still am."

"Sure. Does this story have a point?"

"Taking nothing away from the things Sasha could do to me, you're a better lover than she was. You amaze me."

Kárin said nothing in return, but the corners of her mouth curled up, and her dimples showed up and creased more deeply that I'd ever seen them.

We picked up Lidi and made our way home. Kárin and I both worked on cooking dinner for the first time instead of one or the other doing it.

"Stay tonight? Please?" I asked.

Kárin gave me a quick kiss on my cheek.

"I'll think about it."

After we set all the food on the table and were sitting down, she looked at me.

"Oh, all right. I don't really want to, but if you *really* need me to, I'll do it."

Catty woman! Lidi looked up from her plate.
"Do what?"
"Never mind, Lidi, just eat your dinner."
By the time the kitchen was cleaned up and our things from the weekend had been unpacked and put up, it was time for Lidi to go to bed.
"Can I sit with Mommy Kárin for a few minutes first?"
"For fifteen minutes, then you have to go to bed. It's already past bedtime."
Lidi scrambled up onto Kárin, sitting in her lap facing the television, and Kárin had her arms around Lidi.
Kárin leaned down and whispered something to her. Lidi nodded, turned her head around, and kissed Kárin.
"Night-night, Mommy Kárin. I'll see you tomorrow."
Lidi came over to me and scrambled up onto the chair with me, giving me a kiss and a hug.
"Night, Mommy. See you in the morning," she said as she hopped immediately back off and went into the bathroom to brush her teeth.
"What did you say to her?" I asked Kárin.
"I told her that I loved her, but it was time for bed."
"And slick as a whistle she just did what you asked her to do?"
"I guess she understands that she is my daughter. Do you think it's too soon for me to act that way to her? Does it bother you that we're too close too fast?"
"Are you kidding me? You two are like ducklings on their first trip to the water. You both just jumped in and started paddling. I'm thrilled."
"You're sure?"
"Yes, sweetie, I'm sure."
"I don't want you to think that I'm overstepping my boundaries."
I got up, walked over to Kárin, and sat down in her lap. I put my arms around her neck and nuzzled her neck.
"Can I take a nap on you?" I asked.
Kárin put her arms around me and without saying a word starting stroking my hair, pulling my head down against her. I was so incredibly tired, and within a very few minutes was asleep.

CHAPTER FIFTEEN

Tuesday morning, I looked through my contact list on my telephone looking for Zach. I called him and asked if he wanted to come over on Sunday the twenty-eighth for Chanukah. Even though I'd left my old company where we worked together, we kept in contact rather regularly. He said that he and his wife, Julianna, would be there. He asked if I would rather he get a sitter since his son was only eighteen months old.

"Don't be ridiculous. Shut your mouth and just show up. Julie still have her scarf?"

"Now it's your turn not to be ridiculous. She wears it sometimes when we go out, so she doesn't have to make her hair up. She loves it."

"Thanks. I'm really glad you're coming. We haven't seen each other in too long."

"Life has a way of getting away from you, doesn't it?"

Next I called Benjamin to see what he and his wife Rachel were doing.

"Hey, corner-office-man!"

"You heard? Wow. Yeah, it was a surprise when it happened. I had no idea. I was coming back from lunch one day, and this guy was taking my name plate from my old office. I almost died. Then my boss walks up behind me and I asked her what was going on. She said that I'd have to check with HR. A million thoughts went through my head, why were they letting me go, you know? So I went to HR and they told me to sit down and wait a minute. It was almost half an hour. I was ushered to the back by a lady who was smiling. I thought, 'What a total iron bitch.' She had me sit at a table in a conference room. She started talking about terminating my contract at midnight that day and replacing it with the new contract that would bring me into the other business segment. She gave me the name of the person I'd report to. She told me that me that my salary would be about ten percent less that it was at my current job, but that semi-annually we'd get a bonus of from twenty to thirty-five percent, based on the performance of my business unit. Overall, I make about fifteen to twenty percent more. Not too shabby. Of course, I needed a defibrillator to get my heart jump-started. She laughed at me and apologized. They were supposed to have already told me. I'm telling you, I panicked."

"What are you doing for Chanukah this year?"

"Rachel's cousin is going to be in town, so we've asked her to come eat with us. Why? Pulling another surprise dinner?"

"Except this time it's no surprise, and we're already engaged."

"You gotta be shitting me! When did this happen, and why haven't you called either me or Rach?"

"No secret, Benyamin Menken and the lovely Downtown Rachel Brown! We met in September on a Tuesday evening at a gala fundraising event. We had our first date that Saturday, and less than a week later I asked her if she would spend the rest of her life with me."

"Crap, I thought you moved pretty quickly with Sasha."

"I think Sasha and I moved even quicker than we admitted to ourselves."

"Have you ever thought about taking a relationship easy?"

"Not me. Keep in mind, Benny me boy-oh, that this is only the second girl I've ever dated. I went out twice with Estefanía, but even on our first date it was like I was taking my sister out, and we both knew it. I don't consider going out with her as dating."

"Sure. We were going to do our thing here at the house, but let me check with everybody and I'll call you. I'm sure it will be no problem."

"Okay. Talk to you soon."

Last call before I went back to the grind.

"Hello, Aly. How are you and Lidi?"

"We're fine, Mom. Do you want to do Thanksgiving at your house? Kárin and I can help cook and clean, of course. In fact, I insist. We can come over Wednesday after work and spend the night. The three of us can spend the day in the kitchen. Then in the evening we'll eat, and Kárin and I will do all the cleanup. You and Dad and Lidi can just goof off. What do you say?"

"That sounds fine, dear. We don't have any other plans."

"Okay. Just make sure you give Dad a complete list of what to get from the grocery store on Wednesday. They'll be closed on Thursday."

"I will."

"I've got to run. I'll talk to you later. Love you."

"I love you too, dear."

Hearing her tell me that she loved me never got old. It's something I didn't hear for the first twenty-five years of my life.

Without saying anything, Fran came into my office and sat down in one of the chairs facing my desk.

"You're going to love this one," she said, then sat there saying nothing.

"Want to give me any more clues? Colonel Mustard in the study?"

Franny didn't laugh. Neither a tic nor a twitch.

"The deputy mayor is coming here tomorrow afternoon. He wants to meet for two hours. It's going to tear our schedule all to hell, just so that he can come over and talk about what a good job he's doing, and how much better the juvenile system has become with his help. He wants to 'give us some tips and advice' to make additional changes. God give me the fucking strength."

"Fran! That's the first time I've ever heard you say anything worse than 'heck.' "

"That's how I feel."

"You and me both. You just took me by surprise."

"And I need to see if I can squeeze one more appointment in today. At noon."

"Great. Noon? Who with?"

"Kárin Zajac. I believe you know her. She called when you were on the telephone."

"Um...let me think...yeah, I think I can probably do that. It will be a stretch, but I just might be able to fit her in," I grinned.

Without saying a word, Fran smiled and put a message sheet on my desk with the name of the restaurant and the address. About eleven thirty I grabbed my jacket and waved at Fran while heading out of the building. I caught a cab so I wouldn't have to go through the rigors of parking during the day. It took me almost thirty minutes to get there, so I was glad to have taken a taxi. The restaurant served Mediterranean food from Spain and Portugal. Kárin was already seated at a table.

"Hi, honey," she said as she turned her face up for me to kiss her.

"Hey, sweetie. What's the occasion?"

"I quit work today."

"What? What happened? Are you okay?"

"Pretty much something that I've been praying for, for over a year now. Do you remember me mentioning the Frederich and Natalia Wørsc Foundation?"

"Sure, you had lunch with their daughter once, if memory serves."

"She's stepping down from the spot as the chairwoman. She'll still be a member of the board, but she's getting on in years and while she's in relatively good health wants to spend a lot more time with her grandchildren and great-grandchildren, and less time putting up with people begging for their money. People like me, I suppose. So they needed somebody to take over that position. What do you think? Instead of constantly begging for money, I'll be the one deciding who gets all the money!"

"You're the new chairwoman for the Wørsc Foundation? Are you serious? The director of the whole shooting match?"

"You'd better start being nicer to me. I'm now an important person, and don't you forget it," Kárin laughed.

I leaned across the table and grabbed her neck with both my arms and kissed her.

"You've been important from the very first time I laid eyes on you. The fact that you look so much like Sasha was startling, but your poise, your smile, your dimples, your hair, everything, I fell in love with *you* at first sight. I thought it was going to be a straight girl crush that I'd just have to get over. When I found out you were gay, you had me right then and there. When you said you'd go out with me, I just knew that you'd be the most important person in my life."

I kissed her again and then sat back down.

"When does this change take place?"

"January first, just a couple of months away. So my current people are really yelling at me to bring home the year end with a big bang."

"I wouldn't worry. I have faith in you. So, you up to Chanukah at our place? No big deal, just a few of my Jew friends over for the evening."

"I can't believe you just said that," Kárin said with her eyes big.

"Are you a Jew?"

"Yes."

"Are you my friend? And these other people, are they Jews and are they my friends?"

"Maybe not if you keep talking like that."

"I'd never say it out loud anywhere, and it would be while I'm calling myself a cracker."

"You bitch. You just did that to get a rise out of me."

"Do ya think, chickerdoodles?"

"You're naughty. Still going to let me borrow Lidi before we head down to Queens this coming weekend?"

"Of course. I still want to know what you two have up your sleeves, but I guess I'll just have to be patient. You won't even give me a hint, will you?"

"Nope. Just like I'm not giving you hint one about our wedding plans."

"Okay, now you've gone too far. You have to give me something."

"The hell I do."

"The hell you don't," I retorted.

"Honey, I'll let you know when to show up. That's all you need to know."

"Now who's the stone cold bitch?"

Kárin's eyes sparkled at me. I think the waiter had cleared his throat a couple of times before we broke eye contact.

"Do you have a special today?" asked Kárin.

"Yes, we have..."

"Good, bring us two."

"Would you like to hear what it is?"

"Why are you still here? Scoot, bring us two specials!"

"Yes, ma'am. What would you like to drink?"

"We'd like single malt Scotch whisky, but we'll settle for iced tea since we have to go back to work," her eyes already locked back on mine, her hand entangled with mine over the table.

The waiter disappeared into the kitchen. Kárin kept my one hand in hers and took my other hand and began tracing circles on the back of it with her other hand. Then she did something so totally awesome, I blushed as badly as I ever had in my life. Very quietly, but with people around us still able to hear, she began singing Van Morrison's 'Have I Told You Lately.' I wanted to tell her to stop singing, but I just couldn't. Her voice was so pretty, she was so pretty.... It was just one of the world's most perfect moments.

She finished the first verse and once through the chorus and stopped. All around us everybody had stopped eating and talking altogether. When she stopped, everybody broke out in applause. I continued to stay embarrassed, but Kárin never lost eye contact with me.

"Kiss her!" shouted one of the women in the restaurant, who was obviously straight, sitting with a man and two children, assumedly her family.

Kárin pushed her chair back, stood up slowly, never taking her eyes off me, and moved around to my side of the table. Very, very slowly she leaned over me, and ever so softly placed her lips over mine, as lightly as a butterfly touches a flower. The entire restaurant was watching now, cheering. Kárin got down on one knee, held both of my hands, and asked me if I'd do her the honor of marrying her. I could barely breathe. Even though I already knew we were going to, even though we'd already gone to our counseling session with the rabbi, even though we were already wearing our rings, I could barely get it out.

"Of course. Of course I'll marry you. I love you so much."

The house came down with cheers at that point. Kárin got up off her knee and stood up. She pulled me up out of my chair and brought me in close to her, wrapping her arms around me, kissing me. Finally, she sat back down. I couldn't see for the tears in my eyes. Kárin just kept smiling at me, neither of us saying a word. Very quickly after that, our waiter showed up at our table with a bottle of champagne and two glasses.

"From the gentleman over there, with his compliments," said the waiter pointing to a table about three over from ours.

The gentleman was probably in his late fifties or early sixties, sitting with a lady his age, both dressed very nicely. Both raised their glasses to us in salute. Kárin and I waved at the couple. The waiter poured our flutes and told us that our food was just about ready. Within five minutes, our lunch arrived. Apparently the special of the day was a Spanish salad of romaine lettuce, green olives, spiced shredded pork, and goat cheese. It was delicious. We were about halfway through our lunch when the elder couple that had given us the champagne got up to leave. I popped out of my chair and ran over to their table, thanking them both and giving both of them a hug and a kiss on the cheek.

"I just hope both of you girls will be as happy as we've been. Next month will be our forty-sixth anniversary. Somehow, we've managed to wade through all of the bad, keep all the good, and come out shining," the woman said.

"You're both so lovely. Thank you so much...so very much," I reiterated.

After I had sat back down, Kárin looked at me.

"That was very nice of them to give us the champagne."

"Yes, it was."

"It was also very nice of you to fawn over them in return. It wasn't over the top; it was just enough. I tell you, you'd be great at my job. And they're going to need somebody starting in January," she laughed.

"No, thank you. I'm very happy being an attorney. Oh, my God, what am I saying? I used to hate attorneys."

"But that was before you knew that there were some of them out there doing some really good things with their craft, like you."

"I'd like to think I'm doing some good."

"You know, if Sasha truly is looking down upon you from heaven right now, she's very proud of what you've done with her life, taking it upon your shoulders to keep it going. And with how you've raised Lidiya, how your family has grown together."

"Thank you. That's very sweet of you. You, being Jew-*ish*, without getting a rise out of you, who don't believe in heaven."

"Honey, I mean it. As you said, the very word 'attorney' strikes loathing and a bad taste in most people's mouths, but you use your certificate from the Bar and wield it like a sword for justice. Like the statue, you carry scales in one hand, but in the other, instead of the words of the law, you carry that sword. You're a Dame of Justice. Would that be right? I mean, women can't be knights, but they can still be an order of the garter and be a dame..."

"Yeah, yeah, I get the picture. And thank you. I'm glad you think so. I know it's probably hard to be in a three-way relationship with the two of us and Sasha, knowing that it will never change."

"But that's the thing. I don't compare myself to Sasha. I'm only committed to being the best Kárin I can be. I don't try to live up to Sasha; I don't compare myself to her. That's why there's not a speck of jealousy. And you know, I keep traditions, not the total religion. I do believe in God, but I also believe in angels. Like I truly believe that Lidi is being watched over by Sasha. And Aly? I know we've never talked about it before, but I also believe in heaven. Just so you know," she said with a grin and a wink.

"You're probably the only person in New York that understands me…maybe the entire country. That's why I'm so lucky to have finally found you. You saved my life."

"Don't go overboard here."

"I mean it. I also mean it when I say I've got to get my ass back to work. Sorry. But I have to say this was the *best* lunch I've ever had, ever, ever, ever!" I said.

Kárin held her arm up for our check. The waiter made it over in less than a minute.

"Could I get our check, please?" asked Kárin.

"That has already been taken care of by the manager. We hope that you have had a wonderful dining experience today."

"Taken care of?" she queried.

"Yes, ma'am. You've caused quite a stir here today. And he's sure that by word of mouth alone, people will want to come in and have a meal with us. Not only that, but he was able to take in the entire proposal when he happened to come out of his office for a moment, and he was moved deeply. Enjoy the rest of your day, ladies."

We left the restaurant and both flagged taxis.

"Maybe I'll have to sing to you more often when we go out," quipped Kárin.

"Don't you dare!" I yelped.

"You didn't like it? Not at all? I didn't impress you?"

"Well, maybe a little, teensy, weensy bit," I said, holding up my hand with about a half an inch between my thumb and first finger.

"Okay, silly, I have to get back too. Give us a kiss."

"Kárin? Truthfully, that was brave, thoughtful, impressive, sweet, generous, romantic, and much, much more. I love you, sweetie."

"I love you too, hon. See you tonight."

"Oh? You're coming by tonight?"

"Oops. Gave it away. Didn't mean to do that. You didn't have plans, did you?"

"No. Even if I did, I'd break them."

"Good. Bye-bye."

Fran gave me a glare when I finally walked back in.

"Nice of you to join us. Some of us do have to work."

"Sorry, Franny. It's a long story. I'll tell you about it when I get back from court this afternoon."

"Your updated brief, with four copies, is in a folder on your desk beside your laptop, ready to go."

I grabbed everything I'd need and put it in my messenger bag. On the way out, I gave Fran a hug. "Thanks, Fran. I've also got some news for you. I'll tell you when I get back. See you after a while."

Court was a breeze. The prosecutor wanted to hang a kid out to dry for stabbing her older sister a dozen times. I had no problem with that at all; the kid was completely without remorse. All testing in a mental facility showed her to be a total sociopath. She was fourteen and the state was attempting to have her declared an adult for trial in order to keep her incarcerated for a very long time. They wanted to charge her with attempted murder and conspiracy to commit murder, both with malice aforethought. Her attorney, of course, wanted the judge to keep her in a family court. All three of us presented briefs and motions to the judge, who immediately called us into chambers. He rapidly reviewed the documents and put motions and briefs in a folder for the case in what, by now, had become a very large folder. We all returned to the courtroom.

"Before I make a ruling on the documents presented to the court today, I'd like a little time to read them thoroughly to ensure that I've been able to view all medical and legal information needed to render the proper verdict. I am continuing this hearing for two weeks from today, at two o'clock pm, with all parties required to be in attendance. The defendant, in the meanwhile, will remain in remand until that time."

"Your Honor, the defense again makes the motion that the defendant be allowed to be released on bail. We feel that..."

"Mr. Grier, I have already made my ruling. If you disagree with any portion of it, you may take it up upon appeal, which of course you can't do until the continuance is heard. I guess that pretty much covers that. Any further business, gentlemen? Oh, my sincerest apologies, Ms. Aronov-Lockewood, with respect to your gender. I meant no show of disrespect. I should say lady and gentlemen."

"That's quite all right, Your Honor. I was actually quite the tomboy growing up. I take no offense whatsoever."

"Fucking dyke!" the defense attorney mumbled.

"Excuse me? Mr. Grier? If you have something to say, you will address the court, and nobody but the court, is that clear? I find you in contempt of court and fine you five thousand dollars for your behavior today. Would you like to make further comments, which would not only double your fine, but get you thirty days in jail as well as initiate proceedings for having you censured or possibly disbarred for improper conduct?"

"No, Your Honor."

"Good. On your way out, stop by the clerk's office. We accept cash, personal or corporate checks, and, of course, plastic. Have a good day, sir."

On the way out of the courtroom, as much as the counsel for the defense tried to get away from me, the pattern of foot traffic pushed him my way.

"Well, Mr. Grier, how does it feel to have your ass kicked by a 'fucking dyke'?" I asked.

I looked back over my shoulder a bit when I said this and noticed the corners of the judge's mouth turn up slightly. Oh, yeah, this was a kick ass day.

As I walked past Fran when entering my office, I asked if there were any messages. She picked up a stack of them, entered my office, and closed the door.

"First, tell me about lunch. What happened?"

"We turned in our order and were just looking at each other. Kárin started singing to me. Not very loudly, but certainly loud enough for everybody and their dog around us to hear. She sang the first verse and the chorus of 'Have I Told You Lately.' Right out loud. Never stopped looking directly at me."

"You mean by Van Morrison? Now there's a love song."

"Right. Then when she was done, she got up, came to my side of the table, got down on one knee, and asked me to marry her. I tell you, I lost it. I was crying."

"I can tell. Your makeup is smudged a bit."

"Then an older couple bought us a bottle of champagne. And when it was time for the check, the manager had seen the whole thing and bought our lunch for us. Free. I left a tip for the waiter, but the restaurant gave us our meal for free."

"You may have found a keeper in Kárin, you know. It's just possible."

"Don't I know it?"

"Now, skip ahead to court. Did you really tell that supreme asshole Grier that a dyke kicked his ass?"

I laughed a good belly laugh just thinking back on it.

"Wow!! News travels fast, huh? He knew his kid was going down even though the judge continued it for two weeks. He muttered 'fucking dyke' under his breath. The judge fined him five thousand dollars for contempt and offered to double it with a bonus of thirty days and initialization of disbarment if he did it again. When we were walking out, I said 'got your ass kicked by a fucking dyke,' which made the judge smile."

Fran jumped up and came around my desk, giving me a giant hug.

"Uh, you're being touchy feely. That's a little out of your comfort zone, isn't it?" I asked hugging her back.

"I know, disgusting, isn't it?"

"It's already four o'clock. Let's shut this baby down and go home an hour early today. What do you say?"

"I still have a little I need to get done today. I've got an hour and several things to do yet. You go ahead."

"Fran?"

"Yes, Aly?"

"That's an order."

"Well, since you put it that way, I have no choice. Let me just change my telephone message and I'll walk you out."

It was nice getting home early. Our published working hours are until four thirty, but that gives us a half hour buffer from the outside world to polish up what we have on our plate at the moment. We usually worked until five or five thirty. I kicked off my shoes in the bedroom and hung up my skirt and jacket. I dropped my shirt in the laundry basket. I had no energy left. I fell back on the bed dressed in my underwear, drifting immediately into a deep sleep. I was still asleep when Esther and Lidi come in.

"Knock, knock," said Esther from the doorway.

"Oh, forgive me. I must have fallen asleep," I said groggily, grabbing my robe and pulling it on quickly.

"Don't be silly, it's just us girls here. Speaking of girls, mine haven't been that high for thirty years."

I blushed emphatically. My breasts aren't that large by any means, which is probably why they pretty much hadn't yet started migrating as I'd gotten older.

"Well, I missed you yesterday. I hate always imposing on you, but Lidi always looks forward to seeing you after school, and goodness knows you deserved a three-day weekend with..."

Esther was holding up her left hand, wiggling it back and forth. Her ring finger sported what must have been a four carat diamond on a really wide band.

"Oh, my God! What happened?"

"Gideon's plan for a long weekend was a bit more than I expected. I wasn't expecting anything at all. Just a three-day weekend for a change. Saturday morning, we got on a Gulfstream G550 and touched down in Orly. He had a car ready at the airport and we drank local wine on the way into Paris. He took me to Pétrelle's for dinner. Did you know that's where Jorges René got his first Michelin star? After dinner was over, we stayed at the Design Hotel Secret de Paris. Four stars. Then on Sunday morning, we flew to Le Havre. After we had set down, we got driven to a yacht. We went out for a day long cruise, and at sunset, Gideon asked me to marry him. I said yes, and the captain married us on the spot. We'll figure out my house later, but for now he made a couple of calls and when we got home most of my clothes and toiletries were already moved. What do you think?"

I rushed up to her and grabbed her.

"What do I think? What do you mean what do I think? This is fantastic! I mean, as long as it's what you really want. You shouldn't ever be pushed into it. And it's not for everybody, but I love it. Let me tell you what happened to me today at lunch. Kárin asked me to lunch. At the restaurant, she started singing to me, in front of everybody. Then she got down on one knee and asked me to marry her. Even though we're already in the planning stages, she made a huge show of it. And I know how it must have made her feel. After all, I was the one who got down on one knee and proposed to Sasha. I have to tell you though it was still a big shock to me. So you're Esther Aronov. How does it feel?"

"Perfect. It feels perfect. Chanukah will be very special this year. It will be lovely to have the entire family together."

"Actually, I was going to throw dinner and everything together with Kárin and some friends. Sort of like I did when Sasha and I were dating. Is that a problem?" I said with a screwy look on my face.

"How many friends?"

"Me, Kárin, and either four or six friends, depending on how things work out. And three kids."

"So you'll come to our house. It's plenty big enough. And remember that holiday is all about family and being delivered from the desert together."

"Oh, no, we positively couldn't."

"Oh, yes, you positively can and will. And that's the last of it. If you want to help cook, you're certainly welcome. If you want to help clean up, you're most certainly welcome. But have it at our house you shall. I won't hear another word of it."

"Okay, it's a yes. We'll be there."

"I already knew it. It was just a matter of you figuring that out."

"Esther, you're remarkable."

"Mmhmm."

"Come here to me, my baby. How are you?" I asked Lidi.

"Good. We had a fire drill today at school and had to go stand out where it was cold."

"But that was at least different, wasn't it?"

"I guess so."

There was a light knock on the door, then it opened to Kárin.

"Kárin! Kárin, what are you doing here?" yelled Lidi.

"I just came over for the evening. Is that okay with you?"

"You bet."

"Esther, why don't you show that thing off to Kárin?" I said pointing to my ring.

"What?" asked Kárin.

Esther said nothing. She held out her left hand, bent downward at the wrist.

"Great sands of the Sahara! Where's the hidden cables and pulleys to hold it up?"

"Oh, this little thing? I just threw it on over the weekend," said Esther.

"So this was the three-day weekend, huh? You eloped."

"That we did. I hear you had a nice little weekend in the woods."

"We did, in fact. We had a wonderful time. So where did you to go? Vegas? The Bahamas? Aspen?" asked Kárin.

"Actually, Gideon proposed in Paris, and the next day we got married on a yacht in the Mediterranean off of Le Havre.

"Well, la ti da!"

Everybody laughed.

"I better get going. I have a husband waiting for me," laughed Esther.

"Way to go!" yelled Kárin.

After she had gone, everybody sat down on the couch and I turned on the television. Lidi looked up at Kárin.

"Did you really sing to Mommy in a restaurant today?"

"Yes, I certainly did."

"That's silly. Why did you do that?"

"To show her how much I loved her."

"What?"

"Maybe you'll understand it better when you get to be a little older."

"Why do grownups always say that? If you would just explain it, I might understand it. If you don't do a good enough job of explaining things, it's not my fault."

Kárin and I both laughed at Lidi. Out of the mouths of babes...

"How long did you have that planned?" I asked Kárin.

"About fifteen seconds. It just came to me, and I decided to battle the nerves and go for it."

"You? Nervous? I don't believe it for a second."

"You have no idea. I'll talk in front of a stadium of people, I'll sing along in church with everybody else, but I don't sing solos. It petrifies me."

"Well, you sure did a good job today," I said, taking her hand in mine.

"Really?"

"Didn't you hear the crowd? They went nuts."

"I think that was for the effort, not for the quality of my voice."

"Stop it, you have a beautiful voice."

"What's for dinner? I'm hungry," asked Lidi.

"I was thinking of Chinese takeout. I already called them from downstairs. It should be here within five minutes. Lidi, pick out a movie, sweetpea," said Kárin.

Lidi put a movie in the player and we started it. The food came and we all ate while watching the movie. Kárin lay down on the couch and I spooned into her from the front, and Lidi crawled up into the corner of the couch with her legs draped over our feet. It was cozy. Even Puppet came out and got up on Lidi's lap, curling into a ball, begging for attention. Lidi didn't even make the end of the movie. I woke her up and told her to go brush her teeth and get into her pajamas. Kárin and I went in one at a time after she was in bed and told her good night. While I was in, Kárin cleaned up in the living room. When she came out of Lidi's room, she took my hand and pulled me into the bedroom. She pushed the door shut behind us and flipped the lock.

"Don't you think we should wait until she's good and asleep?"

"She didn't even know I went in to say good night. I think we're good to go."

"The singing wasn't planned. Was this?"

"Actually, I don't even know why I said I'd see you tonight. I meant call you. But I figured, hey, why not?"

"Oh, so I'm an afterthought?"

"No, you're a great thought."

Kárin grabbed my shoulders and violently whipped me around in a half circle, throwing me down on the bed.

"Prepare to be mounted."

We both broke out laughing so hard we could barely breathe. Kárin gingerly lay down beside me and brushed the wisps that had strayed, in place behind my ears.

"Thought of any more wants, wishes, needs, or desires for the wedding?"

"Not a thing. What about you? How's the planning coming along."

"Complete. Everything, down to the last detail."

"But we don't even have a date set yet. How can we plan anything else without a date?"

Kárin just smiled.

"What? What do you know that I don't?" I demanded.

She didn't say anything. Not a single word. In response, she reached for the sash of my robe and opened it. I pulled it back tight.

"Spill it. I'm warning you."

"Warning me?"

Kárin swiftly swept her outside leg up and over me, grabbed my hands, pinning them above me on the bed, and put her face right up to mine.

"I know this romance has been a total whirlwind and we've not confessed to everything yet, partly because we haven't had enough time. Did I tell you, among my other talents, that I'm a midnight blue belt in Tong Soo Do? Not to mention being a dan with indigo trousers in Aikido. So don't screw with me, sister."

"I know that Aikido is supposed to be strictly defensive and not injure the attacker, as well as self-preservation, right? Mostly blocks and throws...but what is Tong Soo Do?"

"You know Tae Kwon Do, right?"

"Sure."

"Imagine every maneuver having two forms," she said as she released my hands, but still straddled me.

She brought her hand forward and down with the bottom as the leading edge.

"This is the attacking move. Now invert it and you go from the knife hand to the ridge hand. It's the hand and leg movements as extensions, whereas Aikido is more of a judo style, sort of," she said, inverting her hand and bringing it down again.

"Now, take a front throat punch, like this, and invert it and roll your hand into a fist instead of just your fingers leading. This is still a potential harm to your aggressor, but is less lethal and meant only as a method of stopping the attack, not of attacking somebody else as a primary intent."

"You know what? My fiancée is one of the most totally awesome bitches in the world."

"I agree. Now let's get you out of these clothes so we can continue the lessons in physical confrontation."

"And just how are you going to make me? With force?"

"How's this for starters?" she said, ripping all of her clothes off in an instant and straddling me again, solely in her birthday suit.

"I'd say that's pretty good, actually. Nice technique. Now get off me so I can join you."

I tried to get her off me, but I couldn't overpower her. No matter what I did, I couldn't get her off.

"Okay, now I'm claustrophobic. Get off me!"

Kárin rolled onto her side next to me and in one even move pulled me on top of her.

"That better? Now get undressed and take me."

"Okay. I can do that.

Somehow we managed to plod through the week. Saturday morning Kárin came over in time for a late breakfast and we all sat down to more talking than eating. After we had cleaned up, Kárin called Lidi into the kitchen.

"Hey, sweetpea, go get dressed. You and I are going somewhere."

"What about Mommy?"

"Nope. Just you and me, kiddo."

"Where are we going?"

"It's a surprise. I'm taking the car, okay, hon?"

Lidi expectantly looked at me, but all I could do is shrug my shoulders. I had no idea either.

"Yeah, you've got keys. Go ahead."

After lunch, the pair of them returned laughing and giggling away. They had a couple of bags with them. Lidi put them down on the kitchen table.

"What do we have here, girls?" I asked.

Lidi got up on a chair and pulled out a shadow box frame about an inch and a half deep.

"What's that?"

"It's a display for Mommy Sasha's scarf so it will stay clean and safe, and I can look at it every day on my wall."

"What will you wear then?"

"This," she said proudly, as she pulled a brand new scarf out of another bag.

It was nearly identical, the exception being that instead of having just a pair of blue stripes running across the leading edge, it also had a blue circle in the very center of the front surrounding a blue Star of David.

"Wow, that's pretty. Where did you go to get that?"

"The frame was from a sports store. The scarves were from Liebowitz."

"Scarves? More than one?"

Lidi pulled another out. This one had two stripes across the leading edge, but they were woven into the fabric with all white thread.

Between the two stripes was a continuous row of Stars of David, also all woven into the fabric using the same white thread.

"I may not even get to let her make a choice when she's twelve. She may already be decided with you horning your way in here," I laughed.

"Horning my way? Need I remind you that you're the one that asked me out?" Kárin smarted off to me.

"No, I haven't forgotten, my love," I said as I kissed her.

"Lidi, show Mommy Aly what else you got."

"Kárin, seriously, you can't spoil her all the time. It's not good."

"It's not all the time for goodness sake, and before you go blowing off, why don't you see what it is?"

Lidi pulled out a jewelry box about six inches long from one of her bags. She handed it to me.

"It's mine. Go ahead and open it. Look at it."

I opened the lid, and inside there was a cross the same size as mine, but on a slightly shorter chain.

"Mommy Kárin said I can only wear it to church and if I dress up. I can't take it to school and I don't wear it to temple."

I moved to Kárin, put my arms around her, and brushed her ear with my lips, kissing her gently.

"Thank you, my love. Thank you so much. You're a good mommy."

"Okay, Lidi, since we're going to Grandma and Grandpa's today, you can wear your cross. You can wear it to church tomorrow too, and then it will go on your necklace stand until next month."

"Of course. How can you have a necklace without a necklace stand, right?" I said with a goofy look on my face.

"Yeah, what's a necklace without the stand? Show her, sweetpea."

Lidi held up her necklace stand to show me. It was made of green wire and had loops at the top to hold the necklaces. It was about fifteen inches tall and the green was patterned after climbing ivy vines.

"Wow, that's nice. Did you tell Kárin, thank you?"

"Yes, she did. Several times."

"Okay, put on your necklace then go get ready to go to Queens. We're going to be late if we don't get going."

And to think Kárin was worried about Lidi accepting her. On the contrary, my two girls were bonding perfectly. I should have been more afraid of losing Lidi to Kárin. I knew the new would wear off, and they'd have their squabbles periodically, just like Lidi and I do now. Life isn't a bowl of cherries; I'm not daft.

"Oh, and we got one other thing."

"Okay, now I think you may be going a little overboard for one day's shopping."

"Oh, it's not something we bought. We dropped by my apartment and packed a couple of pairs of jeans, a couple of tops, an old pair of sneakers, some underwear, a pair of flannel PJs, a little makeup kit, some lip gloss, a tube of lip balm, clippers and tweezers, and some, uh...feminine hygiene products. A basic kit to leave at your folks' house. It's in a small duffel in the back of the car to leave in Queens. Do you think it will convince them that I'm sticking around?"

"Who knows? I was with Sasha just short of two years and Mom still wants to 'unbend' me. You heard her at the house. 'Mom! I'm gay!' "

Other than the standard fare of nearly getting run off the road a half dozen times, it was an easy, lazy trip. We pulled up on the street in front of the house only about a half hour later than usual. We got everything out of the car and headed in. I knocked on the door and Dad immediately had it open, welcoming us in.

"You know, pumpkin, during the day we don't lock the door. And if we did, you have a key. You could just come in," he said.

"Just like you have a key to my place. It's for emergencies. I expect you to come inside, go up the elevator, and then knock on the door."

"Hi, Lidi? How's my favorite granddaughter?"

"Grandpa! I'm your only granddaughter!" she laughed. They did this once a month, and had forever, without fail. It was their little ritual I guess.

"Hey, Franklin," Kárin said with a wave of her hand.

"Isn't that a bit cold and standoffish?" Dad said, grabbing her hand, pulling her inside the doorway, and giving her a bear hug, kissing her on the cheek.

I'm not sure what Kárin's exact reaction was. I don't think she thought it would be so different than last month's trip. At least with Dad, but wait for it...Wait for it...There it is....

"Hello, dear. Hello, Karen."

"Mom, it's Kárin. KÁHR'-in. Not Karen."

"Oh, sorry, I forgot."

"Don't worry about it, Mrs. Lockewood. I get it all the time. It doesn't bother me at all."

"Please, call me Eliza. Mrs. Lockewood makes me seem older than I already am. I'm getting too old, too fast, as it is," she said with a slight laugh.

I just observed Mom for a couple of minutes while she talked to Kárin and Lidi. Dad was right. She had bad days and good days, and this didn't look like much of a good day. I pushed her out of the kitchen, telling her to go in the other room with Dad and spend some time with Lidi. I pulled Kárin by the hand into the kitchen, and we took over cooking dinner. The basics were already started, so we pretty much could tell everything she was going to cook already. We added some Jello and finished preparations. When everything was done, I called Lidi.

"Baby, would you set the table for Grandma and Grandpa, please?"

"Okay, Mommy."

She quickly put out plates, silverware, hot pads, ladles, trivets, and glasses with ice in them for tea. I stepped into the living room and called Mom and Dad in to eat. For a change, there was a fairly light banter during dinner.

"You never said before, Kárin, but what do you do for a living?" asked Dad.

"She's a professional beggar," I pointed out.

"What your daughter is trying so eloquently to say is that I work for a group of foundations, and I'm the fundraiser for that conglomerate...at least until January."

"What happens in January? Is your job going away?"

"No, I'm switching to the other side of give and take. I'm moving from the begging side to the giving side. I'm the Chairwoman Elect to the Frederich and Natalia Wørsc Foundation. I'll be in charge of day-to-day operations of a fund that's somewhere around seven hundred million dollars."

"Jesus Christ!" said Dad.

"Grandpa, you shouldn't say that."

"You're right, Lidi. I was just surprised is all. And very impressed, too."

"Lidi, show them the necklace that Kárin bought you today," I said.

"Yes! Look what Mommy Kárin bought me today. It's just like Mommy's. Do you like it?

Dad looked at it, thought it was nice, and said so. Mom sort of looked at it, but you could tell she was trying to process the 'Mommy Kárin' bit. The medication to slow down the dementia wasn't working very well. After we had eaten, Kárin and I ran everybody else out of the kitchen and cleaned it to within an inch of its life. It took us almost an hour. Mom would never have let it get like that, even in the last eighteen months or so. I kissed and snuggled up to Kárin for a minute and then we made our way into the living room. Mom and Dad were both snoozing in their chairs at opposite ends of the couch.

"Lidiya, are you tired?" asked Kárin.

"A little bit. We walked a long way today."

"Come upstairs with me and let's lie down for a little while. We can turn on the television."

The two of them climbed up the steps. I lay down on the couch and flipped through the channels until I found something relatively interesting, but not too lively so that I could take a nap as well. I slept for almost two hours. When I woke up, Mom and Dad were still in their chairs. I quietly snuck up the stairs and poked my head into the bedroom. Kárin was lying down on her side and Lidi was curled up against her, using her bottom arm for a pillow. Kárin's other arm was up over Lidi, and Lidi was drooling on Kárin's lower arm. I quietly sneaked back downstairs and got my cell phone. I managed to get back up without either of them moving. I took a shot from the doorway, and another one leaning over the bed close up showing both of their faces and Lidi's drool. I went back downstairs and sat down on the couch again. I pulled up the apps for all three of my social media pages that I follow and posted the photos with a caption, 'Mommy Kárin and Lidi'. Apparently Lexa was online because it didn't take but two minutes to get a ding telling me there was a response.

'Too cute! So I guess they get along pretty well, huh? LOL'

Then another ding.

'So adorable! Is that what Lidi really calls Kárin?'

I reposted.

'It is. Lidi is the one that started it after our first date. A date that Lidi went on, I'm happy to say. Is that strange to ask somebody out and on your first date, bring your child?'

It must have been a boring afternoon. I left my phone on and had over two dozen replies or likes between the different pages in under an hour. Finally, I closed the apps and went to the bedroom. There was barely any room to be had with the two of them sleeping soundly, sort of sprawled out. I managed to push and shove gently and get just enough of the mattress under my side not to fall off. I stroked Lidi's hair until she started waking up.

"Hi, Mommy," she croaked out with her sleepy little voice.

"Shhh. Don't wake up Mommy Kárin."

"Don't worry, Mommy Kárin was already awake when you took those pictures of us. I just didn't want to acknowledge the world yet. And, by the way, if you ever show those pictures to anybody, I'll kill you."

"Erm...it's a bit too late. I posted them online."

Kárin just gave a big sigh.

"Why am I not surprised?" she asked rhetorically.

"I'm just so proud of the two ladies in my life that I wanted to share it with the world. When you get good and awake, there's something I want to show you on my laptop."

"Go away. Come back in thirty minutes, and I'll consider it."

"I'm going to go get some juice," said Lidi as she slipped off the bed between Kárin and me, and out the door.

I crawled over closer to Kárin, leaning down, and putting my hand on her cheek.

"I love you so much."

I reached up and covered her breast with my hand, gently squeezing.

"Do you want full on, or just a quickie?" smiled Kárin.

"I don't want anything. I just wanted to touch perfection for a moment."

"Then get your hands off or you'll have to make the choice. Damn it, what you do to me..."

"Can't I just love you?" I asked.

"No, you can't. Not like that. You wouldn't want to sneak a hand down my pants, would you?"

"You mean like this?"

"Mmm...now that's what I'm talking about," said Kárin.

"And maybe like this?"

"Mmhmm....'

"And what about this?"

Kárin almost yelped. I kept my hand where it was, but slapped my other hand down over her mouth to quiet the noise. Kárin's arms wrapped completely around me, and she was almost clawing me with her hands.

"Did I find your warm and fuzzy spot?"

Kárin said nothing, but kept nodding her head over and over.

"So I guess you were the one that made the choice after all, not me, huh? I guess you chose a quickie, am I right? Because you're certainly not wasting any time," I said quietly in her ear.

Kárin jammed her top leg between mine, pulled on my arms, and started to shake, over and over.

"Do you feel better now?"

There was no response. Her body just kept trembling. She kept it up for the longest time, and then we heard the stairs squeak. Thank goodness for hardwood stairs. I pulled my hand back and just held hands with Kárin lying there. I was staring into her beautiful face, and she was trying to slow her breathing down and stop panting. Dad popped his head through the doorway. I should have closed and locked the door, no matter what it would have looked like.

"Either of you girls want anything at the grocery store? I didn't get out last night and I need to pick up quite a few things for the week."

"I'll go with you Dad. I'll help," I said.

"No, you two girls just rest here. I'll be fine."

"Don't be silly. Let me get my jacket and shoes, and we'll go together."

Kárin got up and we went to the bathroom. She turned on the water in the sink and washed both my hands and hers.

"They may suspect what we're up to, but no reason to confirm it," said Kárin.

"Meaning what?"

"Are you out of your mind? Even I could smell me on your hands after."

"But it's the most wonderful smell in the world. Well, maybe after Burberry Red. And bacon, of course. Don't forget bacon. Life's all about the bacon."

"You, Chiquita, are a certifiable nutter!"

"To be sure. Do you think we're clean enough now, doctor? Can we enter the operating theater?"

"Don't be a bitch."

"Takes one to know one."

"Come on. Let's get our shoes."

"You coming too?"

"Sure, why not?"

"Well, you just didn't say anything."

"If you'll remember, I was about three seconds past having one of the most intense orgasms of my life!"

"You keep saying that. Is it always going to be the best, most intense, whatever, between us?"

"I'll keep trying if you will."

We romped downstairs and got on shoes and jackets and went to the store, leaving Lidi and Grandma Eliza together for a little while. We talked a little bit about Mom's condition while we were walking the aisles, away from all other ears.

"So that's where we stand. The doctor thinks it will be less than two years until I'll either have to have a day nurse full time, I'll have to take an early retirement, which will cost us plenty, or she'll have to be put in a comprehensive care facility. She'd get a one-bedroom apartment, but no cooking facilities. They'd bring her food three times a day, and the nurse would come three times a day to check her vitals and administer medications. Not exactly what I'd planned for, but things rarely are."

"I'm sorry, Dad. I didn't know how bad things were last month when I yelled at her. I just get so tired of it. After thirty-two years, I would just like, for once, to be treated like an adult and be given credit for my ideas and thoughts."

"Well, if it's any consolation, I give you full credit. Let's talk about something happier. If I pay for them, will the two of you go to the studio and get your photos taken? I'd love to update my daughter's life."

"No, Dad, you're not going to pay for it...we already talked about it, actually. We're going to stay dressed up tomorrow after church and stop on the way home to get it done. It was already our plan."

"Good."

After we had got home, I called everybody over to the couch and asked them to gather around me. I opened my laptop and went to a favorite video from a popular video upload site.

"The first few seconds of this are chopped off because the person shooting it didn't realize what was going on at first..."

A woman was sitting down in a restaurant, holding hands with another woman, and was singing:

Have I told you lately that I love you
Have I told you there's no one above you
Fill my heart with gladness
Take away my sadness
Ease my troubles, that's what you do

"That's Mommy Kárin! And that's Mommy Aly!"

"Apparently this thing has gone totally viral. It's had five hundred thousand hits since last week when it happened."

"What does that mean?" asked Dad.

"It means that it's been viewed by about half a million people. Isn't that mind boggling? Besides posting the two photos of you and Lidi sleeping today, I also posted a link to the video."

"You didn't. Tell me you didn't!" scowled Kárin.

"Actually, I did. Is that a problem?"

"It might have been if I was keeping my old job, but since I'm not, I guess not. Half a million hits? I wonder what people thought of my singing?"

"I don't know what they thought specifically about your singing, but about your whole performance including your proposal? Out of five hundred thousand views, there were two hundred seventy-five thousand likes. Impressive, if you ask me."

"I'd say so. I don't even understand all of this mumbo jumbo, but it does sound awfully impressive," said Dad.

"This really doesn't hurt you and what you do, does it, sweetie?"

"I was just kidding. I'm personally mortified, I'm embarrassed, but I've been out of the closet so long that there isn't a single soul I do a meet and greet with that hasn't already been warned that I'm a big bad 'L-word.' "

"They warn them ahead of time so they won't feel like they're going to get cooties?"

"Or an STD," laughed Kárin.

"Church in the morning, everybody. All hands on deck, ready your sleeping stations."

Mom and Dad went to their bedroom. Kárin and I made up Lidi's bed on the couch. Then we went into the bathroom and changed into pajamas and brushed our teeth.

"So, are you a convert now to long pajamas?" I asked Kárin.

"Probably not in the summer, but I thought for your parents it might be a little nicer if I seemed a little more proper."

"I appreciate it, actually. I do."

I kissed Kárin on the back of the neck while she took out a clean washcloth and got it wet with warm water.

"What's that for?"

She just turned to me and smiled, then walked into the bedroom. As soon as I walked in, she pushed the door closed behind us and flipped the lock.

"I believe that question was, 'Do you want this full on, or do you want a quickie?' Ms. Aly?"

"I'll take 'What is a "Quickie for 500" please, Alex.' At least for now."

Kárin embraced me and kissed me, all the while walking me backward until I was jammed into the corner between the dresser and the outside wall of the house. She thrust one hand down my pants while she grabbed my hair from the back with the other. There was absolutely nothing violent about her actions, neither was there anything gentle about them. All her movements were designed for one purpose, and one purpose only. It was working quickly. I started to get guttural, so she smashed her mouth over mine to quash the noise. The closer I got, the wilder she worked her magical hands on my body. She leaned down to my chest and started biting me gently through my top. It sent me through the roof. Kárin was relentless. Or ruthless. Or both. I tried pushing her away from me, and she still continued. I begged her to stop, and she continued. I tried wrestling away from her, but she was much stronger than me as I'd found out a few days before. Finally, I was whimpering and tears were running down my cheeks. She stopped her movements, put her hands under my arms, and pulled me back up straight against the wall.

"I told you. I want to try and make it better and better."

I had no reply, no response. I merely collapsed into her arms, falling forward. She caught me and pulled me over to the bed, orienting me in the correct direction.

"How does my baby feel? Hmm? Do you feel good? Baby? Honey? Are you okay?"

For the longest time, she just propped herself over me with her arms and waited for me to respond. When I finally did, it was a one-word response. And it was the only word I could think of, "Fuck."

Kárin went to the dresser and picked up the washcloth. She licked her right hand like she'd just had barbecued ribs, making a grand showing of it right in front of me. She finished wiping her hand down with the cloth, then she took it, put it down my bottoms, and cleaned me.

"There. All better. Your turn."

"My turn for what?"

"Our game."

"What game?"

"The full on or quickie game. It's your turn to ask me."

"You have *got* to be kidding me."

"No, I don't. Ask me."

I still hadn't gotten my heart rate down to twice normal. Surely she was kidding.

"What do you want? Full on or a quickie?" I managed to pant.

"Full on. I want us both to undress, and I want you to get on top of me and just do whatever, until we're both calm and serene and at one with the world."

"No problem. But one thing...can you give me about ten minutes?"

Kárin laughed. I didn't. I got up to go and use the restroom first. I came back in and shut the door, flipping the lock.

"Open the lock."

"Now we're going for the thrill of possibly getting caught?"

"No. Come here and get your PJs on."

I was more than a little confused. I got over to my side of the bed and got dressed, noticing where the covers were slightly pulled back that she was still fully dressed. She patted the mattress beside her.

"Come and spoon with me."

"I thought you said full on?"

"There's full on sex, and there's full on making love, and sometimes there's just full on love. Come lie with me."

I slipped under the covers and Kárin spread them completely over me. Not only was her arm on top of my pillow underneath my head, but she also wrapped her top arm around me and placed her hand, palm up, holding my head as well. After we had gotten situated, she gave out a huge sigh. I reached out with my lips and kissed her forearm. She wiggled her fingertips under my head, and that's exactly where Lidi found us in the morning.

CHAPTER SIXTEEN

In the greeting line, without being told, Pastor Douglass noticed Lidi's new necklace.

"That's beautiful. It matches your mother's necklace perfectly. Who bought that for you?"

"Mommy Kárin," she said and took Kárin's hand, smiling, halfway hiding behind her leg.

"That was very nice of her, wasn't it?"

"Mommy Aly and Mommy Kárin are going to get married. Isn't that good?"

"Lidi! Pardon me, Pastor. Sometimes she's not old enough yet to know what's public and what's maybe not," I said.

"Not to worry, it was already information shared with me."

"Of course, Dad."

"Something like that."

"Well, it was nice to see you. Say, when we do it, and if it fits into your schedule, would you be interested in doing a dual service ceremony like I had last time?"

"That's also something I'm already privy to as well. People sometimes think that because I'm a man of the cloth, I don't know what's going on in the rest of the world," he laughed.

His wife, Nathalie, was next in line, with their children on the other side of her.

"I have to tell you, your video has gone wild! I wish Ray had done that for me. It was simply spectacular. I mean, over seven hundred thousand hits in a week!" she exclaimed.

Kárin and I looked at each other in bewilderment.

"Yesterday it was only five hundred," I said.

"Yes, but Saturday night is when everybody that's not out on a date or at a movie, logs in. I know that's when I usually do. The kids are with their friends and Ray's smoothing out his sermon. It's my personal quiet time for the week."

We walked to the parking lot. Seven hundred thousand hits. Wow! After the buffet, we went to Mom and Dad's house to lie around for a while and hold our overstuffed bellies.

"If we want to get pictures taken today, we'd better get going, gang," Kárin said out loud.

"That's true. Go give Grandma and Grandpa L. a hug and a kiss, baby. Then get your jacket and your shoes."

Dad came up behind me and wrapped his arms around me. He leaned into my ear and spoke very quietly so that only I could hear, "I know that you loved Sasha with all your heart. If your mother and I would have taken notice of you all those years, we would have been able to figure you out without having to be told. And I'm very sorry for having taken all those years away from you. You've been so very lonely these last few years even though you've had Lidiya, but you've now grabbed the brass ring twice in your life. Don't do anything to screw this up. Always try your best. I'm convinced that Kárin will fight for you as hard as you fight for her, if not harder."

I turned around and grabbed him by the neck and started crying. "Oh, Daddy. I love you."

"I love you too, kitten."

I managed to pull myself together quickly, but was still very teary. We all got outside.

"What's wrong, Mommy? Why are you sad?"

"Oh, I'm not, baby. I'm happy. Very, very happy."

"Then why are you crying?"

"I know you hate it when a grown up tells you this, but it's one of those things that you don't really understand until you grow up a little more. And no, explaining it better won't help a bit. Okay?"

"I guess so."

Kárin looked over at me with a quizzical look on her face; her eyebrows raised in question. "Care to share?"

"Today I went from ninety-nine percent understanding and acceptance to one hundred percent, at least with Dad. And he told me something else."

"What's that?"

"He was talking about you. He said that most people never find true love, but I've found it twice. That I've gotten the brass ring twice in a row."

Kárin leaned over into my arm as far as her seatbelt would let her. She replied in a very quiet voice, "I wonder if he'd say the same thing if he knew that I was finger banging his daughter in his house?"

"TMI. I don't think it would change his opinion, but I guarantee that he'd chastise you for the TMI factor. Just to bug Mom, several years ago, I asked her if she and Dad still had sex. I asked her if she ever tried a reverse cowgirl on him."

"You didn't!"

"I did. Before she really realized I was talking about sex, she asked me what that was. I told her it was where they both took off their clothes; she mounted him facing away, and yelled 'yippee-ki-yay!' She almost fainted."

"Well, I would imagine she would! That's awful!"

"Well, apparently they did still have relations on a fairly regular basis, but with the lights off...and they never talk before, during, or after the act. So Dad is talking to me on the phone and says he wanted to ask me a personal favor. I said sure. He told me to never, ever, ever mention sex to Mom, ever again."

"Jesus, I'd like to have been a fly on the wall at your parents' house that day."

"She got over it. But you saw the first night we went over. She was hoping that your name was Karl, not Kárin. It's like I disappointed her all over again. I mean, she loves Lidi to death, but she still held out hopes for a 'regular' daughter."

"Actually, Kalista and I used to sit in our room and laugh late at night. Our parents' bed was fairly noisy. They used to go after it like rabbits. All the time. When it came to the talk about the birds and the bees, Kalista said, 'You mean like you and dad?' and my mom just about came unglued."

"Mommy?" asked Lidi.

"What, baby?"

"What's a piss ant?"

"Where did you hear that?"

"During the football game this afternoon. Grandpa said that the man in the green shirt was a piss ant and should just do his job."

I looked at Kárin, barely able to keep a straight face and to keep from laughing.

"You want to take this one, Mom?" I asked, looking toward Kárin.

"Lidi, it's not spelled like it sounds. It's p-e-s-a-n-t. It means worthless. It's called that because it's the French word for a tiny, tiny ant. It's also not a very nice word, so you should probably put it in your naughty words book. For now, anyway."

"Oh. Okay."

"Well played, lover."

"So I passed?" asked Kárin.

"With full marks."

At the photography studio, I was trying to brush through Lidi's hair. Her hair wasn't wavy like Danny's, and it wasn't quite the tight curls of her mother. Sometimes it truly had a mind of its own and you just couldn't do anything about it, not with any amount of water or spit or brushing.

"Lidi, come over in front of me and let me fix that for you," said Kárin.

Lidi walked over and got between Kárin's legs, facing toward her chair. She had Lidi bend over at the waist.

"Now, shake your hair like you're trying to get it to fall out. C'mon, more, more, more, harder. That's it. Keep going! Okay, stop. Now just stand straight up."

Lidi had an absolute bird's nest on the top of her head. Kárin put each hand, fingertips down, in the middle of her hair.

"Now shake your head from side to side, but this time not so hard."

Out of nowhere, this beautiful mane of hair appeared, as though she'd been in the stylist's chair for an hour.

"What do you think? Is that what you were looking for?"

"It's perfect. Is that a Jewish thing?"

"No, actually my roommate in college worked her way through as a hairdresser. It's just a trick she showed me with my hair when I needed to get going, like when I was late for a class, instead of just throwing it in a tab-backed baseball cap. I didn't want to look *too* much like a dyke."

"Kárin, if it weren't for the fact that you just don't wear dresses or skirts that much, I wouldn't have any idea whatsoever. That's why I'm so glad our conversation went like it did, letting me know when we first talked. I have no gaydar at all."

"I don't either. I mean, sometimes a woman looks totally butch, but she's just tomboyish. She might not be. Much easier if it's a guy and he is a total flamer. Still, never a guarantee."

They finally called our name and we went into one of the photo rooms to have our photos taken in various combinations and poses. After we were done, we sat down again and waited to be called to the printing room. There were three printing stations in one huge room. On the wall was a collage of hundreds of photos that they'd taken in the past. Kárin and I had just stepped up to the computer screen to see the shots to choose from, when I heard Lidi start screaming at the top of her lungs over and over and over.

"*Mommy!*"

I ran over to see what was wrong and found her pointing at a photo amidst the others clinging to the walls. It was a photo about seven years old. It was a photo of me and Sasha.

"It's Mommy Sasha! It's Mommy Sasha! Make them take it down! Make them take it down!"

Kárin snatched her up in a second and took her outside to talk to her and try to calm her down. The girl from the studio asked me what was wrong and what had upset my little girl so much.

"That's an old photo that her mother and I had taken together before we got married, and before Lidi was born. About six months after Lidi was born, Sasha was shot and killed in the line of duty. Would it be possible for you to remove that photo from the wall and destroy it? I still have originals so it wouldn't be as if we'd be losing anything, and I'm sure there are many more you could use. Please?"

Before I'd even stopped talking, the young woman was removing it from the wall and apologizing profusely.

"It's okay. This is the first time she's ever reacted like that. Usually she relishes everything that was her mother's: jewelry, photos, an old purse, a religious scarf, and many other things. I guess this one was just so much out of the blue."

I then went a little further into the details of our life together for so long, and then us meeting Kárin, the fact that we were getting married, and that she and Lidi got along so well.

"Would it be all right if I went to talk to her? If she gets upset, I'll immediately leave her alone, I promise," the technician requested.

"Sure. Go right ahead."

We walked out of the shop together. Kárin was walking up and down the sidewalk, carrying Lidi.

"Lidi, baby, why don't you get down and try to walk now. You're getting too big for anybody to carry you anymore."

Kárin gently set her down on the sidewalk. The woman from the studio walked up to her very quietly and held her hand out.

"Hello there. I'm Tami. So I guess your name is Lidi, right?"

Lidi shook her hand, but didn't talk.

"I'm very sorry you were so upset about the picture of your Mommy Sasha and your Mommy Aly, but you know what? All of the pictures on those walls are the ones that we think are the very prettiest ones. So it wasn't meant to take anything away from you. It was a way to honor those people and share them with everybody else because we thought they were so special. I promise you, the photograph is already down off the wall. But now there's a hole on the wall. If you'd let me, I'd like to put up a photo of you and your mommy and your new Mommy Kárin. I'd really, really like to, if you'd let me. Would you let me do that?"

Lidi didn't say anything, but nodded her head. We all went back inside and went to the print station. Kárin held her up to the computer screen. The technician asked her which picture she'd want up on the wall. Lidi pointed her finger to one of them.

"Are you sure this is the one?"

Lidi just nodded. The technician printed out the photo by itself, separate from everything else, and put it on the wall.

"So, do you like that now? Is everything okay?"

Lidi just nodded her head. I suspected that above all else she was just tired after staying up late and then going to church early. We picked out all of the poses and sizes we wanted, then went back and sat down waiting for the finished images to spit out at the end of the machine.

"That will be twenty-five dollars."

"What? Twenty-five dollars? We didn't have a coupon or anything."

"Yes, ma'am, but we also want to make up for any undue discomfort to your daughter."

"Thank you. Thank you very much. You're very kind."

"No problem. Lidi? Can I get a shake before you leave?" the technician said, holding out her hand.

Lidi did shake her hand, but still never said another word until we put her to bed that night. I'm not sure why she was so traumatized, but clearly she was. Something just set off something inside her. I'd never seen her do anything like that before.

"May I talk to her, please?" asked Kárin.

"Sure. Call me if you need anything," I answered and backed out of the room so that I remained hidden, but would still be able to hear most of what was being said.

Kárin sat on the side of the bed after tucking Lidi in tightly and giving her Best Bear to hold.

"So, this has been a crazy sort of day, hasn't it?"

Lidi didn't acknowledge being spoken to at all. She just played with two of her fingers in her mouth, like she'd been doing for the last hour while staring off into space.

"You know, Lidi, I'm not trying to take the place of Mommy Sasha. She was very special, and no matter how hard I tried, I'd never be as good as her in so many ways. Nobody in the world would ever be good enough to take her place. I'm just Kárin, and all I can do is be the best Kárin I can be. That's all. No better than the best I can do. A lot of times it won't be as good as Sasha. And I'm sorry. I'm just not as special a person. If you want me to stay, I'd be so very happy, but listen to me. If you don't want me to be here...if you don't want me to get married to your mommy, then I won't. Maybe you thought that if I came along it would fill in a hole where Sasha was. And now you've figured out that I'm not doing a very good job of that. If that's what has happened, just tell me. I don't want to push myself in where I'm not wanted. If you ask me to go, I will. I'll leave you and your mommy alone. I hope you don't, but if that's what you want, I'll go."

Lidi lay there for almost five minutes without saying anything. Kárin started getting up from the side of the bed, and Lidi went totally nuts. "No, no, no, no, no! Don't leave me. Don't ever leave me. I love you. You're my new mommy. I want you to stay. I want you to live with us. I want you to never leave me, never!"

She kept screaming over and over, even though by that time she'd already jumped out of bed and into Kárin's arms. She was absolutely wailing. Kárin kept trying shush her and kept stroking her hair, but Lidi just didn't stop. After about twenty minutes, she finally cried herself to sleep. Kárin carefully put her down into her bed and covered her up, but as soon as Lidi's head hit the pillow, her eyes flew open.

"Mommy Kárin? Sleep with me, please! Please sleep with me tonight, please?"

Kárin walked over to the wall and switched off the light. She saw me standing right outside the door and rubbed my hand against hers, then she walked over and slipped right into bed with Lidi. She waited a full hour after Lidi had gone to sleep before she tried getting up. I was already in bed, sitting up reading.

"You know what turns me on?"

"Probably, but you tell me what you think and we'll compare notes," I said back to Kárin.

"Chicks in tank tops. No bra."

"That's because you're a lesbian."

"No, I think if I was straight I'd still like chicks in tank tops and no bra."

"You're a freak show, Kár."

"Takes one to know one."

"So, I believe we've definitely put this question to bed, haven't we."

"I think Lidi needs to see a therapist. That's PTSD. I guarantee it. And it will happen again if it's not addressed. It hasn't triggered until now because she hasn't been mentally developed enough to start putting the pieces of it together. But her subconscious is now weaving a tapestry, and parts of it don't make any sense to her. And she's terrified."

"I'd always dreaded this. I'll check into it tomorrow. I'm sure that Diya has friends that she could recommend. I know she's in speech therapy, but I bet she knows people…good people instead of a random finger in the phone book."

"Actually, I see a therapist every two months. I've been seeing her for the last ten years. She doesn't see children, but I bet she'd have a great contact for us."

"I didn't know that you saw a therapist. I saw a grief therapist for four years. I'm not sure whether it helped while I was going, but every time I missed a session because of whatever reason, I had these massive anxiety attacks. I've stopped going because of my new job, but I always knew that I'd have to find somebody else and start up again. I should check into that too, I suppose. So why did you go to therapy?"

"PTSD."

"You have PTSD?"

"Yup."

"From what?"

Kárin hesitated for the longest time. Then she uttered one word, "Rape."

"Baby," I said, throwing myself over her and wrapping around her like a magic cloak shielding her from the rest of the world.

"I know every last symptom and manifestation of PTSD. I've studied it extensively. But knowing it logically, and being able to control it as opposed to a part of your brain that's subjective and emotional, are two different things. I already hated anything sexual about a man before that, but now..."

"Would you sleep with me tonight?" I asked, just as Lidi had asked her.

Kárin reached over and turned off the light. She pulled a sheet up over us and we didn't even get undressed; we just held on for dear life. That night, I wasn't going to let anything or anybody do anything to either one of my girls. Not if I could help it.

CHAPTER SEVENTEEN

After I had prepped for my first meeting in the morning, I called Dad at work. It took a few minutes for him to get to his phone. I had just about given up and was going to hang up.

"Hey. What's going on? Any problems?"

"Yes and no. The first thing I wanted to bring up is a pair of options. I can bring dinner with us on Thanksgiving so that nothing has to be cooked, only heated. The other option is to do something totally different, like bring over some Chinese food, or maybe even a half dozen foot-long sandwiches from Brightman's Deli. They're fantastic sandwiches. Club, ham, turkey, pastrami, corned beef, sliced beef, meatball, you name it. It's also all kosher food. That's all they sell. That way we wouldn't have to clean up, either."

"Well, I'll have to check with your mother, but Brightman's seems like a pretty good idea. I haven't had a great kosher deli sandwich in, I don't know how many years. And it comes with the whole potato fried up, right?"

"Oh, absolutely. Is there any other way?"

"You said yes and no, indicating maybe there is something?"

I told him briefly about Lidi's reaction yesterday.

"Sounds like PTSD to me."

"That's exactly what Kárin said. How do you know what PTSD is? Do you know somebody with it, or just saw a show on television, or what?"

I heard a deep, deep sigh on the other end of the phone.

"You know that I was in the Army for two and a half years, right?"

"Yeah, so?"

"My classification was an eleven-bravo."

"What's that?"

"Infantryman. Rifle-carrying foot soldier. And you know when I was in, don't you?"

"I think in the early seventies."

"I was drafted in nineteen seventy-two. I was released early with the drawdown after the fall of Saigon in seventy-five. They let me go early. Think, kitten. When was I, where was I, what was I...think."

"You never told me you were in Vietnam!"

"Because, just like your little brother, it's something your mother just preferred never to talk about, so it wasn't talked about. I suffered badly from PTSD for several years, but it gradually got better. It hasn't ever gone away though. The images of the carnage that you inflict on another human being, who also doesn't believe in his side of the war, that was also drafted...but the reality of life is that under certain situations only one of you gets to go home."

"So what you're saying is..."

"So what I'm saying, Aly, is just trust me that it's PTSD and get her to a therapist now. Don't waste any time."

"But Dad, what about..."

"Just forget about it. That's my last word on it."

"Okay, okay. This is what I meant before when I was talking about our family never communicating. You didn't protect me by shielding me from everything. If anything, you never let me build up my own resistance so that I could face the world."

"Let's just say we did what we did, and now we are where we are, and move on. What do you say, huh?"

I believe that's the first time my dad ever actually grew a great big pair and showed them off. I was very proud of him! Not that I was going to tell him though...

We'd been able to get Lidi into a counselor quickly. At first she'd be going once a week, at least for the first few months. Then she'd back off to the point she'd go to therapy every two weeks. Then every month. Pretty typical. Kárin and I got pretty in-depth training on signs to look for and ways to diffuse situations like the one at the photography studio. The therapist did say that Kárin did a brilliant job of reacting quickly to the situation and separating Lidi from the trigger. And I think that having the whole week off from school helped Lidi as much as us. The first three days of the week, she'd stayed at Papa and Esther's house.

Thanksgiving did go like Dad and I had talked. We did the kosher food bit, along with some couscous, pita chips and pickles, and both ripe and green olives. It was clean and easy, nothing to clean up. We stayed over until Saturday morning, spending two nights. It was nice to have the extra day of downtime. We drove back to Brooklyn in mid-afternoon to be nice and rested for Sunday's celebration.

On Sunday, just after noon, Kárin reached back behind all of Lidi's clothes hanging up in her closet and brought out three brand new dresses.

"Girls, I believe these are the right sizes and should fit perfectly," she said as she held them up.

"You're in trouble now, girly," I forced a fake growl and grimace.

"What? You said that it was enough for one day, a couple of weeks ago, but you didn't say anything after that about going shopping for us on a different trip. And I've already ironed them," she countered.

"All right, no time for arguing right now."

"Who's arguing? You're the one that's arguing. I'm just saying we need to get dressed. I don't think you win this one, hon because I don't think you quite have a good grasp of the rules."

"You're full of shit."

After I had Lidi dressed and in her shoes, Kárin told her to go get her necklace.

"Uh, I thought that we'd already told her that the cross was for Christian activities, right?"

"No, not that necklace, the other one. The silver one."

Lidi came racing back into the living room.

"Mommy, Mommy, look what Mommy Kárin brought for me!"

Lidi was holding up a sterling necklace with a Star of David pendant on it, sans diamonds, of course. I put it on Lidi and she was tickled pink looking at it. I walked up to Kárin.

"Before Christmas rolls around, you and I are going to have a serious, binding talk about the rules. Do you understand me?"

"Yes, miss."

"I'm not kidding."

"Yes, miss."

I playfully grabbed her by the throat with both hands and shook her neck around loosely.

"Now, if it's not too much trouble, could we leave for Papa's house? We'll be the last ones to get there."

I'd already given the directions and address to Zach and Benjamin. We indeed were the last three people there. The cousins weren't there so Lidi didn't get to spend time with them, but Esther had her grandkids there. They were older than Lidi, but they still enjoyed spending time together. Or should I say, tearing through the house together. Gideon and Esther. Grig and Gabi. Valery, who had the entire night off, with Diya, who was there. Roni with Michael. Zach and Julie, who wore her scarf as she often did. He wasn't kidding. She wore it a lot when she went out, to keep her hair up and off her neck. Ben and his wife Rachel had come with her cousin, Brittany. It was so packed you couldn't swing a dead cat in that place without hitting somebody, just like the proverbial sardines in a can. Papa was wearing his long coat and a fur hat out of respect for traditions, even though he wasn't Orthodox.

Lidi was showing off her new necklace and scarf to everybody. I mean everybody. We sat down to dinner and said the four blessings, along with the lighting of the Shamash and the first night's candle. Lidi had been able to say all four blessings in Hebrew last year, so this year was no big deal; however, it still impressed everybody. We laughed and joked and sang and told stories in the tradition of the Festival of Lights. While we were still singing, the doorbell rang. Esther started to go answer it, but Gideon told her to sit and enjoy, and he'd get it. Without warning, everybody inside heard the hysterical screaming coming from outside. Valery ran to the door to find out what the problem was. He found Katya with her arms around Gideon, wailing at the top of her lungs. She kept it up with no end in sight. Finally, while still acting hysterically, with Gideon on one side and Val on the other, they brought Katya into the house. When she got into the living room, she fell to her knees. Kárin had a better view than I did since she sat two chairs farther over than me.

"Oh, God. Get Lidi out to the car, now!" she said pushing me up.

"What's going on?"

"I'll tell you when we're out. Just go."

I grabbed Lidi by the hand and told her to follow me quickly and not to ask questions until we got to the car. Finally, we were all in the car and sitting there quietly, waiting for Kárin to talk.

"Tell me you don't know Katya. Tell me she's not someone from your past."

"I've never met her before tonight. Did you notice her collar?"

"What about it?"

"It had been cut, like with a razor. I figured you were the last person she needed to see tonight, even if it was her fault that you never got along."

"I don't understand."

"When a Jew cuts their collar or their sleeve, it means someone has died. And the way she was taking it, I think it was probably her mother. Call Zach, call Ben, and call Roni. Make sure she gets everybody out of there and make sure she explains everything to them, and to Gideon. Tell them we'll call them later tonight."

Kárin had chosen to drive home tonight, probably because she just took control of the situation. I really admired her for that. She had that quality. I tried Zach first.

"Hey. Sorry to drag you into this, but I think Sasha's mom died. She did? Did they say how? Well, Kárin caught it nothing flat and got me out of there so there wouldn't be any more drama than there had to be. Yeah. I'm really sorry. Listen, I'll call you in about an hour and a half, right? Okay. Bye."

"Benjamin? Zach just told me. Kárin thought it wouldn't be good for Katya to find me there right now. She's always hated me, and old feuds aside, she's still in pain. Yeah, Kárin picked up on it like a hawk on a field mouse a thousand feet below. She's brilliant, isn't she? I'm so sorry. Yes, I did have a great time up until then. And it wasn't a waste. Tell Rachel it was wonderful to meet Brittany. I'll talk to you in the next couple of days. Okay. Bye."

"Hey Roni. Sorry about pulling the disappearing act."

"I figured out what you were doing, but you scared the shit out of me. You were gone even before we found out what was going on. It was like the earth opened up. Diya and I had turned this place upside down before she looked out the front door and saw your car was gone."

"Kárin saw Katya's collar from the table, all the way into the living room. My fiancée's pretty sharp, isn't she?"

"You're kidding me? Kárin figured it out from that? But how did she know it was mom?"

"Because she wouldn't be carrying on so much for anybody else unless she'd met somebody and then lost her boyfriend or husband. Even then, it was just too intense. It all made sense, so we just split. Make sure once everything has calmed down to let Gideon know what happened to us and why we cut out. Anyway, next weekend is temple. We'll see everybody soon."

"Make me a promise?"

"What?"

"Don't ever pull that again, no matter what the circumstances. For a minute, I thought you'd been kidnapped!"

I laughed at her.

"It's not funny, Aly. It scared me. Really scared me."

"Okay. Never again. I promise. I'll call you tonight about ten, okay?"

"Okay. Later."

I turned to Kárin. She just looked back at me.

"I had to promise. She made me."

"Promise what?"

"Not to ever disappear like that again, under any circumstances."

"I seriously doubt this particular set of circumstances will present itself again. You do know that the burial will be tomorrow, don't you? It wouldn't happen today, on the first day of Chanukah, but it actually could be postponed for an additional seven days, if taken literally. First thing in the morning, I'd clear out your calendar and reschedule, if you plan on going. I'll go with you if you want, I'll stay with Lidi if you want, or I'll just stay in the background if you'd like."

"Where I go, you go, my love," I said, taking her hand.

"Mommy? What's happening?"

"Lidi, you never met her, but Mommy Sasha's mother died today. The woman that came into Papa's house is Mommy Sasha's sister, Katya, just like Aunt Roni. She was just very, very sad. She didn't ever talk to everybody else in the family so she only had your grandmother Aronov, and grandmother A. only had Katya."

"Oh."

My phone rang less than ten minutes later.

"Hi, Roni. Have arrangements been made?"

"Yeah. Tomorrow at eleven in the morning. Papa is going to lay her next to Sasha. Oh, Aly, we hadn't talked for years, but she was still my Mama. Why did it have to be so hard for us? Why couldn't we have talked?"

"Roni, you tried. You aren't the one that made the decision to cut communications. Don't beat yourself up."

"I know. It just hurts."

"I'll be there tomorrow morning about ten fifteen, okay?"

"Sure. Night."

"Good night, baby sister."

As I ended the call, I realized that we were in front of Kárin's apartment.

"Are you going to stay here tonight?"

"Would it bother you if I did?"

"Not really. I mean, if you want to be alone to think or whatever..."

"Tell me the truth. Truth!"

"I don't want you to sleep here. And I don't ever want you to sleep here. It was a rule that I made for you not to move in, and I made it with good intentions, but the reasons why I had that rule have already been fulfilled. As far as I'm concerned, you can move in anytime you want."

"Well, you can relax. The only reason I'm here is to get a suit for the funeral. Why don't you and Lidi just stay here and move the car if a cop comes by? I'll be back in a sec."

"You're a stinker!"

"I can be."

It took about twenty minutes for Kárin to come back down. She had two hanging up bags slung over her shoulder and was dragging a roller suitcase. As she approached the car, I leaned over and popped the latch to the back glass. She stowed everything inside and we drove home.

"Damn, did you bring everything but the kitchen sink?"

"That's what the suitcase is for...it's got the sink. It breaks down into four pieces so it's easier to transport."

"You're a regular comedian. If you had brought the toilet as well, I'd call you a regular commodian."

Kárin glanced over the back seat, making sure that Lidi was still asleep.

"I want you to listen very carefully. What's in the past is in the past. Draw a line in the sand, right here, right now, in this car. There's before now, there's now, and there's after now. And the only thing that counts is after now. No matter how much friction there was between you and Antoniya, no matter how much friction there was between Antoniya and the rest of her family, no matter how much friction there was between you and Katya, guess which two categories that doesn't fall into?"

"I'm going to say now and after now."

"Correct. Tomorrow isn't about you. It's about Katya. If she wants to take something out on you, let her. If she wants to punch you in the chest over and over, don't swing back, and for God's sake, don't turn your back on her even if to walk away and avoid the confrontation. Just stay there and take the pain. Do you understand what I'm saying to you? I know you're not Jewish, but there's six thousand years of drama behind this. You guys have only got two thousand behind you," Kárin finished with a smile on her face.

"Right. Don't react. Don't back down. Don't turn away. Don't retaliate. Sort of like dealing with a bear attack, right?"

"Exactly, except you can look her in the eyes. In fact, that's best. But don't glare or show a hateful face. Show total empathy, if you can. If you can't, show apathy."

"Gotcha, mon colonel," I said, saluting her.

"You think this shit is funny. It's not. I'm just trying to help you. And besides, if she goes just totally ape shit on you, I'll be right there and I'll do the restraining, all right?"

"Aw, I gots my own bodyguard. Ain't that cute?"

Kárin punched me in the leg.

"Ouch!"

"Don't be a bitch."

"Yes, my love."

After we got Lidi into her PJs and into bed, we got all of Kárin's things put away. That's a lie. We got all the important things that had to hang up, hung up, by crushing everything into Lidi's closet.

"We're going to buy an armoire for our bedroom. I know it will eat some floor space, but it will have an additional set of drawers in the bottom, and I can hang up a ton of my stuff."

"Okay."

"I'm sorry. That sounded bad. I'm not trying to boss you around. It was more of a suggestion to myself that I made out loud. Sometimes

I talk to myself when I'm working. I just forget that now there are people around me."

"Don't worry, I do the same thing at work. It used to drive Franny crazy until she sort of got used to it. She was forever asking 'What?' until she got the routine down."

"I think we do need to talk about something though."

"Uh oh. That sounded a bit ominous."

"With you and Sasha, who would you say wore the pants in the family?"

"Neither. I was the chef, and I was the technology person. She was the brilliant one with regard to relationships, street smarts, and defusing situations…like you did tonight. But we weren't like a lot of lesbian couples where one of us was the alpha."

"So with us, who would you say wears the pants?"

"I never thought about it before. I guess we both have strong points. Does there have to be a boss? Now that you ask, with Sasha, she told me several times that even though she was seven years older than me, I was her equal in every way."

"Thank you. That's what I wanted to hear. Only in our case, you're two years older than me, but we're on equal footing. A lot of people consider me a bit...aggressive? Femme, but most definitely a bit of a tough exterior. Probably because of things like tonight. I find myself in a situation, and I quickly react and engage. But if I ever seem to make the wrong decision, or take ahold of the reins, feel free to take them from me if you think of something better to do. Or if you just don't feel like doing anything at the moment, throw the reins to me and I'll drive. Either way."

"How about this? How about shut up and take me to bed. It's late, but we don't have to get up quite as early as normal, so we could stand to make a little playtime?"

"Playtime is good. What did you have in mind?"

"Full on. Only this time, full on sex."

"I could do full on sex. Yes, I think I could."

The next morning at eight fifteen, the alarm went off. It was nice to get the extra hour and a half to at least counteract being up late a little. Everybody got up and ate a bowl of oatmeal and drank some juice first. Then we all brushed our teeth and got dressed.

"Lidi, come here, please..." I hollered.

"What?"

"What would you think about wearing some lip gloss today? Just this once."

"Oh, goody," she said, jumping up and down.

"Hold still now."

I painted her lips with the colored gloss and told her to go and look at it in the mirror. It was a very light pinkish color, so it didn't look garish on such a young child. It really made her day. Kárin and I were both dressed in black, of course. I was wearing a dress and Kárin was wearing a black suit.

"Aren't you the typical lesbian? Pants!"

"I don't have a black dress other than a ball gown. I've got two of those. I do. I just don't think it's quite appropriate for a funeral."

"I'm just kidding. I don't have a black skirt and jacket. I have a charcoal dress, but I thought black would be better. Especially with black hose and pumps."

"Well, I think you look beautiful," she said giving me a kiss.

"Watch out, you'll mess up my lip gloss."

"Probably not. If you used the one that's on the front edge of the cabinet in the bathroom, I used that one too. We should match."

"Cute."

"I thought so. So what are your instructions?" I was quizzed.

"One: don't be confrontational. Two: if struck, don't fight back, take the pain. Three: under no circumstances turn and walk away, that will only exacerbate the issue."

"What else?" asked Kárin.

"I don't remember any 'else'..."

"What's before is before. And be nice."

"Okay. I'll try."

"No, you'll do."

We arrived at the temple where the graveyard was, exactly when we had planned, at ten fifteen. Roni and Michael were already there. Grigoriy and Gabi were also there. Gideon and Esther were somewhere with the rabbi, and Valery and Diya were almost there, according to Roni. There would be lots of other people of course, but not this early.

I walked up to each person, one at a time, and gave them a hug. Kárin and Lidi were right behind me. Kárin shook everybody's hand. Everyone mussed up Lidi's hair just a little bit, so by the time we'd interacted with the family, she looked totally disheveled.

AFTER SASHA

"Roni, look at what Kárin taught Lidi to do with her leefa hair," I said.

"Did you just say leefa hair? I never thought about it before. She does though. You don't hear that word much unless you're in Israel." Roni answered back.

"Go ahead, Lidi, show Aunt Roni."

All eyes were now on Lidi. She turned her head down low and shook her hair violently around while pushing it down with her fingers. Then she pulled her head back up straight, put her fingers in the middle pulling slightly to the sides and shook her hair from side to side. When she was done, her hair was fluffed up a lot, but it was relatively cohesive and looked good to go. She crossed one leg behind the other, put her hands palms out to either side, and did a curtsy like Shirley Temple had so many times. Everybody clapped for her.

"That's amazing, Lidi," said Gabrielle.

The room suddenly got quiet. Too quiet. I turned around and saw Gideon walking toward us with Katya, her arm interlocked with his. Both had a tear in their collars, even though they were both reform. I put my arms down by my sides and took a deep breath. My heart was pounding in my chest. I slowly closed the distance between us. I could almost hear an audible gasp collectively from the group as I did so. The look on Katya's face wasn't very pleasant, but not as bad as it might have been. I got very close to Katya, and in a quiet, calm, even voice, addressed her. "Yekateryna, I am so very sorry for your loss," I said as I moved closer, and although she was very stiff, I gave her a light hug and kissed her on the cheek.

"Thank you. That's very kind."

"I know that this might not be the most appropriate of places for this, but I've had to find out myself how very precious life is, and how short it can be. Would you come with me? I have somebody that would like to meet you."

I put one hand on her upper arm, gently tugging her in my direction, and used my opposite hand to direct her toward our group. She held onto Gideon's arm tightly. Gideon, ever so lightly, loosened her hand from his arm. Katya followed right up to Lidi.

"Yekateryna, this is your niece, Lidiya. Lidi, this is your Aunt Katya. Use your best manners please, Lidi."

Lidi held her hand out eagerly to Katya, knowing none of the history of the family, and so entering the relationship without passion or prejudice.

"Hello, Aunt Katya. I'm Lidi. I'm very pleased to meet you. You're quite beautiful."

Katya held onto her hand for quite some time, and Lidi never made a move to pull back. Eventually, Katya knelt down on one knee in front of Lidi, without letting go of Lidi's hand. She stared at Lidi's face, her dress, both sides of her head, and finally dropped Lidi's hand to pick up her Star of David. Then she looked straight into Lidi's eyes. Her hands came slowly up and pressed into Lidi's back, pulling her tightly to her.

"Sasha. Sasha. Sasha."

"My mommy's name is Sasha. She got shot and died when I was just a baby. I have all of her pictures though. If you want to, I could show you sometime."

"Your mommy's name was Alexandra Irena Aronov?"

"Yes. What is your Sasha's name?"

"Alexandra...Irena...Aronov.... Oh, my God. What have I done? What have I done?"

Katya fell to both knees and practically smothered Lidi. She broke down crying almost as badly as she had at Papa's house last night, rocking Lidi back and forth. You could tell by the look on Lidi's face, it was a bit overwhelming and that she wanted to be released, but she held steadfastly and never tried to break away.

"I'm very sorry about your mommy. I saw you at Papa's house last night. We left so you wouldn't be sadder because my mommy was there."

"Lidi! Shush!" I ventured.

"What?"

"Lidi, it's all right. Don't worry about it. Don't worry at all. I never even knew about you. Oh, you are so beautiful. You look just like your mommy," said Katya.

"That's okay. I still have Grig and Val and Roni. I'm not alone."

"But I was, and I didn't have to be. I never realized until just this second."

Katya got up from the floor and walked towards me. I tensed up, and out of the corner of my eye saw Kárin tighten up her entire body, if need be. Katya walked up so that our nose tips were about four inches apart.

"Aly. How will you ever begin to forgive me? I'm such an awful person. I don't deserve to have a family like you."

I carefully, slowly, reached my hands out, grasped her shoulders, and began to pull her toward me until we were pressed into each other. Her arms were around my back, then I moved my arms down hers and began to return her hug.

"There's nothing to forgive. What's happened before now, is in the past. What happens after now, is in the future. All that's important is how we decide to live in the future. Right?"

Katya nodded her head, but she was weeping nonetheless.

"You're my sister, and nothing will ever change that. Nothing. Brothers and sisters don't always get along. Let's just say that we've gone through that period, and now it's time for us to be proud of each other, okay?"

Again she nodded. Lidi walked up and held onto the back of Katya's leg, and Katya reached down with one hand and played with Lidi's hair. From there, it devolved into a group hug. A family hug. A long overdue hug. I think everybody felt better than they had when the day started. I think the healing could begin for the entire family.

CHAPTER EIGHTEEN

Thank goodness the next week was very, very quiet. Every day Kárin got a little more stuff to bring over after work. And thank goodness the next weekend was totally free of commitments. We didn't have church or temple. We didn't move anything on the weekend. Saturday I cooked a nice dinner and Sunday Kárin cooked dinner. We cleaned the apartment, but we didn't exactly do a spring cleaning; more of a pickup and not much else. We talked about playing hooky on Monday, but we were planning on taking more time off work at the very end of the year, so we decided against it. I had some that I had to use during the month or I would lose it, but I could still get it in between Christmas and New Year's Day.

The following week was pretty slow...dead slow. Kárin's fundraising was sort of at a halt. There were two types of people when it came to donations at the end of the year. One type is the group that are filthy rich and feel an associated guilt. Ones who assuaged that guilt by giving away a mere pittance of what they owned. The other type is the group of people that are still uncertain what the end of the year is going to look like on the financial bottom line. Money had already been depleted for the year, and they would wait until well after

the first of the year to give money away. They usually cut off the year
with the end of December, but there was also the accounting work to be
done to find out how the previous year actually ended up by comparing
actual money with projected and budgeted amounts.

And for me, there were very few court cases. We still had some
important work to be done, but quite frankly there was a lot more
dancing and prancing for deals to be struck, avoiding separations of
families and institutionalizing children. Everybody in the system was
fairly lenient and congenial, which was almost always to the benefit of
the children. And that's what it's all about, after all.

The weirdness started on Friday night. Weirdness? No, maybe a
more appropriate word was freakiness. Out of nowhere, Kárin told me
that she wanted to spend Shabbath with the family. I told her I'd call
Papa and ask.

"No need. I already have."

I was surprised. Out of the blue she wanted to do this, and she'd
already set it up. Of course, this is typical of Kárin I was learning. It
was why she'd been appointed to become the new foundation CEO. So
we drove over to Papa's house, dressed nicely. Not overdone, but more
than casual. Everybody was there. Even Val, which was a rarity on a
busy night for the restaurant. And Grig—he was supposed to be out on
sea trials. I wondered about that. I figured I'd corner him later in the
night and find out what the story was. Either that or maybe talk to
Gabrielle. And then I saw her, looking differently than I'd ever seen
her before. Katya. She looked...elegant. I know that I'd not seen her
for the better part of seven years, but she'd matured really well. She
was as beautiful as Sasha had been, but in her own, unique way.

For the first time since the funeral, she told us the story of her
personal journey. She and Antoniya had been relatively close at first,
but as she got older, their relationship had begun to deteriorate. Two
years after she and Antoniya pretty much splintered from the rest of the
family, she felt nothing but anxiety and depression. She saved every
penny she could for a year, then bought a one-way plane ticket to
Israel. She lived in a Kibbutz for two years, farming. She studied
Judaism with great intensity, and although she still considers herself
Reform, she undertook all the education she could for those two years,
and an additional year when she moved to Haifa. She'd met a young
man in Haifa, but their relationship had not been a serious one. He'd

wanted to get married, but she still didn't know where she was going in life.

There is only one rabbinical shul in the United States that is both Reform and accepts women, and it's here in New York. It totally blew us all away when she quietly told everybody that she was in her second year. She was going to be a rabbi! When we heard the news, everybody shouted out their congratulations to her. She visibly blushed and hung her head.

"Please, everybody. I have a request, and I know that it will be very hard for some of you. I know now what Sasha felt, being shunned. In my case, I made the conscious decision to shun myself, so to speak. I ask for your forgiveness, as I've asked God for forgiveness every night for the last five years during prayers. Everything that we stand for as Jewish people, I've acted against. I've been trying to find the way to approach the family since coming back to America. I think I'd planned to wait until I graduated from shul, as if that would show you the changes I'd made. I mean, really being able to show you positive proof. But I realize that I should have come to your door the first hour after my plane landed back here."

"There is nothing to forgive, my child. Nothing. You are a part of me just as my right hand is. My heart was heavy and pained for the last years when I thought that I'd lost you forever, but you were always with me, closer than you ever will know," came the healing words from Papa.

Katya ran from her chair to Papa's side and embraced him tightly for a long, long time. Finally, she went back to her seat, and everybody along the way reached out to touch her hand, her arm, her cheek. Grig took her hand in his and kissed the back of it.

"Enough of this. This is Shabbath! Shabbat Shalom!" hollered Papa.

We did the whole bit. Lidi and I knew many of the prayers and blessings for this, and we enjoyed it immensely, especially being with the family, which is what it's all about. For somebody who was 'sort of' Jewish by 'tradition' only, Kárin knew everything. Reform, sure, but she remembered everything. Like she'd said herself on more than one occasion, she was a pretty smart cookie. Just when I thought everything was settling in for a late night, Papa rose from the table and announced that it was probably time for everybody to split up for the night.

"Tomorrow will be a busy day and everybody needs their sleep. Go in peace, each of you, and remember every one of the people at this table tonight in your prayers."

It seemed a little odd, but I gave in to his will. Kárin, Lidi and I loaded into Kárin's SUV and headed home. I never did get a chance to find out what changed with Grigoriy's plans. Kárin put Lidi to bed, then came back into the living room with me.

"Lover, I don't know why, but I'm beat. Would you mind if we went to bed early?"

"No, that's perfectly fine. You know I'll do anything for you. You don't have to beg," I smiled at her.

"I know. I really do."

I got up and took her hand, following her into the bedroom, turning off lights on the way. Kárin reached under the pillows and got our pajamas out. That in and of itself was sort of strange. I guessed that she really was tired if she just wanted to get dressed for bed and die on a weekend night. Still, I walked to her side of the bed and undressed her, put her clothes in the hamper, and gently, lovingly, caringly dressed her for bed. I peeled back the covers and held her hand while she climbed into bed. I changed, went around to my side, and got in beside her. I turned the light off immediately. We were facing each other. I put my hand up on her cheek.

"Sweetie?"

"Hmm?"

"Are you all right? Really?"

"Of course. Why do you ask?"

"You just seem subdued tonight. It's not like you. Just having a night?"

"Not at all. I'm just tired. And lying next to my lover makes me feel better than I've ever felt in my life. So relaxed. Believe me, I'm good."

"Good night," I said, leaning over her and giving her a lasting kiss.

She put her arm around me and scratched lightly on my back for a few seconds, then drifted off.

I wasn't that tired and sleep didn't come that quickly for me. I was probably awake for another hour, maybe more, but I didn't want to move so as not to disturb Kárin.

I heard the alarm go off in the morning. I was confused. I didn't remember setting the alarm.

"Did you set the alarm? I don't remember doing it."

"I sure did. Get up, sleepy head. Let's go in the kitchen and get some breakfast."

"Oh, God. Give me a few minutes. I'm dead."

"Nope, get your ass out of bed. Now!" she said, grabbing me by the hand and pulling on me hard and fast, once again, demonstrating her brute strength.

"What the hell is going on?"

"You'll see. Go to the kitchen."

She went into Lidi's room and sat on the side of the bed. She started gently shaking her, telling her to get up, it was going to be a special day. Immediately, Lidi sprang to life.

"Is it today? Is it going to be today?"

"Shhh. Remember, don't say a word."

"I won't!" whispered Lidi, although I heard her as I walked toward the kitchen.

Coffee was ready pretty quickly, and by the time it was ready to pour, there were bagels and creamed cheese on the table waiting to be eaten. I looked up at the clock on the stove.

"Are you freaking kidding me? It's not even eight o'clock yet!"

"I know. We don't have much time. We need to get up and get ready now. Quickly, quickly, children!"

Was I in a dream? Had I really gotten up? The Freak Show, Part II, carried over from last night.

"Okay, okay, okay...let me get this straight...Papa said everybody get sleep because tomorrow was going to be a busy day. And we're not going to temple, right?"

"That would be correct, sir!"

"Stop it, Stimpy! Would you like to explain to me exactly what's going on?"

"I would not. Eat, eat!"

Lidi was grinning the whole time, like she was a cat that had just swallowed a mouse.

"What the *hell* is going on?"

"First, don't be cross with anybody. Second, eat, eat. We need to get ready."

I gave up. I ate as quickly as I could without choking on my bagel. Without me asking, Kárin had taken a cherry chip bagel, spread cream cheese on it, and put it on my plate. I didn't even question it. I ate most of it. I just didn't want to argue with her anymore.

When we were done, while Lidi was still in her PJs, Kárin took her into the bathroom and sat her on the counter. She painted Lidi's fingernails a light pink. Again, I refused to ask any more questions. I figured there wasn't any way I was going to pry it out of her anyway, so why try? Lidi brushed her teeth and then got dressed in jeans and a long-sleeved top. Kárin dragged me into the bathroom, put toothpaste on both of our brushes, and began brushing her teeth. I brushed mine as well. I was getting more confused by the minute.

After our teeth, Kárin took fingernail polish remover and cleaned off my chipped polish, going back after that and putting on a fresh coat of crimson.

"You know, I'm not your little doll that you can dress up and make up and everything else."

"I'm going to tell you this one time and one time only. Shut up," she said, poking me in the chest with her pointer finger, hard enough that it hurt the smallest bit...

I let out a deep sigh. She used the curling iron on my hair, enhancing my natural waves, then put in a few bobby pins and a pair of barrettes, and sprayed the whole thing when she was done. She took a warm wash cloth and cleaned my face well, drying it after with a face towel. She had the nerve to put on my makeup. Everything from base to rouge to eyeliner to mascara to eye shadow. I felt like a little teenager being made up by her mother. She pointed to the side of the tub indicating I should sit while she did her nails and hair and makeup, although with her hair, she just brushed it out well and then sprayed it a little. She did put a long barrette in the back that reached nearly from side to side.

"Go to the bathroom. It might be a little while."

I was going nuts. Absolutely nuts. When we went into the bedroom, she got out underwear for both of us. I put mine on while she did hers.

"Would you like to dress me, Mommy? Or should I do that myself?"

"Just pick jeans and a sweater."

Nice makeup, fresh nail polish, and jeans? I put the back of my hand on her forehead.

"What is that for?"

"Just seeing if you're sick or something."

"Nope. Hurry up. We're already running a little behind."

She made me and Lidi scurry through the bits and bobs, and then shooed us to the Murano. Seriously?! The woman was deranged. But whatever she had in mind, Lidi knew what it was. You'd have thought she'd gotten to see the real Santa Claus. Kárin drove us down some streets I wasn't familiar with.

"Where are we?"

"You'll see soon enough."

Gawd! I just watched the scenery without saying another word. Finally, she slowed, then turned into a parking lot beside a large building with a sign in front proclaiming, 'Polish Community Center.' Aha. Seeds began germinating…but I was wrong. Boy, oh boy, was I wrong. I couldn't be more wrong if I tried. We weren't the first ones there. Upon entering, I found that Roni and Michael were already there. Bri and Danny were there. Lexa and Bobby. Zach and Julie. Penny. Martha was there with Beryl. Estefanía and María-Elena. Franny and her husband. Mac, and several people I didn't recognize. All of them were really dressed up, with the exception of me, Kárin, Lidi, Estefanía, and María-Elena.

I was ushered back to a room by Bri. I noticed that somebody I'd never met before was escorting Kárin to a different room. And Estefanía and María-Elena were being split up as well. Lidi went with Kárin. After we had gotten into the room, I grabbed Bri by her upper arm and got into her face.

"You tell me what the fuck is going on here right damned now or I'll rip your arm off and shove it up your ass!"

"Tsk, tsk. Such language. And I thought you were a lady."

Before either of us could say another word, there was a slight knock on the door and it opened. An elderly woman stepped in with a dress wrapped in plastic, a pair of shoes, a veil, and a bouquet.

"Don't tell me!" I said with my voice raised.

"Okay, I won't. Now let's get you dressed, missy!"

Brianna pretty much took over the situation, helping me into the dress. Diya had done a perfect job. It fit me as if it were painted on, to perfection. It was even more beautiful than I'd ever imagined. I slipped my feet into my shoes and she placed my veil on, although to the back for the moment.

"Oh, sweetie pie, you are so beautiful. I know that Sasha is looking down on you right now and she has the biggest smile on her face. I almost think that she's sent you an earthbound angel in the form of Kárin. It seems so perfect."

My eyes started tearing up.

"No, no, no, no. Don't make your face run! Suck it in!"

I blinked several times to get it to stop.

After we were done, Bri kept looking at her watch.

"So what time is this whole thing supposed to go down?" I asked.

"What thing is that?" she said in reply.

"This surprise wedding thing being sprung on me."

"Oh, I don't think you know half of it yet," she said, cackling maniacally.

"Jesus. This day just keeps getting better and better," I mumbled half under my breath.

Bri looked at her watch again. Finally, there was another knock on the door. It was Papa and Dad. I noticed that they weren't just dressed up, they were both wearing tuxedos. Ah. It was all was starting to all come together. The question of whether I had any desires for the wedding. The fact that Kárin was going to take care of everything. The fact that this weekend was 'not available' to Rabbi Abrahamson, although he had a twinkle in his eye. Everything. I'd been duped.

"Exactly eleven thirty. That's only about eight minutes. We should hear the music," Dad smiled broadly at me.

I hugged him tightly.

"Papa. Sasha never quit doing good. Through all of you. You've done so much for us. And I love you all so much. So very much."

"And why shouldn't a father love his daughter?" he said, embracing me back.

Now it was Papa, Dad, and Bri all three looking at their watches constantly. Finally, it was less than two minutes away. Papa gave me a final kiss and headed for the main hall. Dad walked up to me and looked me smilingly in the face, his eyes watering.

"You know, I meant it when I said you caught the brass ring twice. But Aly? In your case, I think both times your ring was pure platinum."

Man, you talk about coming as close to the edge of losing it as possible without going right over! He brought my veil down over the front of my face. Bri gave me one last hug and a kiss and dashed off.

"Good luck, babe. See you at the altar."

Of course. She was my matron of honor! Finally, it was time. Dad walked me to the doors of the large hall, taking my arm in his. There were large double doors on either side. As we got to the doors, I looked to the other side. Also being escorted there was María-Elena, dressed oh so beautifully, in a traditional wedding gown with a train and a long veil, and holding the same Akito white roses in her bouquet that I held. It was going to be a double wedding! Estefanía intentionally kept their engagement a secret after Kárin approached her about the double wedding. Yeah, ain't she a sharp cookie? I realized for the first moment, although they were totally different women, this was exactly the same feeling I got with Sasha, but perhaps magnified by the presence of Lidi, which Sasha gave me.

María-Elena smiled at me and waived. I smiled and waved back. She had her hand over her mouth like a giggling little schoolgirl. It was a precious moment. I can't describe the rush I had. No words would ever do it justice. Then the music started. They were playing The Prince of Denmark's March, commonly called The Trumpet Voluntary. We both started walking down each side of the auditorium, which had the chairs set up to make two aisles about fifteen feet apart. I had met her escort once before, Manolo Escobar. He was the host of the first PFLAG meeting I went to with Kárin.

Set up at the front was a sort of stage with people on it. Rabbi Abrahamson was on one side, and Pastor Douglass was on the other side. The rabbi was in a vest and a Jewish waist coat, the pastor in a dark grey suit. I wondered who was filling in for the rabbi, and how Kárin had convinced him that our wedding was more important than his services for this day.

As we approached within about fifteen feet of the altar, out of a side door came Estefanía escorted by Martha, who looked really sharp in a dark blue three-piece suit, and my lovely bride, Kárin along with her friend from her fundraising efforts. Just like the two of us from our end, Kárin was wearing more of a casual dress and Estefanía was wearing a traditional gown with a train and veil. All four of us were in pure white, and all four of us carried the same white roses. It couldn't have been timed more perfectly. Kárin and I came to a halt, side by side, directly in front of the rabbi at the same instant that the other two came centered upon Pastor Douglass.

Standing by me, as my matron, was Bria. Her dress was a nice turquoise color. Kárin's matron was Sheila Wørsc, also dressed in turquoise. Estefanía's maid of honor was Mac, dressed in turquoise as well. And on the far side from me, María-Elena's maid of honor was Denise. You guessed it…dressed in turquoise. It was almost like being in a Disney fairytale. Immediately prior to us coming out, they'd collected my rings. I assumed, of course, that was so Kárin and I could place the rings on each other's fingers during the ceremony. Behind me, I heard a noise and turned my head.

"Hi, Mommy! You all look pretty!" she said very loudly.

The entire auditorium erupted with laughter. In her hands was a white velvet pillow about a foot square. Laid across the pillow, in order, were the rings for each of the four of us. She was dressed in a white dress and was wearing both her cross and her Star of David. I couldn't have been prouder of my little girl in a million years.

"You look pretty too, baby. If your Mommy Sasha could see you now, she would think you were the most beautiful girl in the whole wide world."

"I know." Lidi said obviously trying to whisper, failing miserably.

The auditorium erupted again at the humor and the innocence of Lidi. Kárin squeezed my hand. I looked at her and mouthed the words, 'Thank you.' She replied by squeezing my hand again and nodding her head a little. I then mouthed, 'I love you.' She mouthed back, 'I love you too, honey.'

The rabbi started off.

"Shalom and welcome, all of you who gather today for the marriage of these two couples—couples who have come forth to be witnessed in this ceremony of marriage, couples who pledge their love for each other and commit themselves to the lifelong journey of matrimony. I'm Rabbi Abrahamson, and I represent the Jewish component of this grand display of dedication with all of you as witnesses today. It is unfortunate that the Holy Roman Catholic Church still does not recognize the union of same-sex marriages, for both Estefanía and María-Elena are lifelong, dedicated, loving members of that institution. For this reason, the pastor and I will officiate for them as well. We are all God's children, equal in his eyes."

"Good morning. My name is Pastor Douglass. I am the voice of all of the Protestants gathered today. Although we may be severely outnumbered today, still, we'll do our best to hold up our end."

Once again, the auditorium gave a good round of laughter.

"I feel very comfortable being here this morning. I perform many marriage ceremonies. Some I do gladly. Some, to tell you the truth, I've performed with a little trepidation. Even with premarital counseling, I don't always get the same degree of comfort and feelings from couple to couple, but today, I bring you glad tidings. I don't feel, I simply know. I know it my heart. These couples before you today will keep their promises, made before you and in the eyes of God, that until death do them part, they will remain faithful and true. Welcome."

The rabbi began to speak again, "Sanctus, Sanctus, Sanctus Dominus Deus Sabaoth, plenisunt Caeli et terra gloria tua. Hosanna in excelsis. Benedictus qui venit in nomine Domini. Hosanna in excelsis. In nomine Patris, et Filii, et Spiritus Sancti. Amen. Welcome one and all. These words are the words that would have been spoken had these two women been able to consecrate their union within their church. They are not words that belong to the church, at least so I believe. They belong to the people of the church. Words of God. And so I mean no disrespect. I say these words so that they may be shared and experienced by those who come together today to be wed."

"We must remember that there are two important principles at work today here in this building, and they work in an intricately woven harmony to each other, as though they were one. The first is that God is the divine wisdom, spirit, leader, father to all man, and creator of the heavens and the earth. The second is the bond between those to be wed. These vows seem to be written on paper far too often, instead of etched in granite to stand for all time. Today, they will be carved in stone before your very eyes as a tangible, visible proof of the miracles that God gives each of us in our daily lives," Pastor Douglass followed.

Rabbi Abrahamson poured a glass of wine for Kárin and me, and Pastor Douglass poured a glass of wine and brought two wafers for Estefanía and María-Elena. Kárin and I both drank from the same glass first as the rabbi gave a blessing in Hebrew. When we were done, he took the glass and set it back on the temporary dais. Mac and Denise helped Estefanía and María-Elena kneel down at the edge of the stage. Pastor Robinson first laid a wafer on each of their tongues, then poured a small drink of wine in their mouths.

"This wine, as it has been blessed, has become the blood of Christ. And the wafer, also offered as a sacrament and having been blessed, has become the body of Christ. Eat this and drink this as a display of devotion and reverence to our Lord, Jesus Christ, and the Father, and the Holy Spirit," spoke Pastor Douglass.

The rest of the ceremony was done before I knew it. Everybody had taken rings from Lidi and exchanged them between each of the pairs. Kárin now broke the glass we'd drunk from twice, in the traditional handkerchief. Both the rabbi and the pastor had read numerous blessings, both in English and Hebrew. One thing that did stand out in my mind though, was when Kárin and I were facing each other, standing sideways to the stage, and I could see all of my family. Mom and Dad, and all of the Aronovs, including Katya, sitting next to Papa with her arm interlaced with his, and both were smiling. In the front eight to ten rows on Estefanía's side were dozens of Hispanic attendees. I never, in a million years, would have been able to predict this spectacle. That's what it was...a spectacle. Absolutely spectacular! Finally, all four of us raised back our veils and kissed our respective brides. Cheers went up through the crowd.

Rabbi Abrahamson presented Kárin and me, and Pastor Douglass presented Estefanía and María-Elena next.

"Friends, may I present to you today, Kárin Cecylia and Alison Jeanette Aronov-Lockewood. Mozeltov!" Kárin had decided to just take her last name and use it as a third middle name.

Everybody in the crowd shouted mazeltov in unison. Pastor Douglass presented the other girls next.

"Amigos y familia, les presento, Estefanía Paulina and María-Elena Julieta Alvarez de Medina. Felicidades!"

Everybody in the auditorium stood and cheered for the four of us. Suddenly, seemingly from nowhere, about a dozen people started grabbing the chairs and setting them up in rows around the outside of the huge room we were in. And when I say huge, I mean huge. As I said, there were probably around three hundred people in attendance, but there could easily have been another hundred with no problem. Other people opened the double doors and tables were brought in laden with food. Additional tables were brought in and immediately two girls started spreading out glasses and filling them with ice. As well, wine glasses were being set out on yet another table. And the most amazing thing was that all of the staff were dressed in traditional Polish costume. It was delightful, and all moving at the speed of light.

Mom took the ring pillow from Lidi and put it in her large purse for safe keeping and to keep it clean since it was white velvet. Dad was talking to Papa. Katya still stood, like a leach, with her arm through Papa's crooked arm. Diya and Gabrielle were chatting away. Val and Grig were talking animatedly among a group of about ten or twelve other men. I still wanted to know how Grig got to be here. Estefanía and María-Elena were talking to the members of the Hispanic community. The rabbi and my pastor were talking, with Abrahamson holding his hand on the pastor's shoulder; both were talking back and forth and nodding their heads constantly. I began to walk towards the family and suddenly, Kárin shrieked at the top of her lungs.

"Oh, my God! You're here!"

She apparently wasn't the only one who could work a little magic. Estefanía had arranged, without Kárin's knowledge, to have Kárin's parents flown in from Denton, her sister, Kalista and brother-in-law, Kyle, from Seattle, as well as her Babcia and Dziadek from Maryland. She hadn't expected them until at least Christmas, if then, but she kept in constant contact with them so they knew all about me and our relationship and most everything else. She let go of my hand and ran to them, hugging them around the neck, holding on for dear life. Estefanía caught my eye, winked at me, and gave me the thumbs up sign. I took both my hands and put them over my mouth, then opened them wide towards her like I was blowing her the biggest kiss. Kárin ran over to me, practically jerked my arm out of its socket, and dragged me to her parents. We got along famously from the word go.

About five minutes later, Kárin pulled away and ran over to Estefanía and her beautiful bride. She dragged them over to us. She introduced them to her parents.

"Actually, we've spoken on the telephone many times. She's why we're here. You should thank her, kochanie. She's wonderful, isn't she," Mrs. Zajac said with a wink, rubbing Estefanía's cheek with her fingers, her hand balled up loosely.

"Wait a minute, I need to check something before he gets away," I said to anybody and everybody.

I looked around and panicked. I didn't see him, but then, he wasn't that tall. Finally, I spied him talking to a different group of men. I rushed over to Grigoriy.

"Spill it. Why are you here today? What happened to your sea trials? That was such an important job. It could have meant so much to your career!"

"Опускается, мало сестра. Lower your voice, little sister. I've been on my ship and I will go back. The ship is operating with a carrier battle group in the western Atlantic. We haven't broken loose with cruiser escort to go farther east. They flew me by helicopter to the carrier Teddy Roosevelt. From there I flew on pretty much a mail plane, a C2 Greyhound aircraft. They brought me to Patuxent. Then Papa sent a driver for me. I'll spend the night with Gabi and the kids, then I'll fly back out the same way I came in. So see? Никаких проблем. It's no problem"

Even as short as he is, I still had to reach up to kiss him on the cheek.

"Thank you so much for being here."

The floor in the middle was cleared, with people being moved out to the chairs in concentric circles. People were eating, drinking, and talking. It made quite a din. Then from nowhere, also dressed in traditional Polish costumes, dancers came running and tumbling out in the middle of the floor to the music of a couple dozen musicians that followed immediately behind them. They performed a Mazur first, then an olender, and next was a szot. Then they started playing the music for a cena. One of the musicians took a microphone and announced to the crowd that this would be the first dance by the Aronov-Lockewoods. I looked at Kárin, shaking my head.

"Don't do this to me. I don't know this."

"I've arranged for that. Just watch me and everybody else, and follow. I'll lead. Imagine that I am one of the men in the hats, and you are one of the ladies in the dresses. Okay?"

As if I had a choice. Fortunately, Kárin had arranged for the song to be started at about a quarter of the normal speed. There are about eight stages of the dance, with circling, promenading, twirling, and various other combinations. I felt a little more secure, that is until they sped up the music to half speed. I had trouble keeping up, but somehow I managed.

"See? I knew you could do it!" Kárin yelled at me so that I could hear her.

"You're killing me!"

She threw her head back, cackling. Before I knew what was going on, the music picked up to full speed. I felt like I was a rag doll being thrown around by a little girl. Finally, the damned dance was over. I was panting like a dog on a hot summer's day. Everybody applauded as we left the dance floor.

The man with the microphone then made the next announcement of the first dance of the Alvarez de Medinas. Obviously, Estefanía was deeply rooted in the marriage conspiracy. She'd already met with the band and given them sample music of the chacarera style of Argentina, followed by a smooth transition into a tango, native to both Argentina and Uruguay. Again, when they finished, there was applause. Then there were various combinations of dancing. Friends, family, every permutation that could be. One of them was me dancing with María-Elena and Kárin dancing with Estefanía, then we switched partners. While I was dancing with Estefanía, she looked me straight in the eye and told me that she loved me and would for all time. She was so happy, and she knew I was so happy, and at that moment in time, everything was perfect. Then she kissed me and rubbed her hands up and down my back, laying her head on my shoulder.

"I love you too, sweetie. If we'd never met, my life would be so much less complete. I'm so glad you found María-Elena. You look so beautiful together, and you both look so beautiful today."

"Pardon me, but I need to dance with my beautiful мало братской, my little sister. I don't have long before I must spend the little time I have remaining with my family and fly back to the waiting waves of the beautiful, deep ocean," Grig laughed.

Estefanía smoothly twirled herself out of contact, leaving my hand in Grig's. I looked over Grig's shoulder as we were dancing and saw Kárin holding Lidi, whirling around the dance floor. Lidi looked happier than she ever had. In fact, I knew it deep down. As the song ended, Grig kissed me on the cheek and bade me a wonderful, long, and happy life, and told me that he would see me in a couple of short months once again. All afternoon and into the evening, one person after another had pretty much just taken over and picked one, or all of us to dance with. Some we knew, some we didn't. Some were exceptional dancers, some not so much. The musicians had played a wide variety of music: from traditional Polish to jazz, to tangos and merengues, to the old standards, and to Hungarian dances. They suddenly changed styles and started playing Jewish music. I felt a tapping on my shoulder from behind. I turned around to find Yekateryna.

She was standing with her head held slightly down, with big blue eyes pointing up to me, looking like she didn't know whether to smile or cry. She was petrified, so much so she was shaking. She held hands out as if to be led. I took her hands and moved them so that she would lead. I pulled her chin up so that she no longer had her head pointing down, then kissed her cheek. I moved into her, put her one hand on my back and took her other hand and put it out, then put my hand on her back and reached out to accept her leading hand lightly. She was a little awkward at first since she'd never taken the lead dancing. I took her leading hand and pulled up against my body, more intimately. I leaned into her ear, "It's okay. Let it go. Everything is wonderful. Enjoy yourself and loosen your body. Move to the music fluidly. Act like you like me, even if you don't really."

Katya's eyes began welling up.

"Do you remember when you two had the fight at your old house and you thought she was going to kick your ass? She ended up pinning you against the wall and kissing you and squeezing your breast? I think that was the funniest thing I've ever seen in my life!"

"Oh, God, do you have to remember that? How horrible. How could that have even been me? If somebody today told me a story about that incident—if it hadn't been me, but somebody else—I would offer to counsel them. Isn't life funny? Maybe a little sick, but funny?"

"See, you *can* smile! Like I said the other day, what's past is past and what's now is now. The only important thing is what we do tomorrow. Right?"

She gave me a hug. Then I felt a tap on my shoulder again. I turned halfway around, and there stood an elderly gentleman I'd never met before. Well dressed and looking distinctly Jewish. Katya patted him on the shoulder.

"Hiya, Pauli. How's work?"

"Good, Katty-Kat. Good…as long as your father gives out good bonus checks this year!" he said, roaring with laughter.

Katya waved very demurely by just curling and uncurling her fingers several times, and walked away. I felt so bad for her at that moment, but I saw Estefanía reach out and take her hand. I don't know that Katya had truly accepted the gay community, or ever would, but she was clearly no longer a homophobe. She appeared to be Chatty Cathy with Estefanía as they danced.

Finally, the man with the microphone spoke one last time for the evening.

"This will be our last dance for the night, ladies and gentlemen.... We're going to bring up the tempo and take you to a Euroclub. So get up and shake to the music!"

Val pulled Diya out onto the floor right next to Kárin and I. The next thing I knew, right beside us were Martha and Beryl, Estefanía, and María-Elena, Denise and Mac, Lexa and Bobby, and Grig, Papa, and Katya.... I could keep going on, but it would just take too much time. Everybody was there. It wasn't so much couples dancing, as everybody in the entire crowd dancing. All of us undulating to the music, separately, yet together, in tight quarters, twisting and turning and moving around slightly so that at any given time we were in front of any of the others dancing, banging into each other constantly. The last song wasn't so much a single song, as it was about a half hour upbeat improvisation. When the musicians finally stopped playing, everybody gave them a huge round of applause, and most of us lined up to shake hands with them all. They had truly been the best performers I'd ever seen. This was the same magic that I felt the first night I went out with Sasha to see the New York Opera.

Kárin took my hand and smiled. She leaned over so I could hear her over the din in the room, "Take me home, Goose, or lose me forever!"

"You know, I had an equal crush on both of them. Even though I was gay way back then, when that movie came out I had a boy crush on Tom Cruise and a girl crush on Kelly McGillis. I think the biggest difference was with Kelly, I thought I was really in love." I giggled.

"You and me both! On both accounts," she laughed back.

It took almost an hour after that for everybody in the auditorium to find a way to say their goodbyes to every other person there, but finally the room was down to only about two dozen. The four brides went back into the rooms we used to change in and put our street clothes back on, and then we rejoined the crowd. Beryl told everybody goodbye and asked Martha for the keys. She said she was completely tired and wanted to go to the car, lay the seat back, and listen to some quiet music. Martha dug out the keys and handed them to her.

"I'll be right there, sugar. I love you," she said as she kissed Beryl.

Mac, Denise, and I all did a double take. Did one of New York's finest, Detective Captain Martha Devonshire, just tell someone that she loved her? And did she kiss her in front of everybody? Had the world gone completely mad? Or maybe Martha's just getting older and calmer and wants more stability?

"You know we saw that, don't you?" asked Mac.

"And your point would be?"

"I don't think in all the years I've known you I've ever heard you tell someone that you love them, much less kiss them in public. I've heard them tell you that they love you, and by the following week they're out the door. What gives?"

"You know, maybe it's because I never met the right woman before. Beryl is soft and sexy and feminine, but she doesn't take shit from anybody, even me. She stands up to me and she never nags me, pushes me, or tries to change me. She loves working for the fire department and loves that I work for the police department. I don't know where it's going to go, but I'm willing to find out."

"So when did you know it might be?"

"We'd been dating about four months. I guess I was in a bad mood. Looking back, I think I wanted to act out to make her want to leave me so it would be her idea. She sat me down and held my hands and told me she didn't know what was wrong, but that we'd work through it together. I never laid a finger on her, but still, I was abusive. She got up in my face with that finger of hers and told me that I should be ashamed of myself, that she knew she was only half my size and couldn't physically defend herself. She told me the mental abusiveness was twice as bad because, unlike a broken bone, sometimes those wounds didn't heal. I told her she might want to go home for the rest of the evening and sleep at her own place. She told me not to be such a pompous ass and that our relationship wasn't going to be spoiled because I was having a bad week. I literally screamed at her to get the fuck out. She informed me quietly that she was going to stay for another week, and at the end of that week, if I still wanted her to go, she'd do so with no protest. By day four, she was sitting on the couch, after a dinner that she'd cooked by the way, as she had all week long. I looked at her face and it just touched my heart. I knelt down on the carpet in front of her, put my hands on her knees, begged her forgiveness, and told her that I'd never been in love before I'd met her. I told her I wanted to keep loving her as long as I could, and I asked her to stay. That was about five months ago."

"Bee-otch, you been holdin' out!"

"No, it's just nobody's business but ours."

"Don't you want to tell the world how you two feel about each other?"

"No. Not particularly one way or the other. It's no big deal to anybody else. I love her. She loves me. We spend most of our free time together. And I know that everybody takes one look at me and sees this big butch dyke with short, spikey hair and a departmental ball cap on, wearing combats instead of shoes, and figures I've got to be the 'man of the family,' but when it comes to that, Beryl treats me as an equal, and she's a magnificently tender lover."

"Okay, TMI. Time for you to go take her home and get some of that tender mercy," I proclaimed.

Lidi had been stretched across three chairs put together side by side and asleep for about an hour, despite all of the noise. We woke her up, said good night to Mom and Dad, and then the entire Aronov clan. Estefanía had planned to avoid the expense and coldness of a hotel, so Kárin gave her and Mariá-Elana the keys to her apartment for the night. We both hugged them and told them to call us when they got up on Sunday so they could come over and we'd fix a big lunch for everybody and figure out what our plans for the next couple of days would be.

Even Katya approached me. "Shalom. I'll see you at Papa's house."

"I'd really like that, and I know Lidiya will too. Thank you for accepting us."

"The two years I worked at the Kibbutz...there were several gay women and one pair of gay men there. They didn't approach me to change me. They didn't try and tell me that they were no different than anybody else. The *showed* me. They worked the soil. They gathered the crops. They sold the produce in the market. They were stronger than me: in physical strength, in mental fortitude, in their religious beliefs, in every way. I learned that maybe they had something to teach me. Eventually, I tried to learn. That is why I am here today, and that is why I'm at rabbinical school."

I stared at her for a few short moments, then inched up to her, hugged her, and rubbed my hands up and down her back. Shortly after I started caressing her, I felt her hands come up to my back, rubbing up and down in unison with mine. We both let out a big sigh simultaneously, a cleansing breath. I smiled at her and placed the palm of my hand against her cheek. She finally turned and went to find Papa, dragging him by the arm over to where Lidi was sleeping soundly on top of a couple of coats on the chairs. She knelt down and shook Lidi gently.

"Lidiya? Hey, Lidi?"

"Hi, Aunt Kat. I'm sleepy."

"You should be. This has been a very busy day. You look so pretty dressed up in your white dress. It's almost like you were getting married today along with everybody else."

"That's what Mommy Kárin said. She said that we're all doing this together and that we'll all be a family. She said she would be my real mommy. She's going to adopt me."

"Isn't that so special! I have to go home, but I promise you, I'll see you very soon, okay?"

"Okay. Will you come to Papa's house?"

"I can't always come because of my school, but I will try whenever I can."

"Good night."

"Good night, sweet child," she said and tickled her, making Lidi laugh.

Finally, it was just the people working at the Polish Community Center cleaning up the evening's festivities, and Kárin and me. Bri and Danny had taken Lidi for the night so that she and Ingrid could spend the whole day playing tomorrow...and so that Kárin and I could have the night alone. We were finally in the car ready to drive home. She took my hand and leaned over, facing me.

"So tell me, lover...is it as good as being married to Sasha?"

I'm sure that all color left my face. I wouldn't say that I got angry, although I'm not quite sure what I felt at that exact moment. Then, actually flying into a rage, I put the flat of my hands against her chest. Bolting straight out of my seat, I pushed her all the way against her car door. I think it surprised us both that I was able to do that, especially considering how powerful and muscular she was.

"Promise me. Right now. Say the words. Say you promise."

Kárin was still startled.

"Promise what?"

"Never compare yourself to Sasha ever again!"

"I'm sorry, honey. I never meant to say that I could in any way replace her..."

"You stupid idiot! Sasha was perfect...at being herself. And you...you're perfect at being you. And quite frankly, as perfect as

Sasha was for me, if anything, you're more perfect. Just be yourself. Don't compete with a shadow on the wall. What you did here today, with everything you accomplished...don't you realize what a total fucking miracle it was for you to pull this off? Even if you are used to planning and arranging and making deals, and everything else you do.... You're thirty years old, and you did something that maybe a dozen people in all of the city of New York could pull off. Did you see Estefanía and María-Elena and how happy they were? Sure, Estefanía helped you on this, but it was all you. I know that I asked you out first, but don't you realize you picked me up a broken carcass of a person and you breathed life into me? You resurrected me. You are so completely different from Sasha...I don't even have the words. Like the northern and southern hemispheres—both are beautiful places, but in no way are they like each other. Both fit together to form a perfect world, and that's what I think of you and Sasha. You've both fit together to form my perfect world. Now, my wife, my bride, my lover, my partner, my girlfriend, my best friend, my soul mate...take me home. Take me home and take me in your arms. Love me. Make me happy."

For two or three minutes, I sat there pushing Kárin against the door, not moving my hands, not letting up the pressure. Then she finally took my arms in her hands and pushed me back with ease. She practically crawled up on top of me, forcing me now to my door. She put her face right into mine. For the slightest moment, I thought I'd gone too far without meaning to. I'd just reacted.

"I promise. For somebody who didn't have the words to describe what she wanted to say, you sure did a pretty darned good job. So now I'm going to take you home, I'm going to love you, and I'm going to make you happy. Forever and a day. I promise."

Before she could raise back up, I had my arms around her neck and was kissing her. The lights in the parking lot were on, but it was still dimly lit. We were parked at the outside edge toward the back end since we'd gotten there so early, so we were pretty much in the shadows.

"Have you ever made love in a car?" she asked me.

"Truthfully, that's one thing that's been on my bucket list for a bunch of years..."

"Sweetie, get ready to scratch it off!"

~THE END~

ᑭ About the HollyAnne Weaver ᑫ

Ms. Weaver has worked for many years in a scientifically-based career writing technical documents. An avid reader from a very young age, she gradually began writing poetry and fiction, one of her current passions. Growing up, Ms. Weaver was always fascinated with books and the ability of an author to write fiction. A sequence of emails with a close friend led to her writing longer pieces, eventually culminating in her first novel being completed in 2010. Ms. Weaver's main writing focus is on lesbian fiction, although she has projects for mysteries and historical fiction already planned.

If you have enjoyed **AFTER SASHA**
please look for HollyAnne Weaver's novel **COMING OF AGE**
from
Shadoe Publishing:
We have a chapter here for your enjoyment.

CHAPTER ONE

COMING OF AGE

I thought I was sitting in quite a pretty position. I'd just finished with University about four months before and the whole world was waiting just for me. I was young, not unattractive, moderately intelligent, and got along with most people...

Well, I thought that until the next two months passed as well and I still couldn't find a company willing to give me my first chance. I looked high and low. From companies in small little squares where you can wear trousers all the way up to the nose-in-the-air shops in the centers that still make you wear tights and skirts every day.

I'm relatively average, I guess. At twenty-two years old, I'm about five feet five-and-a half, and weigh a bit over eight stone. I've got mother's facial features but I have Dad's athletic figure. And his Irish black hair and emerald eyes. I don't stand out in a crowd, but I've never wanted for attention either.

I have had a couple of boyfriends in the past. None serious though. I was keen on a couple of boys, but it wasn't the end of the world when it didn't go farther. And one of the boys in my college had eyes for me and was so sweet, but he was way too juvenile in my opinion. Nonetheless, we dated for quite a while.

I worked part-time for a local antique shop, which I dearly loved, but would never pay well at all. And I had still lived at home since Regent's was close and would be cheaper than my own flat, so I wasn't on the straits quite yet. But I was getting thoroughly demoralized. This night was particularly harsh. I'd been to a follow-on interview and been highly encouraged. Yet when I called to find out if I'd gotten the position, not only had I been passed over but they treated me as if I had an icky disease or something; they were very rude and acted annoyed that I'd called them.

I called a couple of mates to meet at a pub. "Oh, yes, let's!" I got there on time at half seven for drinks and maybe a bit of starters. Then eight came round. Then half eight. I felt worse than I had ever in my life, I truly believe. I'd found the lowest point in my adult life. I'd moved from Coke to alcohol. People always laugh at me, but I've always liked cherries. So my usual drink is either a tequila sunrise or even just a glass of grenadine with ice. Mmm… Cherries that glow going down.

I'd had three or four of them, but certainly wasn't drunk. I got up and turned to go, taking the last sip from my glass. I caught my heel on something and managed to pour what was left of my drink straight onto a woman in the pub wearing a white shirt, black leather skirt, and black leather boots. "Oh, God, I'm *so* sorry, I'm *so* sorry" I kept saying over and over. We headed toward the loo, my with a stack of napkins and her holding her doused blouse away from her body.

As we got into the ladies', I started furiously rubbing at the stains with the napkins, with my hand under the material where I was swiping. "Hey, are you a fucking lesbian? Get your fucking hands off my tits!" First I froze, absolutely unable to move. Then it started. Tears rolled down my cheeks. I don't mean a few, I mean a non-stop rain shower, streaming down my face, puddling on the floor.

"Are you a total ninny?" She was staring at me like I was a freak of nature.

I never sobbed out loud, but somewhere from deep inside me a quiet little mouse managed to squeak out, "No. I'm not a lesbian. I'm not… It's just… I've just had the most terrible day in my life and I'm just… not…"

I told her I was so very sorry about her blouse. It was a lovely shirt. I really only noticed for the first time that her shirt was made of beautiful silk, with a woven pattern all through it much like clouds in the sky, and it was nearly but not quite transparent. I could tell she was wearing a lacy bra because of the scalloped edge tracing its way underneath the flimsy top. And what that bra held in place was more than I had to offer.

"Well, just let me pay for having it cleaned. That's the very *least* I can manage." I'd blurted out that I'd pay for her shirt, certainly, since I was the one that ruined it, and I *was* sure it was ruined. I dug around in my handbag and came up with a piece of paper I tore from an envelope and scribbled my name and mobile number on it. I handed it to her and told her to call me if it didn't come clean, which I knew it wouldn't, and I'd buy her a new shirt. She put the paper in her skirt pocket muttering something I couldn't hear and I managed to pull away. I went over to the sink and rinsed my hands off. By that time she was pretty much finished cleaning herself. She straightened up and walked back into the pub.

I wanted nothing more than to slip out of the building, and that I did. I ran all the way to the underground, slipping from there to the tubes, and caught the train back to the flat. I let myself in the door, ran into my room, dropped my trousers and jumper, and slipped between the sheets. The next I knew it was morning and late at that. I nearly always wake without the aid of an alarm but it was nearly ten o'clock when I managed to pry my lids apart. Then the tears started streaming again.

I got out of bed and slowly went about my day. Coffee and toast, got dressed, went to the antiques shop where I work, went home, ate dinner whilst avoiding the prying eyes of my parents. Mum and Dad could tell something was wrong, but they've always been brilliant and pretty well left me alone. I finally scooted back under the duvet once again and drifted off to sleep after an hour of tossing and turning. Then I slipped into a series of dreams, or should I say nightmares.

A week later, I was brought sharply out of my reverie by, "Hello?" I didn't recognize the number. "Sophie? Um, this is Pamela. Pamela Browning." Pamela Browning???

"Sorry?" I asked.

"Pamela Browning. Um, the shirt incident. In the pub?"

"Oh, I'm sorry, I never got your name the other night. Right! The shirt... It's ruined, isn't it? It's absolutely ruined, right? Well, I said I'd buy you another and I will. I promise you I will. I work this morning, but I can go in the afternoon and…"

"Slow down! Christ Almighty! There's no constable coming round to take you away for blitzing my shirt for goodness sake. Would you relax?"

"I'm sorry, I'm just sorry for..." And then I couldn't talk again. The tears were streaming, the cat had my tongue, and there was a voice on the other end repeating, "Hello? Hello?"

"No, I'm here," I managed to say. "When do you want to meet?"

"That's what I was asking you. Look, Sophie, I did take it to the cleaners but they didn't manage to get all the red quite out, but it's not like you hit me in a carpark with your Vauxhall, is it? I mean, is it really?"

"No, I suppose not. It's not that. Truly it's not. It's just everything, I suppose. It's just been really tough on me lately, yeah? And then we did our dance with the glass and it just made it worse. That's all."

"It must be really bad for you to be so upset. Has there been a problem in your family? A death? Divorce? Medical problems?"

"Oh, no, nothing like that."

"Well then, what's so bloody bad then?"

So I started talking with her. Before I knew it, I'd been talking for near half an hour. About not much of anything. I'd told her of going from my A Levels to University to nothing with all my high expectations dashed. Her next question I didn't anticipate. And my answer was even more off the walls.

"So, what *do* you want to do?" Pamela asked.

"I want to go to the zoo. It's been ages. I want to go to the zoo and have it be just like it was with me and Dad years ago. Everything was so fun and I had no troubles or worries."

"Ha ha ha. I meant what do you want to do in general!" Pamela had such a warm voice. I was just beginning to realize this. But then again when you're not getting yelled at it's easier to notice things like that. "So, I don't want to bug you about this blouse bit, but are you free this afternoon?" Pamela asked.

"Oh, yeah, sure. I mean, like I said, after lunch, I'm done for the day."

She asked me to meet her at the St. Paul Station at two o'clock. I said I would, and I somehow felt much brighter than I had in days. Weeks, really. I looked in my wardrobe and pulled out a powder blue jumper and some jeans. Then out of my drawer, I picked out something I hadn't in a long, long time. Matching cotton bra and knickers, in a bright yellow colour. They were my 'cheery-dearie' under things. Hmmm... Was I cheery? I wondered.

✤ COMING OF AGE ✤

Work was just an average day. Taking in just a few items. Asking our few customers if they needed assistance. Usually we do most of our business on the weekend. I found myself actually anticipating my rendezvous with Pamela. Rendezvous... What a strange word to have picked.

But finally lunch rolled around. I grabbed my bag, and headed toward the station. I jumped on the train and off I went. I mounted the stairs and walked around to the plaza in front of St. Paul's. I panicked! Oh my gosh! What did Pamela look like? I practically memorized the shirt. The stain. Even the evidence of the bra underneath. But I couldn't even tell you the colour of her hair! What would I do?

I knew! I would call her. I didn't have her number... Oh, it's on my incoming calls list. But what if she had called from her home phone? The lump in my throat began to rise. My heart started racing. Then behind me was a voice that I recognized as if I'd known her forever, although I'd only talked to her twice; once in the pub and once on the phone.

"Sophie?" Oh such a relief. My heart was really racing, but now because of the relief you feel after a small crisis. And then when I turned around my heart went to a completely new level. It was pounding though my chest. Cor! Pamela was a goddess! Her hair wasn't just a beautiful shade of brown, it was the colour of a beautiful chestnut carriage horse. And something I certainly didn't remember: it was cut short in a pixie. How could I not have noticed this? I was just so upset and absorbed with the situation, I never looked at her face. Or maybe I did but didn't take any notice.

She was taller than I am by an inch, maybe more, but she still gave the image of a magical little faerie! And her skin was so very pale and clear, like a statue that suddenly stood up in the gallery and walked out into the street. And contrasting her pale skin she wore red lip gloss. Not too bright, not too dark. But perfect. She had on a pale blue sundress that let her shoulders show the world that she was proud of her body, along with a pair of smart low heeled Italian slippers.

Oh, I was so jealous! But then again, I'm at least attractive enough that I don't usually wear makeup. I have a natural ruddiness in my cheeks, and my eyelashes are very long and thick and with my black hair it gives the appearance as though I've put on mascara. If there's anything I would change about myself it's that my hips are a bit too wide and my hair is a bit too straight. I do have strong thighs, due to my workouts and playing both rugby union and football side at University, but I always thought the spread of my hips made me look like I'd already born a child.

But back to Pamela. She stood before me smiling, saying nothing. "So. Here we are. Should we get cracking?" I asked. She replied, "Are you sure you don't have anything to do today? Or this evening? Shopping can get like that, yeah?"

"No, nothing to do. I'm so glad you're here, really. Like I said on the phone, I've been just traipsing across the city looking high and low for work and working at the shop. I could really use a break from all that."

"So," she asked, "were you a bad student or something?"

"No, certainly not! I got high marks in all my classes. Always high even in classes that weren't in major. Even the science and maths that I had to study, always high marks."

"I was just asking. So, let's go grab the tubes." And we did.

We chatted along, sometimes freely, sometimes a bit strained and paused, but we kept going. I never bothered asking where, as I assumed that Pamela was directing the show to the shops now to look for a replacement blouse. I started wondering, though, especially as we changed lines twice. When the overhead announcement came for the Baker St. station, Pamela stood up and gathered her things. I followed suit and stood with mine.

When we left the station I looked about. I've been to this area before, but it had been several years. I didn't know of any boutiques right at hand, but maybe there was something new. I began moving around to the left as we exited the station out of old habits from previous visits. Pamela turned right instead. I quickly caught up and slipped in beside her. Around the corner we went again, and down the street. Down York Terrace, York Gate… Then left into Regent's Park. What? I stopped in mid-sentence dead in my tracks. Pamela stopped as well.

"If the shop is on the other side of the park, why didn't we just take a train up to Camden Town station?"

"Because, Sophie, the zoo is in the park."

I stood for perhaps fifteen or twenty seconds staring straight at Pamela, possibly without any look on my face whatsoever, quite likely with my mouth completely agape. She said something, but it must have been in Hindi or Japanese, or some equally foreign language, because at first I didn't understand her. Then it hit me like a skip of bricks. "The zoo?" Surely I sounded like a little school girl, as I jumped up and down and clapped my hands and squealed! Then I stopped and stood still for another fifteen seconds, though now I had a huge smile on my face. After that I jumped straight up into the air and threw my arms around Pamela, hugging her close to me.

She didn't exactly stiffen, but I'm sure she didn't expect to hug me back either. I stopped and dropped back to the ground. "I don't understand, Pamela. I don't get this at all. I'd never met you until two days ago, I assaulted you in a public house, and now you bring me to the zoo. I don't know what to say."

"First, Pam. Just Pam. And don't ever call me Pammie. My sister used to call me that when we were little. She tormented me. I don't like it. Secondly, don't try and figure it out. I have my own past, my own history. It's just that under the degree of stress you were in, the only thing you wanted was something that would only cost a few quid and a half a day's time. So I decided to just go with it and see what came about. And besides, I'll pick a more expensive shirt than the first one!"

"Oh, I bet you will!" I was laughing now. Not a care in the world. I was… Happy. Imagine: me—happy.

I pulled back away from her, realizing that I was in her space a bit. I started walking way over to the side of the wide walkway. She asked me if I was trying to get to the animal park via a different route. I laughed and said no, and moved in closer to her as we walked along from then on. She told me that she was very apologetic about yelling at me in the pub. Apparently it wasn't her yelling at me, it was the multiple glasses of gin, and she was three sheets to the wind pissed drunk when it happened.

I told her it was okay, and that I wished I had handled it better than I had. She came closer to me draping her hand around my back on my shoulder as we walked. "Thank goodness you didn't cross paths with me when my husband left me."

"Husband? You must have gotten married really young."

"Yes, I did, and no, he didn't stay long. I picked *him* up when I was twenty-four and he dropped *me* when I just turned twenty-six"

"Twenty-six? You don't look more than twenty-three or -four now!"

"Thanks for that!" Then she gave me a hug. Nothing big, but a hug. I've had mates forever. Some I've known since we lived in Dover as a wee tiny tot, some since secondary school, but I felt as if I'd known Pam forever and a day. And unlike my mates who'd stood me up the night that fate cast Pam and I together, it was an adult relationship. For the very first time, somebody that would treat me like an adult and somebody I felt I might count on. At least I hoped.

The next two and a half hours passed so quickly. I wanted to stop the clock. I wanted to make time stand still, but the more I prayed for it to do so the more it sped up. We chatted about family life. About school. About the end of summer approaching. It was as if two long lost friends had re-united after forty years and were catching up on decades of events.

Then it happened. We were standing by the window watching the tiger walk by. It was one of those thick glass enclosed walls that the animals couldn't break, like bank glass. And as the tiger strode by, he was within inches of you. The conversation had come to a lull. I more felt Pam's gaze on me than saw her. I turned toward her. She reached out and put a few strands of hair behind my ear that had blown loose in the breeze.

"So you know I was married. And I've told you about a couple of my boyfriends, yeah?"

"Sure."

"And I told you at the pub, even if it was in my eloquent French, that I wasn't a lesbian, right?"

"Uh-huh…" I wasn't sure where this was going.

"And you've mentioned casual boyfriends that you've had."

"Right."

"And you're not a lesbian, right?"

"No, I'm not a lesbian. I like boys."

"Are you bisexual?"

"I don't think so. I've never really considered it one way or another. I just assumed I was straight."

"Well, I'm in a dilemma."

"Are you bisexual?" I asked Pam.

"No. Just like you, I never even considered the possibility. Until now."

"Until now?" I asked. "What do you mean?" I managed to croak out in a tiny little voice.

"Because something's happened to me, something I've no idea how to deal with."

"What is it? What's happened?" I don't know if she could even hear me now; I was so quiet.

"I've fallen in love. Love at first sight. I mean, I've been infatuated before, and I thought I was in love with Derek when we got married. But now it seems as if all that was preparation for now, for what's happening to me. For what's going through me right this second. I think I'm truly falling in love. No, I'm already in love. With a woman. And I don't know what to do about it."

"But why tell me? Surely your mum, or a best mate, or somebody else would be a better choice to tell. Somebody older than I to give you advice. Why me?" I asked her.

"Because, silly goose, it's you. I'm in love with you. I've never even so much as gotten a thrill in school when all us girls were showering together or when I've watched blue films with Derek." She stood, waiting for my reaction. Then she reached out and touched my hair again. I took her hand in mine and pulled it away. I could see the disappointment in her face. The hurt in her eyes. Then I held it against my cheek. I rubbed it against my cheek softly. Tenderly. My eyes averted, staring at the pavement below. I pulled her hand out in front of me, and held it flat, palm down, with my left hand. With my right hand I traced over the back of her hand. Then I turned it over, brought it to my lips, and ever so gently kissed her palm.

I could hear a sigh escape her. I then took her other hand. I held it palm down as well, tracing over it as I had the other. And after a minute or so, I turned it over, and kissed her on her palm again. I reached out and took both of Pam's hands into mine and just held them for a moment. She didn't move her hands at all, but let me direct them. When at last I looked up, I was amazed at what I saw. Now it wasn't my turn to bring on the tears. It was Pam's. Rolling freely off her cheeks. Hitting the pathway like drops of rain. I moved very close to her, put my arms gently round her, stood up on my tip toes, and whispered into her ear, "Do you have to be such a ninny?"

Pam laughed and punched me in the side. We laughed and laughed. And then laughed some more. Pam's hand came, found its way to the back my neck, and gently rubbed my neck under my hair. "You have beautiful hair."

"Pam, everything about you is beautiful."

"So what happens now?" Pam asked.

"I'm not sure. Didn't you listen? I told you I've never done this before either!"

"So is this because we both need something in our lives just now? Or is this something more? I mean, I don't want to make you do something you'll regret."

"Stop! If I feel uncomfortable at any point, I'll just tell you. That's simple enough, yeah?"

"Well how about this..." she said suddenly, changing subjects. "I'm hungry. Let's go to Picadilly and grab dinner! There's an Italian restaurant across from the theatre that serves a fabulous calzone! Do you like Italian?"

"I like most anything. So long as it's not too hot."

Pam hooked her hand around my arm, after I stuck my hand in my front pocket. I'd walked like this before with my girlfriends going places. But this was different. This time, it was with my girlfriend. I mean, like a real girlfriend, not just one of my mates.

We made our way to the restaurant. It was pretty sparse, even though it was still during holiday season. It was drawing to the end of summer so the majority of the tourists had come and gone, but it was also a Wednesday night. The sun was just touching behind the buildings as we chose one of the three tables on the walk outside.

We ate, we drank, we laughed, we smiled. We rejoiced. I was flying. What a journey! A few days ago I'd had the worst day of my life. Today was the best day of my life. But then the inevitable happened.

"I hate to break up this little shindig of ours, but I *do* have to go to work very early tomorrow," Pam finally said. "Give me your mobile."

I gave her my phone, and she entered a number. Then she saved it. And another. And another. She then scrolled down through my saved numbers, showing me as she did so. Pam – Home. Pam – Mobile. Pam – Work.

I smiled. She reached out once again, put my hair behind my ears, and then took my hand. She squeezed my hand, holding it between both of hers, and then brought her hand to her cheek with mine between them. She stood up, and walked away. As she walked away, she smiled, and waved at me. Then she dug into her bag and pulled out her phone. When my phone rang, it showed Pam – Mobile. I answered the phone and said, "Hallo? Who is this?" laughing.

Cackling wildly, she answered, "This is your wicked girlfriend. And you still owe me a shirt." And then she was gone into a crowd. I was sad to see her go. There was now something missing. There was a hole where she had been that would remain empty until she returned. But I was positively happy. So very happy. So very much in love.

~End Sample Chapter of COMING OF AGE ~
For more go to www.Shadoepublishing.com to purchase
the complete book or for many other delightful offerings.

~ Because a publisher should stand behind their authors~

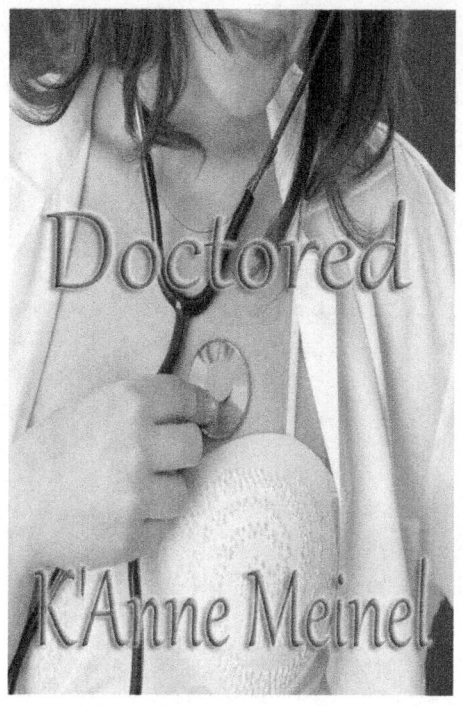

A brilliant child protégée, she dreams of becoming a doctor and a surgeon...and accomplishes her goals. Unfortunately, her youth and round, child-like face work against her. No matter how skilled she becomes, how knowledgeable, the old school, male-dominated medical hierarchy wants to keep her in 'her place.'

Deanna has worked hard to become an expert in her chosen field, but few believe this 'child' capable. Specializing in infectious diseases, she travels the world—from the States to Europe to South America—honing her skills before winding up in Africa where her skills are desperately needed.

Meeting a nurse by the name of Madison MacGregor, she finds they share an insatiable curiosity and a love of helping others, but falling in love was not what she intended. Later, when she loses Maddie to a misunderstanding, she is haunted by the one that got away...

Ten years have passed and both the doctor and nurse have moved on with their lives, but fate intervenes when they find themselves working at the same hospital. Their friendship is revived...can their love be rekindled? Will the past haunt them or bring them closer? Will the secrets that both harbor keep them from realizing a future together?

www.shadoepublishing.com

What do you do when you meet someone who changes everything you know about love and passion?

Paige Harlow is a good girl. She's always known where she was going in life: top grades, an ivy league school, a medical degree, regular church attendance, and a happy marriage to a man. So falling in love with her gorgeous roommate and best friend Alyssa Torres is no small crisis. Alyssa is chasing demons of her own, a medical condition that makes her an outcast and a family dysfunctional to the point of disintegration make her a questionable choice for any stable relationship. But Paige's heart is no longer her own. She must now battle the prejudices of her family, friends, and church and come to peace with her new sexuality before she can hope to win the affections of the woman of her dreams. But will love be enough?

www.shadoepublishing.com

~ Because a publisher should stand behind their authors~

As I watch the wormhole start to close, I make one last desperate plea ...
"Please? Please don't make me do this?" I whisper.
"You're almost out of time, Lily. Please, just let go?"
I look down at the control panel. I know what I have to do.

Lilith Madison is captain of the Phoenix, a spaceship filled with an elite crew and travelling through the Delta Gamma Quadrant. Their mission is mankind's last hope for survival.

But there is a killer on board. One who kills without leaving a trace and seems intent on making sure their mission fails. With the ship falling apart and her crew being ruthlessly picked off one by one, Lilith must choose who to trust while tracking down the killer before it's too late.

"A suspenseful...exciting...thrilling whodunit adventure in space...discover the shocking truth about what's really happening on the Phoenix" (Clarion)

~ Because a publisher should stand behind their authors~

In the male dominated sport of Formula 1 racing, Samantha 'Sam' Dupree is struggling to make her mark against the boys. She hears about a driver who is making a name for herself in NASCAR and goes to check her out. Little does she know that she's in for the race of her heart.

Addison McCloud wants nothing more than to drive. She doesn't care about fame or fortune; she just wants to be fast enough to get herself and her family away from her abusive father. Meeting Sam changes her world and revs her life into overdrive.

When the two women meet, sparks fly like the race cars that they drive. Will they be able to steer their relationship into something more and win the race, or will their families make them crash and burn? The boys of Formula 1 are going to learn that Southern girls are a force to be reckoned with.

www.shadoepublishing.com

~ Because a publisher should stand behind their authors~

WARNING ~ book contains graphic violence towards women

A serial killer plagues the gay community and leaves a trail of dead bodies across state lines. Agent Danni Pacelli and Agent Parker Stevens rush against time to catch their killer and stop the body count from increasing.

Agent Parker Stevens life was perfect when transferred to a new city and new location which offered her solitude from the grief of losing her partner and children to a predator. But, while hunting down her suspect, she meets Samantha Petrino who takes the once closed off Stevens and opens a world to new love. The charming advertising agent breaks down her defenses, and no matter how hard she fights to protect her heart, she finds herself falling for the beautiful and intelligent woman.

New to the FBI, Agent Danni Pacelli's struggles to balance her personal life along with the job, to save her relationship, she convinces her new partner to bring in Annabel and utilize the young detective's skills to track down their killer or risk losing Annabel all together.

The heroic efforts of two agents who hunt down a serial killer, but find more than they bargained for.

www.shadoepublishing.com

~ Because a publisher should stand behind their authors~

Carrie flees from the demons of her present, trying to protect the ones she loves.

Frankie hides from the demons of her past, and the memory of loved ones she failed to protect.

A modern day princess thrown to the wolves, Carrie's only hope is the rancher who had spent the better part of a decade in self imposed, near total, isolation. Frankie's history of losing those she tries to save haunts her, but this madman threatens her home, her livestock, her sanctuary. She knows she can't do it alone, has she still got enough support from her oldest friends?

www.shadoepublishing.com

~ Because a publisher should stand behind their authors~

In a world on the verge of being told that everything they once thought was merely myth is real, can one teenage girl cope with life changes she never saw coming?

Seventeen year old Kyndle Callahan began her year as a typical high school senior. Well, as typical as a girl can be while living life as a werewolf. She wasn't bitten or scratched as most people believe all werewolves are made, no, she was born into the pack that's always been her extended family. She's never seen the people she grew up with as the monsters of myth and legend but everything in her life is thrown into a tailspin when her father springs some shocking news on her. Suddenly, reality as a werewolf is much scarier than the stories humans tell. Stunned by the prospect of spending her life bonded to someone she can't even stand sharing the same space with and devastated at the thought of losing the only love she's ever known, can Kyndle settle into who and what she is in time to set things right? Can the girl that grew up knowing only pack law stand up, embrace her true calling, and become the woman she was meant to be despite going against everything her family believes?

With the help of her best friend Abbey, Kyndle must navigate a confusing world of wolf culture, teenage drama, and coming out in a group that believes her lifestyle is unnatural. Follow her journey through pain, heartache, several states, and the fight to be with the girl she loves and take her place in the world.

www.shadoepublishing.com

Roberta Pena finally has her dream job of being a Biology Teacher at the high school that she once attended, but something sinister lurks in her classroom. She begins to have unusual paranormal experiences. Is she simply losing her mind or is there a ghost trying to make contact? How will she deal with the mystery of the room that often smells of death and where she has begun to have so many unsettling and ghastly sightings? Will she solve the mystery or be forced to leave her career that she worked so hard to achieve? Might she find love in the process?

www.shadoepublishing.com

~ Because a publisher should stand behind their authors~

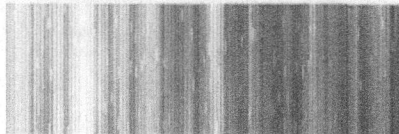

GENTA SEBASTIAN

A Children's Novel for ages 8-11

Horse crazy Lily, eleven years old with two out-loud-and-proud mothers, is plump and clumsy. Her mothers say she's too young to ride horses, she can't seem to get anything right in class, and bullies torment her on the playground. Alone and lonely, how will she ever survive the mean girls of Hardyvale Elementary's fifth-grade?

Across the room Clara sits still as a statue, never volunteering or raising her hand. To avoid the bullying that is Lily's daily life she answers only in a whisper with her head down, desperate to keep her family's secret that she has two fathers.

Then one day Clara makes a brave move that changes the girls' lives forever. She passes a note to Lily asking to meet secretly at lunch time. As they share cupcakes she explains about her in-the-closet dads. Both girls are relieved to finally have a friend, especially one who understands about living in a rainbow family.

Life gets better. As their friendship deepens and their families grow close, their circle of friends expand. The girls even volunteer together at the local animal shelter. Everything is great, until old lies and blackmail catch up with them. Can Lily and her mothers rescue Clara's family from disaster? Or will Lily lose her first and best friend?

www.shadoepublishing.com

~ Because a publisher should stand behind their authors~

When U.S. Marine Dakota McKnight returned home from her third tour in Operation Iraqi Freedom, she carried more baggage than the gear and dress blues she had deployed with. A vicious rocket-propelled grenade attack on her base left her best friend dead and Dakota physically and emotionally wounded. The marine who once carried herself with purpose and confidence, has returned broken and haunted by the horrors of war. When she returns to the civilian world, life is not easy, but with the help of her therapist, Janie, she is barely managing to hold her life together...then she meets Beth.

Beth Kendrick is an American history college professor. She is as straight-laced as they come, until Dakota enters her life, that is. Will her children understand what she is going through? Will she take a chance on the broken marine or decide to wait for the perfect someone to come along?

Time is on your side, they say, unless there is a dark, sinister evil at work. Is their love strong enough to hold these two people together? Will the love of a good woman help Dakota find the path to recovery? Or is she doomed to a life of inner turmoil and destruction that knows no end?

www.shadoepublishing.com

If you have enjoyed this book and the others listed here Shadoe Publishing is always looking for authors. Please check out our website @ www.shadoepublishing.com For information or to contact us @ shadoepublishing@gmail.com.

We may be able to help you make your dreams of becoming a published author come true.

Made in the USA
Monee, IL
24 March 2020